A DOUBLE LIFE

All in all, she thought, as she got ready for bed, she had her life beautifully organised – her lives, rather, for she had two, back to back. A Double Life. By day she was Eleanor Jordan, spinster of this or any other parish, who, once seen, was instantly forgotten. By night, she was Cleo Mondaine, high-priced call girl, with a face and body – always displayed to best advantage – matched only by her sexual skills.

Vera Cowie was born in County Durham. She lived and worked in London for some years before giving up full-time work to write, and moving to Hertfordshire. She has always written – her first novel was started when she was twelve – and the first novel she had published was *The Amazon Summer* in 1978. *A Double Life* is her eighth novel.

VERA COWIE

A Double Life

Mandarin

A Mandarin Paperback
A DOUBLE LIFE

First published in Great Britain 1992
by William Heinemann Ltd
This edition published 1993
by Mandarin Paperbacks
an imprint of Reed Consumer Books Limited
Michelin House, 81 Fulham Road, London SW3 6RB
and Auckland, Melbourne, Singapore and Toronto

Reprinted 1993 (four times), 1994

A CIP catalogue record for this title
is available from the British Library
ISBN 0 7493 1105 3

Printed and bound in Great Britain
by Cox & Wyman Ltd, Reading, Berkshire

This book is for Deb, whose idea it was,
and whose technical knowledge and advice,
freely given, was of inestimable help.

My thanks also to other friends for
their experienced information and advice:
Kath, Wilf, Majella, Jim, Sonia and Alan.

I told you all contributions
would be gratefully acknowledged!

BOOK ONE

1979

I

The man behind the desk stood up, came round it to greet the woman his nurse ushered in. She shook his hand, smiled, but he saw her eyes go beyond him to his desk and the brown folder lying on it.

'Do sit down, Mrs Waring. Would you like a cup of tea?'

'No, thank you, but if your news is bad then I shall require a double whisky.' Her voice was low, throaty, carelessly commanding; the voice of one used to giving orders.

She took the chair in front of the desk, crossed a pair of thoroughbred legs, placed her black alligator handbag on her lap, folded her black-glacé kid-gloved hands on it and said: 'All right, then. Give it to me straight. I am too old to have any interest in beating about bushes. What is (a) the diagnosis and (b) the prognosis?'

Tough as old boots, the eminent brain specialist thought, but admiringly. And it is a great pity, a very great pity. Damned good looking woman, in the prime of life. But he was too old a hand to go all sentimental. She had asked for the truth and he would give it to her because this was not the kind of woman to scream or faint. She had undergone some pretty nasty tests without complaining – except for the occasional pair of cold hands – and not one but two spinal taps. Now, the scan had delivered the final verdict, and it had fallen to him to pronounce it to her.

'The diagnosis is as we feared. There is a brain tumour and it is inoperable, situated as it is in that part of the brain – I will not confuse you or confound the issue with medical terms –

3

which is much too dangerous to play around with. It is also too deep to reach without doing even more damage. The prognosis is that you have a minimum of one and a maximum of two years.'

He held her intent gaze, his own as uncompromising as she could have wished for, hers steady and curiously fixed as though for support.

'Will it be sudden?' she asked.

'No. Gradual for the most part; the last three months will see the most marked deterioration. You will lose control of sight, movement and hearing in rapid succession and will go into a coma.'

There was a silence. Then: 'I see,' she said. Her voice was under control, almost thoughtfully calm.

He got up, went to a sideboard, opened it to reveal various bottles and glasses and poured a double Johnnie Walker Black Label. As she took it: 'I trust this is included in your fee?' she observed dulcetly. She sipped. 'Well, at least you have left me enough time to earn enough to pay it.'

'I would rather not have earned it, in this particular instance.' He hesitated then said: 'Which prompts me to ask a question of my own. What sent you – or should I say who sent you to me? I would have thought there was a plethora of excellent men in my field in London.'

'There are, but I have reasons for not wishing to consult any of them, and you are English – or were until the vagaries of the National Health Service grew too much for you and you came to the Land of the Fee.'

His laugh was genuine.

'I came to you because when I made enquiries your name was mentioned by every one of the people of whom I did enquire. They all said that if anyone could perform miracles you could. They did not know – nor did I – that in my case even a miracle was too much to hope for.'

'Had you come to me six months – a year ago – I would have told you the same thing. There are certain types of brain tumour still beyond even our present state of technology. Perhaps in twenty years – maybe fifteen . . . but at this present time . . .' His shrug said it all.

'No excuses,' she waved a hand before burying her nose in

her glass. Ice tinkled as she lowered it. 'Will I be able to work?' she asked abruptly.

'I would have to know what kind of work?'

'I am in – public relations; the entertainment side.' She regarded him guilelessly. 'I – er – soften them up for the kill.'

'Then I see no reason why you should not continue to use your softening agent for the foreseeable future. You may find the occasional loss of mobility; being unable to grip, for instance, and sometimes a lapse of memory or a momentary loss of balance, but this will not be immediately noticeable. I think at least six months before you begin to notice that all is not as it should be.'

'I have to entertain quite a bit. Will I be able to continue to do that?'

'Until you find you are having difficulty picking up things, yes.'

'And what about sex?'

'What about it?'

She levelled a look. 'I have an active sex life, doctor. How long can I expect to continue that?'

'Until your co-ordination begins to give you trouble. You will know. You will not feel things in the same way. Your responses will change, your sensitivity will lessen, you will lose sense of your surroundings and what you are doing. But it will be gradual. You will sense its onset, and fortunately it will be slow, giving you time to prepare.'

'Prepare . . .' Again her voice was thoughtful. She set down her glass, got up and went to the window; dusk was falling and New York was lighting up for the night. She stared down at the lights of Fifth Avenue, this far up, on the 34th floor, a hazed blur. 'You said a minimum of one and a maximum of two. Would you care to risk a more accurate figure?'

He considered. 'Your general health is excellent, your muscle tone and organs in first class condition considering – '

'My age?'

Tactfully: 'You have taken excellent care of yourself.'

She laughed. 'I had help.' Turning from the window: 'So? You still have not made your bet.'

He steepled his fingers. Twenty years in the United States

had not shaken off the influence of his first Senior Consultant. 'Nearer two than one,' he said finally.

Her breath was shaky but obviously relieved. 'Better . . . I always did believe two was better than one.'

Really, he thought admiringly, she was remarkable. Forty-six according to her file; but until you got up close you would have accepted thirty-five. Time and money, of course, and the sort of dedicated self-love that sexy women invariably had. It was a damned shame because she really was something. Still slender and taut, no double chin, no sagging ass, no lines until, again, you got real close. Why was it always those with most to live for who drew the short straw from the fist of Life? And I'll bet she'll give it a run for its money. There were some people nobody could defeat and he had the feeling that this feisty woman was one of them. I hope so, he thought, because he was a lover of women and would never get used to giving them death sentences. He waited for her next move. Some-times it took them only a little while to accept what he had told them; sometimes they never accepted it. This was one of the calm ones; the kind who understood that the game was over and they had lost. Gallant, he thought, using a very English word from his youth.

She turned away from the window, elegant in her Chanel suit, her crisp blonde hair immaculate, her face a perfect example of the beautician's art. Public Relations, he thought amusedly. That's a new name for it. Private is what I heard, and very private at that.

'Thank you for being so frank, Doctor,' she said. 'I came to you because they told me you didn't do it Forest Lawn style. And they are right. I love this country but I can't stand the way they do plastic surgery on the truth. I fly back to London on Wednesday, can you let me have your bill before then?' She smiled wryly, yet it was wholly amused. 'Seeing as I have not got all that much time to get my *affairs* straight.'

Elizabeth Waring let the doorman hail her a taxi feeling as if she was seeing him from behind the walls of a glass jar. Everything seemed to be blurred and fuzzy. She was not aware of giving the cab driver the address of a particular bar on 3rd Avenue, or of arriving there; it was not until some time later that she emerged from her darkness to realise where she was and what she was doing. Trying to drink herself into oblivion.

Discipline reasserted itself. She checked her Cartier Rivoli watch. 6.45 p.m. Her appointment with the doctor had been at 4.00 p.m. She felt light-headed but clear-thinking, though thinking had been what she had wanted to avoid, which was why she had come to this bar in the first place. Now, she shook herself mentally. She had an appointment for nine. Time to get the show on the road.

Back in her suite at the Regency she got under a tepid shower which she gradually chilled to cold and then to freezing for as long as she could stand it. Then she mixed herself a potion which her father — a veteran of many a sodden night in the mess — had sworn to her would bring a corpse to life, shuddered after she had downed it and then, setting the alarm on her bedside clock, lay down on her queen-sized bed for exactly forty minutes. When the little alarm beeped she opened her eyes and knew exactly where she was and what she should be doing.

As the door of the Cadillac Seville was opened for her, Elizabeth flung the black velvet cloak she was wearing around one shoulder and swept up the long flight of entrance steps leading to the great house without so much as a backward glance, leaving an eddy of expensive fragrance in her wake. Once inside the marble hall she let the cloak gape, revealing the knee-length frou frou of her scarlet dress, a mass of sequins that glittered like diamond fire, the sheer black stockings, the stiletto heeled scarlet satin shoes. Around the bob of her thick butter-blonde hair was a scarlet satin headband, and in her ears long chandeliers of first-water diamonds.

A butler approached her, bowed, indicated she was to follow him. He led the way upstairs to a pair of double doors, one of which he opened to allow her to enter, closing it silently behind her. Seated at a table under a low shaded light was a man, dressed in the striped jersey and navy pants of a sailor. He was dark, swarthy and obviously waiting for her, because when he saw her he rose eagerly and started forward. There was a bar behind the table, but no bartender, and the rest of the room was in darkness; only the table and, on the fringes of the light,

7

the outline of a big double bed were visible. Everywhere else was black velvet.

As he reached her she evaded him, teasing yet tantalising. She held out a hand. He put one of his in his pocket, drew out coins which clinked as he dropped them into her palm. Putting a foot up onto his chair she drew up her skirt, revealing the rolled stockings, the frilly black garter into which she put the coins. From somewhere in the darkness came a faint sigh.

The sailor went to an old fashioned phonograph, circa 1910, and set it to playing a tango. They danced, bodies tight, eyes fastened to each other's, dipping and swaying, gliding and shuddering. When the music stopped, the sailor was obviously sexually aroused. He took his partner's hand, pressed it to his crotch. She smiled, secretive, full of promise and swayed away from him, turning her back suggestively.

At once he was there, his trembling fingers pulling down the long zip. The dress fell. Underneath it she was naked but for her black stockings and scarlet shoes. The sailor fell to his knees as she turned, seized her by the hips and buried his face into the guinea-bright floss at the juncture of her thighs. She took him by the thick black hair, lifted him off, slid her eyes to the blurred outline of the big double bed, brass-railed and many-pillowed. Even as she looked, the light above the table went out and that above the bed brightened until it was lit by a warm golden glow. The sailor and the girl moved to it and for the next hour, using every variation known to man, they used each other sexually, their bodies and actions exposed by the bright glow of the red-shaded lamp. They never spoke; the only sound was that of their harsh, frantic breathing, the slap of body against body, the rising moans, the deep, pleasure-filled groans, the sharp intakes of breath and, towards the end, the frantic springs of the big brass bed and one last exultant combined shout-scream. Then the light went out. From behind the black velvet curtain at the end of the room there came a sound; half moan, half groan, but of pain rather than pleasure. Then there was another long sigh and finally, the faint sound of a door closing. For a few moments more there was silence, then a rustling, another door opening and closing. After another thirty seconds the light above the table went on, but dimly. The girl was alone. Swiftly, the red dress was donned once more, the hair tidied, the lipstick re-applied. Finally, the black cloak was flung over the sequins and the double doors were re-opened, revealing the butler standing outside. Once more he bowed, but this time he handed her a long white envelope before preceding her down the stairs to the front door through which the big black car could be seen waiting at the bottom of the steps.

The car delivered her to the canopy of the Regency Hotel on Park Avenue. In her suite, she locked the door behind her, leaned against the door with a tired sigh and kicked off the red shoes. 'Those goddam things kill me,' she muttered. Then she ripped open the white envelope to reveal a thick wad of English fifty-pound notes. Twenty of them.

'Dear old Alfonso . . .' she smiled. Her brows drew together. 'If only he lasts as long as I do . . .'

The old man had been her client for eleven years now, and always the scenario was the same. A sailor – who looked as the old man had when young, the blonde whore in the red sequined dress done up in the style of Clara Bow; always they enacted the same mime; always it lasted one hour and always she used what the blonde whore had been famous for in Rio: her mouth and her tongue. It was for this reason she was so expensive and why the boy had never been able to afford her; part of the reason why he had sworn to have so much money he could buy *anybody*. And money was all he had now. His wife was dead, his son too, his daughter a nun in an enclosed convent in Sao Paulo. Four times a year he sent for Elizabeth Waring from wherever he happened to be: New York, Los Angeles, Hong Kong . . . And always the envelope filled with fifty-pound notes, sometimes a present if her performance had managed to bring him to the nearest he ever got to orgasm nowadays. One of them had been the chandelier ear-rings she had worn; they were not paste but first-water diamonds. She took one from her ear now, laid it across her palm. 'You may have to go,' she told it regretfully, 'and a pair of Butler & Wilson fakes take your place, but that has all to be worked out yet.' She clenched her hand around the ear-ring, feeling platinum dig into the soft flesh of her palm. Two years, she thought – and that is the maximum. For a moment she wanted to

scream, to howl, to tear her hair because it was not fair . . .
not now, when she nearly had it all after so much hard work.

You are supposed to be the hard nut, Elizabeth Waring, she
reminded herself, so where are the pension fund, the offshore
account(s), the share portfolio? I could still do it, she thought
confidently. I have the contacts, God knows. Sell these, and
that pink sapphire necklace . . . yes, but they would not bring
in enough. You have had the house and the villa; the car(s), the
clothes, the regular stints at Champneys and the little nips and
tucks of your rearguard action against time. You need an
absolute minimum of fifty thousand a year net to maintain
your lifestyle. She bent to pick up one of her shoes. 'Take these
– a thousand pounds the pair because of all the handsewn
sequins – two and a half thousand for the dress and that was
wholesale, for God's sake! No, you need more than half a
million to invest, my girl. You need something substantial,
and nobody must know or else business will wither on the
vine.'

Elizabeth got up, reached to unzip the dress which slid to
her knees where she caught it before stepping out of it. It was
heavy because of all the sequins, and seemed to weigh much
more than it used to. Wearing it for any length of time
nowadays invariably produced aching shoulder muscles, while
taking it off was like removing a ton weight. She moved her
shoulders as if to free them from a long-cramped position,
rotated her neck in a circular motion, yawned tiredly as she
hung the heavy dress away, treed her shoes.

For some time now, her energy levels had sunk considerably
from their original high, and if she was honest, she reflected,
so had her enthusiasm. As she sat down on the bed to roll
down her stockings – pure silk and seven pounds fifty the pair
– she caught sight of herself in the big mirror behind her
dressing table, stared blankly at the drawn face staring back at
her.

The strain was showing, but whether it was because of her
years or her condition she could not say and was far too weary
to deliberate. Sleep was what she needed; lots of lovely, restful
sleep.

She drew off her frilly garter, which clinked, reminding her
of the coins the sailor had slipped into its tiny pocket. Reaching

into it, she drew out five small gold coins, the Brazilian equivalent in 1924 of five dollars; a lot of money for a whore in those days, which was why she had had the monopoly on the foreign sailors. 'And did *you* die rich?' she asked out loud. 'That old man will for sure.'

She tossed the stockings aside; she would rinse them through later – no one else ever saw what she termed the tools of her trade. Now, all she wanted was to get to that big, wide bed and sleep. But first she had necessary hygienic things to do.

More men than my entire family have had hot dinners, she thought ironically, as she lowered herself blissfully into hot, fragrant bubbles, and I have to die of a brain tumour.

The thought struck her as funny and she began to laugh; she laughed until she began to cry and once she did she found she could not stop.

2

The girl in the black leather microskirt shivered as a cold wind swept around her legs in their black fishnet tights and thigh-length boots, huddling deeper into the thin material of her imitation fur jacket and stamping her feet. Her eyes scanned the cars as they swept past her up Bedford Hill and she tried to put a sway to her hips as she sauntered – very slowly – in the opposite direction. Trade was slow tonight; too cold and with the threat of rain; a February night when it was best to be indoors with the fire lit and the telly on. Then her eyes, experienced in spotting the potential customer, saw a car that edged in towards the kerb as it came up the hill, flashed its lights at her. Thank God, she thought, I don't want Mickey going off at me again for another poor showing. She switched on her most seductive smile, bent to look in through the offside window, letting her jacket gape so that he had a good look at the full young breasts in their deeply-vee-necked black sweater.

'Looking for business?' Her smile was enticing, her voice sexy. He was probably on his way home and he fancied a quickie, no more.

'How much?' he asked with brutal impatience.

'Ten?'

'For what?'

'Straight-up.'

'I'd want more than that for a tenner.'

'Try somebody else then!' She straightened, angry. There were some things that even the thought of Mickey and his punishment could not make her do. And she didn't like the look of him anyway.

'Choosy, are we? A whore like you?'

'Get lost!'

He told her to go and do something anatomically impossible and roared away. She resumed her saunter. She had a mere fifteen pounds in her purse and she'd been working the hill for forty minutes. Not a good night. In the summer she could quadruple that in the same length of time. Another car approached; she smiled into its headlights but he changed his mind, accelerated and roared past her. She hated Bedford Hill but Mickey had told her it was her beat as a punishment; he knew it was not one of the top earners: Park Lane, the Edgware Road, Shepherd Market – you could really charge there, but Bedford Hill was a through road and trade depended on the passing motorist or those who knew it was a red-light district and came looking deliberately, even on a night like this when it was cold under the trees on the common and the back of a car was not the most comfortable of places. In the summer, a lot of men liked it up against a tree or in the grass. She shivered again, rummaged in her bag for a tissue to blow her nose and as she did so a car drew up.

'Got a cold, love? I don't want you giving it to me.' A cheeky grin. 'I had something else in mind.'

His car was an Audi; he was well dressed. Nell bent down again but this time her smile was nice, her voice different. 'Twenty pounds to you,' she said, making it sound as though she was offering a lifetime's bargain.

He pressed a lever and the door clicked open. 'Hop in.'

'Oh, nice . . .' she said gratefully. 'Nice and warm, I mean.'

'Oh, I'm always warm . . . hot in some places.' He took her hand, pressed it against his already rigid penis. 'I'll soon warm you up . . .'

She directed him to her favourite spot; dark enough not to be seen from the road but not far enough away to be unreachable should a customer turn nasty. He was in a hurry; one of those who had come looking. He had her spread on the back seat almost before she could get her pants down. Although he was a big man he was surprisingly small. It was soon over but he seemed satisfied and paid up from a wallet fat with notes. Within ten minutes she was back on her beat.

She caught the last tube to King's Cross and then a bus to Islington. When she got back to the flat Mickey was sitting at the kitchen table drinking coffee. Two of the other girls were there – Maureen, who worked the Edgware Road, and Cindy whose beat was Queens Drive. On the table were piles of notes divided into various denominations; twenties, tens, fives and ones. He looked up as she entered. His lake-blue eyes were very cold and unblinking, the pupils contracted. She recognised the signs and her flesh tightened.

'God, what a cold night,' she said brightly. 'I'm dying for something hot to drink. Is that coffee . . .?' She made for the stove where a pan stood over a low flame but suddenly there was a white, flexible cane between her and it.

'First things first.' Mickey's voice was as flat as his eyes. She caught Maureen's eye and also the faint shake of her head. It meant bad mood; watch out.

'Oh, sorry, Mickey . . . the cold has addled my brains . . . here you are . . .' She counted out eighty pounds onto the table. 'Slow night, I'm afraid. Too cold for the punters . . .'

The stick hit the table with a swish and a crack. 'Eighty pounds! You go out for four hours and come back with eighty fucking pounds! Where's the rest of it?'

'That's all there is, Mickey, honestly. It was a slow night . . . bitterly cold and not many punters. I'm freezing from standing there on that road.'

His hand cracked across her face snapping her head back. 'Lying bitch!' From the corner of her eye she saw Cindy and Maureen melt away and knew what she was in for. He used his fists on her body, the flat of his hand on her face, his thin white cane on her exposed limbs, all the while screaming obscenities and demanding to know if she took him for a fool. He didn't send her out to sit in cafés drinking coffee; he sent her out to work and either she worked for him or he would see to it that she would never be fit to work for anybody. She defended herself as best she could but when she crawled under the table he kicked it over, sending cups and cold coffee flying; when she curled herself into a ball he kicked her. He did not stop until he was exhausted. Only then did he slam out of the

14

kitchen and across the landing into his room. She lay there, unable to move. Her nose was bleeding and it was hard to breathe, her ribs hurt and so did her legs. Each time she tried to move she moaned in her agony. She heard the door open and then a gasped: 'Oh, my God . . .' Somebody bent over her.

'Oh, Christ, Elly, what's he done to you . . .' That was Maureen, her thin, bony face that looked thirty but was in reality ten years younger, regarding Elly with horror, her usually blanked-out, overwashed blue eyes for once filled with shock as she saw what Mickey's fists had done.

''is dealer didn't come round, did 'e, so poor Mickey's desperate for a fix,' Cindy said defensively. She was Mickey's girl. 'You know what 'e's like when 'e ain't 'ad no fix.'

'And what 'e's like when 'e 'as,' Maureen said grimly. She was the same age as Cindy but years older in that she had learned from experience and like Paula, had both time and interest to spare for people beside herself, especially if, like Elly, they were outside that same experience. She had been kind in a tolerant yet admiring sort of way, giving helpful little hints and pointers as to how to make a sale and what to do if it turned out to be a wrong-un. She loved to gossip, so Elly had bridled her tongue, but she had a kind heart, and it was obvious that it had been dealt a shock by the sight of Elly's battered, bleeding face and body.

'Can you sit up, love?' she asked, tender with anxiety, torn between solicitude and fear of what Mickey might do if he caught her. She was kind, but never at her own expense. She could not afford it.

'No . . . it hurts,' gasped Elly, finding it was also painful to speak.

'Give us a hand, Cind, she's better off in bed.'

Between them they managed to half support, half carry Elly into the other bedroom, the one she shared with Maureen. Cindy slept with Mickey.

'Go and get some warm water in a bowl – and some cotton wool,' Maureen ordered Cindy, who went reluctantly.

'God, you are going to have a technicolor face,' Maureen observed, as she wiped away blood. 'He's split your lip and your nose looks funny.' She touched it. Elly yelped, which made her jaw hurt so she groaned. 'I don't like the look of this.' Maureen said worriedly. 'I think he's broken your nose and done something to your jaw . . . I think you should go to hospital.'

'No . . .' Elly managed. 'Be all right tomorrow . . . rest . . . sleep . . . just let me rest . . .'

'Paula will have a look at you when she comes back,' Maureen told her reassuringly. 'She did two years of nursing so she's good with things like this. She's Park Lane tonight so it'll be late but she'll know what's best to do.'

Elly nodded, eyes closed. She ached everywhere and her nose felt as if it was stuffed; she had to breathe through her mouth. But she managed to drop off to sleep and when Paula came back at half past three in the morning Maureen took her into their room. Paula, as the longest established girl in Mickey Shaughnessy's stable – she had been with him two years and was the only one he didn't abuse because she was his best earner – had her own room and certain other rights and privileges as Leader of the Pack. She was twenty-five and had once been a nurse, but a medical student had impregnated her and she was forced to abandon her studies. Her four-year-old daughter was with foster parents and Paula worked to keep her. She stayed with Mickey because he was her cousin and only took a percentage of her earnings whereas he took every penny the other girls earned.

Now she looked at Elly and drew a sharp breath. 'God Almighty . . . he's gone too far this time.' She touched the puffy nose gingerly. 'That's broken for a start and look at her jaw, that's not hanging right. I can't do anything for her; she's got to be seen to properly and that means a doctor.'

'Mickey will kill us if we bring in anybody from outside.'

'And if she dies – '

'It's not that bad, surely!' But Maureen sounded afraid suddenly.

'Look at her ribs – that bruising. She could have internal injuries. She's got to go to hospital, Maureen and that's that.'

'Could we take her to one in some other part of town . . . South of the river . . . there's hospitals everywhere out there. Somewhere with a casualty department. We could say we found her in the street – been mugged . . .' Maureen chewed at a nail. 'And what do we tell Mickey? He'll go spare if he finds out what we've done.'

'Then we must make sure he doesn't, but since all he can think of at present is getting a fix now's the time to act, get her to a hospital.'

'How? I'm not goin' against Mickey . . . you know 'ow 'e is . . . It's different for you; you earn more'n any of us and get special treatment. I don't want 'im givin' me a hidin' like 'e done Elly.'

Paula saw the justice in Maureen's argument. Mickey could be a very nasty customer but he did control a profitable series of beats. When she'd tried it on her own she'd been run off either by the girls or their pimps, who did not hesitate to use force. Only with Mickey as her protector had she been able to earn enough to support her daughter – her reason for everything she did.

'All right, I'll have to do it, then. But shtoom, mind. Especially around Cindy. She'll blab for sure because she'll use anything to bargain with to improve her lot.'

'Not a word,' Maureen promised, relieved to be off the hook.

Paula gazed worriedly at Elly, eyes closed, breathing through her open mouth, both eyes blackened, cheeks lividly bruised, chin oddly crooked, ribs darkly discoloured, legs and thighs striped with red weals. 'I always knew she'd be trouble. I told Mickey back at the beginning I had my doubts. She's not like us. She's far too educated for a start.'

'You got O-levels, aint' you?'

'One or two, but she's way beyond me. Have you seen the stuff she reads? What's a girl with brains doing whoring for Mickey Shaughnessy?'

'Lil brung her, you remember . . .'

'I know *that*! But there must have been other things she could do besides tomming.'

'Perhaps there ain't.'

'Rubbish! I said from the start that she wouldn't fit in here and I've never changed my mind. Well, there's nothing more I can do for her tonight except make her comfortable, see she gets a good night's sleep.' She made Elly swallow a tiny green pill, then left her to its powerful narcotic effect.

★

Mickey was out of the house early next morning, his mood still trigger-happy. As arranged with Paula, Maureen took Cindy off to C&A at Marble Arch to look at a dress she had her eyes on if Mickey would come across with the price: Cindy devoted all her interest to her face and figure, especially her nails. Paula went in to Elly.

'Coast's clear . . . can you sit up?'

'I think so . . .'

It was slow work but Paula helped Elly get her clothes on. 'Pull your scarf over your face and wear these sunglasses, they'll hide your shiners. I don't want a nosy cab-driver asking questions.'

'Where are we going?' Elly mumbled as best she could.

'Hospital. I'll take you there but that's as far as I go. I can't afford to get involved, Elly. I've got my Cheryl to think about. I'll take you as far as Casualty but once there you're on your own. You're a clever girl. You'll think of a story.'

Eyes met: dark blue and – within the panda bruising – freshly-washed cloud grey.

'Thank you,' Elly mouthed.

Paula nodded, her mind on her task.

Elly could walk, but only slowly and it took time to get down the three flights of stairs – the flat was at the top of a big Edwardian villa gone to seed – and down the steps from the front door to the pavement. It seemed to take ages to walk her to the corner and down to Upper Street but once there Paula hailed a cab and with relief – for she had expected to see Mickey in hot pursuit any minute – she told the driver to take them to King's Cross. From there they took the tube to St George's, in Tooting, where Paula had done her student nursing. At its entrance she said: 'Right, Elly, you are a long way from Mickey. I doubt if he has ever been this far south. Casualty is just down this corridor; they'll look after you. I don't suppose we'll see each other again because I can't see you coming back to Mickey, can you?' Elly tried a smile but it hurt so she grimaced instead.

'Best of luck, love.' Paula patted Elly's shoulder clumsily. She was eager to get back now, to establish that all was well and to 'discover' that when she had gone to the chemist to get some ointment and painkillers, the 'patient' had managed to abscond.

'Thank you, Paula,' Elly mumbled. 'I hope you get away with it.'

'Let me get back first.' Paula waved as she turned to go and Elly heard her high heels clicking away down the tiled corridor. Then she made her slow way into casualty.

She told them she had been beaten up by the man she was living with but she refused to name names or press charges. She told them she had provoked him into losing his temper; that it was her own fault because she knew how combustible it was. Even when the police came she refused to tell them anything, writing her answers on a pad, for by then her jaw was wired, her nose splinted and taped and her ribs strapped, her bruises and contusions seen to. She said there was no one to notify; her parents were dead and she had been on her own since she was seventeen. She had lived with this man since then and yes, it had been all right but he did have this temper . . . She knew he loved her and would be terribly sorry but in the meantime a little tit-for-tat would not come amiss and she knew that when eventually she did go back he really would be very sorry for what he had done. It was difficult because she could not speak, but her large grey eyes told them of her implacable stubbornness. Since it was a case of domestic violence, as the law stood they were unable to do anything unless she was prepared to make a formal complaint and lay charges, so they had to accept her attitude.

'Stupid little cow,' the policewoman said to her colleagues as they left the ward. 'I'll never understand these girls. Nineteen years old and already hard as nails. I'd hit him with every charge on the statute book and a few more I'd invent. If there's one thing I can't stand it's women who accept violence from men as proof that they love them.'

Her voice was loud enough – intentionally – for her words to reach Elly, who wanted to shout after her: 'What's love got to do with it?' You don't know the half of it, she told the policewoman's broad back as it disappeared down the corridor. Just as I didn't know any of it when I got off that bus at Victoria Coach Station two and a half years ago . . .

*

She had known no one, had nowhere to go, a total of £2.50 in her purse. She carried one small case in which she had a single change of clothing, her hairbrush, a toilet bag and a photograph of herself and her mother, taken in happier days. She had no destination, no friends in the city, no relatives to ring and ask for a bed for the night. She had left in a hurry because the opportunity had presented itself; because a certain door had been left unlocked and a certain lightbulb removed by a tough street urchin named Jenny who was absconding from yet another temporary In-Care hostel while enquiries were made to try and trace her family.

When Elly had known Jenny was absconding that night she had begged to go along.

'I can't afford no passengers,' Jenny had told her. 'And you're green. Don't know nothing, not been in care before. I do, see. This is the fifth time they've tried to cage me and it won't work neither. I'm off up to Scotland, but I'll leave a trail that leads to London.'

Awed and impressed: 'How will you do that?' Elly had whispered.

'Ask no questions and I won't tell you no lies.' The fifteen-going-on-fifty eyes eyed Elly with some puzzlement. 'What you doin' in care, anyway? You ain't no runaway. On remand but too young for a Remand Centre? Waitin' to go into Residential? Ow old are yer, anyway?'

'Seventeen.'

'Blimey, you don't look it! I thought you was my age.'

'How old are you?'

'Fifteen – almost.' Jenny had eyed the well-spoken, frightened girl.

'You an orphan, then?'

'My mother is dead, yes. My father . . .'

Jenny said what Elly found difficult to speak out loud. 'Don't want yer, right?' A sniff. 'With me it's me Mum. Says she can't 'andle me. So why d'yer wanna leave this nice cosy home, then? It's a cold 'ard world out there, you know, and if you don't know 'ow to 'andle it gawd 'elp yer.'

'I want to get away from here – right away. Make a brand-new start.'

'That takes money. You got any?'

'No, but I know where there is some.'

'Where?' It was razor-sharp.

'Back ho – where I used to live. My father always kept money in a tin box in the bottom drawer of his desk . . .'

"'ow much?'

'I don't know, but there was always quite a thick bundle of notes each time he opened it in my presence.'

'Anybody in the 'ouse?'

Elly shook her head. Her father and her sister had both gone to different destinations but she had no idea where, leaving a locked and empty house.

'You got the keys?'

'No.' She had never had a key. Her father had not allowed her one.

'What sort of a place is it? Big, small, 'ouse, flat – '

'A big house – four floors.'

'What kind of windows?'

'Sash.'

'Double glazin'?'

'No.'

Jenny nodded, satisfied. 'What's the address?'

Something made Elly say: 'I'll take you there if you'll take me with you.'

There was a grudging respect in Jenny's laugh. 'Not so dumb as you look, are yer? All right then. Tonight. Once lights is out and we're in bed.'

'What about the other girl?' They slept three to a room.

'She won't say nothin'. Too scared. I know 'er type. But we don't talk in front of her, right? I'll tell you once and if you don't remember that's your look-out.'

Under Jenny's watchful eye Elly had eaten every bit of her supper – 'Don't know when you'll get your next meal, see?' and put her nightie over her clothes. The third occupant of the room, a fat and stupid fifteen-year-old who had been picked up when she solicited a plain-clothes policeman, was snoring stertorously when Elly followed Jenny as she used her pur-loined key and crept through darkened corridors and out through a ground floor window.

Then it had been a long, keeping-to-side-streets-and-shadows walk through an area that Jenny seemed to know better than Elly, though she was not native to the district. 'I got a good sense of direction, see. An' I been 'ere seven months. Would'a stayed longer if the nosy old bag where I was stayin' 'adn't took a look in me room while I was out and seen the stuff I 'ad there.'

'What stuff?' Elly had asked naïvely.

'From the shops, stupid! What I half-inched! Shopliftin'!'

'Oh . . .'

'She called the police and next thing I know I'm back in care again. It's in and out like a bleedin yo-yo and me mum won't 'ave me back, I know she won't. Told the old bill I was more trouble than I was worth and she didn't want no more to do with me. I don't know why they bother. I'll only do another runner . . .' She looked round at the big, silent houses. 'Blimey! Is this where you live?' Suddenly very suspicious she asked: ''ere, what you doin' in care, then?'

'It's a long story,' Elly said evasively. She stopped at a big Victorian pile. 'This is – where I lived.'

'Right. Show us the winders, then.'

While Elly kept a trembling look-out, convinced they would be pounced on any minute, Jenny did her breaking and entering, helping Elly climb in after her.

'No lights.' Jenny warned. 'But you'll know your way around, I 'spect.' The desk drawer was locked – Elly's father had always kept the key on his watch-chain – but Jenny knew how to force the lock, opening the drawer and sighing with pleasure at the sight of the japanned cash-box. There was a little over sixty pounds, and they split it. 'Fair's fair, and you wouldn't even be 'ere if it weren't for me.'

'Just so long as I have enough for my bus fare to London and a room until I can get a job.'

Jenny said nothing. Let her find out the hard way, she thought. I did, didn't I, and a damned sight younger than she is. Won't last five minutes, she thought scornfully. Knows nothin', been nowhere. Talk about babe in the woods! Talks like she had marbles in her mouth. I should'a left her where she was. Innocents like her belong in care; on account of they've always been brought up in handfuls. Oh, well, she'll learn. And she taught Elly her first lesson by stealing the money left in her purse, which was in the bag she asked Jenny to guard while she went to buy her bus ticket.

When Elly came back her bag was where she had left it but no Jenny, which Elly did not take amiss since Jenny had said she never spent money on travel but always hitched. 'Not you, though,' she had said bluntly. 'First ride you took they'd find your body in some layby on the A1. You stick to the bus.'

Elly had appreciated the advice but when she opened her purse to put her ticket away along with the £2.25 change, it was empty but for a piece of paper torn from a sandwich wrapper, and on it was written in capitals: DON'T TRUST NOBODY!

Elly was so shocked she was speechless, then terrified because all her money was gone, then plunged into black despair. Blinded by tears she made her way to the Ladies where she sobbed her heart out, leaving her cubicle only when she heard the announcer asking passengers to board the London coach.

She remembered nothing of the journey; she was too blanked out with a mixture of shock and despair. By the time she got off the coach at Victoria she was numb with hopelessness.

She looked about her bewilderedly, wide-eyed and obviously terrified. The motherly, plump woman seemingly waiting to meet somebody spotted her at once. Elly became aware of somebody struggling with several shopping bags and her good manners came into play. 'Here, let me help you,' she said.

'Oh, you are a kind girl. Not many like you around. If you could just see me across to that bench there, I'll get myself sorted out.'

Elly did so but made no attempt to go about her business. She just sat there, staring about her, chewing her lip and twisting the strap of her case.

'Haven't your folks come to meet you, then? Perhaps your bus was a bit early. They are sometimes, though more often than not they're late. I came to see my friend off and her bus was late leaving. Tell you what, I was about to go and have a nice cup of tea. Why don't you have one with me. We can sit at the window, there, and you can see if your friends come.'

Elly was dying for a hot drink. Her last meal had been

23

supper the night before, but by now Jenny's warning had been branded on her consciousness. DON'T TRUST NOBODY. But this was a middle-aged – well, elderly really, lady, with grey hair and a nice motherly face. Somebody's granny . . .

'There's nothing like a nice hot cup of tea to do you good,' somebody's granny said.

'Thank you,' Elly said, making up her mind. 'That would be very nice.' She had not one but two cups of tea and the lady treated her to a piece of succulent apple pie.

'There now, that feels better now, doesn't it?'

Elly smiled for the first time. 'Yes, much better, thank you.'

'I don't know what's happened to your folks, though. We've been here half an hour and I haven't seen you looking for them. Are you sure you have got somebody coming to collect you?'

Elly went scarlet, shook her head.

'Granny' clucked her tongue. 'Nobody! Well then, you tell me where you want to go and I'll tell you how to get there.'

She was not surprised when Elly mumbled that she was not going anywhere because she had nowhere to go.

'Nowhere to go! Oh, dear me . . . don't tell me you've run away from home!'

Granny was not sounding the note of condemnation; instead, her voice was so compassionate that Elly felt her eyes well and spill. 'No . . . not exactly . . .' she faltered. Which was true. She no longer had a home.

'Where are your parents, then? Don't you think they'll be worried?'

'My mother is dead and my – my father – my father has gone away.'

'Oh, you poor thing . . .' More clucking. 'So you've got no other family then? No aunts or uncles – or a grandma . . .?'

'Nobody. Nobody at all.'

'Oh, dear, I *am* sorry.' The lady gave a decided nod. 'Then it's just as well you met up with me. London is no place for a young girl all on her own. I know just the place for you. Somewhere you can stay until you get your bearings and find yourself a job and a place of your own. You don't mind sharing with three nice young girls?'

'Oh, no . . .' Elly was fervent. She would have shared with

24

thirty if this comfortable, kind, endlessly reassuring granny had said so.

'What's your name then, dear?'

'Elly . . .' It was the one she had decided to use; a variation of her real name but not one that had ever been used by anyone who knew her.

'Well then, Elly. I think we'd better go and get our bus. It'll be rush hour soon and there'll be no getting on them once the offices empty.'

She gathered her bags, profuse in her thanks when Elly offered to carry several of them – and led Elly to a bus-stop. When it came they rode a fair distance, and the lady insisted on paying Elly's fare. When they got off: 'Which part of London is this?' Elly asked curiously.

'Islington, dear. North London. N1. The girls live just a few minutes walk away. They're a cheerful lot, take life as it comes and one more won't make no difference, you'll see.'

When they arrived at the tall narrow house, which Elly saw uneasily had seen better days a very long time ago, they climbed three flights to the very top. But there was light and warmth and the sound of chattering voices and the chink of china and at once Elly's unease gave way to relief, which reached staggering proportions when her benefactress opened a door and ushered her into a big room, once two but now running from back to front of the house. The television was on, in one corner a young woman was ironing a bright pink blouse, on the somewhat sagging moquette sofa another girl, younger, vapidly pretty, very blonde, was painstakingly painting extraordinarily long nails – they reminded Elly of the talons of a bird of prey – with glitter polish in bright fuchsia pink, and a third girl was in the act of filling a teapot with boiling water.

'Hello Lil!' she hailed the motherly lady. 'You always time it right, don't you? I think you must smell the tea. And who's this, then?'

'This is Elly. I found her at Victoria Station, poor thing. Got nowhere to go and no family to turn to. All on her own she is, so I knew you wouldn't mind putting her up for a day or two – just till she gets her bearings and finds her feet . . . This is

Paula, Elly, and that's Cindy on the sofa and Maureen ironing her blouse.'

It had been like being stranded on a desert island without food or water and seeing a rescue launch coming straight for you. They had been kind, cheerful, unquestioningly accepting, although Paula seemed worried at first until Elly assured her that there really was nobody to bother about her; that she had not a single relative in the world.

'Nobody at all! Everybody has somebody who cares,' Paula had protested.

'Well, there's my sister,' Elly had admitted shyly, 'but – you see she's retarded and they've taken her to live in a special Home . . .'

'Oh, you poor kid. You really don't have anybody . . . Then you must stay here. We don't mind, do we girls? You can share with Maureen – all right, Maureen?'

Maureen said cheerfully: 'It's a double bed; just so long as you don't snore.'

'I don't – at least, I don't think I do.'

Lil had stayed to supper – a big panful of spaghetti bolognaise – and as they ate Elly had innocently answered the artfully inserted questions. When, at about nine o'clock, the girls began to 'get ready' Elly asked in surprise: 'Do you work at night, then?'

'S'right,' Cindy said laconically. 'Every single night.'

'Are you on nightshift, then?'

They had laughed, making Elly feel as if she had said something very stupid until Lil told them off. 'They're in the entertainment business, dear, that's why they work nights.'

'Oh . . . I see . . .' That explained everything. 'Could they – I mean – would there be a job for me? I could learn whatever has to be learned. I'm a very quick learner.'

'Well, we'll see, dear. Get your bearings first, settle in and then we'll see.'

When Mickey Shaughnessy arrived, at about ten o'clock, he was introduced as 'Paula's cousin' which he was. He was a good-looking Irishman with dark red hair and an accent that sounded to Elly like music. He had a pair of beautiful Irish eyes as blue as the lakes of Killarney and he was very interested in Elly. When the girls had gone off to work he sat on at the kitchen table, drinking coffee and chatting with her and Lil. When Lil got up to go Mickey said he would see her home; just a few streets away but she was better off walking with him than alone.

'You go to bed when you're ready,' Lil said, as she gathered her bags. 'The girls won't get home till the early hours. You can lock the door behind me, they've all got keys . . .'

'Thank you,' Elly said passionately, taking hold of one of Lil's hands. 'It was a miracle, meeting you. I don't know what I would have done otherwise.'

'Go along with you. As if I could let a pretty young thing like you get lost in a city the size of this one. Now lock the door behind me.'

'I'll be seein' you.' Mickey said, as he went out. 'I come by most days.'

Elly washed the dishes – nobody seemed to have bothered, just stuck them in the sink – and tidied up. She did the same in the bedroom, which had clothes flung everywhere, draped over chairs, magazines on the floor, make-up – lots of it – littering the dressing table. Elly hung away clothes – brightly coloured and cheap looking to her taste – and picked up underwear. She had not seen stockings like these before; she thought everyone wore tights. But these were black and very sheer and all the shoes had high heels. Elly had never owned a pair of high heels – her father said they were bad for the feet – so she tried a pair on, staggering round the room until she became used to teetering on the stilettos. Not for her, she decided. They really were uncomfortable.

But she had gone to bed feeling more comfortable with herself than she had in a long time. She had made the break; she had been taught a lesson – but she was glad Jenny had been proved wrong about the NOBODY, for had she not trusted Lil she would not be here now, warm and comfortable.

The bed was lumpy and the sheets nylon where she was used to linen, and the pillows were some kind of foam rubber, but she *felt* safe. She had really fallen on her feet; she had not expected to find such generosity. Had she not met Lil she might be in police custody: Lil had told her they patrolled all the London main termini looking for runaways.

Elly decided she would stay with these kind people as long

27

as they would let her, and until she got a job she would keep house for them. There was nothing she did not know about that for had she not done so for her father from the age of eleven, and wasn't he the *most* particular of men? Then, once she knew her away around she would get a job. As a waitress, perhaps, or a shop assistant. She knew enough about medical terms thanks to her father to be able to work in a chemist's. There was bound to be something she could do. She would ask Mickey. He seemed to know everything. Perhaps she could even get a job entertaining, like Maureen and Cindy and Paula . . . She yawned, pounded the pillow and, suddenly feeling very alone, wondered where her sister was, how she could manage to find out. She turned her face into the pillow and let the tears she had been holding back for so long well and flow freely. I'll find you and we'll be together again, Margaret . . . I promise, she wept. Wherever they've taken you I'll find you and I'll explain it all so that you'll be able to understand why I did what I did . . .

She wept herself into exhaustion and finally, sleep, and by the time Maureen slid into bed at 2 a.m. she was too deep in sleep to surface.

From her hospital bed, Elly Mark II looked back at Elly Mark I and grieved for her unworldliness, her naïveté and honesty, for what had she known of *anything* of the world? Her father had kept her on leading reins all her life, even within the confines of 17 Warwick Road. *That* had been her world, and she had not known how different the big one outside was until she learned. The hard way.

The girls and Mickey had been like Prince Charming and the Three Witches – all good ones – to Elly. They took her to see the sights, they praised her housekeeping, they let her try on their clothes, exclaimed sympathetically when she told them how her father had always chosen hers; had never allowed her jeans, or short skirts, or any of the fads and fashions.

Her life at home had been hollow with emptiness and aching with loneliness, since her father, who had no need of anyone but himself, failed completely to understand his daughter's need of the companionship of her peers, or that a retarded sister did not give Elly the feedback she needed. She loved

Margaret dearly, looked after and protected her to the best of her ability, but she was just not enough. While the other girls at school had made friends, invited them home, gone places together, Elly had not been allowed to do this. Her father saw no reason to invite strangers into his home.

Patients were different; besides, they never got any further than the surgery. Nell had been at a loss to understand why people came to see her father in his coldness and aloofness, his unbending authority, his unwavering belief that **he** and only **he** knew best and that either his patients did as he told them or they could go elsewhere, until she understood that some people liked to be told what to do since it absolved them of all responsibility, especially where their health was concerned.

'He's got no bedside manner, God knows,' she had heard one patient say to another as they left the surgery, 'and he's about as warm as an iceberg, but he gets you well again, and in the long run, where a doctor's concerned, that's all that matters. If he wasn't such a good one I wouldn't have him near me, and that's the truth of it, he's such a cold, arrogant man.'

Nell did not elaborate on her father's shortcomings, but it was obvious to the others from the way she blossomed in the warmth of their very company, that she had been long starved of the normal give-and-take of ordinary human life. Paula, from her vantage point as Mickey's Number One, was the one whose knowledge and information Elly stored away. Apart from the fact that it was obvious that Paula's intelligence was that of the other two combined, Elly liked her matter-of-factness, her acceptance of the limited choices she had and her determination to wring every last advantage from them. Paula made a good role model and Elly watched, listened, learned and copied, the latter as discreetly as she could.

Maureen, number two in ranking, had a kind heart but the kind of mentality that tended to believe what she read in the papers, and she read every tabloid every day. She was good-natured and easy-going just so long as it involved no risk. She could never have stood up to Mickey the way Paula did, but she good-naturedly gave Elly one or two tips, and was always willing to give advice if it was safe to do so. She was very wary of Mickey. But she stood in awe of Elly's obvious education, since her own had been sketchy, to say the least. Cindy, on the other hand, stood in awe of nobody. Her life was dedicated to herself and her onward and upward progress. As soon as she saw how the land lay where Mickey's territory was concerned, she made sure that she had her own particular acreage, but then stupidly went and fell for him in a way that instantly blinded her to his every fault. For the first week or two she watched Elly like a hawk, ready to defend her territory and her man, relaxing only when she was sure there was nothing to be afraid of. From then on she ignored her, regarding her as an innocent whose education had been a waste of time. All a girl needed were the necessary physical attributes to ensnare some fool of a man (for apart from her besotted view of Mickey, her opinion of men in general was that they were only good for one thing) who would, if she went about it the right way, give her all she wanted without her having to fight for it herself.

Of the three girls, Cindy was the only one who enjoyed her work. Sex was as necessary to her as breathing, and getting paid for it was even better.

It was only when, much later she looked back on events, that Elly realised how deliberately and skilfully she had been softened up for the fall, ready to be introduced to the Life.

'Do you like boys – men?' Mickey had asked Elly casually one evening as the girls were getting ready for work.

'I've never known any. My father said I was too young to have any contact with them.'

'Then we'll have to see that you meet some, won't we? Would you like that?'

Elly looked at him; suddenly her grey eyes were very knowledgeable. 'You mean like Paula and Maureen and Cindy do?'

Well now, and isn't she the quick one, Mickey thought. 'That could be arranged.'

Elly stared into the distance, thinking. 'Does it pay well?' she asked finally.

Paula raised her eyebrows at Mickey who said: 'It depends on what the punter wants you to do.'

Elly looked directly at him again. 'Such as?' she asked.

The girls looked at each other. Such straight from the

shoulder, gloves-off curiosity was most unusual in runaways like this one. Maybe, Mickey thought, she's not so green as she's cabbage lookin'.

So he told her. She did not blush or look away, displayed no revulsion or fear as might have been expected. It was Paula who said:

'Your father being a doctor I suppose he told you all about sex?'

'Yes.' Just the one word in a colourless tone.

'But 'e wouldn't let you go out with boys?' Cindy sounded incredulous.

'No.'

Casually: 'Do you think – if you were shown how to go about it – that you could pleasure men?' Mickey asked.

'I . . .' Elly chewed her lip. 'I could try,' she said eventually.

'With your looks it would be easy. Men like pretty girls like you – you could earn a lot of money.' He paused, let that sink in then struck. 'And we've spent a lot of money on you, Elly. Food, lodging, taking you here and there, fares, tickets – that £2.50 you handed over was not even a drop in the bucket. I reckon we've spent fifty times that much on you over the past week.'

Elly looked stricken. 'I had no idea . . .' Her voice wavered.

'Well, you are obligated to us.' He glanced at Paula who took up and increased the pressure.

'You could pay that back with a couple of nights' work,' she said airily.

Round-eyed, Elly clutched at the straw. 'I could!'

'Easy. Then you'd be all square with us and have money of your own to spend – on clothes and make-up and records; all the things your father wouldn't let you have. Live like a normal teenager instead of Cinderella.'

'But – '

'And we'll teach you *everything*. We know it all, don't we girls?'

'And more,' Cindy said laconically.

Eyes wide and sounding doubtful: 'You really think men would *pay me* for sex?'

'Yes.'

The silence lengthened and they let it stretch Elly's indecision

31

even tighter. When it snapped she would have decided one way or the other. Her head was bent. Mickey peered at it. He had expected to see tears; she was such an unworldly creature, and other girls, confronted so brutally with what was essentially an ultimatum, often produced a tearstorm. But she was not crying. She was staring down at her hands, at her fingers twisting and untwisting themselves. Then he saw her shake her head in a helpless gesture that might have been either 'What choice do I have', or 'I can't . . . I'm sorry I just can't' but when she raised her head her face was calm if colourless.

'All right,' she said very quietly in an equally colourless voice, as if she had packed herself away for the duration. 'Whatever you want.'

What a fool I was, Elly thought now, torn between contempt and pity for the helpless, hopeless creature she had been at seventeen. They knew what they were doing. I only thought I did. For within a month she was deep into the life, and though she had earned many times more than she had owed Mickey that very first week, he kept taking her money for 'necessary expenses . . . all those clothes I bought, and it cost me to have your hair permed and then there's the make-up.'

It seemed she would never get out of debt until she finally came to understand that she would never get out, period. That she was trapped. Mickey ceased to be kind and understanding; he became a hard taskmaster who had no hesitation in punishing what he saw as transgressions: like a girl not earning what he expected. She discovered he had a cocaine habit whose costs escalated almost daily, and that he had a temper you did not rouse if you knew what was good for you.

She tried to save, found it very difficult for Mickey handled all the money. He even bought their condoms – 'I can get them for you wholesale' and she was reduced to keeping back the occasional fiver. She dared not try for more; Mickey knew exactly what she was supposed to bring him and woe betide her if it fell short.

She made no attempt to trace her sister until she had passed her eighteenth birthday; that way they could not put her back into care. The day after she gained her majority she rang Mrs Robson, who had done the heavy work at 17 Warwick Avenue and had done her best – without crossing the good doctor's strictly drawn guidelines – to bring a little cheer into the drab lives of his daughters. Elly lied and said she was staying with her godmother – the truth was she had never even been christened – and was fine, but that she was eager to learn what had happened to Margaret. She cut off all protestations and expressions of shock and stuck to what she wanted to know, giving Mrs Robson no chance to indulge in her favourite occupation – gossiping. Elly was taking a risk in ringing her in the first place so she kept it short, and learned that Margaret was in a home for the mentally handicapped. Mrs Robson knew the address and the telephone number. Elly thanked her and hung up before she could ask more questions, then she called the Home where, after being passed from person to person and asked some searching questions she was finally told that her sister was in excellent health. Yes, she was permitted visitors but it was as well to ring first. Now and again Margaret had – episodes – and had to be isolated. When Elly asked what was meant by episodes she was told that at irregular and unexpected intervals her sister became violent.

When she left the phone box Elly had to go and sit down on a nearby bench. Margaret violent! Placid, docile, at times unreachable Margaret had turned violent! No . . . no . . . it could not be. Except she knew very well it could. She had made it her business to find out as much as she could about people like her sister, and had read many books on the subject of autism. So much for her hope of having Margaret to live with her one day. She walked blindly back home, and for a day or two was so withdrawn and silent that Mickey thought she was sickening for something, and became – for him – quite solicitous, and when, one afternoon, she could not get out of bed, became so alarmed he did the unthinkable and allowed Paula to call a doctor, who diagnosed a minor collapse. 'She's been living in nerves. Let her rest – she'll probably sleep a lot – and feed her up. There's evidence of recent and drastic weight-loss.'

'It's nothing – catching?' Mickey wanted to know.

'It's nothing physical. Has she been under some sort of strain?'

'Strain!'

'She's been very worried about her sister,' Paula explained.

'That explains it, then. Rest, sleep and good food, and this twice a day. It's a vitamin supplement and a mild tranquilliser. Tell her to come and see me in about a fortnight and I'll give her a thorough going over.'

When he'd gone: 'What's this about her sister?' Mickey asked.

'She found out where they'd put her and rang to see how she was. I think it wasn't one hundred per cent.'

'Oh, that's all. Just so long as it's not something she can pass on.'

Selfish bastard, Paula cursed, as she went in to Elly. She did look somewhat fine drawn, eyes shadowed, cheek-bones prominent, Paula thought, as she pulled the quilt up around the sleeping girl, but then she had always looked as though a good puff would blow her away. It belied an inner strength which, Paula now realised, she had been drawing on over the past months since she became part of Mickey's stable. And God knows why you did that, Paula thought. I've seen all sorts and kinds in the Life, but I've never met one like you before.

When Elly was up and about again after a week she never referred to her sister again, but there was a new grimness about her, a determination that chilled. Only Paula noticed it, and she said nothing.

Thanks Paula, for then and now, Elly thought, as she shifted her position to ease her aching ribs. Now I'm free . . . She closed her eyes and felt she was floating. Two and a half years of slavery and an endless procession of faceless men. No more. I've managed to gain my freedom, even if in a painful way, although even that has its compensations because I'm not going to get out of here for a week or two and that will be my very first holiday since . . . since I was born, she realised in shock. Her father had not approved of holidays. 'An unnecessary and needless extravagance.' Which reminded her. Carefully and gingerly she reached for her big black plastic handbag. Folded thinly and inserted in its handle were two twenty pound notes. She had managed to do Mickey down after all! She could afford the occasional magazine, perhaps a bar of chocolate. Just to know the money was there made her feel good. And when she was all healed up, whatever money she earned in future would be hers and hers alone. Never again will I be at the beck and call of any man. Never! she vowed. I have learned my lesson. I shall get four square meals a day and uninterrupted nights of sleep while I am in here. Best of all Mickey has no idea where I am. Paula won't split on me and neither will Maureen. The one who would – and with pleasure – doesn't know where I am either so she can't. That part of my life is over. Never again. I did what I had to do – and let's face it, what else was I fit for? – but I've served my sentence. I'm free at last. My life is my own. All I have to do is decide what to do with it.

3

Elizabeth Waring arrived back at Heathrow on the evening Concorde and took her usual taxi back to Central London. It was raining, and the night air was raw. She shivered inside her sable coat and was glad, once she closed the front door of what the estate agent who had sold it to her called a 'bijou' residence but was in reality a converted coachhouse, to realise that Lulu, her West Indian daily, had left the central heating turned up to HIGH.

She left her single bag in the hall while she went to check her answering machine. Among the messages were two from clients due in London within the next ten days and hopeful of her having time to spare for them. Since one was a very generous Texan and the other an equally open-handed Australian she was happy to return their calls and answer in the affirmative.

The last call was from her oldest friend, Philip Faulkner. 'Still not back from the flesh-pots?' his velvet voice chided archly. 'I hope you intend to ask me round to dinner when you get back. I am in dire need of a fresh fund of stories else yours will soon be the only house I shall ever be invited to. *Do* ring the *moment* you get back. I am simply dying to know All. *A bientôt.*'

The rest of her messages were mundane; a reminder from her dentist, another from her oculist about her contact lenses, a third from a shop she patronised for her dry cleaning saying that they regretted they could not remove the stain from the black pure silk chiffon dress no matter how they tried. Perhaps if she could enlighten them as to what the substance was . . .? After taking off the Bonnie Cashin wrap-round, uncrushable stone-beige jersey one-piece in which she had travelled she donned a favourite robe of raspberry red quilted velvet with matching slippers, then went downstairs to the kitchen to make herself a pot of Earl Grey which she took into the big sitting room. Seating herself at her Regency writing desk she unlocked its central drawer to remove a red leather ledger of the kind used by accounts clerks. Opening it she rapidly ran down the black figures on the left hand page, the red ones on the right, before entering in black the total of her latest earnings. She was busy calculating incomings and outgoings when the telephone rang. She picked it up then exclaimed with pleasure: 'Pa! This is an unexpected surprise – but a nice one. How are you?'

'Calling to complain,' her father barked, in the staccato voice of an army officer, and a high-ranking one at that. 'Haven't seen you in a month of Sundays. Thought I might propose myself for this coming weekend. Got a Regimental on the Friday so I need a bed for the night and the Club's not what it used to be – besides being a damned sight too expensive. That all right?'

'Of course it is . . .' Elizabeth had made no plans that could not be altered. Her father was always welcome. 'We can have one of our "undressed" weekends.' This meant old clothes, no visitors, and a couple of hours in her local before traditional Sunday lunch.

'Fine . . . one thing, though. Might have to bring old Tiger with me. Gettin' old, like me, and doesn't take kindly to being left in Mercer's hands.'

Mercer was the Brigadier's batman, a dog-hater. Tiger, for his part, loathed Mercer but since both were indispensable to their master they had no choice but to get along as best they could.

'He will have to sleep in the kitchen,' Elizabeth warned. 'I am not having you sneaking him upstairs. He leaves hairs absolutely *everywhere*. Lulu goes spare!'

'Well, we'll see,' the Brigadier said vaguely, which Liz knew meant she would not see Tiger after all.

'Do you want me to meet you?'

'That would be nice. I'm giving Mercer the weekend off; wants to go and see his daughter.'

'Which train?'

'Thought the 3.15; gets me into Paddington at 4.45. That all right with you?'

'I'll be there with bells on.'

Her father made a sound like a bark that was his way of laughing.

'As long as it's not balls.'

Elizabeth laughed dutifully at her father's still subalternish sense of humour.

'Until Friday, then.'

But her father was disposed to talk. 'Seen anything of your brother?'

'About six weeks ago.'

'I haven't seen him in six months. Always says he's busy.'

'He is. He's a Q.C. with a very busy set of chambers.'

'All I ever know of him is what I read in the papers.' It was a grumble but it was also a plea. Her father, Elizabeth realised, was on one of his periodic – if infrequent – Family Matters quests. And then she remembered. It was the anniversary of her mother's death next week.

'Tell you what, I'll do my best to get him to come to dinner.'

'That would be nice.' Her father tried to sound offhand but lost.

'Don't count on it,' Elizabeth warned. 'You know how full his social calendar is.'

Her father made a rude noise.

'He is hoping to be appointed to the bench next year.'

'Good. Then he can fix my parking tickets. Damned warden hides when she sees me coming – and me a Justice of the Peace! I –'

'Pa I have to go.' Elizabeth was in no mood for a 'When I was young' dissertation.

'Oh, all right then.' He sounded so down that she felt guilty. To make up for it she offered to cook him a curry. 'Your very own recipe.'

'Now that's more like it! Never get a good curry nowadays. Mercer says the smell hangs around too long. Truth is he doesn't like it; didn't like India, come to that –'

'Till Friday.' Elizabeth interrupted before hanging up. 'Oh, God,' she groaned, 'now what have I done?' Then an imp of mischief took her. She picked up the phone and dialled again.

'You sounded desperate, so I had to put you out of your misery,' she said when Philip answered.

'I was!' Then, teasingly, 'How come you never invite me to accompany you on one of your little jaunts? You could cash in Concorde for two Business Class seats and still have enough to pay my hotel bill.'

'If you think I am risking a long-standing client even for your long-standing friendship you've got another think coming.'

'Would that I had something – or should I say someone coming,' Philip Faulkner said in a mock-mournful voice.

'Oh, dear. Not pipped at the post again!'

'Not so much pipped as peeled and quartered.'

'Poor you! I *am* sorry. Tell you what, come to dinner on Saturday. You can cry on my shoulder.'

'No tears left, but a couple of bottles of that Gevry-Chambertin of yours and I will be as lachrymose as you wish.'

'One bottle. Pa is coming.'

There was a silence then: 'Bitch!' Philip reproached.

'I can't cope with Pa on my own right now,' Liz said.

'Oh, why not?' Philip Faulkner could discern the distress signal of a bat a thousand yards away.

'Not over the telephone.'

'Then you do have something to tell!'

'Yes, and you are the only one I can tell it to.'

'Is it good or bad?'

'No hints, and I can't tell you in Pa's hearing, but if you help keep my sanity while he *is* here then all will be revealed. I'm going to try and get Boy to come too.'

'From what I hear he takes every opportunity.'

Elizabeth laughed. Philip could always be relied upon to lighten her darkness. He was very self-absorbed, and shudder-ingly cynical, but he would give her a dispassionate opinion as to her future course of action. Besides, it was always fun when he and Boy got together. It was through her brother that she had got to know Philip, for Boy had been his fag at Eton. Elizabeth had been awed by the languid swell that Philip

Faulkner was in those days; by his waistcoats, his eyeshadow, his cigarette holder.

'Forty years out of date,' her brother had said pithily. 'He thinks he's a reincarnation of the golden twenties but can't decide whether it is of Stephen Tennant or Cecil Beaton! Now I ask you – who in his right mind would be either?'

But Elizabeth had liked him at once; his hedonism, his wide-eyed belief that the world owed him, not merely a living but a bishopric; that to claim his acquaintanceship was to mark you for life (Yes, like dirty laundry, her brother had said). He made no bones about his ambition, which was to be The World's Best Kept Man, and when young, his epicene beauty had brought him both fame and fortune. Now that the beauty had gone, in spite of a whole series of preservation orders, so was his only way of ensuring he lived the life he believed he deserved. But he was always hopeful because he had the tenacity, the nerve – brass-bound and polished daily – to endow him with a confidence that would crush stone. And when he put his mind to it he could still bedazzle even the most jejune of prospects.

From Philip, Elizabeth knew she would get a ruthlessly reasoned summary of how best to cope with not only what was wrong with her but the short time she had left in which to do so. Brisk self-interest was what she needed right now, for there was no way she could tell either her father or her brother; neither would understand. They had no idea she was a high-class whore, either. Her father thought she lived on what she had got from her divorce from Miles Coxe-Waring (Elizabeth had dropped the Coxe when she took up whoring because the connotations were so risible as to be risky), but that had gone years ago. Her brother thought she worked in Public Relations and was so preoccupied in climbing the legal ladder that it never struck him that he had no office number or address for her. He gave her free legal advice if and when she needed it, but they had never been close because they were so dissimilar.

Philip was her style; he had helped her get started as a courtesan; introduced her to men who could afford her. She, in turn, had kept her eyes and ears open on his behalf, and when they got together they had laughed themselves silly at the vanity and stupidity – not to mention cupidity – of the human race. Of which Philip, that much older and therefore that much more experienced, had enormous knowledge. They came from the same strata of society: Philip's family was of ancient lineage, while Elizabeth could trace ancestors back to Henry VIII. Her father had been a brigadier in a very fashionable cavalry regiment when he retired; her mother the youngest daughter of a twelfth baron, but the land had long gone and the money with it. The Harvills, her father's family, still owned the house they had lived in for the past three hundred years, but the brigadier's pension and the small annuity from his mother's estate were not enough to keep it in order. There had been barely enough to send Boy to Cambridge after Eton; Elizabeth married when she was twenty-one; the very eligible and rich Miles Coxe-Waring who was very handsome, very thick and very boring. But in 1954, marriage was what was expected of a girl, and Elizabeth Harvill had been considered to have done very well for herself at her fashionable wedding at St Margaret's, Westminster (paid for by the groom). White stiff faille, six bridesmaids in paper taffeta, and a reception at the Dorchester.

But she had found on the first night of their honeymoon that she had made a terrible mistake; sex was so utterly disappointing that she almost left there and then. Two years later she did finally bolt with a young French ski instructor who showed her that sex with the right man could be incredibly satisfying. Her husband, with daring rare for the late fifties but pushed into it by his mother, began divorce proceedings citing the Frenchman, but Elizabeth, who had been putting two and two together and getting an A-level in sussing out her husband's real nature, had him watched and then countersued, claiming that his homosexuality was what had driven her to find fulfilment elsewhere. He hurriedly dropped his petition, put together the usual farce of a professional co-respondent and a hotel in Worthing and allowed Elizabeth to divorce him while her brother, via the senior partner in his chambers, extracted a sizeable settlement as hush-money.

For Elizabeth, the sixties were the peak of her life. She lived for the moment and chased it wherever it went, for she had discovered that it had not been sex she had loathed but Miles Coxe-Waring. With other men she could not get enough, and

41

as she did not mind what she did or what was done to her as long as it did not hurt and gave pleasure, she was in constant demand. She had such *joie de vivre*, such an open-hearted lust for life; she loved everything and everybody but she never *really* loved anybody in particular until, in the summer of 1963, at a Guards Club polo match, she met Jose-Luis de Santos. It was a *coup de foudre* which took her utterly by surprise. She liked men enormously and adored what they carried between their legs and what they could do to her with it, but she had never loved one of them before in such a way that had he never laid a finger on her she would still have worshipped the ground he walked on. And what she saw in the bandy-legged polo player, who *said* he was from an Argentine family who had fled Spain during the reign of mad Queen Isabella, nobody could understand. For a start he was about as aristocratic as a backyard moggie if every bit as randy, and the 'de' in his name was self-invented. He was a gaucho, which was why he rode so well and scored so many goals, but he was also a consummate liar, a deceiver of women on a grand scale and, according to continental gossip, a con-man of great skill and much experience. To Liz Waring, who had laughed and loved her way through dozens of light-hearted *affaires* he was the love of her life, and from the day she met him she never looked at another man.

He put her through hell. He did not call when he said he would; he borrowed money which he never repaid; he saw other women as and when the fancy took him and he was not above belting her if she 'whined'.

But she was besotted with him. Her parents could not understand it, her brother could not believe it. 'For God's sake, Liz, the man is an absolute shit! Everybody knows it but you. He's nothing but a common gigolo! He sells himself to the highest bidder and once you have spent your last penny you'll see him no more. He is battening off you shamelessly. You let him use the house Miles bought you – and I'll bet he doesn't pay a penny in rent; you feed him and for all I know clothe him. Where's your self-respect?'

'I'd rather have him.'

He flung up his hands in despair before flinging out of her house, the lovely house in Cadogan Square which had been part of her divorce settlement and which, some eight weeks later, she sold so as to pay off Jose-Luis's gambling debts. Her mother worried so much she had a heart attack from which she never really recovered. When she died her father bitterly accused her of selfish cruelty, of not caring for anything and anybody but that 'randy, bandy polo player' which caused a rift which was not healed for years. It was not until some five years later that the rotting relationship collapsed. He came to her one night to say he was leaving, going back to South America. He had no choice; he had lost a great deal of money at the tables and the man to whom he had lost it was not the sort to look kindly on anyone who could not pay his debts. 'If I don't and stay here I am a dead man socially. I have no choice . . .' He had stopped, flicked her a look then said: 'Well . . . I do have one choice but it involves you, I am afraid.'

'What can I do? You know I'll do anything for you, darling.'

The thought of losing him was not to be borne so she said: 'If you go back to Argentina I'll come with you. I can get a job.'

'No. I cannot deprive you of your family and friends – '

'My family don't speak to me and apart from Philip there is not a friend I would miss. As long as we are together, darling, that's all I want.'

'You do not know Argentina. I do not want to go back there but if I do I go alone.' Pause. '*If* I do . . . You and you alone have the power to save me.'

'But – how? I have no money left . . . I've sold all that would bring a decent price. What have I got that would be worth money in the sums you need?'

He looked at her, and it was then, for the first time that she noticed what it was that had always troubled her about his expression. It was curiously blank; as if dead behind the eyes. And in that same instant she knew what it was he wanted her to sell. But she made him say it just the same.

'What have I still got to sell?' she repeated.

'Not sell . . .' he said reproachfully. 'I prefer to think of it as a trade.'

'Trade what?' she repeated as if puzzled, but suffering the deepest, cruellest pain she had ever known. Say it! she commanded him silently. You *will* say it, you bastard! You will taste those words or else I absolutely refuse. Relief almost had

43

her dizzy when he seemed to hesitate. He can't say it, she thought joyously. He can't bring himself to say it because he finds it unsayable! He does love me, he *does*!

'My IOUs will be burned if you spend the night with him.'

Elizabeth felt his words turn her to stone. 'Rather an expensive fuck,' she said harshly. 'He must be rich. How much was it you lost to him?'

Jose-Luis mumbled something.

'I didn't hear it. How much?'

'Ten thousand pounds.' Now he was irritable, soon he would be angry. Oh, how well she knew his moods and oh, how long she had put up with them. Why? she keened silently. In God's name why?

'He must think I am worth it. Have you been singing my praises?'

'He finds you very attractive.'

'So do most men. But I have never met one willing to pay ten thousand pounds. You had better tell me who he is. I am not selling myself blindfold even for that amount of money.'

He said a name, softly, almost hesitantly, as though the walls might have ears.

'Oh, yes, he *is* rich . . . all that oil, of course. And what is ten thousand pounds for a woman to a man who has recently paid a million for a horse!'

Jose-Luis shrugged, but it was again impatient, and with her newly scale-free eyes she saw that he had never doubted she would agree; that the deal had probably been agreed even before they got up from the table and that it had not been the Sheikh who suggested it, but the Love of her Life. Jesus Christ! she shrieked inwardly. Love! How can I have loved this piece of shit? Boy was right but I either could not or would not see it. How come I can now, then? Because this really is the absolute end. I have wasted years of my life on you; I have spent all my money on you, sold my house for you, lost my friends and alienated my family for you. She wanted to jump to her feet and beat him about the head; she wanted to tear his eyes out, rend and claw that smoothly golden olive skin; see him bleed except she knew now that he wouldn't; his blood was too cold to run freely. But her voice was calm when she said: 'So explain to me the arrangements for this little deal?'

'You go – I take you – to his house in The Boltons; you stay, I leave with a cheque.'

'No,' she said, flat calm and absolutely decisive. 'I go, you don't – and no cheques. Cash. Given to me. I am the one worth the money; the least I expect is to be able to see it, handle it before I pass it on.'

He frowned.

'My way or not at all.' She used her most cuttingly superior voice touched with flat boredom, and it was perhaps the worst thing of all to see the way he agreed instantly. His Mistress's Voice, she thought, quelling a laugh because she knew if she let it go she would have hysterics.

She despised him so much it was choking her, but what made her feel sicker was the depth of the contempt she felt for herself. I have heard people say they would sell their grandmother for a pint, she thought dazedly, but you are the first man I ever knew who would sell the woman they profess to love in order to settle a gambling debt. Which was when she made up her mind.

A week later a big black car came to the Cremorne Gardens flat where they now lived and Elizabeth got into it alone to be driven to The Boltons. She was delivered back exactly one hour later, and as she entered the flat Jose-Luis jumped up eagerly. 'Well?'

'Yes, very well, actually. He is a charming man and very virile.'

His smile was ostensibly relieved but his eyes were no longer dead. They were alive with greed.

She dropped her faille evening coat onto the sofa. 'I am seeing him again,' she said. 'Next week, for a much lesser fee, of course. You always did tend to exaggerate, and while I know he is a very rich man it does not do to be greedy. And why did you lie about it being a gambling debt?' There was a tut-tut in her languid, unhurried voice. 'You offered me to him, that's the truth of it. You had seen him watching me and saw a chance to make a profit.'

She swung then, pivoting on her heel, her extended arm rigid, her palm connecting with his unsuspecting face full force so that the crack was like a bone snapping and the blow so

45

violent he was knocked backwards and fell over the footstool, a look of shocked surprise on his reddening face.

She stepped across the footstool to bend over him, face contorted, eyes burning with loathing. 'You greedy, self-serving son-of-a-bitch! You thought you'd turn pimp, did you?' Her laugh poured scorn. 'Not on my account you won't. If I decide to earn money whoring then it is *my* money, do you hear? *This* money?' She brandished the thick wad of notes she took from her black brocade evening purse. '*I* earned this, not you! No man takes what I earn, with the sweat of my brow, or the juice of my cunt! You oily toe-rag! Get out of my house – no, don't try it'. He had jumped to his feet and raised his own hand. 'Philip!' she called.

The flat door opened and Philip Faulkner, followed by a beautiful young man built like a scrum-half, entered the room.

'Out!' Elizabeth said, to her erstwhile lover, on a jerk of the head. 'Of my flat, of my life. And one word . . . one measly, stinking word and reports of certain matters concerning the seventeen-year-old daughter of one of our belted earls will be laid before the police. Do I make myself clear?'

The onyx eyes flicked from her to the two men and back again. He called her a string of very ugly names in Spanish but he moved, giving the two men a wide berth even though they moved to either side of the door, and was through it in an instant. They heard him taking the stairs two at a time.

'Wonderful!' Philip applauded. 'Bette Davis to the life!'

But Elizabeth burst into tears and buried her face in her hands.

'Now then, come come . . . I thought you had wept yourself into a drought the other day . . .'

'So did I, and I'm so glad I told you because if I hadn't I wouldn't have known about the pimping part or about Lucinda Coleport.'

'Ah, but I did and that's all that matters. Oh, now please . . . this is a new dinner jacket and I do not want watermarks on these lovely satin facings, here . . . use my handkerchief. Robin, a drink I think?'

'I'm not crying for him, don't think that,' Liz sniffed, wiping her eyes. 'these tears are for me; stupid, besotted, infantile me. I was told and told and told but would I listen? You told me,

Pa told me, Boy told me – even Baba Fellowes told me and she *never* gives good advice.'

'I think we must put it down to the temporary insanity which possesses one when deep in the coils of love. I know whereof I speak having been there myself. One's faculties are blunted and one's eyes dazzled. And we must all go through it at least once.

'I am never going through it again, *never*.'

'Foolish one,' Philip murmured indulgently.

'I mean it. And do you realise what I earned tonight? I know it was a one off but – *ten thousand pounds!*'

Liz giggled. 'And I'll tell you something else. I enjoyed tonight. I was good – bloody good if I say it myself. I threw myself into my work and it was obvious he was pleased.' Another giggle. 'Because he gave me a tip. Look . . .' At the back of the thick wad was another, thinner one. 'An extra thousand pounds!'

Philip said urbanely: 'I would have expected no less.'

'It satisfies me because it pays back some of the money I spent on that – that – '

'Yes, we know what you mean.'

' – so I can pay off my own debts, but this . . .' she held out the thin bundle, 'is for you. I really am grateful, Philip. I knew that somehow the idea originated with Lover Boy but it would never have occurred to me to think he was pimping. I thought he really had lost money gambling.'

'Hardly. He cheats.' Philip nodded at Liz's open mouth. 'Oh, yes. Since you ceased to be able to subsidise him that is how he has been making his money – until he saw a chance to blackmail old Hugh Coleport, of course.'

'Is she really pregnant?'

'I'm afraid so. I gather Coleport actually took a horsewhip to the Gaucho when he had the temerity to say he would make an honest woman of her for the right price. He really has lost out all round.'

Philip sounded eminently satisfied, especially with his thousand pounds. 'I will accept this because beggars cannot be choosers,' he acknowledged matter-of-factly, 'added to which I consider I earned it. We are both in the commodity business;

yours is bodies mine is information.' Their eyes met, minds too. 'Yes . . . I could provide you with customers – '

'Clients.'

'Very well – clients – for an introductory fee of – shall we say ten per cent?'

'Agreed!'

They shook hands on the deal. 'You see, dear boy,' Philip turned to the beautiful but silent young man, 'that is what is known as seizing your opportunity. Never turn one down. They take umbrage so easily and never return.'

Liz was deep in thought. 'I think about a dozen don't you? Clients, I mean. And I visit them, otherwise I'm going to incur extra expense. It is going to cost me enough to dress the part as it is – '

'Robin, dear boy, this is much too old for your young ears. Wait for me in the car. I shan't be long.' He blew a kiss. 'I will make it up to you, promise . . .' To Liz, on a creamy sigh: 'Such a dedicated pupil . . .' Then all briskness: 'Now, to business . . .'

Liz came back from the past to hear Philip saying '. . . will come.'

'Sorry? I missed that.'

'I asked if you are sure Boy will come. He will go to such extraordinary lengths to avoid me. I cannot for the life of me think . . .'

'You know very well why! You terrify him. Always have done, always will do. But to answer your question – yes, he'll come all right. He doesn't see Pa nearly enough and I know just the right spot to press on that calloused conscience of his to give him a bad case of the guilts . . .' Liz put the receiver back down but did not return to her figures. She sat staring into space, her mind still back in the past.

Philip would be anything but impressed when he learned how much time she had devoted recently to thinking about money. She had never saved a penny. She lived high and spent the same way. Her champagne she ordered by the case and if she wanted black truffles at £100 for two ounces she bought them. She spent £50,000 a year on clothes, another five on shoes, and her jewellery was the real McCoy. Her car was always the same model; a red Mercedes Sports, and it was replaced every year. Her converted coach house was in the right postal district – SW1 – and no expense had been spared in decorating it. Her handbags were by Hermès and her hair was shaped and kept the right shade of butter-blonde by the skilled hands of Michaeljohn himself.

She went regularly to health farms; the Golden Door in California, Shrublands in England, the Greenhouse in Arlington Texas or the Bircher-Benner clinic in Zurich, where she would look around at the much married women in the process of shedding one rich husband and getting themselves in shape to start the hunt for the next one. Sometimes she would smile to herself for they were the wives of clients who had no idea how she earned the money which allowed her to share a steambath or a hot tub with them, and she would reflect that in reality they were both in the same trade. She would look at some fifty-year-old woman who had worked her way up through four husbands and feel nothing but contempt, because she regarded women like that as predators. She had never liked or trusted women much, especially the ones she encountered in such circumstances, reeking of conspicuous consumption, eyes assessing the jewels of the other women to see whose were the best; women who were about to be dumped by a husband for a newer model and so were intent on losing pounds and wrinkles so that they could acquire their own latest model. The married whores, she had dubbed them, for they sold themselves every bit as much as she did only they hypocritically demanded the badge of respectability – a wedding ring – to hide the fact.

She made no bones about what she was, because she was the best. You had to be able not only to afford Elizabeth Waring but to live up to her. And now it would all soon be over. The occasional lack of feeling in a hand, a stumble when there was nothing in the way, now and then an attack of double vision were what had sent her first to her own doctor, a Frenchman who knew her occupation and gave her a twice-yearly top-to-toe check-up, and finally to a diagnosis she did not at first believe. How could she possibly have an inoperable brain tumour? She, who was as healthy as the proverbial horse – who never even got the common cold, for God's sake!

It's not fair! she had cried, the eternal protest. It was not that she was afraid of death, it was that she loved living so much. She had no belief in an afterlife; death was the last, eternal sleep, and at least that was all that would happen to her. A gradually deepening coma from which she would never emerge. As deaths went it was as good a way to go. Painless, she had been assured, though she would need nursing for the last few months because she would not be able to look after herself. It was the fact that she did not want to have to leave that enraged her. If she had believed in a stern God, like the Jews, she would have thought she was being punished for her lifestyle, but she did not believe in an arbitrarily malignant fate. Life was what *you* made it and she had made a damned good one hadn't she, using such assets as she had? And she had never cheated, never short-changed, always given full value for money and, she had been told time after time, much pleasure and, would you believe it, happiness. Why, then? *Why*? Elizabeth was not given to analytical thought, but she did not like unanswered questions either and she was resentful that there seemed to be no answer to this one. I will talk it over with Philip, she thought now, and found the knowledge comforting. He had such a concise mind, uncluttered by any of the modern-day shibboleths; he thoroughly concurred with Mrs Patrick Campbell's dictum: 'It should not concern anyone else what one does as long as one does not do it in the street and frighten the horses.'

We are a pair, she thought, and found that thought amusing. He a kept man, me a high-priced whore. Thoroughly reprehensible by some people's standards but not by ours. He'll advise me how to handle it; when and how I tell Pa and Boy . . . or even if I need to. Yes Philip will know. He always does.

4

Elly had a surprise visitor at the end of her first week in hospital. She was deep in Bleak House, which she had found on the book lady's trolley, and so did not at first realise that someone had stopped by her bed. Of all the beds in the ward hers was the only one that never had a visitor's chair because no one ever came to see her. Now she heard someone say: 'Do I sit on the bed, then?' and looked up to see Maureen, smiling at her brightly and dressed in what she obviously thought was the appropriate apparel for hospital visiting; unrelieved black, which did not suit her pallid skin and pale fawn hair, and only served to emphasise her long nose and bony features. But her faded blue-denim eyes regarded Elly with the unabashed curiosity and eager interest of one who was dying to know all.

Yes, it would be Maureen, Elly reasoned. Paula was too circumspect and Cindy too selfish. Maureen was always the one whose shoulder was on offer. Or had Mickey sent her to snoop? Her eyes must have expressed her alarm since Maureen hastened to dispel it.

'It's all right, Mickey don't know I'm 'ere. Not that it would do him any good if he did. He's in jail, on remand.'

Elly sat up, reached for her pad and pencil, for as her jaw was still wired she could not speak. 'How?' she wrote. 'Why? When?'

'You'd never guess in a thousand years. Cindy shopped him.'

Maureen nodded happily in the face of Elly's astonishment.

'She knew he was meetin' his dealer for a supply so she told that butch sergeant – you know the one I mean – with the frizzed hair – well, she's arrested Cindy so many times they are almost friends, so Cindy rung the station and arranged to meet her then told her about the drug meet – where and when, like. They got him with a fat little bag of almost pure cocaine and a couple of dozen amphetamine thingummys so they arrested him and the dealer.'

'Why?' wrote Elly. 'Cindy, I mean.'

'He hit her. Complained she weren't keepin' the flat proper. You know how she is about her nails? Well, he broke two of them. She went berserk! You'd a thought he'd broken her fingers! Anyway, she bided her time and when he went out so did she. Kept out of the way till they had him then come back, packed her things and legged it off back up North. So I thought I'd come and give you the good news. How are you, anyway?'

Maureen examined Elly critically. 'Well, the bruisin's a lot better but your nose don't look too good and what's them wires on your teeth?'

'Jaw broken,' Elly wrote. 'That's why can't talk.'

'Paula was right, then. She's in Sutton today with her kid, but we don't know what'll happen now what with Mickey gone. Probably Tony'll run things while Mickey's inside. He did before when Mickey got sent down for poncing. At least *he's* not on drugs and he don't beat you up . . . I brung you these . . .' It was a bunch of mixed flowers and a couple of magazines, the kind with pictures rather than words.

'Thank you,' Elly wrote.

''ow d'you eat, then? Through a straw?'

Elly wrote: 'Liquids – soups, milky drinks, etc.'

Maureen wrinkled her nose. 'Nasty . . .' Then, curiously: 'So 'ow long you going to be in 'ere, then?'

'Don't know, for sure. Another week at least or until they need the bed.'

'Just as well I didn't bring you no fruit,' Maureen giggled.

Just then a nurse came up the ward to issue a reprimand. 'Sitting on the beds is not allowed. You'll have to find yourself a chair.'

'Where from?' Maureen asked impudently.

The nurse looked round. There were none. 'You can both

go into the dayroom,' she ordered. 'Miss Jordan is allowed to spend time out of bed.'

Maureen helped Elly into the hospital dressing gown, which gaped at the back. 'Blimey, you're strapped up like a mummy. He give you a goin' over and no mistake.'

The dayroom was empty so they took two chairs by the window and Maureen lit a cigarette, first opening the window a crack. 'Just in case.'

Elly wrote on her pad: 'What happened when Mickey found out I was gone?'

''e done 'is nut! Give us all the third degree but I didn't know anythink did I, neither did Cindy, and Paula lies with the straightest face I've ever seen. Anyway, 'e played hell for a couple of days then this drug business come up and you was forgotten. Cindy's the one for the 'igh jump if and when 'e ever catches up with her, and that's not likely since she's scarpered back up to Salford where she come from in the first place. She won't be back in a 'urry, that's for sure. Anyway, it give me the chance to come and see you and put you in the picture, so to speak, and to say that if you was to want to come back I'm sure Tony would 'ave yer. Mickey's looking at a year inside at the least on account of 'e was on a suspended sentence anyway because of the last time they done 'im for poncing. Tony ain't bad, and 'e treats his girls decent.'

Elly shook her head in a way which left Maureen in no doubt of her refusal.

'Oh, well, suit yourself. I suppose it would be for the best, seein' as 'ow Tony and Mickey is mates.'

Best? thought Elly. There is no best around Tony Panacoulis. He had given her the creeps the very first time she had ever set eyes on him . . .

He had been sitting at the kitchen table, thoroughly out of place. Too sleek, too smart, too moneyed for his shabby surroundings, and yet she had known at once that he was as cheap as they came. He had a face like an over-ripe fruit, with a pasty-complexion and a pulpy mouth under thick, tightly curled hair that had more grease on it than a headwaiter's palm. But Mickey's attitude told Elly at once that she was in the presence of someone who could break Mickey with a flick of the wrist.

She knew they had been talking about her when Mickey said heartily: 'This is Elly, Tone . . . wasn't I right? Isn't she a bit of class? And a born actress! Sure and the Abbey Theatre would be takin' her if she was to audition for them.'

Mickey's enthusiasm bounced off Tony Panacoulis's indifference and fell back stunned.

'Come over here, then . . . let the dog see the rabbit,' snapped Mickey.

Elly looked at Paula, sitting on the sofa, who nodded slightly. Her look said: watch this one.

'Take your coat off, then . . . give Tone a good looksee.'

Elly had taken off her cheap coat, revealing her slender body in a checked mini and a tight ribbed sweater with a polo neck. It clung to her young breasts. Her long legs were in thigh-length boots and between them and the skirt there was a good eight inches of firm young flesh. She stood under Tony Panacoulis's black-olive eyes as they travelled over her, leaving a slimy trail. She forced herself to stand still when what she wanted to do was make a run for it. Her instincts – and what experience she had gained in the past few months – told her not to have anything to do with this man.

'Tony's looking for a new face for his movies,' Mickey announced, with all the portentousness of one who had just been told he'd been nominated for an Oscar.

'Oh? What kind of movies?' Elly asked.

She felt Tony Panacoulis's obsidian eyes as they flicked over her but she kept to her role. Five months in the Life had not totally erased her naïveté or capacity for innocent surprise – or so she was at pains to have people think, for underneath the shining-surface-innocence the carapace of experience was already forming a hard shell behind which all she really was could be protected.

'Didn't you hear me, girl? This is Tony Panacoulis!' Mickey turned to his Lord and Master. 'I sometimes think Elly comes from another planet! She knows a lot about a lot of things but not one of them of any importance to people like you and me!'

'Tony makes the best hard porn in the business,' Paula said.

'Oh . . . I see . . .' Elly let a frown appear, one of distaste.

'Now don't you be wrinklin' your nose up before you know what's what!' Mickey warned sharply. 'Tony pays his artistes well. You could make a fair bit from just one appearance.'

'*I* could?' Elly asked.

Mickey's eyes narrowed. 'Don't you get lippy with me, my girl. Of course I'd take my cut. I'm giving you the chance, aren't I?'

'One I must refuse,' Elly said politely. She turned to Tony Panacoulis.

'I don't think I could give you what you want,' she told him. 'But thank you for the offer.' It was perfectly polite but it was definite.

'Now look here . . .' Mickey blustered.

'S'all right, Mickey,' Tony Panacoulis said in a voice as soft as his pudgy hands. 'Elly's entitled to her opinion, and if she doesn't believe in what she's doing she won't give the sort of performance I expect. Maybe, when she's had a bit more experience at the job she'll think again. Quite frankly she's a bit young for the part I had in mind right now.' Mickey's face cleared. 'Right, you're the boss, Tone. Whatever you say. Maybe in another six months or so?'

'We'll see,' Tony Panacoulis shrugged.

Not if I see you first, Elly thought. Never in her life had she taken such an instant dislike to anybody, but she had learned to trust her instincts and right now they were red for danger.

She knew, as her clear grey eyes met the shiny black ones that he would come back; that he would ask her again, and if she refused it would go against her.

Later, when she had the chance, she asked Paula about him. 'Who is he?' she asked.

'Mr Big. Runs a string of girls – at least a dozen, but makes his pile from porn – as hard as it comes. Cindy's done a few.' In a cynical voice, 'Cindy will do anything if the money is right.'

'Have you done any?'

'A couple . . . when I didn't know any better. Tony's clever, he starts you off on the ordinary stuff – one or two straight-forward orgy two-reelers – then you graduate to the bondage and the rape and the sadistic stuff. You were right to turn him down. I didn't have the courage when he asked me and I was older than you.'

'He gives me the creeps,' Elly told her on a shiver.

'I know. It's those dead eyes.'

'Why is Mickey so nervous around him?'

'Because Tony can be very unpleasant if you are not pleasant to him. His goons are martial arts experts. More than one man has been crippled for life, and I know of at least one who was castrated. The thought of that turns Mickey bright yellow. Also – though I can't prove it – Tony is where Mickey gets his cocaine.'

Elly had waited with dread once the six months were up. She was coming up to her first anniversary in the Life; she was harder, a lot less trusting, and her former naïveté had long since been sentenced to solitary confinement. She was also more confident in that next to Paula, who had a regular list of punters, she was Mickey's highest earner; as much as Cindy and Maureen together. He had promoted her to Park Lane where her classy looks stood her in good stead. It all depended on Mickey, whose habit now was costing him more than he could afford. He owed Tony Panacoulis a lot of money.

When Tony did not take up his option, she was relieved enough to ask Paula what was happening with him these days.

'He's got some new interest,' Paula told her. 'Very hush-hush, so they say. All I know is that there is money in it – a lot of money.'

'More than pornography?'

'Rumour has it—' Paula shuddered, 'he uses children.' At Elly's expression, 'You too? I keep thinking of my Cheryl. I'd kill any man who laid a finger on her or so much as looked at her that way. It gives me the creeps, sex and children.'

Elly saw Tony Panacoulis a few times after that, but though he always looked at her in a way that had her heading for the bathroom and the loofah, he never repeated his offer. It was obvious that he knew what her answer would be.

'. . . what are you going to do then?'

Elly came out of her thoughts to find that Maureen had been chatting on. 'I mean, it's not as though you've got any trainin' except what we give you.' She giggled.

'I'll think of something,' was all Elly wrote.

But she lay thinking about Maureen instead, after she had gone, realising how deeply touched she felt that a girl with whom she had nothing in common should take the trouble to come to a hospital a long way south of the river in order to set her mind at rest concerning the man who had put her there. But then, Maureen was, always had been, the kind one.

From Paula, Elly had learned to expect impartiality and an almost clinical judgement as to her worth; from Cindy she had never expected anything. She was grateful to Maureen and appreciative of her good deed, but her paramount emotion was one of relief that she was free; of them and of the life she had been forced to live with them, though they had given her her first taste of what it must be like to live as part of an ordinary family. She knew by now that her own had been anything but.

They had been kind in their way, but if the price of her freedom was to lose that 'family's' hold on her then she was willing to pay the price.

She turned her mind to thinking about how she could manage to live in the future, and to the lady who had recently been to see her, obviously prompted by someone on the hospital staff. Some kind of a social worker, she had offered Elly a place in a hostel for girls like her – 'who have nowhere else to go. You will receive Social Security and help in finding a job while you are there. The maximum stay is six months, I'm afraid. There are so very many young girls like you, but when the time comes to leave they will help you find alternative accommodation. Would you be interested?'

'*Would I!*'

'Then I will see what I can do. The hostel is funded partly by the GLC and partly by the London Diocesan. Their aim is to give practical assistance to girls in your position.'

She did not say that she knew Elly's usual position was on her back but Elly had no illusions as to her cover being blown. Probably because of the police. She had been cautioned twice by them, after all.

'I think you will like it. There are rules and regulations, of course, and certain duties – household duties to be performed – the hostel is a large house, actually. You understand that you will not be free to come and go as you please. There will be supervision.'

'I understand. And I am still interested.'

'Excellent.' The lady had been pleased. One more rescued soul.

But Elly was content because it meant she had somewhere to go other than the streets. As for rules and regulations . . . I could tell you all about them, she thought sardonically. My father had more of them than the Army.

One way or another she was never going to be at any man's beck and call ever again. She had run away from home only to end up in the clutches of Mickey Shaughnessy. She would not do *that* again. No more taking orders. No more being told: 'I run things around here.' I am in nobody's charge but my own from here on in.

I'll get a decent job this time, and whatever I earn will belong only to me. And I'll save because this time I will be able to. No more handing over everything I earn to finance a greedy man's drug habit. And I'll have my own place where I don't have to share. I will be all on my glorious own, and the door will be one I can lock. Oh, yes, she thought, all but delirious with joyful anticipation. I've learned my lesson. I know what to do now, and what not to do. Once is bad luck, twice is unfortunate, if I let it happen a third time I deserve all I get! Only I won't let it happen again. I'm no longer the trusting innocent I was when dear old motherly Lil – the best scout in the business – saw me at Victoria Station and only had to give me a nudge and I fell right into her outstretched hand. Jenny did me a greater service than she will ever know and I still didn't heed her warning. But I will in future. Nobody will *ever* use me again . . .

5

When Liz met her father at Paddington she was shocked by the change in him. Suddenly he was an old man. Whenever she thought of her father it was as the professional soldier; band-box smart, buttons bright enough to put your eye out, leather gleaming, shoes shined to a mirror finish, hair smooth and sleek, moustache trimmed to the mathematical millimetre. Now he was stooped, his moustache straggled and he leaned rather heavily on his stick. His suit needed both cleaning and pressing and he looked about him bewilderedly.

'Hello, Pa.' She went up to him, hugged and kissed him.

'Ah, there you are . . . don't see so well these days. Damned glasses need changing again, I suppose. Still, at that I see a damned sight better than Mercer.'

No wonder he looks so scruffy, Liz thought on a pang. He is seventy-eight and Mercer is only two years younger. They are two old men.

'Give me your case,' she said. 'I've managed to find a parking space but this is warden territory so let's get away before I'm caught.'

He who had once walked so briskly now tended to shuffle, and getting him into the car took ages, but finally – still free of a ticket – Liz drove off back to town.

He was glad of the whisky she brought him, and with that inside him brightened somewhat, enough to launch into a diatribe against British Rail and the state of their first-class carriages. He had another whisky and then went upstairs to bathe and change. Liz unpacked his case with something like alarm, but when she took out his mess dress it was immaculate; decorations unspotted, insignia gleaming. Mercer might have to let some things go but never anything to do with the Regiment.

She let him soak for fifteen minutes then took him up another whisky.

'I say, this is service,' he said appreciatively. 'Mercer never lets me have more than two; says it's too expensive.'

'This is an occasion,' Liz told him. 'It's been too long, Pa. I'm sorry.'

'Well, you've got your own life to live, and from the looks of things you're doing it very well.'

'I can't complain,' Liz said truthfully.

'Pays well, this public relations?'

'Very well.'

'Good, good, because there's not much I can leave you and the house and land are entailed to Boy.'

'That's not something I expect,' Liz said. 'I don't need your money, Pa. I have enough of my own. But what about you?'

'Well, army pensions never were intended to allow one to live in the lap of luxury but I must say it gets harder and harder to get the damned ends to meet. Always something needs doing to the house and as for the gardens . . . Too much for me and Mercer but I had to let old Forbes go; couldn't afford him any longer.'

There and then Liz resolved to speak to her brother about giving their father some sort of quarterly allowance. Boy was doing very well at the bar and she had enough to be able to afford what – £250 a quarter say. With the same from Boy that extra two thousand a year would make all the difference. She would go down to Wiltshire and have a quiet word with Mercer. He was a born manager. The Brigadier never had been much good with money, and Liz had inherited his attitude to it. It was meant to be spent. She would make a one-off gift so that the most urgent repairs could be carried out. All right, so that was really Boy's responsibility, but he had an expensive wife who loathed the country and would give him hell if she thought her husband was wasting money on a white elephant she abhorred. She would see that the family home was sold once it became his. I really have neglected Pa of late, Liz thought guiltily, watching him relish his whisky.

So she made sure that he went off, smart and erect and every inch the Brigadier, even if he had been retired for twenty years; that he had an extra couple of twenties in his wallet, and knew there would be a cab waiting for him once the dinner was over. He came back well oiled, so she helped him up to bed and into it once he was undressed, and next morning she let him sleep late, taking him breakfast in bed; a full English breakfast with all the trimmings which she had cooked herself.

Afterwards she took him to Harrods where she bought him some new shirts and a couple of ties as well as some new underwear. Mercer had darned even the darns, she saw. She gave him his curry for lunch, and in the afternoon they went to a movie, a western because the Brigadier loved westerns, especially if they involved the Seventh Cavalry. On the way home, he gave her a long, reasoned critique of the Battle of the Little Big Horn and the character of General George Armstrong Custer, and demolished a large tea before going up to rest for a while before it was time to change for dinner.

Boy and Philip turned up on the doorstep together, Philip taunting as ever, Boy still resentful after all those years.

'Wouldn't have recognised you, old chap,' he said, emphasising the old. 'Had another face lift?'

'Not since you had yours.'

'Put away the rapiers,' Liz ordered. 'Pa is here and this is for him, he doesn't get out much these days. *Don't* go on about selling the house, Boy. That day will come soon enough, and Philip, lay off the cracks about all your beautiful young guardsmen. Go and pour yourself a drink; I want to talk to my brother.'

'Now what are you after?' Boy asked when they were alone.

'Money. Pa is positively threadbare.'

'Is it surprising? It's that damned great house! He just can't afford it any more and he only lives in one wing of it anyway. He could sell it and live in luxury for the rest of his life. I don't want it. I've told him he can break the entail if needs be.'

'You know that's the last thing he will do, it's been in our family for three hundred years, so it is up to us to help out.'

'How much?'

'Only a thousand a year each.'

'Only! The boys are both at prep school now, you know, with Eton coming up for Jeremy. I'm not made of money, my girl. The law is not public relations; I have to work for *my* screw and damned hard.'

Boy Harvill took after this mother; he had not his father's height or leanness, as Liz had; he was just above middle height and he would run to fat if he did not play squash twice weekly. His plump face bore rather a high colour and he had a sulky mouth. Right now it was turned down at the corners, a sign his sister, who had seen it often enough in childhood, recognised as indicating the sulks. It was his invariable response to situations he did not like, and being forced to sit down to dinner with Philip Faulkner was high on his list. All his life he had envied Philip to the point of hatred. In Philip's presence he felt diminished, a fact Liz had noted the moment she opened the front door to them. Philip wore clothes with the ease of one who knew he would have looked sensational in sackcloth and ashes. Boy always looked as though his nanny had forced him to wear last year's dinner jacket, now far too small for him.

He had his suits made by the same Savile Row tailor, but since he had no idea how to wear clothes he might as well have gone to any high street chain. The only time he acquired dignity was in his silks and wig but that, Philip was wont to say, was because while everyone knew Boy Harvill was a pompous ass, they also knew that the law was an even bigger one.

Liz sighed inwardly, but with impatience. She saw little of her brother nowadays; truth to tell she did not like him very much; never had, since he had been both a cry-baby, a tell-tale and easily bullied by a stronger personality. Such as his wife. Liz had known better than to invite her if she wanted Boy to come across with the necessary cheque. Boy Harvill was run by Mrs Harvill, and she held a very tight grip on the pursestrings. But Liz wanted to make her father financially secure and she needed Boy's money to help her do it, so she ignored the sulks and the petulance to say briskly: 'Don't try and flannel me. This is your sister you are talking to. I know how well you are doing. That libel case you just settled was worth a very hefty fee. You will give me an extra thousand a year for Pa *now*. God knows it is little enough. I will match it. That way he will be sure of a few creature comforts.'

Liz's voice was so harsh that Boy was taken aback. Normally she never got het up over anything; her attitude to life was very much one of laissez-faire; too much so in his wife's opinion. She and his sister did not get on. 'She doesn't earn all that money in public relations; I can't prove it but I'm sure the kind of relations she has are those conducted in private,' his wife had said in the course of their latest argument about money.

Boy had been furious and told her not to say such things, but he had heard one or two others that made him quite sure that Liz's job was a subject best not brought up. He had his own career to think of, and in law if one did not know and could honestly swear to the fact, there was no case for perjury. But now he saw that her normally pale face was flushed and her mouth a thin line. Their father's welfare was all of a sudden very important to her. And it's not as though we saw much of him when we were children, he thought aggrievedly. He and Mother always stationed somewhere abroad, and us here at school. I was fully grown before I ever spent any amount of time with him. And he doesn't have to hang on to that barn of a place. I won't, that's for certain.

'What's all the rush?' Boy protested.

'He's an old man and – and time is precious. I want him to have a few luxuries in his life. A whisky when he wants it, decent clothes, decent food. And you'll give that thousand or by God I'll rubbish you where it will do you the most harm. Do I make myself clear?'

Boy got out his cheque book, wondering how he was going to explain *this* to his wife.

'Laying down the law, were we?' Philip murmured when they joined him in the sitting room. 'Going in for a little rôle reversal? Ah . . . Brigadier. How nice to see you again . . .' His voice changed beat without a falter as Elizabeth's father came in.

The food was good – it always was at Liz's house – and the wines superlative. It was obvious from the way her father appreciated both that it had been a long time since anything like it had come his way. She knew he did not go out much because he could no longer afford to entertain, and he was very sensitive to what he thought of as charity. Only from friends old enough to drop the pretence did he still accept invitations.

Liz saw to it that he ate and drank well, and that Boy did not argue when his father talked about: 'When you take over.' One darkling glance from his sister was all it took – for Boy was at heart a moral weakling who had always been afraid of strong women. He reminded Liz of a client whose pleasure was to be dominated unto subjection.

Liz feared for her father; for a future where she would not be there to do what little she could for him, even if it was only money. Better late than never, she thought, feeling anger well again, so much that she had to leave the table with a murmur about coffee and go into the kitchen to stab a knife into a baking potato to relieve her feelings. Oh, Pa, I don't want to go, she wept silently. There are so many things yet to do. I've been neglectful of you; now I have so little time to make it up and when I do go I have to leave you to the tender mercies of a man who will do exactly what his wife tells him and that will be to let you get on with it. And I can't be too obvious because you will twig. It's not as though we have ever been close. It was you and Ma who practised togetherness while your two children were packed off to school. But I could have been more of a daughter all the same, especially since Ma died. She disposed of the remains of the potato before taking the coffee tray into the living room.

Her father began to nod over his second glass of port, and Boy made it his excuse to go. When he had, Liz said to Philip: 'Give me a hand to get Pa upstairs, will you?'

The Brigadier protested but leaned on Philip nevertheless, and was grateful for his help in doing what Mercer normally did.

He patted Liz's cheek when she leaned down to kiss him goodnight, 'You're a good girl.'

Liz felt the lump in her throat squeeze tears from her eyes.

Downstairs again: 'Right,' said Philip, 'it is time for explanations, your unwanted sentimentality, for one thing. I am aware that you have a certain affection for your father but this display of daughterly reverence is a bit much, even for you. The one thing that bound you to your father was the distance you kept. You left his paternal care when you were twenty-one and that is now some twenty-five years past. I trust you are about to enlighten me?'

Liz poured them each a brandy. Then, using the words the doctor had used to her, she told him. He was silent for some time, the only sign of his inner disturbance being the slight frown which engraved three vertical lines between his eyebrows. Normally that particular facial expression was proscribed.

If I had had eyes for anything other than myself I would have seen the signs, he thought. Like the fact that Liz's glow had gone. One of the remarkable things about her was that she seemed to have a light inside her, illuminating her face. For some time now that had been switched off. And she was thinner. Her Jean Muir scarlet silk dress no longer fitted her perfectly. Its exquisitely cunning, softly draped folds no longer hung right because she had obviously lost weight. Truth to tell, he thought angrily, she looked haggard, driven. Which of course, she is. In Death's coach and by his very own coachman. Talk about appointments in Samarra!

Anger flooded him. The world overflowing with oiks and fools and people no one would ever miss and Liz had to be the one to receive the tap on the shoulder. He raged with despair at the sheer bloody *unfairness* of life. His silver eyes glittered with a light that had been compared to that of the Medusa, but he forced himself back from the brink. Anger was futile and not what his dearest, closest, and only *real* friend needed right now. Remorse threatened to strangle him. Look at her!

Her glow had gone; there was a dryness about her, as though those lovely juices which had coursed through her for so long were drying up. Anguish was a feeling he had been careful to avoid all his life; now it rolled over him like a tidal wave, but his voice was calmly controlled when he said finally: 'Well, as the song says, everybody dies, but where you are concerned I would rather it was later – *much* later – rather than sooner.'

'So would I.'

They looked deeply at each other. Philip held out a hand.

Liz grasped it. Both held on tight. Then Liz said in an unsteady voice: 'I have to decide what to do, Philip. How best to use the time I have left and even more important – how to do it in the style to which I have become accustomed.'

'You never would buy that umbrella.'

'But you do see that I have to hold it over Pa too.'

'Confrontation with one's imminent mortality does have a very salutory effect on the conscience,' Philip smiled. 'But then, you do have one, do you not, hence your bi-weekly stints as a ministering angel.' He pursed his lips judiciously, drained his brandy. 'I think a general audit is called for. You need to know exactly what your assets are, what your liabilities. You must achieve as accurate a figure as you can of future earning potential and how long you are likely to be able to go on earning. Pencil and paper, please, and your books of account – the true story please. Not the popular fiction you give to the gentleman who does your books.'

'I pay my taxes!'

'Yes, dear, so do I.' Philip was unimpressed, but he had a head for figures and knew her business as well as she did. She appreciated his matter-of-fact approach. Right now she could not have handled unbridled emotion.

She brought him her books, refilled his glass, sat by his side while he added, subtracted and multiplied, thinking idly of ways and means and going over the dinner, her thoughts interweaving, until suddenly something her brother had said locked into her consciousness with an audible click. Her shoulders straightened and her face lightened as if somebody had switched on a light.

But she waited until Philip picked up his brandy glass, drained it then set it down with a decided thump.

'This,' he said shaking his head at her ledger, 'will never do. You have no sizeable debts. But nor have you any capital except this house and your jewellery, and you need the one to live in and the other as proof of your solvency. You simply cannot go on living at your present rate and put aside sufficient to see you through your last months, unless you intend to entrust yourself to the tender ministrations of the National Health. You have no other recourse but to cut back.'

'Oh, but I have,' Liz said.

'If these are not your true books – '

'Of course they are, but this has nothing to do with the red and the black. This has to do with earnings and I know how they can be maintained.'

Philip laid down his pencil, surveyed her with the patience of one humouring an invalid.

'I take a pupil,' Liz said.

Ten seconds ticked by. 'You what?'

'I take a pupil. It was something Boy said tonight that gave me the idea. About pupillage, young barristers learning their trade by watching and helping the experienced ones who know it inside out.'

'*You* propose to take on an apprentice?'

'Why not?'

'To teach what? The art of fucking?'

'The arts of a courtesan,' Liz corrected, riding his derision.

Another silence. 'And to whom do you teach these arts? Where will you find your pupil? I do not think that what you teach is on the careers list of many young women – although . . .' A shrug. 'I am sure there are one or two.'

'Didn't it head yours?' Liz asked sweetly.

Philip's smile glimmered. 'Touché, but mine, as you must admit, is a somewhat specialised field.'

'So is mine.'

'Needing a very special pupil.'

Philip contemplated her at some length. 'You will, I take it, charge this pupil a fee, for that is the object of this – exercise is it not?'

'I shall take fifty per cent while she is under my wing. Once she knows enough to fly on her own then all she earns she keeps. By then I will be beyond the need of money.'

'Ah . . . I see . . .' Enlightenment dawned. 'This is to see you through your – shall we call it a lay-off? To cushion the last months.'

'Of course.'

Philip's smile broke free of his pained disapproval. 'Now that's more like it! You almost had me believing that you were a convert to that earnest group who worry so about the gradual dying out of so many of our ancient trades – like thatchers and such like. I am infinitely relieved to hear that you still practise that of enlightened self-interest.' He wagged an admonitory finger. 'You had me quite worried for a moment.'

'*You* are worried?'

'My dear girl, neither of us has ever called a spade anything but its proper name and neither of us is the kind to wish to devote our last months of life to performing good works and repenting of our sins. What we must ensure is that your "apprentice" is intelligent enough to learn quickly.'

'Time is of the essence,' Liz agreed.

'Would that it was,' Philip sighed, 'and that I had a phial full of the lovely stuff.' He squeezed her hand. 'I would share it with you, my closest friend and *only* confidante.'

Liz was touched. Normally, Philip was generous only with advice.

'He poured them both a fresh brandy. 'So,' he said, in his most practical voice, 'where do we look to find this paragon?'

'I don't want one of those. I want a blank canvas on which I can create The Courtesan. I want her to have experience but not too much; she has to be young – I thought late teens early twenties, and personable, of course, but the body is more important than the face because that is what she is working with.' Liz sipped her brandy. 'Nor will *my* clients want a bimbo. She has to be able to talk on whatever they care to talk about and to make intelligent conversation or, should they prefer it, not talk at all but listen. She has to be able to become whatever it is they are paying for – more, want to pay for again.'

Philip pursed his lips and shook his head. 'I hope you realise that by the time you find this paragon – because that *is* what you are looking for, there might not be time to teach her?'

'That's why I have to start straight away.'

Philip brooded. 'At first thought I cannot put forward a single candidate. Let me think on it. How wide am I permitted to cast my net?'

'Haven't I always trusted your judgement?'

'A difficult one. What we are seeking, my dear old friend, is another you, and I doubt if she exists.' He raised her hand, kissed it.

'If you make me cry I'll never forgive you,' Liz's voice was not steady.

'Have you any tears left?'

'It would seem so, though I can't think how . . .' Liz stood up. 'So I must now shoo you away. I haven't cried in public since – '

'You ended one chapter and began another.'

'The final one,' Liz said more cheerfully, 'and I always like a book to have a cliff hanger finish – plus a Happy Ending, of course.'

'I shall do my best,' Philip told her, as she helped him on with his cashmere top-coat. 'But do not expect miracles.'

'I don't,' Liz told him dryly, 'else I would already have asked for one.'

Next day, the Sunday, after a couple of hours in the pub and Sunday lunch, followed on the part of the Brigadier by a post-prandial snooze, Liz drove her father to the station, saw him onto his train and promised to come down to Wiltshire very soon. 'I mean it this time, Pa. I've got something important to do over the next couple of weeks but once I've got it sorted out I'll be down.' She hugged him fiercely. 'Give me a ring when you are home so I'll know you got there safely. Mercer is meeting you at Broadwood, isn't he?'

'Yes, yes, he'll be there. Lovely weekend, Lizzie.' He called her by the name nobody else ever used, patted her cheek. You're a good girl.'

That was praise indeed. She stood until the train had disappeared round the bend and then went back home. In the still watches of the night a name had arisen in her mind and she wanted to check it out.

By that strange osmosis which existed between Philip and herself, there was a message on her machine when she got back and it mentioned the very same name, so that night they went to the Claremont – Philip was a member – where that person was likely to be since she loved to gamble. She was known to them, and though she was not in the same league as Liz as far as her clients were concerned, they were men of the type for whom it was only a matter of time before they were able to look higher and pay more. Now, ostensibly out for nothing more than a little light entertainment, Philip and Liz watched their quarry. In the cab going home they looked at each other: 'No,' they both said.

'Too common,' was Philip's verdict, 'even if her father is in Burke's.'

'Too obvious,' was Liz's opinion. 'And she drinks too much.'

'Ah, but that could have a lot to do with who she was with.' Philip shuddered. 'He would drive me to drink, that one.'

'Strike one name,' Liz agreed.

They looked at two more over the next two nights and gave them the thumbs down. One was too experienced in certain sexual disciplines – 'and I do mean discipline,' Liz said with a distastefully wrinkled nose.

The other was someone they had not seen for some time; her clientele was strictly international and she travelled to them, besides which she had spent the last year in the United States and had become very transatlantic. 'No,' Liz said reluctantly. 'She's a stunner and that body is incredible but – not my style either. What does for Dallas does not do for Deauville.' She chewed her lip. 'All three are far too experienced; too set in their own particular ways and with too good a set-up to want to exchange it for another. I think I am going to have to lower my sights somewhat if I am going to take on board someone I can make-over.'

'Not a novice, surely!'

'No, but downmarket rather than upmarket.'

'Not some little tart from the street!'

'Good God, no! But perhaps somebody from one of the Houses . . .' Liz quoted the name of a well-known Society brothel. 'She always has stunners and none of them is over twenty-one. There might be someone worth my while.'

Philip agreed to give the project his attention that day while Liz saw one of her oldest clients – and one of the easiest. All she had to do was treat him like a dog – including putting him on a leash. She had to receive him in a room that was a mess and make him clean it up; she had to talk to him as if he was a fool instead of the multi-national industrialist he was, and she had to beat him if he did not perform his housekeeping duties to her satisfaction.

She would don a white glove to run a forefinger over every surface when he had finished. Always she would find fault, always she would command him to bring her hairbrush, order him to bend over and then beat him – hard – with the bristle side. His erection – which had grown with each abasement, would be such that his hand would stray in its direction only to be swatted by the brush, making him howl with pain. He would plead with her to let him touch his throbbing phallus and she would refuse, finally sending him away unfulfilled – and straight to his wife, who had no idea how he had been primed, and bragged to her friends about her husband's incredible virility.

All part of the fantasy, and all strictly confidential because otherwise his City reputation as a ruthless entrepreneur would be in tatters. It was as much for her silence as the strength of her wrist that Liz earned her fee, but it brought her, she reflected worriedly as she drove home, no nearer to solving her own problem.

6

Thursdays, to Elly, were Book Days. That meant two new books to read (three if the lady came to her last and there were indeed three she wanted). She read voraciously, always had done. Books had been her way of escaping. Every day, on her way home from school she had gone to the library to change her book. 'Heavens!' the librarian used to say. 'I never knew a girl to read so much or so fast as you!'

She read every minute she got; in between chores, on the bus, in bed at night, though this was against her father's rules and had to be done by stealth. In the hospital, she had gone through every book in the dayroom book corner, mostly romances or westerns, and the books she got from the trolley did not last long.

Now, she waited with keen anticipation for the rumble of the trolley wheels, but when at last it came the lady pushing it was not the usual one. In fact she was most unusual. She was model-girl elegant for a start, though she was obviously no longer a girl but a woman of what the French termed 'une certaine âge', and dressed in the kind of clothes Elly had seen only in the tattered copy of *Vogue* she had found in the dayroom. A nubbly tweed suit of vivid, crushed-strawberry pink with a cropped jacket and a short straight skirt, and with it she wore not one but several ropes of pearls, and there were pearls in her ears. Her blonde hair was short, thick and glossy and as she bent forward it swung like a bell only to fall perfectly into place as she straightened up. As she picked out books Elly caught the flash of nails as scarlet as her mouth, and there was about her the crackle of a vivid personality. One of those up-market do-gooders, Elly surmised. Doing her bit to help the less fortunate. If I handle her right I'll get three books out of her. It's worth a try, anyway.

Intrigued, she watched the trolley make its slow way up the ward, stopping by every bed even when there was no request or no books to exchange. Some of the women knitted, one embroidered and another did crochet; one or two had visitors. The new lady chatted agreeably to them all before moving on.

When the trolley stopped by her bed she gave this lady her best smile, proffered her three books and said: 'I don't suppose you've got any Georgette Heyer, have you?'

'Let's have a look.' The voice matched the appearance; ring-of-crystal clear, with the kind of vowels that were unmistakably Upper Class. Elly herself had no accent: her father had been despotic when it came to sloppy diction – and she had very quickly learned to hone her own. She had no trace of regional accent either, though she had lived the first seventeen years of her life in the North East. After the first few jeers, which turned into resentful slaps, from Mickey, she had soon learned the obligatory glottal stop. Now, though, she spoke as her father had taught her.

'I've got *Bath Tangle* and *The Toll Gate*,' the lady said. 'Any good?'

'I've read them both before, but if you haven't got anything that's worth reading once then I would prefer to read them again.'

'Take a look,' the lady said cheerfully, 'and help yourself.'

'To whatever I like?'

'I won't tell if you won't.'

Elly's eyes ran over the titles, spotted a book of short stories by Somerset Maugham and another by John O'Hara as well as a tattered paperback copy of *Gone with the Wind* which she had already read twice but which would last her a good couple of days. Together with the two Heyers she had enough to absorb her until the trolley came round next time.

'Thank you,' she said to the book-lady in such a way as to make her say amusedly: 'They are only books.'

Elly shook her head. 'Books have never been "only" to me.'

'I'm more of a magazine sifter, myself.' The lady's bright

73

blue eyes – the colour of the bluebells that used to grow around Elly's father's rockery – examined her with frank curiosity.

'What happened to you? Walk into a door?'

'Something like that.'

'You sound a bit strangulated . . . oh, I see . . . your jaw is wired.'

'Not as much as it was before. Then I couldn't speak at all, but they've slackened the wires so I can speak even if I only move my lips.'

'You poor thing . . . *and* a broken nose! You have been in the wars.'

There was genuine sympathy in the light, clear voice and a sincerity to which Elly felt herself responding. The nurses were kind in their brisk way but she got short shrift from Sister, who made no secret of the fact that she disapproved not only of Elly but her injuries and the way she had received them, and since the ward – all women – took their cue from Sister, its attitude to Elly was one of ignoring her presence when the little group of ambulant patients congregated in the day-room and whispering about her when they got together around one of the beds. She had heard the word 'whore' more than once, never spoken directly to her but sent winging in her direction. Only one old lady had ever spoken to her; quite deliberately told her in a loud voice 'not to take no notice of that lot of narrow-minded hypocrites', but she had been discharged shortly afterwards so that the book-lady's sympathy was the first Elly had received since then.

'I hope to be discharged next week,' she volunteered, 'that is if my nose has set properly this time. Something went wrong with the septum so they had to re-set it, otherwise I would have been discharged already.'

'I know. Hospitals are bores, aren't they?'

Not to me, thought Elly. It has been a happy holiday as far as I am concerned, in spite of the aches and pains.

'Thank you for the books,' she said. 'I'd better put most of them away otherwise you might get into trouble. I've got five and two is the limit.'

'Oh, never mind that. What are two books to a genuine reader? Sister is a sweetie if you treat her right.'

Elly smiled faintly and the lady laughed; it was more of a gurgle.

'Comes down hard on you, does she? Probably because you are so young and pretty – or will be once you've got that splint out of your nose and the wire from your jaw.'

Elly found herself flushing. Nobody had ever said she was pretty.

'I've never seen such long hair . . .' The lady lifted Elly's plait – she wore it that way because it was easier to cope with in bed – and said – 'so beautifully old fashioned. I hate the way young girls your age let their hair over-hang their faces like a shroud. What do you do with yours when it's not in a pigtail?'

'I either wear it in a ponytail or pile it up.' Elly eyed the book-lady's thick, butter-blonde hair enviously. 'I can't have it short because it is so fine and thin.'

'Mine is so thick I have to have it thinned every so often.'

The woman in the next bed, who had been having a bath, now came up to the book-lady.

'If you don't mind there's others would like the chance of a book,' she sniffed, giving them a look that made it seem as if she had a bad smell under her nose.

'Oh, I am sorry. Do help yourself.' The lady said pleasantly. She was obviously not in the least put out. There was a sense of conspiracy in the blue eyes which danced mischievously. The woman, seething with curiosity, made the matter of choosing a book into a lengthy business, obviously intent on eavesdropping.

'Enjoy your Regency romances,' the book-lady said. 'I went right through the lot myself when I was once laid up with a broken leg – a horse decided it was not in the mood for jumping – and I fell in love with more than one Regency rake. I think my favourite is the one in *Regency Buck*.'

'The Earl of Worth', Elly said, face glowing, 'he's my favourite too.'

'And I adored the *Grand Sophy*. A lady after my own heart – and a good hundred years before her time.'

The book-lady checked her watch – Elly recognised it as Cartier, having pored over that particular model in *Vogue*. One day . . . she had promised herself. 'I must go . . . I have two more wards to do.' She took hold of her trolley. 'If I don't see you again, best of luck,' she said to Elly. Then to the eavesdropper: 'Have you made up your mind?'

'Nothin' there I want. All the good ones is gone.' She shot a rancorous glance at Elly, who stared back without a flicker, then sniffed and took herself off back to her own bed, where she got into a low voiced conversation with her neighbours on the other side, both of them turning to stare in Elly's direction.

She stared back defiantly then happened to glance at her new found friend of short acquaintance only to meet a pair of eyes so hungrily curious as to give her a shock. Then the curiosity was gone and they were smiling again. 'My name is Elizabeth Waring,' the lady said. 'What's yours?'

'Nell Jordan.'

'Short for Eleanor?'

Nell nodded. Nobody but her father had ever called her Eleanor. Elly she had chosen quite deliberately as her name for the streets; a name that was not, never had been hers in that other life, and she now would never use again.

'Well, Nell, if you are such a great reader I might be able to put you in the way of a whole slew of books. Would you like me to?'

'If you want,' Nell answered automatically, still upset about the curiosity and saddened too. She was sick and tired of being exhibited like some exotic creature in a zoo, as though a prostitute was an endangered species. She felt as if she had been let down. She had thought the interest, the friendliness, genuine but it was just another case of 'a street-walker! Really! Oh, I must go and see for myself.'

So her goodbye was polite but no more, and as soon as the trolley went back down the ward, picked up *Bath Tangle* and began to read.

'I see you spent some time with our star patient,' Sister said in her superior way when Liz went in to say that her book round was over.

'Star patient? Why is that?'

'She's a prostitute who got beaten up by her pimp.' Sister nodded in a 'thought that would make you think' way.

'She doesn't look like a prostitute,' Liz said noncommittally.

'Oh, butter wouldn't melt. Nineteen going on ninety.'

'How do you know she is a prostitute?' Liz asked.

'The police. They've twice cautioned her for soliciting.'

'He must have been a nasty piece of work,' Liz commented. 'A broken nose *and* jaw.'

'Her own fault for consorting with such a person.' Sister was not one to waste her sympathy.

Liz shrugged. 'You pay your money and you take your choice,' she said. 'Oh – I told her I'd bring her some books – she's a great reader evidently, so I'll probably stop by tomorrow if that's all right.'

'You and your lame ducks, Mrs Waring!' Sister's reproof was lightly given – Elizabeth Waring was a close friend of the hospital's most senior consultant – but there was a sting to it.

'I've been lame myself so I know how it feels,' Liz returned blithely.

Nell was well into *The Toll Gate* the following afternoon when she felt something drop on her bed and looked up to see half a dozen books lying on the blue and white counterpane and Elizabeth Waring, her arms full of magazines, smiling at her. 'Don't look so surprised,' she chided. 'I said I would bring you some books . . .'

'Yes, but – not so soon!'

'I was going to bring these to the hospital anyway to add to the trolley so you may as well have first go.'

Nell reached for them. They were all brand new. The latest novels of half a dozen best selling novelists, English and American, none of which she had yet read. 'Oh . . . manna from heaven!' she exclaimed. Her face was, for a moment, totally unguarded, and for the first time showed Liz the long-lost teenager behind the carefully and deliberately maintained façade of a mature woman.

'I have a friend who has a standing order with Hatchards for all the new books, but once she has read them that's it, so I always commandeer them for the hospital.' Liz told the lie without a flicker for she had that morning herself bought them.

'I shall have to read them on the double because they are discharging me on Monday.'

Liz drew up the chair which had now appeared by the bed. 'Where do you live?' she asked casually.

'I've got the chance of a room in a sort of charity hostel.'

'Good heavens! I didn't think there were any of them left.'

'This one is run jointly by the GLC and the Church.'

'Oh. Are you religious, then?'

'No, but if I have to go to church to get a roof over my head I'll do so.'

Liz took careful note of the sudden edge to the lovely young contralto, surprisingly deep for a teenager, and diagnosed an acute shortage of cash.

'What do you do for a living?' she asked, taking care to sound interested rather than curious.

'I'm between jobs right now.' The guard was up again.

'You are not going back to your boyfriend, then?'

Nell's eyes flared as she shook her head, but Liz's did not flicker. Of course they told me, hers said.

'Sensible girl. I will never understand why women stay with men who abuse them physically.'

'Nowhere else to go, probably.'

'There is *always* somewhere else to go – even if it is only the police. Once you lodge an official complaint they have to do something.' Liz sighed. 'Well, if you are already fixed up then there is no point in me telling you about my own proposal.'

Nell's surprise got the better of her suspicion. 'What proposal?'

'I do a bit of welfare work as well as my book round,' Liz fibbed smoothly, 'and it was mentioned to me that you were, as they say, of no fixed abode and did I know of a nice room in a decent house where you could stay for a while.' She saw the 'pull the other one, it's got bells on' look begin to turn Nell's surprise into scepticism but sailed on regardless. 'It so happens that I do know of such a room; in a very nice house and with a very nice lady.'

'Probably beyond my means. Once I leave here my first port of call is the DHSS.'

'No, her rates are very reasonable. She regards it as her own bit of welfare.'

Nell was totally unconvinced. 'Such as rescuing fallen women?'

Liz threw back her head to laugh and her hair shimmered. 'Good God, no! That's a Victorian idea if ever there was one.

To paraphrase Dorothy Parker "if all the world's fallen women were laid end to end I wouldn't be at all surprised".'

Nell's sense of humour got the better of her and she grinned. 'Nor would I.'

Liz said impulsively: 'Oh, it *would* be a pity if you didn't take up my proposition. I know you would be happy there. She is a very understanding lady; does not judge.'

'Who told you I had been found wanting?'

'My dear, this is a hospital. You had the police to see you, and the Vice Squad at that.'

'I have a place already.'

'A hostel? No privacy; rules and regulations; social workers?'

'Beggars can't afford to be choosers.' The logic was overlaid with matter-of-factness but it told Liz much about the kind of life this girl had been leading.

'My friend does not expect you to beg but to pay your way – once you get a job.'

'As what? Lecturer in Fornication?'

Liz rode the anger. 'I am sure there is something worthwhile you can do. All we have to do is find out what it is.'

Nell was still suspicious. Short on trust, Liz thought. Been taken for a sucker once too often. I know the feeling. She is convinced there has to be a catch because up until now there always has been, and she has been left hanging on it.

'Think about it,' Liz said, rising to her feet. 'I'll come back tomorrow, if I may, and we can talk again.'

Nell gave no quarter. 'Suit yourself.' She was aware she was being ungracious but she had been taken in twice. No way was she going to be made a fool of a third time. Why would an obvious lady like this one bother with a tom? And whoever her friend was she had to be of the same ilk. Remember how kind and motherly Lil was? Elly writhed at the thought of how naïve she had been. Even this lady could be a con. She has to be. A pound to a penny she's got some kind of ulterior motive. Remember your motto: DON'T TRUST NOBODY. How do you know she isn't some upmarket Madame? Perhaps she thinks you are some kind of diamond in the rough? That all you need is polishing so she can sell you and make a profit too! No way!

Liz had watched the conflicting emotions chase each other across a face that was still far too expressive for a girl with her

79

background. Not nearly as hard as she would like me to think she is. Reaching out she took hold of the stubborn chin, tipped it so as to look deep into the storm-cloud eyes. 'I'm on your side,' she said quietly. 'Please believe me.'

Nell watched her walk away down the ward. In navy blue today, a long jacket and short skirt. Probably cost more than I ever earned in a month, she thought. What can she possibly know about *my* kind of life?

She picked up her book again but found that her interest had gone. All she could think of was that, in spite of all she had said, all she had told herself, she still had a choice to make.

7

'I've found her,' Liz said to Philip that night, when they met at the Connaught Grill.

'When? Where? Most of all – who? Do I know her?'

'No, you don't know her. Nobody does. She's a streetwalker who got on the wrong side of her pimp and landed up in hospital with a broken nose and jaw and battered, cracked ribs.'

Philip fell back in his chair, covered his eyes, felt for his glass of champagne – his favourite, Krug – and drained it. After a moment he set down his glass, opened his eyes. 'I'm sorry; I could have sworn you said you decided to adopt a common little street tart.'

'She's anything but common. There's quality there. She's intelligent, too. This is not your average scrubber, Philip. By no means. She doesn't look like one or sound like one or behave like one.'

'How would you know? Have you seen her at work?' Philip's voice was thin with scorn. 'I am aware you have an inoperable brain tumour, my dear Elizabeth, but I had not realised how far it has already affected your reasoning.'

His spite curled round her like a whip, but Liz did not flinch. 'I know what I am doing.'

'Not if you do this, you don't!'

'She's the perfect blank page, Philip. All she knows is the streets. I can teach her everything about the villa, the hotel suite. And she has got the kind of face that can be made over into anything you want. Best of all she is young – nineteen

81

going on twenty. She has a lovely voice and she has been educated.'

'Next thing you'll be telling me she was stolen from her crib in the castle by a wicked witch!' Philip threw up his hands. 'Elizabeth, you really *must* stop believing in fairy tales.'

'This one hasn't got a happy ending yet. I have yet to persuade her to agree.'

'You did not tell me she was endowed with commonsense.'

'She doesn't trust me. In her world there is always a catch. As yet she hasn't found mine, but I'll bet she is doing a thorough search.'

'Sensible girl. I begin to warm to her.'

'I did the moment I saw her. You know that funny feeling I get at the nape of my neck.' Elizabeth put up a hand to demonstrate. 'It prickled like mad. She's exactly what I want, Philip, I *know* it.'

'Like you knew Jose Luis de Santos?'

Liz withstood the blade. 'That was entirely different. I was not capable of thinking around him. I've done nothing else since I met Nell.'

'Nell! Good grief! Next thing you'll be telling me she sells oranges!'

'What matters is that I think she can be trained to sell what I know how to sell. She has a brain, and in my profession that is every bit as important as the body.'

'Just how much have you told her?'

'Nothing – yet. She would have laughed in my face. I have to get her to accept me before she can accept anything else. She needs somewhere to live; I offered her a room – she thinks in the house of a friend. Unfortunately some welfare worker has got her a place in a hostel so all I can do is wait and see which she chooses. I did not dare go too far in case I really frightened her off. I want her to trust me and feel confident about me before I tell her the truth.'

Philip poured more champagne. 'Mad!' he pronounced. 'Quite, quite mad *and* bad. Are you aware that you have a time limit? How long is it going to take to change this little scrubber into a lady your clients will accept as your replacement? Have you for one minute really thought about the enormous quantity of information she has to acquire? Not only the sexual skills –

for hers cannot be more than basic, to say the least – but the manner, the attitude, the – the sheer pinnacle of perfection such as you proclaim when you are on the job?'

'Yes. And I am sure she could do it. She has imagination, a very necessary quality when you are dealing in fantasies. She is nothing right now, don't you see, which is what makes me confident that I could make her into something.'

'Provided she wants to become something.'

Liz sighed. 'Yes, always provided that.'

Their waiter approached to tell them their table was ready, and drew out Liz's chair to allow her to rise.

'I think I had better see her at the earliest possible opportunity.' Philip decided.

'Not until I know I have her acceptance. You *would* frighten her off.'

'I?' Philip sounded hurt.

'You. This is for me to handle until I tell you different. Down, boy, and muzzle that curiosity.'

She preceded him to their table.

When Liz returned to the hospital next day she found Nell's bed empty and for a moment disappointment had her stuck to the floor, then she saw that the pile of books was still there and her heart started beating again. Of course, she thought. The day-room . . . Nell was there, but so were half a dozen women from the ward – every ambulatory patient in it, in fact, and it was obvious from the way they were clustered together that they were keeping an eye on Nell and waiting eagerly for the next instalment. The flowers Liz carried, the box of chocolates, had the desired effect, but when Nell said: 'I think these had better be put straight into water,' leading the way into the room where the vases were kept by a big stone sink, their fury was patent.

'No – ' Nell cautioned as Liz followed her in, 'don't shut the door. That's the perfect cover for eavesdropping.'

'It reminds me of school,' Liz said amusedly.

'I don't want my business gossiped about by all and sundry,' Nell said, filling a china vase with water. 'They've nothing else to do in here because most of them are long-term patients. I'm here because it is the only spare bed they had.'

'I wondered why you were the only chick in a yard full of old boilers.'

Nell giggled, then sobered. Paper rustled as she unwrapped the shaggy headed daisies, cheerful cornflowers, vivid blue iris, red carnations and yellow tulips, then began to place them in the vase.

'Have you thought over my offer?' Liz asked.

'Yes.'

'So?'

Nell turned her head to look at Liz. 'Why?' she asked. 'Why are you so keen to help me, of all people? Is it me in particular or just another good deed in general?'

'I'm not particularly altruistic; this is the only 'charitable' work I do apart from contributing on flag days. Something about you caught my interest.'

'Hadn't you met a common or garden prostitute before?' Sarcasm dripped.

'I've known several – and I know one in particular very well.'

Nell was obviously surprised, then she said: 'Not on my level, though.'

'No.'

'More of a courtesan, I expect.'

Hiding her surprise: 'Yes. That is exactly what she is,' Liz said.

'Is she also the lady with the room to rent?'

'Yes,' Liz answered. I told you she was bright, Philip, she exulted.

'That makes more sense,' Nell said, sounding satisfied. 'Are cases like mine part of her charity work?'

'Her offer has absolutely nothing to do with charity,' Liz answered truthfully.

'Is she retired and looking for something to do?'

'No, but she is intending to retire shortly.'

'Am I supposed to be groomed to be her companion or something?'

'She does not lack for companionship.'

Nell stood back to contemplate her flower arrangement. It was obvious that it was not one of her talents.

'Here . . . let me.' Liz moved her to one side and with a few deft repositioning movements really arranged the flowers into a beautiful mass of colour.

'How do you *do* that?' Nell asked.

'My friend will teach you if you like.'

Once again Liz met the clear grey eyes, and this time they were sardonic. 'And what else will she teach me?'

'What would you like to learn?'

'It is what I would like to unlearn that matters. I am *not* going back on the streets. I was put there because I didn't know enough to know better – and that was an offer I should have refused. Every instinct is telling me I should know a lot more about yours before I make up my mind about it.'

'Take a look-see at what she is offering, then. See the house, find out what you want to know and then decide.'

Nell had obviously not expected that. 'No strings?' she asked, suspiciously.

'Absolutely no strings. If you decide it is not for you then you take up the vacancy at the hostel.' Liz laughed at the expression on Nell's face. 'You thought it was some sort of white slavery conspiracy, didn't you?'

'It goes on. People may ridicule the idea but it does go on.'

Something in Nell's voice told Liz that she was speaking from knowledge rather than belief.

'I have never had anything to do with it,' she said truthfully. 'Nor has my friend. Honestly. I give you my word.'

Nell was still struggling. No sooner did she make up her mind as to one course of action than the virtues of the other began to loom large. Not used to having to make decisions – they had always been made for her – she was finding it hard. On the one hand she liked Elizabeth Waring; felt drawn to her, at one with her, trustful of her. On the other she remembered how it had been with Mickey. First of all granny-Lil, so understanding, so sympathetic, so helpful; then Mickey, listening to her patiently, leaving her alone, feeding her up, letting her sleep, gentling her along and then – wham! She was back in the cellar of 17 Warwick Avenue, suspended by her wrists from its huge central beam, naked feet just grazing the floor, her father disappearing up the steps, impervious to her wild pleas, the door shutting, the key turning in the lock . . .

'Look – why don't you come and see the house; a visit, no

more. Let me show you what is on offer and then you can make up your mind.'

'I'm not allowed out of the hospital.'

'Oh, I think they will let you go with me, and you are being discharged in a couple of days after all.' For a moment Liz had a moment of her own doubt. The girl was so *young*. Have I the right to set her on a road of *my* choosing? This is what *I* want, after all. And once she sees what is possible she will want it too, her other self argued. What has she got now? Nothing. What is she going to if she goes her own way? Nothing.

But Liz found herself saying: 'I won't pressurise you, honestly. You must make up your own mind in the last analysis, but don't turn me down sight unseen, I beg of you. Come and take a look at the room on offer. Then make up your mind.' She quelled the sardonic thought that once seen, the room on offer would sweep the hostel right out of sight.

Nell stared at the shaggy-blue cornflowers in the vase; they reminded her of her new friend's eyes. Except this is no cornflower, she reminded herself. This is more your hot-house orchid.

Which had her saying: 'All right. I'll come. But you'll have to get permission.'

'Of course. You put the flowers by your bed and I'll go and have a word with Sister.'

Not that Nell had any doubts as to the permission being given. Elizabeth Waring had that steam-roller confidence which surrounded people who always got what they wanted. And there was always the chance, should she decide to stick around it, that some of that confidence would rub off on her.

'Right,' Elizabeth said, when she same back. 'We can go now as long as I have you back for supper, so you have got a whole day of freedom. Now, where are your clothes?'

They were in Nell's locker, and the moment Elizabeth took them out Nell was loathe to put them on. They looked so *cheap*; proclaimed what she was in neon. Micro-skirt, thigh-length boots of imitation leather, a short red jacket trimmed with what was supposed to be fur, and a leather-look shoulder bag. 'Oh, you can't wear this,' Liz frowned as she held up the jacket. 'It's got blood all over it. Wasn't it taken away to be cleaned?'

86

Nell thought: By whom? And for why? And who would pay? More important, who would care?

'Well, you can't go out in that,' Liz said. 'It's only fit for the bin.' Which was where she put it. 'Here, you'll have to wear this.' She picked up her own short, blue-fox jacket and held it out.

'Oh, I couldn't wear that!' Nell was obviously horrified.

'Why not? That thin sweater won't keep you very warm and it is not exactly hot out there, which is why I brought it.'

'I might get it dirty.'

'Sitting in a car? Don't be ridiculous.' Liz was impatient. She almost had her quarry and the sooner she could pin her down the better. She held up the coat and unwillingly Nell slid her arms into it. At once one of Liz's suppositions turned into fact when she saw the way Nell folded the coat about her, nestled her chin into the soft fur, straightened her shoulders, tilted her chin. Yes, the girl definitely had an appreciation of the good things of life. She *wanted*. All I have to do is show her how she can *have* and she's mine!

This was further confirmed when they got downstairs, after walking the gauntlet of a ward full of stunned eyes and leaving behind a maelstrom of outraged gossip, to the car park, where Liz led the way to a glossy, beautifully maintained red car which Nell, who had lingered in front of the showroom when working the West End, recognised at once as a Mercedes Sports. The leather of the seats was ivory-cream and the dashboard fascia of silky walnut. She waited while Liz unlocked her door which released the lock on the passenger side then she got in. At once, the smell of real leather mingled with the expensive perfume clinging to the fur jacket. The smell of money, Nell thought, suddenly awash with a fierce hunger to have enough of that to possess such a car, such a coat.

She had associated this particular car with luxury, riches and the good things in life ever since the night she had been waiting for punters who were thin on the ground. She had been working Park Lane, and as she slowly walked up towards Marble Arch her eyes had scanned ahead. As she got to Brook Street the lights changed and she had to stop to let the traffic pass; as she did so her eye alighted on a red car, the colour of blood, waiting on the other side. A girl had been at the wheel, not much older than herself, but oh, so different. Her hair had been thick and blonde, much like Elizabeth Waring's, but longer, and she had been beautiful. She was alone in the car, but somehow Nell knew she was going to meet some man; there was a glorious, exultant, anticipatory quality to the smile she tossed Nell as she put the car into gear and roared on down towards Hyde Park Corner. It had left Nell feeling desolate, hollow with envy and sick at heart. How was it that some people had all the luck; found things came easily, never had to struggle? That flower face had never had to fight every step of her way through life; things had come to her without effort and the man waiting for her would not be some stranger; impatient, greedy, callous or contemptuous, but kind, loving and in love, rapturous and worshipping. Nell had found herself bitter with envy and filled with resolve. Some day, somehow she would be the girl in the Mercedes Sports, on her way to meet a man for much, much more than sex. As the years passed, every time she saw a red Mercedes Sports she thought of that girl but knew, with every passing hopeless day, that her dream of emulating her was just so much pie in the sky.

Now, here she was actually sitting in such a car, on her way – could it be – to begin that new life? Eyes and ears open, mouth shut and perhaps you can learn a thing or two. Courtesans don't walk the streets. Men go to them. And their fees are high. Yes, but what do they do to earn those fees? What do you know about that kind of sex? Perfumed, luxurious, *monied* sex. Whatever I don't know I can learn, can't I? she told herself.

Hark at you, a little voice taunted. Leaving the streets, are we?

Yes, about that I am very, very definite, she told herself. But if there is money – and I mean *lots* of money – to be made inside the house or flat then that's the way I go. I've been kept on short commons all my life. Whatever I do in the future, however I earn my money I am not handing over most of it to somebody else. Those days are over. And let's face it, what else do I know about? What else am I fit for? Beggars can't be choosers, just remember that.

She had been so deep in her thoughts that she had not

realised they were through Balham and Clapham and heading towards Battersea Bridge, which they crossed before heading for South Kensington. But the car headed up the Kings Road then turned into Sloane Street before turning off at Cadogan Square, finally to enter, through an archway, a small cul-de-sac with houses on one side, the left, a high cream-painted wall surmounted with spikes on the other.

'Some eastern country's embassy,' Liz said, as she saw Nell staring. 'Very security conscious but nice and quiet.'

They had come to a stop outside a small house painted sugar-almond pink, its red window boxes filled with flowers; pansies, geraniums, lobelia, carnations, bluebells. It had a white trim and its front door was as red as the window boxes.

'Oh, how lovely!' It was quite involuntary but Nell had finally set foot in her own personal fairyland and her reactions were all spontaneous.

'Yes, it is nice, isn't it?'

Nell was wide-eyed and bowled over and then suddenly her face hit the ground as her dreams evaporated. What on earth would anybody who lived in this house want with somebody like her? She would stick out like a sore thumb and the neighbours would complain. She was not SW1 she was SW12. And how could she possibly pay the rent that would be expected of her for a room in a house like this? She had let her dreams run away with her. That red Mercedes had done it again. She would never be the blonde, *never*. Disappointment hit her so savagely her eyes blurred, and on its heels came anger at being duped yet again. It seemed she would *never* learn.

She turned to say as much to Mrs Waring, but found that she was already out of the car and unlocking the red front door. Her blue eyes met Nell's suddenly accusing glacier gaze. 'Yes, it is my house and I am the lady with the spare room – along with everything else. Please, come in and let me tell you the whole truth and nothing but the truth.'

Nell did not move.

'We cannot talk in the street,' Elizabeth said reasonably.

'You tricked me,' Nell accused. 'I don't like being tricked. That's how I ended up with – I don't like being lied to.' Her voice had been low but now it rose.

'I did not lie. Every word I told you was the truth. I just did not tell you that I was the "friend" and that is not strictly a lie. I am my own friend – my best friend apart from one other.' Liz took a step towards Nell. 'Please, come in and let me explain everything.'

'What do you want with *me*?'

'Just give me a chance to explain, but inside, please.' Elizabeth's voice was reasonable, quiet but firm. 'Ten minutes of your time is all I ask. If you don't like my explanation then I promise to take you back to hospital.'

Eyes met and held, and for some reason she could not explain Nell suddenly felt ashamed for doubting.

She followed Elizabeth into a tiny hall which opened off at once into a large light sitting room with floor to wall french windows at one end giving onto a pocket handkerchief-sized garden. There were flowers everywhere, in china bowls, in vases – some crystal, some porcelain – in wicker baskets, and the general air was of comfort and solidity, from the chintz of the loose covers to the sheen on the parquet floor. A lovely carved mirror hung above an elegant fireplace and there were pictures on the walls. It looked for all the world like a room in a Laura Ashley catalogue and it was the most beautiful room Nell had ever been in in her life.

'Come and talk to me while I make coffee,' Elizabeth suggested, tossing her bag onto a chair and her keys into a blue and white bowl on a spindly table whose wood glowed from centuries of sunlight imprisoned within.

Terrified to brush against anything, Nell hunched her shoulders, clasping her big leather bag close to her chest. The kitchen too was out of a magazine *House and Garden*, perhaps; a far cry from the 'kitchen' of the house where she had recently lived: nothing more than the landing outside the rooms she had shared with 'the girls' with only a stone sink under an Ascot heater. This room was big and square and had windows on one side, curtained in filmy voile tied back with crisply starched bows in sunshine yellow and white check. The walls were lined with fitted cupboards above and below a worktop tiled in the same check as the curtain bows. In one of them was set a double electric oven and a microwave. The hob was on the big, square cooking-cum-preparation core occupying the centre of the floor, and from the ceiling hung a myriad of copper pans along with bunches of herbs, strings of garlic and onions and various cooking implements. There was also every electric gadget known to man; a percolator, a cafetière and a filter machine; a Kenwood plus attachments, a slicer, a blender, a toaster, a waffle iron.

'Yes, I like gadgets,' Liz said amusedly, watching Nell's face.

'Don't *think* of adding me to your collection!' It burst out in spite of Nell's determination to keep calm.

'That is *not* what I have in mind.'

'Then what do you want with me? I'm a streetwalker, you are a courtesan. I'm lucky if I get twenty-five pounds; I can't even begin to guess what you earn.'

'My fee is one thousand pounds minimum,' Elizabeth said calmly, measuring beans into the grinder. 'How do you like your coffee, by the way? Strong? Medium? This is Blue Mountain but I've got some continental blend if you would prefer it?'

'Blue Mountain would be fine, thank you. My – '

'Your what?'

'My taste does not run to very strong coffee,' Nell improvised. She had been going to say 'My father always drank Blue Mountain' but it would not do to open up just yet – if at all.

'Nor mine, except after a good dinner.'

Neither spoke over the highspeed whine of the grinder but as Liz measured out the coffee into the cafetière she said: 'I am in the business of realising fantasies and the men who are my clients have the means to do so. That is why my fees are so much higher than average.'

'Higher! They are astronomical,' gasped Nell, but her interest had been well and truly caught. She had not realised that money could be earned in such amounts by women selling sex.

'To you, perhaps, but I am expected to maintain a certain standard, and every penny I earn is needed to maintain it.'

The kettle Liz had filled first of all now began to whistle and she poured boiling water over the ground coffee.

'Is that why you need to let your spare room? Because I might as well make it quite plain here and now that I doubt very much that I could earn enough to afford the kind of rent you would charge.'

'We will get to that eventually.'

Liz set the cafetière on a glass-topped tray by the cups and the cookie jar before lifting it to carry it into the sitting room, but suddenly her left hand seemed to lose it strength and the tray tilted dangerously, the cafetière sliding downwards towards her arm and wrist. Only Nell's quick thinking in stepping forward to take hold of the left-hand side prevented it from falling.

'Oh, thank you . . .' Liz's voice trembled slightly. 'This damned wrist of mine . . .'

'Have you a weakness in it?'

'Now and then.'

'I'll carry the tray, then.'

'Thank you,' Liz said again.

She showed Nell where to set it down, on the big coffee table between twin two-seater sofas on either side of the fireplace.

'Shall I pour?' Nell asked.

'I think perhaps you'd better.'

Nell not only poured but set down the cup in front of her hostess.

'You've done this before,' Elizabeth said humorously only to be rewarded by a sudden closing of what had been a concerned face. Ah, she thought. That touched a nerve.

'Help yourself to biscuits,' she said, helping herself to cream. She sipped, relished then went on: 'Tell me, when you first saw me, what did you think I did for a living?'

'I didn't think you worked at all. I got the impression of enough money to render working unnecessary.'

'Good, that's the impression I try to give, but the reality is quite different. Like you, I sell sex, but on a different level – more upmarket, shall we say.'

'How did you get there?' Nell asked, her curiosity getting the better of her. 'I can't see you as ever being on the streets.'

'I wasn't. I have always been what I am now, with a regular clientele though that took time to build up. I go where I am sent for, and that means New York, San Francisco, Europe, of course, Hong Kong, Singapore – my clientele is international.'

'And they pay your expenses?'

Oh, yes, she is bright, Liz thought happily. 'Every penny,' she said.

She let Nell digest that, ostensibly enjoying her coffee but in reality monitoring every nuance, every flicker of expression.

'You walk the streets, I answer the telephone,' she went on. 'You don't know the men you have sex with, I do. I don't know what you do to earn your money but I doubt if it is anything else but – to put it bluntly – a quick fuck. I do a great deal more than that. One does not get paid a thousand pounds for something that is available for one tenth of that – and from a skilled professional. I am worth every penny I earn because I am good at what I do. I also happen to like sex and when I found I could make a very good living by providing it to men who had the money to pay my price, I had no hesitation in taking it up full-time.'

'Tax free?' Nell asked, awed.

Ah, so money *is* important to her, Liz thought, as she answered: 'No. I have an accountant, and according to the books he keeps I am a Public Relations Consultant; certain cheques I receive are paid to me in that capacity and on those I do pay tax. But the majority of the money I earn is in cash.' Laconically: 'I am part of what the Revenue call the 'black economy' and they are right because the books of account I keep myself are definitely in the black.'

But Nell did not smile; she was too busy calculating.

'You are wondering how much I make a year, aren't you?'

Nell had the grace to blush.

'I will tell you, because it has an important bearing on what I propose to discuss next. My income over the past ten years has averaged out at around £150,000 a year.'

Nell's jaw dropped. When she could. 'And you get to keep it all to yourself?'

'I do not have, never have had, a pimp.'

Nell let out an admiring breath.

'I meet my clients by recommendation and referral from existing clients, but all the same I always do a check on them. I do not go in for S&M, bondage, or any of the revolting peculiarities of the darker reaches of sex. But I do do fantasy –

in fact, that is my speciality, and in that respect I am reckoned to be one of the best *femmes dominatrices* in the business.'

Liz finished her coffee and set down her cup before reaching to lift the lid of a silver box, from which she took a cigarette. This she fitted into a black lacquer holder before lighting it with a matching silver lighter.

'Prostitution has made me a very good living for the past dozen or so years, but the time has come when I have to – think about retirement.' She drew hard on her cigarette. 'In fact, it is not a matter of thought any more, nor choice, come to that. I am being forced to retire.' She blew smoke at the ceiling. 'That little episode in the kitchen was symptomatic of my illness. Every now and again something like that happens; not always an arm. Sometimes it is a leg and it is nothing I can control because –' she drew another deep drag, 'because I have an inoperable brain tumour.'

Nell could not stop her sharp hiss of indrawn breath but she said nothing.

'I have at the most two years, during which time I will deteriorate slowly. The occasional weaknesses will become regular and progressively worse. Towards the end I shall need round the clock nursing. All this I have arranged for. It is about the intervening time I wish to speak to you.'

But Nell asked: 'Is the tumour malignant or benign?'

'Malignant. How come you know about things like that?' Liz asked in surprise.

Nell did not answer at once then, reluctantly: 'My father was a doctor.'

'I knew it!' Liz was triumphant. 'I said to Philip that you were not your average streetwalker.'

'So it is too deep for surgery?' Nell asked, still pursuing her own tack.

'Yes.' Curiously: 'Was your father a brain specialist?'

'No, but he was an out-of-the-ordinary GP. After – after my mother died he used to discuss his more – interesting – cases with me. He wanted me to follow in his footsteps.'

'Why didn't you?'

Another pause. 'Other things – intervened.'

'You say your father was a doctor? Is he retired now, or – ?'

'He no longer practises medicine.' Nor am I answering any more questions, her voice said.

'So illness does not, as the Americans would say, faze you?'

'My mother died of multiple sclerosis when I was eleven and she was in a wheelchair from the time I was seven. I know about illness.'

Something in the dispassionate tone chilled Liz's blood and she had a vision of a seven-year-old being acquainted far too early on with the harsh realities of life. How old was she, for God's sake, when her father discussed his more interesting cases with her? And why is she a streetwalker? Her brain buzzed with questions but she tranquillised them and concentrated on the matter in hand. Time enough, once she had what she wanted, to find out all the myriad whys and wherefores. One question had been answered to her satisfaction anyway. There was no doubt as to the ability of this girl to learn, and learn well.

'Anyway, it is because I am on notice, so to speak, that I am looking for a – let me say pupil. Someone to whom I can pass on my skills and my client list, should they be agreeable, of course. Someone who will live here with me, absorb my – ambience, if you like. Study me, listen to me, understand what makes me tick, and most important, what makes me a great courtesan.'

'Is that your – *estimation* – of yourself?'

'Rather my classification. When people think of a prostitute they visualise somebody like Irma la Douce or Sweet Charity; cheap, common, easily used and quickly disposed of. A courtesan is not to be used so lightly. She costs more, for a start, and when you pay a lot for a thing you take care of it.'

'Like those of *La Belle Epoque*?'

'Exactly. You know about *Les Grandes Horizontales*?'

'I've read about them.'

'Then you are halfway there.'

'Except there are no longer any Kings or Grand Dukes to squander fortunes on jewels, castles and an estate or two.'

'No, but there are merchant princes, and they are our modern equivalent.'

'And they are your kind of client?'

'Yes.'

A faint yet steel-tipped smile. 'So it is the money that lifts you up? Changes your name? Grants you status?' The smile became a razor-edged laugh. 'Of course it does. Money is the one thing with the power to change almost anything.'

'I am glad you said almost. It cannot change a damned thing for me and it is not for want of trying.'

Nell's face sobered. 'No. Life is the one thing which cannot be bought, no matter how much money you have.'

'You are not a complete cynic, then?'

'I like to think that there are some things over which we have no dominion, even while I am well aware that I would like nothing more than to be rich – independently rich.'

'So you can be if you agree to my proposition.'

'I'm listening.'

'I take you under my wing. You come here to live with me and over the next few months I give you the benefit of my experience – and my arts. Once you are ready, you gradually take over my client list and during that time and up until the time when you are on your own, you give me fifty per cent of your fees.'

No reaction.

'That means you still get to make far more in one night than you can hope to make on the streets in a month of Sundays. And I will have to incur the initial expense of dressing you, making you over, housing you, feeding you. You pay nothing while you are a . . . student. But once you begin to earn, I shall probably be curtailing my own activities and it costs a great deal to maintain my lifestyle. Fortunately I have insurance to cover my last nurse-run months and my doctor's fees, but until then I propose to gradually withdraw from the scene. You will become the breadwinner. And since I have no dependents I shall probably leave you this house. It is mine. I have only the minimum mortgage that allows me tax relief. If you wish to pay that off – ' Liz spread her hands.

'You said "make-over",' Nell reminded. 'Just how much would I be changed?'

'Totally. Your hair for a start. It is a pretty brown but not dramatic enough. A wig can change all that. We don't know how your nose is going to be once that plaster comes off; it may require corrective surgery. Your make-up will have to be created for you, and you will have to dress the part.' Liz saw

Nell's eyes glow with a kind of fire down below. 'You like clothes?'

'I would like to be able to dress well, though I don't agree with those who believe it must cost a fortune to do so. You don't have to have money to have taste. But you can have money and no taste.'

Liz was amused. 'Is there anything on which you don't hold firm views?'

A faint brush-stroke of colour washed Nell's creamy skin. 'I know what I like.'

'And what you don't like? Don't hesitate to tell me what you don't like about my proposition.'

'At first glance – nothing. A fifty per cent split is, as you point out, far more than I could ever hope to earn if I went back on the streets, but I did not intend to do that anyway.'

'Can I ask you how you got on them in the first place?'

When Nell did not reply, 'You came from a good home, surely,' Liz pursued. 'So why the streets?'

'It was all I was fit for.'

'You mean you were straight from school . . . Untrained for anything?'

'Yes.'

Liz had a strong feeling that these ostensibly simple facts covered a complicated tangle of reasons but she did not press for them. Nell's terse voice and body language were making it very clear that she did not like being questioned too closely about her background. Why? wondered Liz, before asking: 'And did you receive any training from your pimp?'

'He showed me what was expected of me.'

'Can I ask you – I have to know exactly how sexually experienced you are, you do understand that – just exactly what you charged for and how much?'

Nell told her, factually and even clinically, but Liz noticed yet again that when Nell talked of sex her face took on a curiously remote expression as though she was dissociating herself from something she would rather not do but since she had to – well then, she would do but not feel. It was Liz's first disappointment and it was a big one, for her own knowledge and experience told her that with this girl, it was all mind and no emotion. Which would never do, because in the fantasies

97

she created Liz entered heart and soul, not only because she liked (a) sex and (b) playing a part, but because she was being paid a great deal of money and believed in giving full value for it. Her disappointment was all the more acute because she was sure that in this girl she had found the perfect fit to her specification.

'How do you see prostitution as such?' she asked.

'I have never given the matter much thought.'

'So it is nothing more than a job like any other?'

'I suppose so.'

Liz shook her head. 'No good, I'm afraid. I am not looking for an automaton. My clients will not pay for someone who does nothing more than go through the motions. You have to give a performance, yes, but not with just technical skill. You have to mean what you do.'

Nell was listening intently.

'Let me give you an example,' Liz said, and described to Liz her South American client with his fixation on the whore of his youth.

'To him this woman represents the summit of his young dreams and it is my belief that he goes back to her again and again because never in his life since has he met a woman who got such a stranglehold on his emotions. He never had her in reality because he could not afford her; in his fantasy he has her again and again and again in all the ways there are – and she loves it! *He* is the young man who brings her to glorious orgasm over and over and over . . . He is at last fulfilling his youthful fantasy; giving that woman something to remember him by as he has never forgotten her. If I went through the motions he would know at once and I should lose him as a client – one of my best. Once you enter into whatever part you are playing then you play that part to the hilt; you become whoever it is your client is paying you to become. Do you understand?'

'Yes.' There was no hesitation.

'But could you do that?'

'Yes.' Again without hesitation.

'*Really* enter into the spirit of whatever the game – for fantasies are game-playing – asked of you? Not so much play a part as become it?'

Liz persisted because it was important. 'Not for a moment must you do less than wholly believe in what you are and what you are doing.'

'I can learn any part just so long as I know what it is – and who it is, of course.'

Again there was that hint of remote controlled certainty. 'Have you done some acting, then? School plays and such?'

'Yes. I've done some acting.' This time there seemed to be an almost unholy amusement underlying the words. If she was laughing – and Liz was not absolutely certain – she was laughing at herself. 'I like it, acting, I mean. I like becoming someone else.' Now a smile appeared. 'That is *my* fantasy.'

For a moment Liz felt a chill. What have I got myself here? She wondered uneasily. She wanted a chameleon, but not one who never revealed her true colours.

Now Nell asked a question: 'You think I can be made to look the part? Look like you?'

'I am certain, but if you have doubts, would you like me to illustrate?'

The grey eyes glowed, as if someone had turned on a lamp.

'Come on, then.'

Liz led the way upstairs, Nell following but pausing on the threshhold of a bedroom the like of which she had seen only in magazines or on the movie screen. Acres of fitted carpet, a bed that was a four-poster swagged and swathed in shot silk that now was pink, now lilac, now turquoise. One whole wall of mirrors which slid back at a finger touch to reveal fitted wardrobes. A dressing table that was spotlit from a dozen angles by powerful unshaded bulbs, a whole bank of windows occupying two corners and an all pervading fragrance of expensive perfume. She stood in the doorway, unwilling to track dirt across a carpet that was a drift of the same delicate, subtle colours of the bed-hangings and curtains. It must have cost a *fortune*, Nell thought, and then: Yes, but isn't she earning one?

'Come on in . . . I don't charge admission, you know,' Liz chuckled.

Nell pulled off her boots first.

'That's better,' Liz said, 'I thought we were about the same height. I'm five seven, what are you?'

'Five eight and a half – these boots add three inches.'

'And a size twelve?'

'Yes.'

'Again the same as me. Good, My clothes will fit you, then. Now, let me see . . .'

A mirrored door slid back at a touch revealing more clothes than Nell had ever seen outside of a boutique. 'Let's try black . . . you've got that beautifully transluscent skin . . . I know. This one.' She reached in to the crowded hangers, each one holding a dress shrouded in a plastic cover, drew out one which had Nell drawing a deeply appreciative breath before taking off her outer clothes. Underneath her black skirt and sweater she wore only bra and pants – black nylon – from Marks & Spencer, and her tights.

'Right – this goes on first.' It was a black velvet leotard with a polo neck and long tight sleeves, and it fitted like the proverbial glove; hugging the figure, outlining Nell's firm young breasts. With it went a black taffeta skirt, yards of it, which tied at the waist in a big black bow and opened as the wearer moved giving flashing glimpses of sheer black nyloned thigh and leg.

'No – don't look yet, first I want to do something with your hair. Sit down but turn your back to the mirror.'

Nell did so, sat blissfully – for she loved anyone handling her hair; brushing it, combing it, styling it – while Liz pinned it up. Then just as swiftly, with the skilled ease of long practice, Liz made up Nell's face. Finally she said: 'One last touch . . .' and put into place ear-rings that were a cluster of baroque pearls and diamonds. As Nell stood up: 'Hang on – you need shoes. Try these on.' Nell slipped her feet into a pair of black satin four inch heel plain court shoes and then Liz said: 'Right, now you can look at yourself.'

Nell turned, saw a woman she did not know reflected in the mirror wall. Tall, slender, stunningly elegant, her lovely face made up to emphasise its high cheekbones and wide-lipped mouth. Even the plaster over her nose could not diminish the overall effect. This woman was a head-turner, definitely worth a second – even a third – glance. She was also – and this was quite unmistakable – a lady. Her hair was piled up on her head, seemingly carelessly but with cunning art, small fronds framing her cheekbones, through which the pearls gleamed haughtily, and the grey eyes glittered like mint-new silver.

Nell looked for a long time and Liz let her, knowing full well what the silence meant.

'I had no idea,' Nell said finally, and her voice was as stunned as she was stunning.

'I didn't think you did.'

'You saw this – I mean – ' Nell lifted the taffeta wrap-around skirt, twitched it in an enticing rustle, smoothed the velvet of one sleeve, touched the ear-rings. 'You knew this could be achieved from what I was at the time?'

'Yes.'

'How?'

'Let's just say I know what to look for. You have a quality that is as essential in top models as it is in top courtesans: quality itself. To put it crudely – you've got class, and to the discerning eye it shows.'

'Yes, but I have been massively aided. This . . . these . . . everything is – well – a sort of camouflage.'

'No. If you have that indefinable something it cannot be camouflaged. I spotted it in you.'

'I wasn't working at the time.' The sardonic note was back.

'No matter. What you were was no secret, but had it been I would never – never – have put you down as a tart.'

'Is this the sort of thing you wear – "on stage"?'

'Yes. I have a client who likes me to wear black, black and only black. Even the bed has black silk sheets.' Liz shrugged lightly. 'Who can explain your average – or unaverage – male fantasy? I only know that black plays a large part in it. Fortunately you can wear it. You have the colouring. So have I. It positively extinguishes some women. But we'll find out your colours by trial and error.'

Attacking from her position of strength: 'Look, I know you are not your run-of-the-mill streetwalker. It's not that your father was a doctor: mine is a Brigadier (retired) but I am still a whore, like you. The difference between us is that I get very well paid for the sex I sell, and as we both know, money has the power to change anything and everything. You said before that you had intended to leave the streets. I am offering you the chance.' Liz paused. 'Or did you mean you were leaving prostitution itself?'

Nell nodded, her eyes still fastened to her reflection, as if she had fallen in love with it. Which she had. 'Yes. That's what I meant.'

'And now?'

Nell did a slow, model girl's twirl, the wrap-around skirt billowing, revealing legs that began under the armpit and a well-indented waist. 'I think,' she said, as she came to a stop, moved her head so that the ear-rings gleamed and glittered, 'that you have just made me an offer I can't refuse.'

Liz was at the hospital to collect Nell on the Monday morning and drive her back to the house. There was just one small plaster on her nose, but she was instructed to keep it there until she returned to Outpatients in another week's time, and the wire on her jaw had been further loosened. This too would be re-examined in another week. She could now eat soft food – scrambled eggs, yoghurt, thick broths, and talk a little more clearly.

'Better,' approved Liz, 'but we won't really know about the nose until all the plaster is off.'

Nell felt as if the car flew northwards. *She* was sitting in a red Mercedes Sports; it was *her* hair which blew in the wind, *her* smile which dazzled a man waiting for a lights-change. Liz glanced across at her and they exchanged a grin.

'I feel like I am about to start a great adventure,' Nell confessed, exhibiting a child-like eagerness for the unknown.

'Eventually,' Liz agreed. 'I can't remodel you overnight, you know. We have got weeks – months – of work ahead.'

'All part of the adventure. Oh . . . I feel so *good*. Do you know – ' Nell stopped short, an arrested look on her face.

'What is it?' Liz asked in alarm.

'I can't remember the last time I felt like this – or even if I ever have.' That simple admission told Liz much. Her heart wrenched. She took a hand off the wheel, placed it over Nell's, lying on top of the black shoulderbag which contained all she had in the world, and squeezed it. 'From now on it is a feeling you will come to regard as completely natural,' she promised.

Nell's eyes were very bright suddenly, like water behind

glass, but her voice was steady when she promised: 'I won't let you down. This is my chance to make a new life. I won't lose it! *I won't*! I'll strangle it before I'll let it go!'

Her fierceness told Liz more than all the words she had been so careful to control. This was a girl – yes, a girl, for that was all she was behind the artificial ageing of the streets – who had not had much out of life beyond hard words and even harder actions. She concealed a child's vulnerability behind a cold eye and a watchful façade. She had learned far too young that trust could be betrayed; lies could be spoken in seemingly honest voices, promises broken without a second thought. I'll bet that behind the–butter–wouldn't–melt façade there are feelings she learned – the hard way – to keep well hidden. But she's got guts. And then some. Not nearly as tough as she tries to be, but her determination is very real.

Lulu was cleaning the windows when they got back, and Liz introduced Nell. Lulu examined Nell from head to foot then smiled, revealing blindingly white teeth. 'I got coffee on,' she said, in her lilting Barbadian accent.

'Good.'

'First things first,' Liz said, tossing her bag on a chair and making for the stairs. 'I've looked out some clothes for you. Then we can get rid of those awful boots and that nasty skirt.'

'Mickey made me buy them – '

'Oh, I know they are not your taste. I hope these few things are . . .'

They comprised several pairs of trousers; two pairs of cords, one black, one French blue; another pair in bronze velvet and a last pair in vivid pink crepe. There were also two pairs of jeans, several sweaters in assorted colours and a couple of big shirts, one white and one taupe.

'All your size,' Liz assured, as she helped Nell carry the clothes across the corridor to the room she would use, decorated in Wedgwood blue and white, with *toile de juoy* curtains and matching bedspread.

'Lulu does the housekeeping,' she said, as she helped Nell hang the clothes, 'but I like a tidy house. A place for everything and everything in its place, my old nanny used to say.'

'You had a nanny?'

'My parents were abroad most of my childhood, since my

father was a regular soldier, usually stationed in countries he thought were not the place for young children, so until I went to school Nanny Roberts looked after me and my brother. She had been my mother's nanny too. I adored her. She was mother *and* father to me.' Liz slid a shirt on to a hanger. 'Your mother died when you were very young, didn't she?'

'I was eleven, but she had been ill since my sister Margaret was born, when I was seven.'

'You have a sister!'

'Yes.' The pause was a little longer. 'She's autistic and lives in a special school.'

'I don't see much of my brother. We have nothing in common; never did. I've never subscribed to the belief that because someone is your brother and sister you must love them. I never even liked my brother all that much and I was terrified of my maternal grandfather. I just knew he did not have time for children.'

'I never had any grandparents. My mother's mother died when she was a small child and her father just after she married. My father's parents had been dead for years before I was born – they were middle-aged when they had him. And there were no other relatives that I knew.'

A lonely childhood. A father who was the product of elderly parents. More pieces to fit in the jigsaw Liz was slowly but surely compiling. 'Right, let's go down and have a cup of coffee and discuss strategy.'

'I'll just change first . . .'

'All right.'

Nell quickly stripped off her skirt and sweater and tried on a pair of the jeans. They had obviously been bought only to be discarded because they fitted perfectly lengthwise as well as around the hips and waist. Over them she put on the taupe shirt. The only shoes she had were her boots, but in the bottom of the wardrobe she found a shoe-rack where Liz had placed a pair of brown Bass Weejuns which were a little tight but would wear in, and a pair in black. The black ones were better, being half a size larger. An American nine. She brushed her hair, tied it back and was pleased with her reflection. Picking up the hated skirt, boots and sweater she took them downstairs with her.

'Where's the dustbin?' she asked.

'You give them here,' Lulu said. 'I know somebody glad of them.'

'With pleasure,' Nell said, handing them over.

Lulu went to put them in her bag. 'Does she know what you do?' Nell whispered.

'Of course. Lulu can be trusted. I've been doing so for a long time now. She's even more pragmatic than I am and is always urging me to up my fees. She bemoans the fact that she never got to be so lucky; that she – and I quote "give it away free".' Liz sat back, swung her legs up on to the coffee table. 'This is a House of Whores,' she said happily. She offered Nell a chocolate biscuit which she had to refuse. 'Still too hard to chew.'

'Dip it into your coffee. I won't mind. I love dunking. I always do it with doughnuts, like the Americans.'

'Do you have many American clients?'

'Four. Two in New York, one in Chicago and one in San Francisco.'

'Do you see them often?'

'About six times a year each – or when the urge takes them. I get a phone call, followed by a return ticket on Concorde and a car meets me at JFK or O'Hare or wherever.'

'How long do you stay?'

'Again, it depends on what they want. Sometimes only the one night, others a weekend, occasionally a whole week. Once I am sent for I am at their disposal – literally.'

'Do you think they will accept me?'

'If I do it right. That is my part of the agreement so don't you worry about it. I know them all; what they want, how far they will go, what they will accept. I am not going to face them with a fait accompli. I will prepare the ground and over a period of time gradually phase myself out and you in, by which time I will, I hope, have taught you all I know.'

'Do they ever come here?'

'Never.' Liz was emphatic. 'This is my home. I don't do business at home. Nor will you. You go to them. Wherever they want, for as long as they want, and you charge commensurately. I once came home from San Francisco with ten thousand dollars, and the dollar was worth about 1.40 at the time. I went for one night but he would not let me go.' Liz sighed. 'He's dead now. But I got an equally good referral from him.'

Nell was full of admiration. This woman knew her own worth; no signs here of either an inferiority or superiority complex; she saw and understood herself for what she was and saw no reason to feel ashamed. She had the calm assurance that came with years and years of steady, continuous success. Even her own predicted death did not frighten her. How many other women would have handled it with so much practicality, so much sheer common sense? For one, brief blinding moment Nell saw and recognised her good fortune for what it was before her innate caution shouldered her vision aside and told her irritably not to let her optimism get the better of her.

'Tell me some more about why you are a courtesan,' she requested.

'First and foremost, I like sex,' Liz said. 'I always have. It is just about the most pleasurable activity I have ever engaged in. What about you?'

'No.'

'No what?'

'No, it is not my most pleasurable activity.'

Liz pursed her lips. 'That's a pity,' she said finally, 'because it is absolutely essential that you seem to be thoroughly enjoying what you do; that you took off your inhibitions with your clothes and your only aim right now is to give and get as much pleasure as it is possible for two people to gain from each other.' She stood up, began to pace, her voice flat. 'On the streets you are not required to do more than provide the necessary friction; my clients expect a great deal more than that, not in the least time spent, attention to detail given, ambience appreciated, fantasy revelled in. You have to like the male body in all its forms because, once again, this is not a quick fumble – what Erica de Jong calls the zipless fuck. One thing I must make clear is that most of my clients are men who will never see fifty again. It takes time to make their kind of money and by the time they have they are at the age where fantasy satisfies more than reality. Most of them have had several wives and/or mistresses and without exception they are men who need sex – hence their willingness to pay for the kind they like. If you have a problem with that now is the time to say so.'

Nell was silent, thinking, but when she spoke it was not what Liz had expected to hear.

'Want I can understand. Need . . . need is – at present anyway – beyond me.'

'Then we have a problem.'

'Why? You said I have to play a part. Well, I can play any part once I understand what is called for. I can give as good a performance as any man has a right to expect for a thousand pounds.' Her smile was mordant. 'And I know all about fantasies.'

Oh, yes, Nell thought. I could tell you about fantasies. I was very young when I started to act out my own. It was the only way I could handle a hideous reality.

'I know all about fantasies,' she repeated. 'I can be all things to all men once I know what is required of me. Start me off with your most difficult client. If I can't send him away not only satisfied but raring for more then you can find yourself another girl.'

Her voice was passionate, her eyes brilliant and she had colour in her normally pale cheeks. Oh, yes, she has feelings all right, Liz thought, even if they are buried, and I mean *buried*. This girl is a positive tomb when it comes to buried darknesses . . . But she's the one. I felt it when I first saw her and I knew it when I saw her just now in that black dress. As she looked at herself in the mirror I saw her change; the eyes enlarged, the face took on a glow, the defensive body stance relaxed to a lazy grace and when she twitched the skirt, swayed her hips, lowered her lashes . . . and she won't need false ones, that's for sure – she was as sexy as any man could hope to die for. I don't know what makes her tick and she is going to take a deal of knowing but she is the one, nevertheless. When she puts her mind to it – and that, Liz knew instinctively was the key to this girl – she has a sensuality that raises the temperature. She had watched the uptight, suspiciously defensive girl merge – like a slow-dissolve in a movie, into a soft, curvaceous woman who exuded sex. Which was when enlightenment dawned.

'You wanted to be an actress, didn't you?' she asked.

'Yes.'

'But your father wouldn't let you?'

'He abhorred the very idea.'

'So – you see this as your chance to act out your own fantasies?'

'Without the client ever suspecting.'

None of the others ever did, she thought but did not say so because it was neither the time nor the place. I've given performances the like of which even you have never seen, Nell thought. But then, I had the ultimate in teachers.

'I can do it,' she said now. 'Just give me the chance.'

But Liz no longer needed convincing.

8

It had been many years since Philip had seen Liz so het-up over anything, and while he was happy for her he knew how impatiently impulsive she was. Liz had a vivid personality; as full of fizz as her favourite drink, but there was a febrile reined-in quality to her now; had been ever since she had brought this unknown quantity home with her. For his part, he was willing to be convinced, but equally sure that since it was one of Hercules' hardest labours to convince Philip Faulkner of anything about which he had doubts, he would not have placed a bet on it, no matter how small. He had arrived to meet the 'protégée', only to find she was out shopping. He had another cup of tea and a third piece of chocolate cake to console his impatience.

Nell had had a lovely time wandering around Harrods; not a shop she had ever been able to afford. Window gazing was as far as she had ever got. Now, after buying everything on the list Elizabeth had given her, which took her through the food halls, she browsed in the pink marble of the perfume department, accepted a spray of Estée Lauder's newest, admired the crocodile handbags and promised herself 'one day', fingered the Hermès silk scarves and made a similar vow, then treated herself to a quarter pound of hand-made chocolates before hefting her assorted green carrier bags and starting back along the Brompton Road, reflecting that nobody in Harrods had given her a second look – except a man buying perfume for a wife or girl-friend. He had not so much looked as stared, and in admiration rather than affront, for her trousers were well-cut and her sweater cashmere (another cast-off from Elizabeth) both obviously expensive, as was the tweed jacket, once part of a Karl Lagerfeld suit. And the big bag over her shoulder was coach hide, not vinyl. Clothes do maketh the man or woman, she reflected. The way Mickey made me dress proclaimed what I was because it was his idea of what a prostitute looked like and he had picked that up from the cinema/TV stereotype. Nobody in a million years would take me for an apprentice courtesan because I don't look the part. And nobody in their right mind would take Elizabeth for what she is. In time, I will be accepted, taken as what my clothes proclaim me to be – and my manner of course. Confidence, Elizabeth had told her seriously, is an absolute must. If you appear confident to others they will take you at your own valuation. Never let anyone see your fear, or your nervousness, or your uncertainty. You, and only you, are in control. And that's how I like to be, Nell thought contentedly.

When she turned in through the archway of the mews she saw the coffee-coloured Bentley in front of the house and knew Elizabeth had a visitor, knew also that it was probably Philip Faulkner. Elizabeth had mentioned that he would be 'dropping by'. To drop me in it, Nell thought – if he can. Except that is the last thing I will allow him to do. He may have a lot of influence with Elizabeth, but who is it needs who? She squared her shoulders, chose from an assortment of smiles and got out the key Elizabeth had given her.

'I'm back,' she sang, as she entered the hall, but she went into the kitchen to unpack her carrier bags. She took her time. So much that Elizabeth came looking for her, though it was ostensibly to get more boiling water.

'Did you get everything?' she asked brightly.

'Yes – but only a dozen quail eggs; it was all they had left.'

'Never mind . . . It will be enough for us two. Care for a cuppa?'

'Yes, please.'

'Come on, then.' Over her shoulder Elizabeth added carelessly: 'Oh, Philip's here, by the way.'

'Yes, his way,' Nell fretted to herself, determined not to let him persuade Elizabeth to put her back on the streets. The past week had been enough to show her that after being thrown out of the window, not only had she landed on her feet, she had done so in front of the one woman in the world likely to see something more than just a bedraggled stray she had proceeded to take home to a lap of luxury such as Nell had never known. Her childhood home had been comfortable, middle-class, but gloomy, in keeping with her father's anti-social outlook, and because the house and its contents had been inherited from his father, likewise a doctor.

Nothing had been changed in the years since it was bought and furnished in the days before the First World War. It was an Edwardian monolith, frozen in time, as cold as charity and dark as a cave. It had taken courage to take a bath in the enormous bathroom, all mahogany, brass piping and flower-decorated porcelain; freezing cold in both summer and winter, its tiled walls and floor daring the faint heat from the towel rail to raise the temperature by as much as one degree. In Elizabeth's jewel of a house the temperature was constant in every room and it was possible to move from one to the other – like from her bedroom to the guest bathroom – stark naked, and not raise a goosebump, whilst the beds were a dream of comfort, unlike the hard Edwardian mattress in its striped ticking that had never, over the years, yielded to the body, in which she had slept for the first seventeen years of her life. And Elizabeth's kitchen was light, cheerful and labour saving. The one at 17 Warwick Avenue had been lofty, gloomy and painted in the original dark green and brown, its original big black range still in use, for her father refused to waste money on either a gas or electric replacement and for years Nell's first job had been to see to the fire in it, always banked up at night but often as not out next morning and requiring the laborious effort and toil of relighting.

Elizabeth's house practically ran itself; there was no effort involved in its maintenance. Warwick Avenue had been hard physical work, for though her father employed a daily to do the cleaning, Nell had been saddled with the cooking and the washing. Her father was particular about his shirts and would not hear of them being sent to strangers to launder; no, Nell had washed, starched – for her father was old fashioned in his dress as well as everything else – and ironed them, a clean one every day. From the age of eleven, Nell's day was never less than twelve hours long.

The only place in the house which had ever held any light and warmth had been her father's surgery, for it had originally been the house's conservatory and he had left the upper half of the glass walls and ceiling alone when converting it. In Nell's memory the dark and gloomy house had been lit by her mother's presence. After she died there was nothing and no one to counteract her father's pessimism and cold logic. Or his power.

Now, as she followed Liz into the sitting room she knew she was about to meet a second powerful man, one who, like her father, was difficult to please. 'Not that he will change my mind, you understand,' Liz had hastened to reassure her. 'It's just that – well, Philip's approval is absolutely essential. There's nothing and nobody he does not know.'

'How did he do that?'

'Because,' Liz met Nell's eyes head on, 'when he was very young he set out to become the World's Best Kept Man. And he succeeded.'

Nell laughed until she saw that Liz was deadly serious.

'You would not have heard of Philip because you know nothing of the world in which he and I move. In it I have some standing and a certain reputation, but Philip – Philip is the stuff of myth and legend.'

Nell was by now utterly fascinated. 'You mean there are Kept Men as well as Kept Women?'

Liz was amused. 'You really have no idea, have you? Philip has been used by four different novelists of considerable literary standing as a character in a novel; Cole Porter once wrote a song about him – not the kind that would *ever* get onto Top of the Pops – and he can number kings, princes, dukes – millionaires by the dozen – among his patrons. When Philip was young, he had the sort of looks that had people standing on chairs to stare.'

'I thought they only did that with Lily Langtry.'

Liz smiled. 'That describes Philip perfectly. He is the male equivalent of what Lily Langtry was.' The smile faded. 'One thing you must understand: there is an inner, secret world and once you throw in your lot with us that is the one you will inhabit from then on; Philip occupies a very special place in that world – '

'A sort of elder statesman?'

Liz nodded. 'That is it exactly. He has been there, you see, before anyone else and for a much longer time. So – '

'Be careful?'

'Just remember who and what he is. Some people may see nothing more than an ageing queen. Don't make that mistake. But don't be frightened, either. Philip has great contempt for fear. What I hope you will do is convince him that you are indeed everything I have told him about you.'

Watching Nell, Liz could not read the well-schooled face, which showed only close attention, but she knew her protégée well enough by now to know that a great deal went on behind the attentive façade. She was not holding back where Philip was concerned because in all conscience she could not let any lamb cross Philip's path without warning, but more than that because she was convinced that Nell would do better if she clearly understood the formidable task she was undertaking.

'All right,' Nell said at last, mustering her courage. 'I can only do my best.'

Nell's first impression, on entering the sitting room and meeting the very pale, very cold blue eyes of the man enthroned – yes, enthroned is the word, she thought, in the centre of one of the twin sofas flanking the fireplace, was as Liz had predicted – one of enormous presence. He sat at ease, sipping his tea, one leg crossed over the knee of the other, and he radiated the massive, unshakeable calm of the absolutely confident. Her second impression was of greyness; his suit – and Nell compared it with every other suit she had seen and knew she had never seen a *real* suit before – was grey, and his shirt was the colour of the first faint flush of a newly opened magnolia, while his hair was ash, worn slightly longer as became an older man but in the style of his youth: short back and sides but cut so as to flatter the rather long, aquiline featured face, with its deep-set eyes and wide yet exquisitely-cut mouth – a mouth which had given rise to many a fevered imagination. He had a red rose in his buttonhole and it was the perfect match to his plain, silk tie, whilst the small *cabochons* in his cuff-links were the dark red of rubies. His socks were of grey silk and his shoes reflected the chintz of the sofa, so brightly did they gleam. His watch was wafer thin and on a plain crocodile strap, and he wore one ring; a heavy signet on the little finger of his right hand. As Nell shook it she saw that it bore a crest. He held her hand when she would have withdrawn it and for a moment they looked deeply at each other.

Nell felt the icy eyes slide into her and she wanted to shiver, but she forced herself not to. Then Philip smiled, and Nell blinked. It was like coming out of a cold room into hot and humid sunlight. Then she saw what he must have been like when young and it awed her. His eyes were slightly hooded she saw, holding them as if mesmerised, and they were not blue; they were silver with ice-blue flecks. Mercury, she thought dazedly, remembering sixth form science and the way it used to form a pool of multi-colours that coated its silver surface. She could see her own reflection in them, and it brought her back to herself.

'How do you do, Mr Faulkner,' she said, giving him the smile she had decided on.

He inclined his head. 'Miss . . . Jordan?' He waited until she had sat down then re-seated himself. Frowning, Nell looked down at her forearm; it felt as if an insect was crawling up it yet there was nothing there. It was her reaction to his voice, which was of a depth and timbre that stroked the flesh. She flicked a quick glance at Liz who caught its meaning, which was: 'You have not told me the half!' Every preconceived idea went out of the window. This, Nell realised, she would have to play by ear. Never in her life had she met a man like this one and she was therefore out of her depth. She would just have to tread water and watch for sharks.

She took the cup of tea Liz handed her, shook her head at the plate of shortbread. If she took one he was sure to catch her with her mouth full. Her father had numbered several fee-paying patients in his files, and Nell had seen most of them at one time or another when they came for their private consultations. They had arrived in big cars and most of them had been in the same age group as Philip Faulkner, possessed of power, influence and wealth, but not one of them had poleaxed her as this one did, which was when she realised the secret of

Philip Faulkner. He was potently attractive to women as well as men. Is this what they mean by sex appeal? she wondered, gulping hot tea and keeping her eyes on her cup in case she missed her mouth.

Philip knew exactly the effect he was having – it was something he had worked on, long and hard – but his own surprise was equally as considerable as the experience which enabled him to hide it. He had dismissed Elizabeth's encomiums as being those of someone who tended to let her enthusiasm run away with her. There was never any careful thought between her instant 'Yes, that's the one I want' and her realisation, once she got it home, that it would not do at all. But he could see why she had been bowled over. This leggy, undeniably classy girl was not the Predator Bird he had expected who, having seen her sucker, had at once proceeded to attach herself by her own and proceeded to drain dry. This was an innocent. She can't have walked the streets looking like *that*, he thought. She'd be picked up by the police within five minutes as being in need of care and protection. But he put his imagination to work, re-styled the thick, dead-straight shiny hair into a mass of artfully untidy frizz, painted the face, shortened the skirt by a good twenty-four inches and lowered the neckline by ten, then grudgingly decided that yes, she would pull in the punters. But to do what? She looked as if she would not know what on earth to do once a man had himself out of his trousers. Yet she must have, for had not Elizabeth said she had been on the streets for two and a half years. Ah, but perhaps that is her forte . . . The world is full of men who like little girls, and under all the paint and surface shellac she probably looked as if she wanted to put her thumb in her mouth and suck. Oh, yes, he thought, understanding at last. They must have come for miles . . . Clever, he approved, satisfied he had found the key, the one that would unlock the cupboard containing all her secrets.

'Such a pretty, old-fashioned name, Nell. Dickens used it to such powerful effect. I don't know when I have laughed so much . . . Or did you take it from an earlier age? Carolinian, perhaps? Charles II must be given credit for not wishing his pretty, witty Nelly to starve, even if nobody else gave a damn. As for the Jordan . . . another royal connection? Are you perhaps one of these peculiar people who think there is something magical about royalty? I believe there actually are such people?'

The viciousness of his onslaught had Nell reeling, but she fought back manfully.

'Eleanor Frances Jordan is my real name,' she told him steadily. Her resentment at his preconceived notions firmed a voice which was for a moment on the verge of shaking, when she said: 'If I had intended to re-name myself I would hardly have chosen the names of two women who were dumped by their royal lovers. Nell Gwynne died penniless while Dorothy Jordan was given the elbow, along with the ten children she bore the Duke of Clarence, as soon as he became William IV. If Liz thinks a new name is needed to match my new persona then I might borrow one from a really successful *grande horizontale*. Liane de Pougy, perhaps or Cleo de Mérode.'

Put that along with the rest of your jaundiced misconceptions, Mr Faulkner, she told him hotly. She did not mind voluntarily putting herself on other people's level but what right did this sneering, supercilious man have to place her as belonging on the bottom shelf with the rest of the cretins. He was as snide a snob as she had ever met, and she'd met a few of them in her time. Superior shit! she thought angrily, keeping her voice calm and her expression pleasant. If he was needling her deliberately – and she would put nothing past this spiteful man – then she would die rather than let him see it. Liz *won't* change her mind, she told herself fiercely, but if she does at the insistence of this nasty piece of work then you are well out of it because that means she is not the woman she seems to be, either.

'Obviously you aspire to great things,' Philip purred in his loin-stroking voice. 'What a pity there are no longer any kings left to help you attain them.'

'Yes . . . I understand you had the last of them,' Nell heard herself saying. It was out before she could stop it. 'That ready tongue of yours will be your downfall, Eleanor,' her father had been wont to say. Frequently. Well, it was done now. Nell tilted her chin and prepared for the worst. Only to find that Philip Faulkner was laughing. He made no sound; he merely shook.

'Watch out,' he said, sounding amused as he did so, 'it bites.' He turned his silver eyes on her and for a moment they bathed her in molten fury. Which was when she knew she had made an enemy. Confirmed when he turned to Liz to say, his flexible voice as cutting as a riding-crop: 'I had thought to find you had brought home some scruffy mongrel, much like that awful terrier you had some years ago. What was its name?'

You know damn well what its name was, Nell thought, curling a mental lip. You always know exactly what you are doing. And saying.

'Heinz . . .' Liz said. 'All fifty-seven varieties . . .'

'Yes. That one.' Philip turned his head to give Nell a judge's scrutiny. 'But I see that you have rescued a borzoi.'

Liz laughed delightedly. 'True. Nell does have a long face and somewhat elongated eyes. Best of all, borzois are invariably long pedigreed.'

And bitches, Nell thought. As their eyes met she saw Philip smile when he saw she had caught his meaning.

Philip passed his cup to Liz for more tea.

'So, it is obvious you know something of our country's history. What else do you know and where did you learn it? What was your school? Do you have any – what is it they call the matriculation these days?'

As if you didn't know, Nell riposted silently. '"O" and "A" levels' she answered his question. 'And I have nine of the one and four of the other, gained by ten years at a former grammar school founded by Henry VIII. Would you like to know the subjects?'

He held up a traffic-stopping hand. 'Thank you, but no. I have qualifications in just about every subject that is not on any school's curriculum. Do you read?'

'As much as I can.'

'And what do you read?'

'Anything I can get my hands on that is worth my time and attention.' And I don't remember a character like you in *any* of them.

'Have you travelled?'

'No.' Her father, like George V, had been of the opinion that 'abroad was bloody'. It also cost far too much.

'Have you any accomplishments? Are you good at sports, for instance? Do you ride? Play golf? Tennis?'

'No, to all of the above.'

Nell was well into her stride by now. She could toss a conversational ball with the best of them. Working the streets you soon learned the art of the verbal.

'Do you play bridge?'

'No. I used to play Happy Families with my sister.'

Once more she saw the molten flare to the eyes, like sunspots. He knew what she was doing and he did not like it; he did not like it at all. Too bad, thought Nell, watching her boats blazing away. But I promised myself a long time ago that once I was truly free I would never allow another man to ride roughshod over me. Liz may think you sit on the right hand of God but I was brought up by a man who had no use for religion, organised or otherwise, since organised religion is man-made and therefore suspect. Any other kind is usually created out of desperation. You don't frighten me, Mr Faulkner. I spent seventeen years with a man who *really* knew how to frighten.

'And where do you come from?' Philip asked next.

'A small town some fifteen miles from Bristol.' It came off her tongue with all the readiness of truth though it was all part of the lie she had created for herself a long time ago, when she used to spend the time waiting for punters in creating a whole new, credible and believable background for herself. She had no further use for her real one, which in reality lay some three hundred miles to the north.

'And who or what are or were your family?'

'My mother is dead. My father was a doctor. I have one sister, seven years younger than me. She is retarded and lives in a special Home.'

'Other relatives?'

'None.'

'And where is your father now?'

'Retired.' There was a fractional hesitation. Liz missed it completely but Philip, who had a bat's radar for errors and/or omissions, picked it up at once, filed it away for future reference and eventual classification.

'But you no longer see or communicate with him?'

'No.'

'Why is that?'

'He ran my life for seventeen years; and I mean ran. He wound me up and placed me on the tracks he set every morning. Finally, the morning came when I had had enough. So I left.'

Philip nodded as if he could understand *that*, replaced his cup on the tea tray.

'The preliminaries being disposed of, now tell me how you came to be a whore.'

My God, Philip, but you are going your ends this afternoon, Liz thought appalled, until it came to her that he was being intentionally hard; testing Nell to her limit. Probing for her weak spot, no doubt. On which he would press hard once he found it. Except that Liz had the feeling that in this seemingly fragile girl he had met his match.

Philip was watching Nell assimilate the brutality of his question. Really, she is very pretty, he thought, even as he listened intently to her story. Her skin is like the inside of a shell. Something will have to be done about the bump on her nose and whoever did her jaw made a clumsy job of it but that can be put right by a competent man. Eyes her best feature . . . remarkable clarity and brilliance. Mouth well-shaped if a trifle wide. Taken separately her features are by no means perfect, but together they make a face well worth a second look. Something pre-Raphaelite about her but without their dreadful monotony of expression. No suggestion of a mournful horse here. Masses of hair, but very fine. It will need the very best cutting. Too slender for her height and not much in the way of breasts but nice long bones and an exquisite neck. Yes. Liz was right when she said there was raw material here. And once she knows her place – *and mine* – I think something can be done.

'So,' he said briskly, when her tale was told, 'now tell me what you think of Elizabeth's proposition.'

'Too good to be true.'

Philip shrugged. 'Understandable. But do you think you can provide what we are looking for?'

'Yes.'

'Tell me why.'

Liz poured fresh tea for them all. Nell picked hers up and sipped gratefully. Her mouth was dry. Philip Faulkner had that effect. He picked a bone cleaner than any vulture. Years of practice, she surmised.

'I like the idea of becoming someone new,' she said at last. 'Of being re-created, playing a part.'

'Is that how you see it?'

'Isn't that what it is? The job of a courtesan is to please a man sexually for a large fee. What else is that but a piece of acting? Especially since Liz's speciality is fantasy.'

'You are "in" to fantasy?'

He had an impression she smiled but her face did not change its serious expression. 'I've *always* been into fantasy,' she said.

'And you obviously consider yourself enough of an actress?'

'Yes.'

'Ah . . . the confidence of youth.' Philip's sigh was wistful. 'So you would have no difficulty in entering into the fantasies – whatever they might be – required of you at any time?'

'None.'

'Even if their instigator was, shall we say – unprepossessing – unattractive, even. Would such things affect your performance?'

'The fact that he could afford me would provide enormous inspiration.'

Philip threw back his head as he laughed, with evident enjoyment. He rated a sense of humour very high, and she obviously had one, along with a vivid imagination if the fairy story she had just told him was anything to go by. She was hiding something, of course, but then, weren't most people? What she had told him was her own, carefully edited version of the truth. She was far too intelligent to lie about everything, but she had most certainly lied about her reasons for leaving home, though she had not lied about her acting abilities. Liz was totally convinced. Yes . . . an actress indeed. It was probably her air of fragile vulnerability; she looked like a waif and stray in need of care and protection. Those big grey eyes would melt stone, until, as you talked to her, you became aware of the granite under the gossamer. But then, two and some years on the street might well have turned Joan of Arc into Jack the Ripper. Which brought him back to what intrigued him most. *Why* had she so easily taken to prostitution? The idea of becoming someone else? Which means she cannot have liked the self she was. Dear old Sir explained all that to me years ago. 'I loathed myself out of make-up, dear boy. Such a relief to hide myself in a well-written part. Oh, the sheer pleasure to be obtained from make-believe . . . to feel the love of an audience flowing towards one. Is it any wonder that the theatre is so full of misfits and monsters, able to transform themselves once in full make-up, able to make the audience hang on their every word? Very addictive, that kind of love. Comes of not having any at the proper time.' Yes, thought Philip smugly. I did not spend five years with one of England's greatest actors and not learn all about the craft of acting.

He laid down his cup and saucer. 'Well, it has been delightful but I must take my leave. Binkie Lassiter is having one of his *soirées* this evening and you know how they are. I must prepare myself for the feast.'

Yes, Liz thought dryly. An assortment of exquisite young men served *au naturel* on a bed of your own choosing, but she said: 'And what do we feast on? Suspense? Have I your approval or not, Philip? Will you help or do we go it alone?'

She saw Nell's set face melt under the brilliance of her relieved smile. So did Philip.

'My dear Elizabeth, I thought you knew me well enough by now to know when I am for rather than against.' He turned to Nell. 'You have possibilities; we must make them certainties. Are you willing to give of your very best?'

'Yes.'

'You wish to become a high-priced whore rather than a cheap one?'

'Yes.'

She saw his mobile mouth tighten. Stab away, Mr Faulkner, she told him silently. You can't butcher what is already dead.

'Have you any record with the police which might affect

your future activities? Have you ever been arrested for soliciting?'

'No. But I have been cautioned – twice.'

'Elucidate, if you please.'

She'd been working York Way, beside Kings Cross Station, still nervously new to the job after six weeks, still not up to all the tricks of the trade explained to her by the others, so that when the car drew up beside her and she saw the navy blue uniform her heart had taken refuge in her throat. Then she saw that the officer getting out of the car was a woman; plump, middle-aged, not unlike dear old motherly Lil. Nell had waited, frozen with fright, expecting to have the handcuffs on her wrists before being bundled into the car and taken into custody, but the sergeant said mildly: 'Not doing very well tonight, are you dear? That's the third car I've seen you bargain with.' She had taken out her notebook. 'Right, what's your name?'

'Elly . . . Elly Little.' It was the one she had decided on. Nobody ever gives their right names, she had been told.

'Address?'

She gave it.

'How old are you?'

She lied; said she was eighteen. She was terrified of being taken back into care; worse, sent back where she had come from.

The sergeant eyed her, then seeing the obvious white-faced fear she said on a sigh: 'We can check, you know.'

Not without my real name you can't, some cool part of Elly's brain reminded.

The sergeant wanted to know her height, had she any tattoos, any distinguishing marks. Her complexion was noted, whether or not she wore glasses – everything about her including her race – IC1 – white – Then the sergeant cautioned her officially for soliciting; warned her that she could be cautioned only once more. After that, the next time she was picked up she would be arrested.

'You know what that means, don't you?' the sergeant asked, as if hoping Elly did. 'It means that you won't be just a name on a caution register; it means you will be photographed, finger-printed, given a number. You will have a police record. Is that what you want? What's a young girl like you doing tomming on York Road? Is this the best you can do? I am authorised to help you find something better. Let me give you the name and address of an organisation designed to help girls like you get off the streets. I've sent quite a few girls there and it was always to their advantage.' In a kindly voice. 'You are far too young for this kind of life, love.'

She saw small white teeth bite down on an over-lipsticked, pathetically vulnerable young mouth. My God, they get younger and younger, the sergeant thought. This one can't be a day over sixteen in spite of what she says and her real name is probably not the one she's given me. Scared stiff and thrown in the deep end.

'Ring these people,' she urged. 'Go on . . . put that bit of paper away safely in your bag . . . give them a ring tomorrow. They'll help you. That's what they are there for.'

She got a quick nod, a hunted look round.

'Somebody keeping an eye on you:' the sergeant asked knowledgeably. 'New to the job, aren't you? Stands out a mile. Don't get in any deeper otherwise you'll be in so deep you'll never get out. Do something while you've got the chance. Ring these people . . . Save yourself while you can and use them to do it. Now don't let me catch you again and remember – one more caution is all you'll get. After that you'll have a police record . . . for the rest of your life.'

When the police car had driven off, Maureen, who had been working in tandem with Elly and been watching from the other side of the road at a safe distance, came hurrying across.

'Did she caution you?' she asked.

'Yes.'

'And give you a song and dance about leavin' the streets before it's too late?'

'Yes . . .'

'That's "Ma" Parkes. She does that to all the girls. Got some sort of religion; sees it as her life's work to save as many souls as possible. Did she give you a name and address?'

'Yes.'

'Then for Gawd's sake don't let Mickey see it or 'e'll do 'is nut.' Sharply: 'You ain't thinkin' of goin', are yer? I wouldn't if I was you. All you'll get is lectures on the sins you committed and a hairshirt to wear. I know a couple of girls as took the bait but they were back on the streets before you could miss 'em. They find out where you come from and bung you back 'ome.'

'But – she said – '

'You never believe a copper, love! Where's your common? They are supposed to get us off the streets and they'll say and do anythin' so as to show they've done it!'

DON'T TRUST NOBODY. Nell had never forgotten that warning, even though she had been horrified at Jenny's cynicism, but more and more, experience was proving that tough street urchin to have been absolutely right. She took the piece of paper from her bag, tore it into confetti, let the wind take it.

She never saw Ma Parkes again. Mickey took her off York Road and put her on Queen's Drive. It was almost a year before she was demoted back down to Kings Cross for daring to argue with Mickey, who liked obedience and showed her, for the first time, what he did when it was not forthcoming. She had been very careful since then not to incur his wrath, just as she had been very careful to avoid the police, learning as she went along, knowing enough to be alerted by a parked, unmarked car. It was not some punter making up his mind; it was nearly always the police.

So the second time she was cautioned she was taken completely by surprise. She was back on York Way for the first time in many months and she knew enough now to recognise a car that could be dangerous, but this one ambushed her. It was an expensive car, to start with. An Audi, so she stood on the edge of the pavement, hip sprung, one hand on her hip showing off the tight leather-look skirt and the narrow ribbed sweater. When she bent down to smile invitingly at the driver through the window he lowered, she got the shock of her life. Underneath the expensive navy blue top coat was a police uniform. He was off-duty but he was still a policeman and if he had taken the bother to stop it meant he had her dead to rights. But she had come a long way since Ma Parkes. She smiled nicely, said with evident relief: 'Oh, thank heavens, a policeman. I wonder if you can help me, officer. I'm lost, and I don't know this district at all. I'm looking for Coram Street. Can you direct me, please?'

She saw him smile; knew he was not fooled for a minute. He had very blue eyes and they laughed too. But only for a moment until he said sardonically: 'I thought your granny lived in the woods.'

'Granny?' Nell sounded blank. 'I don't understand . . .'

'You are Little Red Riding Hood, aren't you?'

'What do you mean?' Nell straightened, stepped back, wondered if she could do a runner as some instinct told her to. This was no motherly Ma Parkes.

'The fairy tale you are telling me about being lost.'

'I am most certainly not!'

'Suit yourself.' He opened the car door, got out. Standing he was still a head taller than she was in her four-inch heels, and when he shrugged off his coat, reached for his cap, she saw he was an inspector.

Oh, no . . . she groaned inwardly.

He took out his notebook. 'I have to tell you you are being cautioned for soliciting.' He began the official procedure, but when he asked: 'Name?' and she said 'Little. Elly Little.' she saw his pen stop and his head come up. 'What?' he asked disbelievingly.

'Elly Little,' she repeated more loudly.

This time he roared with laughter. 'My God, a tom who reads Dickens. What's your real name, Little Nell?'

Elly was flabbergasted. He was the very first person, since she had evolved her new name, to have recognised its origin.

'That is my real name,' she said as indignantly as she could.

He sighed, shrugged. 'All right, if that's your story . . . fond of reading, are you? What do you think of Trollope?'

His voice was innocent but Elly felt the flick of the steel in his voice.

'Right now I'd rather be in *The Small House at Allington*,' she told him sweetly.

This time he lowered his notebook, took a good hard look at her. 'What the hell is an educated girl like you doing on the streets?' he asked. 'Is being a tom the best you can do?'

'In as much as it pays well, yes.'

'Let's have a look at you . . .' He had taken hold of her arm, taken her over to a nearby street light, examined her at some length.

'For God's sake!' he said disgustedly. 'You must only just have sat your A-levels!'

'And passed every single one,' she shot back. 'But almost two years ago, if you must know.'

'All right, turn out your bag,' he snapped coldly.

He counted the condoms – twenty-two of them – 'How many have you done tonight, then?'

'None of your business,' Elly answered curtly.

He pawed through her purse, her comb, her packet of tissues, her small spray of Chanel No. 19, given to her by Cindy who, having shoplifted it from Selfridges decided she did not like it and swopped it for a bottle of expensive nail varnish a punter had given Elly one night – a traveller for the cosmetics company. He lifted it out, commented laconically: 'Well read *and* expensive tastes,' and then found the paperback edition of Zola's *Nana*, which Elly read on the journeys to and from work. 'And ambitious?' he asked, lifting one well-shaped eyebrow, as blonde as his hair.

There was distinct curiosity in his eyes as he examined her. 'Who is your pimp?' he asked.

'Mickey Shaughnessy,' Elly said sullenly.

'You are not his usual pick-up. You know he's an addict?'

'So?'

'He's been done for GBH. Be careful.'

She intrigued him. Far too young; the face behind the paint was that of a girl; her voice was an educated one, she read Dickens, Trollope and Zola yet she was trawling the streets for a well-known pimp who also recruited for a man making a bid for the title of King of Porn.

'Ever been cautioned before?' he asked.

Knowing it would be useless to lie because he would check the register, Elly said: 'Yes. Once.'

'Well this is your last chance. Next time you will be arrested. Do I make myself clear?'

'And loud!'

'Because I'm trying to get through to you, you stupid child!

You've got education, you've obviously got intelligence. Is selling sex the best you can do?'

His voice was harsh and his intensely blue eyes pinned hers in such a way that she could not evade them.

'How long have you been doing this?' he asked abruptly.

'About fourteen months.'

'Then you are already getting in too deep. Why don't you leave while you've got the chance? Did the officer who cautioned you the first time tell you about the help that's available?

'Yes.'

'Then why didn't you take it?'

She did not reply.

'You are sure you are nineteen?'

She would be in a month or two so she answered defiantly: 'Yes.'

'And this is all you can find to do?'

Because it is all I am fit for! she wanted to scream at him. It's all very well for you to talk! How do *you* know what it's like?

'It pays the most,' she said woodenly.

'Is that why you do it?'

For a moment her guard slipped and he got a brief glimpse of the self-hatred he had encountered so many times before in girls like her. Runaways, mostly. Very short of emotional success. Nothing of value in their life. They find they can be successful at something: selling their bodies to men. Their only achievement. Why were they so often middle-class girls from nice homes, like this one? There was no doubt about them being the preferred target of most pimps, though Mickey Shaughnessy, now that he had a very expensive habit to support, took what he could get.

He looked at 'Elly Little'. Her name proved that she had not yet been deadened by the life she was living. Life! he thought. Existence, more like. He'd seen more than his fair share of toms in his two years at the Cross, but this one . . . he could not put his finger on it but she was not your usual tom in any way. Something had made him stop; strictly speaking he was not even on duty, just about to begin his weekly stint on nights, yet something about the way she had been bending forward to speak to the occupant of a car who had not taken up her offer had made him reverse and drive back again.

As if she was aware of his thoughts he saw her straighten, put up a hand to push away the mass of curls which had been artfully arranged to frame her face, at the same time she squared her shoulders, tilted her chin. She appeared fragile but he'd bet there was a goodly proportion of high-grade steel in her backbone.

He snapped his notebook shut. 'You've had your second caution,' he reminded crisply. 'The next time you are stopped it means arrest. Do I make myself clear?'

'As crystal, Inspector.'

'If you'd look a little deeper into it you'd see that this is no life for you,' he said, getting back into his car. 'Try reading the Bible for a change, the bit about the Wages of Sin.'

Then he was driving away, leaving her fuming.

She told Paula about her second caution, because it worried her.

'A caution's a nothing,' Paula dismissed. 'It's being arrested; that's what marks you, and I mean marked. That fingerprint ink *never* comes off.'

'I didn't think inspectors stopped to caution prostitutes,' Elly complained bitterly.

'What was he like?'

'Very tall . . . vivid blue eyes, blond . . .'

'Ol' Blue Eyes,' Paula said at once. 'He arrested me once. For him, I went quietly. I gather he increased the number of toms on the ground at the Cross by a good twenty per cent, all hoping he'd arrest them.'

'Stupid idiots.'

'Didn't you think he was gorgeous?'

'I didn't really notice,' Elly answered impatiently, 'I was too annoyed. He must have been watching me!'

'That's what they are supposed to do, right?'

'You know what I mean.'

'Watching is better than propositioning! Oh, yes, it's done – far more often than you'd think. Coppers are men first, remember. But not Inspector Stevens. I once had a sergeant offer to look the other way if I offered him a freebie and he still turned round and arrested me! Stevens does it by the book –

probably because he's what they call a flyer marked for higher things. If I had to be arrested I'd as soon it was him as anybody.'

As he had done before, Mickey switched Elly's beat once he knew about her second caution. Fines were to be avoided at all costs: he had got to the stage where he could not afford them. Everything his girls earned went to support his habit. He put her on Park Lane; it was where a girl could charge most, and Elly had the looks and the class to do so. It was there, outside the Dorchester Hotel, that she had her second and final run-in with Inspector Stevens.

He was standing on the forecourt in front of the hotel; one of a group of men, all wearing dinner jackets and all having dined and supped extremely well. Elly saw him because of his height and blond hair, but before he could see her she put her head down and scuttled sideways, like a crab, out of range so that if he did happen to turn he would not get a good look at her. Once past the hotel she slowed her pace to its customary saunter, keeping to the edge of the pavement so as to give the oncoming cars an eyeful as well as the few pedestrians, letting her imitation leopard skin coat – lent by Paula – gape, revealing her tight black sweater dress with its deep V-neckline.

She almost jumped out of her skin when a voice from behind her said:

'I thought it was you . . . I recognised the legs.'

She whirled to find him standing there, swaying ever so slightly, hands deep in the pockets of his topcoat, streetlights gleaming on his blond hair.

'You didn't take my advice, I see,' he tut-tutted, 'which means that by rights I should arrest you . . .'

'For what? Walking up Park Lane?'

'The way you walk – yes! Every sway of those hips flashes a For Sale sign!'

'I've not stopped a single car . . .'

'Not for want of trying. You are soliciting; I've wined and dined well but not enough to fuddle my wits that much! I may be off duty but a police officer may act in the performance of his duties should he think it necessary even if he is not on such duty. However . . . I have just been celebrating my transfer to the C.I.D. No more relief. No more shifts. I am now a Detective Inspector.' He moved closer, bent to put his face closer to hers. He had extraordinary long eyelashes and he smelled of something sharp and fresh. 'But if I so much as see you on the street I will arrest you. Am I getting through to you?'

'Perfectly,' Elly said quickly. 'And congratulations, Inspector . . .'

He smiled, waved a lordly hand, swayed slightly.

'Do you want me to flag you a cab?' she asked. He was in no condition to drive.

'No, thank you. I intend to walk until my head is somewhat clearer.' Bending a stern eye: 'I would advise you to do the same.'

'Oh, I'm gone.' Elly retreated backwards until she was sure he was not going to change his mind then she turned her back on him. Before making off at full speed she turned to call 'Thanks . . .' but he had also turned and was walking away in the opposite direction, weaving slightly.

'And that is the extent of your involvement with the police – two cautions?' Philip asked, after she had given him an edited version of events.

'Yes.'

'I am glad to hear it. Cautions are noted but they do not constitute a record. The Metropolitan Police have neither your photograph or your fingerprints on file. The kind of client you will be dealing with in the future is the kind whose only contact with the police is chatting to the Commissioner at a cocktail party.' Philip steepled his fingertips. 'You were indeed fortunate in that you escaped arrest during your time on the streets. How was that, do you think? Good luck or good management?'

'Both.' After a moment: 'And – eventually anyway, experience. I had an excellent teacher in Paula.'

'You were friends?'

'She was the only one I trusted.'

'You have had some trouble with trust in the past?'

'You could say that.' Again and again, Elly thought, remembering Jenny and motherly old Lil.

'Am I to take it, then, that you are not entirely convinced as to the trustworthiness of either Mrs Waring or myself?'

'No; but I know enough, now, not to take things at their face value.'

Philip's joined hands assumed the prayer position just in front of his lips. 'Is not that what you are asking us to do in your case?' he reminded gently. He smiled as he saw, via the lightning flash in the eyes and the tightening of the mobile mouth, that lesson sink in. That will teach you not to play chess with *me*, Philip warned her silently.

Their eyes met, held. Liz, her ears ringing with relief, was the only one who did not hear the clang of steel meeting steel.

Philip turned to Liz. 'I will be in touch regarding details: a timetable; who will undertake what by way of instruction. We will discuss it all thoroughly. He turned then to Nell. 'You,' he said, 'will do as you are told. You have just as much to unlearn as you do to learn. Whatever went before you will discard; slough it off like a dead skin. *Everything* will be taught.'

He kissed Liz, nodded at Nell. There was no handshake. Then he was gone.

'Well?' asked Liz, when she came back from the front door.

'You didn't tell me the half, did you?'

'You'd have run for your life.'

'How he would have liked *that*.' Nell was piling dishes on to the tray.

'But he didn't really frighten you, did he?'

'No. Only made me bristle.'

'That's par for his course. Philip is an acquired taste – difficult to acquire at that.'

'I'm glad you said that because I don't think I shall ever acquire it.' Nell picked up the heavy tray. 'I don't care for the taste of self-importance.'

'Philip tends to use that with a heavy hand,' Liz admitted.

Nell hesitated then asked bluntly: 'Why do *you* care for him so much?'

Liz smiled. 'I know him,' she said simply. 'Probably I am the only person who does. To know all is to forgive all – but for God's sake don't tell him I said that.'

'He's a frightful snob, isn't he?'

'To Philip, the House of Windsor is *parvenu* to a degree; *very* suspect in its blatant manipulation of bloodlines. Philip's is straight and true, you see, for almost a thousand years. Kings mean nothing to Philip: he can bid two in any game of bridge.'

Sombrely: 'He's an impossible man to like and his prejudices are virulent, but what he can teach you is invaluable. And I've never seen anyone handle him as you did this afternoon.'

'I told you. I had seventeen years practice.'

'Was your father like Philip?'

'Only in his absolute sense of superiority and unshakeable conviction that he, and only he, knew the real truth of things.'

Liz laughed a little, but her glance was respectful. 'I see what you mean,' she said. She drummed her fingers, a sign of unease. 'Look,' she said at last, 'if you think you and Philip will be at loggerheads then perhaps I should not bring him in . . .'

Nell paused with the tray. 'But you said he could be invaluable.'

'And I meant it.'

'Then he has to be in. I'll be honest with you; I didn't take to him and not for a moment do I think he took to me, but needs must.'

'I applaud your pragmatism,' Liz praised, 'and so would he. It takes guts to stand up to him, and though he always says he admires it he doesn't, far from it. He regards it as *lese majesté*. Far be it from me to tell you to tug the old forelock, it's just that – if you can bear with him – he can teach you so very, very much. And you want to learn it all, don't you?'

'Yes, yes I do. Very much . . .'

But there were times, in the following weeks, when Nell wondered if it was all worth the effort. Every minute of her day was filled with some purposeful activity or other. The first one had been taken up by a head-to-toe medical examination and the decision to re-shape her nose and jaw.

'You can study while you are in the clinic and until the bandages are off you can't go out which will mean ample time to absorb all you need to know.'

'But why do I need to know about antique French furniture? Or Impressionist painting? Or the difference between a First and Second growth claret?'

'Because you might have a client who wishes to tell you

about a recent purchase he has made of a Louis V chair or a small Manet or a case of Château Latour 1961, that's why. You have to know not only what to order in an expensively fashionable restaurant but how to order it. More important, how to eat it. Do you know how to peel a peach without messing your fingers? How do you cope with a globe artichoke?'

Once she was able to go out again, subtly altered because her new nose had lost its bump and her jaw had a softer curve, she was put into the hands of a visagiste, who showed her how to make the best of her new face. She was warned not to nibble at her nails – which she tended to do when deep in a book – under pain of banishment, and when they began to grow they were shaped and manicured to a perfect oval. She was depilated, massaged, pedicured, manicured, had her face steamed and de-pored, spent thirty minutes of *every* day on specially designed exercises; while her hair took on a gloss like a piece of the mahogany she learned about, the best of which came from the West Indies.

She learned who made the best of everything, who sold it and where. She learned about champagne, hotels, restaurants, where to shop in which city, what to charge and – depending on the client – what not to. And she learned how to dress, but since she was already possessed of an 'eye' and an unfaltering sense of taste it was merely a case of allowing it free rein.

'You seem, my dear Elizabeth,' Philip commented one afternoon when Nell had come out of a *cabine* wearing an ivory pure silk shantung suit with a short straight skirt from which her racehorse legs flashed with an elegance which stunned, 'to have discovered a clothes-horse,' for Nell, in all her glory, was all that Liz could have wished.

She was a knock-out, but even more important, she was a classy knock-out. The long-limbed figure, toned and even re-shaped by all the exercise she had done, was the perfect frame for the haute couture clothes she now wore, and her new face was as unconsciously aristocratic as even Philip could have demanded. She had become, as she had said she would, what was wanted, and Philip had helped her by taking her to lunch at a fashionable restaurant much used by those women whose names graced the gossip columns by dint of the men they were either living with or married to, in all cases for an agreed sum of money.

'That one, for instance,' Philip said with a discreet but pointed glance at a table by the window. 'She arrived here a few more years ago than she cares to admit to hanging tightly to the coat-tails of a certain film director who had been making a film in the Third World jungle she was born in. He passed her on to a box-office attraction who took her in hand, taught her how to dress, how to talk, how to eat, and when he tired of her he passed her on to a teenage idol with whom she blossomed; he was even more common than she was but he had made millions by his so-called singing. She helped herself to a goodly slice, but he would not marry her and made her abort the two pregnancies she had while with him. Then she caught sight of a bigger catch; an Australian entrepreneur who thought she was Cleopatra, for by then she had become very snooty, invented a whole new background and imaginary family and given herself such airs . . . When she got pregnant she blackmailed him into marriage though everybody knows the child was not his. She then had him watched while she made his life hell and got the goods on him the first time he strayed, with a thirteen-year-old, unfortunately, so that she was able to screw a massive settlement out of him. Now she lords it about café society – for that is the only one she will ever be admitted into – as though she were the Queen of Sheba, and all thanks to one not so little thing.'

'What thing?' Nell, who knew him by now, asked.

'Her mouth. No one before or since has possessed such a trained tongue and lips. No female, that is . . .'

Philip caught her eye and smiled, satisfied that she knew whom he meant.

'Now that one, the one with the artfully untidy mane of hair; she is a professional suer. In the past four or five years she has made almost a million pounds out of suing certain tabloids for printing stories she herself has been most careful to plant in the right quarters and then, once in print, has become *most* indignant about. She got her start by a one-night stand with a very famous name indeed and never looked back. She parlayed that into the love of his life story of the decade; all lies, of course, but the gentleman in question is in no position to answer back.'

Nell, being careful not to be seen to stare, took a good look at the lady in question and was amazed, for she was nothing to write home about, though she did have a superb pair of breasts, artfully displayed by the low-cut suit she wore without the benefit of a bra.

'Her companions are also gold-diggers. The blonde is in reality an Anglo-Indian of dubious antecedents – probably the slums of Calcutta – who had her eyes seen to and her skin lightened, all paid for by a rich American who believed she was Hawaiian or some such rubbish but whose taste ran to exotic women. He is now dead so there is no one to call her bluff when she says she *is* Hawaiian. The third was once what they euphemistically call a "starlet" which meant she was there to service the stars. She latched on to a fading luminary who was offered a cameo role in a picture which he proceeded to steal from under the nose of its stars and for the last two years of his life enjoyed a resurgence of popularity – and income, which she inherited when his liver gave out. She is currently the paramour of a very nasty jumped-up lager-lout who got into the property development scene after gathering his experience as a rent collector for a notorious slum landlord. It is difficult to say which of them is the most common. All are for sale to the highest bidder, but they now insist on a legal sale. Collectively they are not worth the price of a box of matches. But that one . . . the lady lunching alone? That is a horse of an entirely different colour.'

Nell, by now hooked and dangling, asked: 'The elegant woman in the hat?'

'Yes. Her. Look your fill, my dear. There will never be another.'

'*She* is a kept woman?'

'Since she was a girl of seventeen, now some . . . oh . . . forty odd years ago. Just before the war. She was a chorus girl, very pretty, much sought after. Now she is the doyenne of this – this job lot. She has been the mistress of some of the most famous and powerful men in the world in the forty years since the war started. Her first was a politician; a household name in his time. Her second was a brilliant American general. The war got him. She was devastated for he was the love of her life, but eventually she met a handsome Italian industrialist of vast wealth who fell deeply in love with her but was, alas, irrevocably married. She was with him for fifteen years. When his wife eventually died his greedy family absolutely refused to countenance his marrying his mistress and threatened to run him out of it unless he married the heiress – 20 years younger than he was – they had chosen. He made his lost love a *very* generous settlement, of course, including the villa they had lived in on Cap Ferrat and the house in Chester Square in which she now lives. She – shall we say "retired" for a year or two after that until she met an exiled king, a widower, with whom she remained until he died. He too, left her very well provided for. But what I am trying to get over is that not once in all those years and with those very famous men, did she ever appear in a single gossip column. Everything she did was conducted with the absolute in discretion. She must have known and learned things that could have earned her a fortune but never once did she betray any of her lovers. They repaid her by seeing to it that she would not suffer by their absence. That, my dear, is a great lady, chorus girl or no. I know her well. Would you like to meet her?'

'Yes, I would, but – if she is so much the lady, why does she lunch here?'

'To remind herself of how lucky she was and to realise how far things have gone to the dogs. She does not do it very often; once every six weeks or so, but her table is kept for her and occasionally, a friend joins her.'

'You?'

'Now and then.' Philip bent a stern glance on his pupil. 'You see the moral of my tale? Today, the belief is that nothing succeeds like excess, but that is put about by people who do not know anything but excess since they worship the God Conspicuous Consumption. The great courtesan is always discreet. What she learns from a man . . . *in extremis*, shall we say, is privileged information, and if she wishes to deal with the highest level of client she will guard that privilege. These – scrubbers have never done that. Consequently, the most they can hope for is the second, even the third-rate. Pop stars,' Philip's voice seared with distaste, 'television "personalities" game-show hosts. The dregs. Here today and – hopefully – gone tomorrow. Tabloid fodder. Your name must *never* appear there. Elizabeth's never has. Nor does she "lunch" here. Not in this place. There are others where it is permissible to be seen. I have brought you here merely to show you how it is *not* done. On our way out I will introduce you to the lady who knew how it was done and did it superbly.'

Nell was pondering on this next day as she walked down Oxford Street in the direction of South Molton Street, where she was due for a fitting for the bras which were being specially made to her measurements. The pavements were crowded, it being Midsummer Sale time, and as she threaded her way through the people coming in the opposite direction she was doing it on automatic pilot. So deep was she in thought that she did not give wide enough berth to a woman coming towards her and they collided, causing the woman to drop two of her carrier bags.

'Oh, I'm so sorry,' Nell apologised instinctively.

'I should bleedin' well think so! Why can't you look where you're going? Some people think they own the bleedin' street!'

Nell had gone down on one knee to pick up the carrier bags but she did not need to look up to know who had spoken. It was Maureen. For a moment she panicked, then common sense asserted itself. Maureen had not, would not, snitch. She rose to her full height, held out a carrier bag and waited for the disbelieving cry of recognition. But it was not forthcoming, and when she forced herself to look into the face she knew so well there was no recognition in the eyes, only resentment. 'I do apologise,' Nell said.

'I should bleedin' well think so!'

'I wasn't looking where I was going.'

'You're tellin' me!' But that was all she was told. There was no sudden suspicion, no dawning 'Well I never!' astonishment. To Maureen, the tall well-dressed girl in the navy skirt, a sugar pink silk shirt under the matching navy jacket with brass buttons, her Gucci shoulder bag matching her well polished loafers, was a total stranger.

For a moment Nell wanted to say: 'Don't you recognise me, Maureen?' but even as it crossed her mind she stood aside and let it pass. That world was no longer hers. Thank God. The thought followed on with indecent haste. 'Sorry,' Nell apologised for the last time.

Maureen was already turning her back. 'Toffee-nosed bitch,' Nell heard her say, then she was lost in the crowd.

Nell turned to continue on her way, but caught sight of her reflection in the plate glass of a shop window, looked at herself with the eyes of the stranger Maureen now was and saw the difference. It was not only the up-market clothes or the voice – her own, and nothing like the one she had used with Maureen and the others, or the sleek, shiny hair, so different from the bird's-nest Mickey had insisted she sported. This girl was glossy with confidence; her head was up, her shoulders back. Always, before, the shoulders had been hunched, the head sunk between them, like the head of a turtle, just far enough out of its shell to see and be seen but on guard and ready to be withdrawn at the first hint of danger.

Toffee-nosed bitch, Maureen had said, recognising not the face or the voice but the attitude, the general air of consequence brought about by confidence. The hard work had paid off. Already she had taken on the colouration of the person – the woman – she would eventually be. She had changed on the outside, and from her reaction she knew that inside the changes had begun there too. She gave herself one last, lingering, committed to memory stare.

'Goodbye, Elly,' she said before she continued on her way.

BOOK TWO

1980

9

In the moonlight the villa gleamed like an ice sculpture, its
formal gardens dark and heavy with the shadows cast by ilex
and cedar, its ancient-yew lined walks all converging, like the
spokes of an enormous wheel, on the fountain at their centre,
its spray drifting like mist in the light breeze, warm and heavily
scented by the massed bushes standing in straight lines, like
soldiers, their branches drooping under the weight of the white
roses they bore. On the wide rim of the fountain a woman sat,
trailing her hand in the water. Her dress was as white as the
roses; flimsy, semi-transparent; close-to, the gleam of flesh
could be seen through it. Her hair was long, almost waist-
length, and black in the moonlight. Her face was pale as marble
but her mouth was full and pink, and her lashes cast curved
brush-strokes on her cheeks. She lifted her head, hair falling
back, and dreamed up at the moon with closed eyes, seeming
to listen.

From the distance, faint but clear, borne by the breeze, came
the sound of a piano. The enormous Great Dane sprawled on
the ground near the woman lifted its head from its paws and
seemed to join in. 'You like the music, Nero?' the woman
asked. Her voice was deeply musical. The dog got up, went
up the steps towards her, butted her with his head. She caressed
him, fondling his ears, and his tail expressed his pleasure.
Somewhere nearer, a clock outspoke the piano and struck four,
sonorous strokes. The woman sighed. 'It is late, Nero. Perhaps, if we go back now, I will be able to sleep.'

They walked back together in the direction of the house, the big dog keeping pace with the woman, her hand resting lightly on its studded collar. They mounted a flight of shallow stone steps, went in through open french windows, which the woman shut behind her, locking them. The dog raised his head, ears pricking, whined softly.

'What is it? Do you hear something?' The woman listened. Silence. Only the ticking of the huge clock in the corner. The black and white of the tessellated floor bore only their shadows and a vast staircase that disappeared into the darkness above. Together, the woman and the dog mounted it and went down a long corridor to a pair of big ornately carved doors at its end. They went through them to the small lobby immediately beyond, where the dog flopped down in front of a second, smaller door which the woman again went through, bidding the dog 'Goodnight, Nero' as she did so.

Her bedroom was big, swathed in silk, the vast bed with gilded and carved bedposts set on a raised dais. Dozens of candles in branched candelabra gave a bright yet soft light, the flames flickering delicately in the same soft, perfumed breeze that stirred the gauzy curtains hanging in front of the slightly opened doors that gave on to a balustraded balcony.

The woman sat down at her dressing table, as ornately draped as the bed which showed signs of disturbed occupancy. She picked up a silver-backed brush and began to sweep it through her hair. Then putting the brush down she picked up a crystal flacon, drew from it a glass stiletto, heavy with a perfume that was exotically erotic, and ran it down the valley of her breasts. She wet her fingertips with the perfume and placed them in the hollow of her temples, feeling the bite of it on her heated skin. She closed her eyes, inhaled deeply, did not see the white curtains swirl as a figure, clothed head to foot in black, stepped through them; black trousers, polo-necked black sweater, black shoes, even black gloves – and a face-concealing mask. He let the curtains drop behind him and stood looking at the figure of the woman sitting with her head bent. As if she felt his gaze her head came up and she looked into the mirror, saw him standing there. In an instant she was on her feet, swirling to face him, hands braced against the glass top of the dressing table, one of them knocking the perfume flacon on to the marble floor where it shattered, sending pieces of glass flying and perfume spraying, drenching the room with its sensuous fragrance. Her eyes were wide, her face rigid, her breasts rising and falling rapidly, clearly visible through the silk gauze of her gown, which was revealed as a nightgown under a peignoir, both of them sheer. For a moment they stared at each other then she made a dash for the door, but he was there first, seizing her by the wrist and flinging her back so that she fell on to the floor. Terrified, now, she scrabbled backwards until she was on the lowest step of the dais on which the bed stood. She cowered against the silk coverlet, staring at him fixedly, like a rabbit trapped by a fox. He walked towards her, bent casually, took hold of her, raised her up. He saw her throat move convulsively and her body was stiff. He put his mouth to the pulse which beat frantically in the hollow of her long neck, and at once she strained back, making fists of her hands so as to pummel him. His mouth came up for a second but only while he leisurely took hold of her futile hands to pinion them behind her back, thus allowing his mouth to explore her at leisure; her throat, her breasts, after first pushing peignoir and nightdress off her shoulders. She moaned, fought fiercely, and when his mouth covered hers bit him savagely. Blood trickled from his lower lip but the mouth, revealed by the mask which ended just below his nose, only smiled. He bent, put one arm under her shoulders, another under her knees, picked her up and tossed her on to the bed, where she huddled in a foetal ball while he went round the candles, blowing them all out but the eight-branched candelabra on the table by the bed. Then he came back to her, and in their light, without a word being spoken, he raped her. Their struggle continued in silence; she fought, she bit, she tried to scratch, but his only response was a contemptuous laugh. Everything he did to her was done with contempt; he used her as an object provided for his pleasure. Her pleasure did not come into it. His savagery said: 'I am the master now.' Once, when he paused in his pounding, stone-hard and hot inside her, he looked into her eyes, saw the rage behind the fear and laughed again, exultantly, before resuming his thrusts.

As he orgasmed, his mouth also erupted in a stream of foul-mouthed abuse, all directed at her, his voice rising to a frenzy even as he did. Which was when the dog began to bark. In one swift motion he was off the bed, adjusting his clothing, and across to the windows, where he disappeared as silently as he had come.

Once he was gone the woman got off the bed, naked now, for the things she had been wearing were torn irreparably, and went into the adjoining room, which was a bathroom. The dog had ceased to bark. The woman ran a bath while she examined her face and body for bruising, frowned as she saw he had left one on her throat where his fingers had gripped just that much too strongly for a moment. The bath filled rapidly, and turning off the taps she added a liberal helping of perfumed oil before turning back to the mirror to remove the wig she had worn, revealing her own, light-brown hair, equally long but fine and straight. She brushed the wig before placing it on the wig-block. Then she tested the water in the enormous bath before lowering herself into its perfumed depths. Lying back with a sigh, 'Another night, another thousand pounds,' she said to herself. She kicked her feet, sending bubbles swirling, then sank down into the water until it touched her chin, and wondered once again what her 'rapist' looked like.

This was the fourth time she had played out this particular fantasy. Her instructions had been explicitly set out in a two-page document she had received the first time she had met with her client's representative. She flew to Pisa, where a car met her and drove her up into the hills of Tuscany, to a Palladian villa miles from anywhere. Its only occupant was an old woman who never spoke, but who conducted the visitor to the beautiful room where she would sleep. It adjoined the room where the fantasy would be enacted. The props were laid out for her. The exquisite hand-sewn nightgown and peignoir, the black curly wig, even the perfume. She had to meet the dog, spend the day with it, familiarise herself with the gardens.

The timetable was precise. She had to be at the fountain by 3.50 a.m.; stay until the stable clock struck the hour then return to the villa where the fantasy would be played out. Her 'struggle' had to be real, though his 'punishment' would be feigned to a certain extent. The one thing that was not feigned was his anger, the contempt he felt for the woman he abused. His hatred was a living thing which had at first shocked until it became clear that his 'victim' was a woman whose memory he was unable to exorcise. Whatever she had done to him had left emotional scars that even now, forty-five years later, were unhealed.

She had no idea who he was; she dealt only with his emissary, who had requested her to sign a document binding her to silence. An unofficial Secrets Act, she had thought. It was the emissary who contacted her, handed over her plane tickets and expenses, paid her in cash. The villa itself was uninhabited but for the silent caretaker. All the rooms were shrouded in silence and white covers. The only person she ever saw was the shuffling old woman who silently brought her her meals. The car which took her to and from Pisa had darkened windows. All she knew was that it was a big, black, chauffeur-driven Mercedes.

Where the villa was situated she had no idea, but it was obvious that the client was rich enough to ensure his fantasy was enacted in total secrecy. After some thought she had come to the conclusion that it was an act of revenge for an act of humiliation. He hated the woman she played but it was the kind of hate that is akin to love. He was obsessed by what she had been, had done to him.

She liked to analyse her roles; that was where she gained her satisfaction. She had not lied when she had told Liz she could become whatever was needed. She just had not told her that it was the only way she had ever been able to endure what was done to her.

Once she was dressed and in make-up she *was* the character she was playing. Only when it was over did she return to her own self and analyse everything.

She found it all fascinating; threw herself into the role with total veracity. She had tried to find out what she could from the villa itself, but the rooms, apart from those used to enact the fantasy, were obviously unused. The only clue was the coat of arms carved into the massive stone fireplaces. Diligent research had established that it belonged to a once powerful Tuscan ducal family, high in the fascist ranks surrounding Mussolini. When he fell so did they. The head of the house had been arrested and sentenced to death but managed to commit suicide; the eldest son was executed by the partisans, the youngest had fled who knows where. The daughter – and this seemed to confirm her theory – had escaped vengeance by enslaving the American major who commanded the troops who made the villa their headquarters in 1944. He had got her out of Italy, then she vanished. The major had been court-martialled for his pains; the woman had been an unrepentant fascist and, it had been rumoured, one of Mussolini's mistresses. This could only be the woman on whom the client took his revenge. A former employee of the Duke, no doubt, for he was not a young man. The body she wrestled with was no longer hard and strong; she had learned not to struggle too hard because he tired easily. But in his fantasy he was young and virile and she was being well paid to help it come true, so she acted accordingly. But even so, the heartbeat under the black polo-neck was a laboured one by the time the 'rape' was over.

You must have been quite a woman, whoever you were, she thought, as she dried herself off, because you imprinted yourself on the mind of a man who still can't get over you years later. We are all the prisoners of our pasts, she thought staring at her face in the mirror. Yours is why you are here in the first place, isn't it?

She wrapped herself in her fleecy dressing gown, for the villa was all marble and without central heating, before going back into her own vast and chilly bedroom where her supper had been set out. Paper-thin prosciutto and deeply pink canteloupe, fresh figs and a small goat's cheese. The bread was warm and crusty and wrapped in a napkin; the wine was cold. She fell to with a will – physical activity always gave her an appetite, and while she ate she read another couple of chapters of *The Leopard*. Dawn was breaking by the time she went to sleep.

She was paying off the taxi when Lulu opened the front door.

'Anything wrong?' Nell asked anxiously.

'She be frettin', is all. You late.'

'I know. My connection was late in from Milan – fog. Is she all right?'

'Can't you hear?'

Through the open door came the finger-snapping lilt of a

bossa nova. Nell's concerned face relaxed into a smile. 'How she loves that beat.'

'Nobody dance to it like her. She a natural.' Lulu snapped a queen-sized hip. 'Like me.'

Nell laughed happily. It was good to be home.

In the sitting room she found Liz, in the wheelchair to which she was now confined having lost the use of her legs some three months ago, her upper body swaying, arms weaving, fingers snapping, eyes closed, a beatific, dreamy smile on her face. As Nell entered she began to sing along to the music, her voice weaving in and out of the melody.

Nell went over to the state-of-the-art music centre and turned down the volume. Liz's eyes snapped open on a scowl until she saw who had done it, when her anger changed to delight. 'Nell! At last . . . I was worried.'

'Sorry. The plane from Milan was late – a whole hour.'

'They always are. That damned city is always shrouded in fog. But how was the trip?'

'Profitable, otherwise another repeat performance.'

'Aren't they all? That's the drawback about this job; it can get to be awfully boring.'

Liz sounded both irritable and petulant; that and the fact that she was playing music as loud as the ears could stand it meant she was not having the best of days. Nell examined her face. It was thinner, as Liz was, and drawn, the skin no longer glowing but dry and tight over her cheekbones, papery-looking and of that unmistakeable greyness that meant ill health, with bright patches above the hollows of her cheeks. She was failing rapidly, and she knew, as did Nell, Philip and Lulu, that her two years had been a pipe-dream. It was just on the year since she had been told and already she was in the wheelchair she had dreaded, and was losing mobility in her hands. She was also beginning to forget words; to search and become increasingly frustrated when she could not find the right one, beating on the padded arms of her electronic wheelchair – imported from the United States and capable of doing everything but read and write – in her anger at herself and her fate.

The one thing she loved, and which Nell had been worried about since she had been afraid it would taste like bitter aloes – was to hear in detail about Nell's trips, especially to those clients who were new, like the Fantasy Rape. Liz had been approached first, but had declined because, she said, her list was full and she was not taking any new clients. However . . . she had herself trained a pupil who bid fair to become every bit as good, and whom she now recommended unreservedly. Nell had gone to Pisa and the rest was history. As for the other clients, some had stayed, others had gone; mostly those who were unable to cope with the transfer of a mainstay of their fantasy. 'It would not be the same', was their reason. They were the ones who, like the unknown Italian client, were paying for much more than sex. Those who stayed still wanted their fantasy, but so long as the participant fitted their specifications did not mind who it was. And Nell had acquired two other new clients of her own, both introduced by existing clients.

One was a man who had never known what it was to want for anything including sex, and whose taste ran to the kind he was not use to. Nell had to act the street-whore, and the street had to be Fifth Avenue in New York. She had to seem to be window shopping; always in shops where a look in the window was all she could afford. The first time it was Tiffany, the second Cartier, the third Bergdorfs. She had to look as well as act the part; an indecently short skirt that was also all but obscenely tight; she had to be blonde with a page-boy hairstyle, and she had to have long, scarlet nails and the highest of heels. To Nell's eyes the whole thing was a parody but it was what the client wanted, including the fact that she had to chew gum. He would stop at the window into which she was staring and she would become aware that he was watching her, but she would give no sign. She would walk on, always westwards, strolling more than walking, and stopping to browse in every window that caught her fancy, until they were deep in the West Side at a sleazy hotel that had seen better days but not since well before the Second World War. She would turn in there, having registered earlier, and go up to her room. All the time he would be following her and all the time she would give no indication that she was aware of him. Not until she was in her room would the knock come, and he would be standing there.

'How much?' he would ask.

'What do you want?'

'What do you do?'

And Nell would smile. 'You want I should show you?' reaching for his zipper. From then on it had to be as whorish as she could make it – talk as well as action, and she had become proficient in the first by listening to a lieutenant who had worked vice for twenty years but made up for it by spending his leisuretime well outside the 13th Precinct and a long way up town with a man who was a long-time friend of Philip Faulkner. He had sent her to the right shop for her underwear; bras with nipple holes and briefs with no crotch, all black trimmed with scarlet. He had even instructed her in the right kind of accent, and the actress in Nell lapped it up, even as the client lapped her. His favourite kind of sex next to her lapping him. It was an all-afternoon job, for though the client was an up-tight, buttoned-down type, the fact that he was with a whore undid every single one of those buttons. He only stayed in character where a return on his investment was concerned, for he was a Wall Street Wizard.

Discussing it with Liz – who liked to hear of Nell's progress – they decided that it was his way of slumming. His kind of up-town, up-market people came down from the High Seventies and Low Eighties to Tribeca and Soho and the whole area below Canal Street, but for him, the Lower West Side was far down enough. And how he liked going down. Obviously it was something his wife did not allow. But since Nell got a first-class round trip on Concorde and a suite at the Pierre, she was happy to service him until her jaw ached, and since it had been reset any heavy use had it protesting.

Through him she had acquired another old New York client, but this one's fantasy started in a singles bar, where Nell, nicely dressed this time but, like every other person there, looking for sex, had to let herself be picked up. After a lengthy foreplay of fencing and flirtation she would let him buy her a drink, then another, until – no names exchanged but intent clear, they would leave for a nearby apartment where the sex would be almost perfunctory he was so ready. With him it was a pick-up that mattered, the cheap – to him – apartment, the game they played, each knowing there was no winner, just two losers. He would leave her, ostensibly sleeping for it was supposed to be her apartment, to go back to his East Seventies town house, but he would also leave on the bedside table a K-Mart envelope containing $2,000 in small denomination far-from-new bills but eminently spendable.

'There is just no accounting,' Nell said now, as she recounted her Italian trip, 'for the sexual fantasies of men.'

'As long as you are satisfying them,' Liz pointed out.

'I find the ledger very satisfying; still in deepest mourning on the receipts side and no longer bleeding on the expenses side.'

'I don't know how you do it,' Liz sighed, 'but don't stop, will you? I've never actually been in credit before. You are a born manager.'

'I learned how to manage a budget at an early age. My father would not spend a ten pence piece where five would do. I bought you this.'

Nell took out a small box which she handed over to the eager Liz who tore at the shoestring red ribbon. Watching her, Nell saw the familiar frustration shove every other consideration aside as her fingers failed to come to grips with the knots and bows.

'I told her to make it pretty but she seems to have been determined to make it unforgettable,' Nell said lightly. 'Here . . . let me . . .'

Her long, nimble fingers soon had the ribbon falling away and handing the box over again.

Liz lifted the lid and exclaimed joyously: 'Oh, my God – Panetone! Quick, Lulu, get the coffee on . . .'

Now that she no longer had to worry about her weight, since (a) she could no longer work and (b) she was losing it anyway, Liz indulged her appetite for goodies, and the rich Italian bread known as panetone was one of them.

'It's from the airport shop at Pisa not Peck's of Milan, but it was the best I could do under the circumstances.'

'Who's complaining?'

Greedily Liz tore off a corner of the rich fruit bread and crammed it into her mouth. 'Mmm . . .' she closed her eyes beatifically.

'I'll just go and get changed – oh, I brought back some

Italian coffee too, and a kilo of prosciutto. I'll give them to Lulu . . .'

In the kitchen: 'How has she been?' Nell asked Lulu.

'Up and down. Fell out the chair twice. Keeps trying to make her legs carry her.'

'What's the latest from the doctor?'

'He come day before yesterday. She say she ain't sleepin' so he give me a prescription for some pills. She take one come bedtime.' Lulu shook her head. 'She fightin' every step of the way.'

'Nothing was said about a nurse?'

'She don't want to hear nuthin' about that yet, and she so light I lift her easy. So doctor don't press. You know how she is when she get all ariated. He tol' me to humour her; ain't nuthin' else to be done.' Lulu poured boiling water into the cafetière. 'Her pa comin' the weekend. Bringin' that dog.'

'Tiger's all right. Just old, like his master.'

'He leave hairs on the furniture.'

'I'll spread his blanket,' promised Nell.

Lulu sniffed, unimpressed. Nell took the coffee in as a peace-offering.

'I hear the Brigadier is coming for the weekend.'

'Yes, with Tiger. He won't be left any more; drives Mercer mad by howling all the time.'

'I don't mind. I like dogs.'

'Well, Pa likes you; that's why he comes, if you ask me. He always did like a pretty face and mine is not what it was.'

The Brigadier had turned up trumps. Liz had not told him until it was impossible not to, but though he had been shocked and it had taken a double whisky to restore the normally ruddy colour to his cheeks, he had from then on rallied to his daughter's colours like the professional soldier he was. He did not smother her in his concern, nor did he pretend that it did not exist. He merely accepted that he was going to outlive his daughter and made the necessary adjustment. Boy, on the other hand, had all but gone into hibernation. He rang regularly, but since Liz had begun to fail he could not bear to see it. His wife sent designer arrangements of expensive flowers but she never came either.

'No loss,' Liz dismissed. 'I think she's a diamond-hard bitch and she thinks I'm the family Black Ewe so what the hell. And Boy always was a coward. That's why he absolutely refused to follow Pa into the regiment. It's Pa I'm concerned about anyway. What is going to happen to him when I'm gone. Boy won't bother and neither will his anything-but-better half. I've arranged an annuity for when I die – I've an insurance that will take care of it, and until I do he's got an extra couple of thousand a year, half of which I screwed out of Boy anyway.'

'I'll look out for him if you like,' Nell had offered.

'Would you? You are so capable I wouldn't have a worry in the world if I thought he had a friendly/concerned eye on him. Mercer is old too, you see, and I dread to think what Pa would do if anything happened to him. They've been together longer than I've been alive. Mercer is Pa's closest and oldest friend. If Pa goes first then arrangements have been made to look after him; but to be honest, I think when one goes the other won't be far behind. They fight like cat and dog but it is what keeps them going.'

Liz's smile had held mischief. 'The Harvills are a feisty lot; nothing they like better than a good fight.'

'So I've seen.'

Liz eyed Nell. 'You don't, do you – like a good fight, I mean? You would rather negotiate.'

'Each to his own.'

'Oh, I'm not complaining. You've done right by me from the start. I'm too soft. I know that; you are not. You'll negotiate but only from strength, and the fact that you've already got us a ten per cent increase in fees proves just how strong you are.'

'All I am, you taught me.'

'No. I gave you the benefit of my experience. You took it and added your own and the result is quite something.'

Nell's clear grey eyes had frosted over. 'You have obtained some feedback?'

Liz had been equally cool. 'Of course – and no, I am not saying who. Naturally I checked! I had to know if the experiment was working, didn't I? When I sent you out that very first time, truly on your own, all I could do was wait and worry. It's all very well saying you can become whatever the fantasy demands but the proof is in the way your audience reacts.'

'And mine reacted favourably?'

'Very much so.'

In fact, Liz had not been able to suppress a pang of jealousy as she listened to the pleasure with which one of her oldest and most valued clients recounted his first encounter with Nell. In his particular case the fantasy was that of Droit de Seigneur, and Liz had to admit that Nell fitted the part of the virginal bride much better than she did. It was not only that she was almost thirty years younger – and latterly Liz had taken to wearing a fine veil over her face – she *looked* virginal. It was the pale, pearlised skin, the huge grey eyes, the cloud of dark hair. The client, a middle-aged Swiss industrialist, had spoken of Nell's accomplishments in the tones of one well impressed. There had been just the right amount of terrified awe covering the hatred and despair she was supposed to feel, which was to turn into awakened passion hot enough to need skin grafts. 'After so many years, my dear old friend, I congratulate you on finding so remarkable a replacement. I had thought you irreplaceable, but you have, it seems, created an all but duplicate who has added her own, unmistakeable refinements.' He had presented Liz with a five-stranded pearl necklace which fastened by means of a *cabochon* sapphire the size of her thumbnail. 'In gratitude.' Liz had been torn between pride and pique, but common sense had won the day. Pride paid no bills. And she had talked out her resentment with Philip.

'It had occurred to me that you had, perhaps, left your own feelings out of your calculations,' he'd said. 'Retirement is never pleasant whatever the reason. It is only natural to feel, as you are right now, resentful, supernumary, denigrated and discarded as well as pleased with your own perspicacity. Perfectly human, my dear Elizabeth.' But she had still cried herself to sleep that night, knowing she was being stupid but unable to help it. The crown had been hers for so long. But at least she was giving it up of her own free will. Nobody had staged a palace revolution. And Nell had been her own choice. She need not fear, now, that her last days would be spent worrying how to make ends meet. No, she'd thought, unable to repress the bitterness of jealousy. Not only will they meet, she'll tie them in a bloody bow! *It's not fair*, she had wept into her pillow. It's just not fair.

For a day or two she had been cool with Nell, who had been at a loss to understand it, for Philip, meticulous in the spite emanating from his own jealousy, said nothing.

It was Lulu who, after Liz had been particularly snappish said practically: 'She don' like not bein' The One any more. That you, now. You takin' her place. Don' expect any jumpin' for joy on that account but don't you worry none neither. She come round. She know which side her bread is buttered.'

Bitter-chocolate eyes gleamed sardonically. 'And she like jam on it too.'

So Nell had left it and in time Liz had come round, though until she did there was an atmosphere which drove Nell out of the house for it reminded her too much of her father's silences. She had hated them too. And then one afternoon she had come home from a movie and heard, as soon as she opened the front door, the sound of Frank Sinatra singing about 'Baubles, Bangles and Beads' and knew Liz had resolved her difficulties. The night they had dined together in perfect charity, sat afterwards and listened to the LP Liz herself put on the turntable. Frank Sinatra singing about the September of his Years; bittersweet songs reflecting on a life well lived and from the perspective of sixty years. Looking back. Remembering. Nell had learned a lot from just monitoring Liz's face but at the end, the result had been a pleasurable sigh and a soft: 'That's how it goes. Nobody lives for ever.' And it was never referred to again.

Now, Liz was too far along the road of no return to have time to spare for jealousy; and much too grateful to Nell for all she did to feel resentment. Nell was not only the provider, she was companion, helpmeet, and at weekends when Lulu did not normally come in – though she now made the exception when Nell had a weekend appointment – chief cook and bottle-washer. She and the Brigadier had fitted like key and lock, and even Mercer, who once he heard Miss Elizabeth was ill insisted on coming along to give what assistance he could, thought Miss Nell (whose cover was that of a paying guest) just what Miss Elizabeth needed.

'So, what shall I cook for the weekend? Will Mercer be coming too?'

'No. He's off to Sheffield to see his daughter. I gather his son-in-law is not too good. But Tiger, as I said, will be along. So remember him when you do the shopping.'

'I'm on very good terms with Mr Morgan at the butcher's. He's always good for the right-size bone and a couple of pounds of shin beef. What about us? The Brigadier likes his roast beef, doesn't he?'

Liz was buttering a thick slice of panetone. 'We had that last time.' She caught Nell's eye. 'Oh, all right, then . . . beef it is, and all the trimmings. But I draw the line at rice-pudding. Let's have crème brulée instead. You make a perfect crème brulée.'

'Right; that's Sunday. I'll check the freezer for the rest. Friday night arrival as usual?'

'Well, afternoon. About four thirty at Paddington.'

'I'll meet him.'

'Take a blanket for that blasted dog.'

Liz no longer drove, though until recently Nell, once she passed her test – (first time) – had taken Liz for drives or to Philip's for dinner. He could always supply a beautifully built young man to carry her from the car and upstairs to his Edwardian flat. These days, however, Liz tired easily so Philip came to her, while the drives were getting rarer and rarer. The last twice, Nell had got Liz dressed only to have her change her mind. 'Too cold,' she had said the first time, and 'too windy' the second, but they both knew that the truth was that she just did not want to be seen.

When people had first learned of her illness the visitors had been constant. People Liz had not seen for years made it their business to repair the omission. Until she could not be bothered. Which coincided with the first physical signs of her deterioration. Now, she saw only Philip, who dined at least once a week, and those of her friends who could be relied upon not to get maudlin. The champagne would be brought out, the music put on, and gaiety would be the order of the day. Only when Nell and Philip saw the strain begin to show would they allow things to begin to wind down.

Of her former clients she saw and heard nothing. 'Only to

be expected,' she said on a shrug. 'I was, after all, only a highly-paid employee. I know too much about them for a friendship to be able to withstand the strain. Their only comfort is that they know I will take that knowledge with me.'

But there was a bitter edge to her voice; some of her clients, like the old Argentine, went back to her beginnings in the Life. When he declined to accept Nell he evaporated into the smoke of his carefully obscured lifestyle. Only one made any sort of gesture; he sent flowers. Every week a huge arrangement was delivered and though there was never a card Liz knew at once who they were from. 'It was his little joke,' she explained softly, her fingers caressing one of the creamy camellias. 'He always called me Marguerite . . .'

'La Dame aux Camelias?'

'Yes. Only she died of consumption . . .'

The massed camellias were always placed where she could see them, and sometimes Nell caught her looking at them in a way that was far worse than any of the tantrums or fits of self-pity.

Otherwise, apart from wanting to know all about Nell's assignments and their success or otherwise, she was content to leave everything else either to Nell, Lulu or Philip. She had never been a great reader, but she liked to flick through the magazines, and for a while she had tried tapestry work but she had neither the patience nor the aptitude and, as her hands gradually lost mobility, the strength. She listened to music a lot and watched television until she could not take any more. What she liked most were old movies, so Nell scoured the video rental shops for what she christened The Great Weepies starring either Bette Davis – Liz's favourite – or Joan Crawford – 'totally over the top' Liz would say happily, or Katherine Hepburn – 'the perfect match with Spencer Tracey' or Greta Garbo. If she was fractious, the sovereign remedy was to draw the living room curtains, produce a box of chocolates – soft centres – and something like *Jezebel* or *The Women* or *The Philadelphia Story* and she would spend a couple of hours in her particular idea of heaven, from which she always emerged with the disposition of an angel.

At other times she would throw things, scream abuse and work herself into a tangled mass of frustration, when the only thing to do was get her to take one of her tranquillisers and go upstairs to lie down. She would invariably fall asleep and afterwards be in an agony of contrition. 'It's not *me*,' she would say despairingly. 'They used to call me Sunny Jim at school because I never lost my temper. Now it seems to be gone for ever . . . How in God's name do you put up with me? I didn't bargain for this, you know . . . not for you to have to act as nurse . . .'

'Not *act*.' Nell said quietly. 'Not with you, Liz.'

Liz's eyes filled and she bit her lip. 'Look at me . . . now I'm a watering pot. My reactions are all shot to hell these days . . .'

The house came to revolve around her. Lulu was of enormous help; her vast bulk and superior strength gave her the ability to lift and carry Liz's increasingly frail body, whilst her stolid character enabled her to withstand the verbal assaults, the tantrums, and the objects hurled at her. 'She got the right, Lord knows,' she would shrug. 'Me, I'd be mad too.'

Each time Nell came back from America she brought things she knew Liz would find pleasurable. The LP of the latest Sondheim musical; an armful of scandal sheets, a pound of Reese's Peanut Butter Cups, a bottle of Tanqueray Gin, a scented-herb-stuffed satin cushion from Bloomingdales. But what pleased Liz most was to hear of Nell's successes – (and occasional failure.) Like the shoe-fetishist.

Nell always met him in the afternoon – it had to be the afternoon, and she was required to wear the sheerest of black stockings hooked to a garter belt, also black, to match her half-cup bra. This she never took off. Then she tried on shoes – pair after pair. Always in the same style; stilt heeled, strappy and fastened around the ankle; gold lamé, diamanté-studded, rainbow silk. She would sit in a big chair and he would kneel at her feet and he would fit the shoes, caressing them, laying them against his cheek, his eyes bright and his cheeks flushed. Each time he fitted a pair she had to parade up and down in them and walk over him. He would lie down, arms by his side, and look up at her as she walked over him, her high heels digging, especially into the erection that strained against his zipper for he never took off his own clothes. He would moan, catch painful breaths but she had to continue. Finally, when all the shoes had been tried on she had to wait while he put them all back in their boxes; she was not allowed to touch them. Then he would watch while she took off her stockings, after which he would bring a bowl of hot water, a fresh cake of soap and proceed to wash her feet, totally absorbed in his task, his fingers probing in between her toes. Then he would pat them dry before proceeding to give her a pedicure. His last task was to paint her toenails a particularly virulent shade of purplish red. By that time, his zipper would be straining under the force of his erection, his eyes would be glazed and his breath would sound as if he had just run a marathon. He would excuse himself then, go into the bathroom and shut the door, leaving Nell to put on the clothes she had worn when she arrived. By the time he came back his colour was normal and his erection deflated.

Then there was the one who was, her referral said, 'in the music business'. He was staying in a big house in Sunningdale, and Nell was conducted upstairs and left outside a door. She knocked, and it was opened by a man she recognised at once. He had been an international singer for the past fifteen years. He was polite, very explicit. He spent at least half of every year on the road, he said, but his wife never accompanied him because she preferred to stay with the children. He missed her like hell, so his solution was to call in a paid substitute. Nell had to wear the wig he produced, and the clothes, make up her face like the photograph he provided, wear her perfume. With the lights dimmed and faces only half-perceived, he could have the sex he needed but pretend it was with his wife. What he wanted, most of all, was to hold Nell in his arms in the big bed and talk, all the time caressing her, until he could contain himself no longer. He told her exactly what he wanted from her in the way of reaction, and when it was over told her seriously that she was the first one who had managed to maintain the illusion. He asked if she would put his name on her list of regulars. And he gave her a tip equal to her fee.

Another client required her to accompany him to auctions. What turned him on was the bidding; if he got what he wanted at a good price there would be no holding him once they got back to his hotel suite. If he failed in his quest he would still pay her fee but there would be no sex. It was as though he only allowed himself to have that when he was successful. Failures did not get rewarded.

'Weird,' agreed Liz. 'But I learned a long time ago that as my old nanny used to say, "there's nowt so queer as folk".'

There was one client whom Nell could not get away from fast enough. Again it was a referral, and from a long-standing client of Liz, who assured Nell that if he recommended someone they were worth taking on.

Nell was picked up by car and driven to a beautiful house overlooking Hampstead Heath. It was empty but for her client, and he took her upstairs to the top of the house, to a room Nell recognised at once as a nursery. A girl's. Everything was pink and ruffled, including the bed, and the toys and the books indicated that she would be about nine years old. On the bed a nightgown was laid out; an exquisitely smocked and be-ribboned affair of finest white lawn. The client asked her to let her hair down, after which he made her sit down while he brushed it. Through the mirror Nell could see him becoming more and more excited, and her horrified suspicions were confirmed when he said in a choked voice: 'Now, let Daddy put you to bed and we'll play a little game, shall we?' even as he took one of Nell's hands and placed it on himself. She flung off his hand, brought up her knee in its place and while he was doubled over grabbed her clothes and ran. In the hall down-stairs she tore off the nightgown and hastily dressed before letting herself out.

The car was gone, so she walked down into Hampstead where she picked up the first empty cab she saw. She was trembling violently, but by the time the cab had made the journey south she had managed to compose herself. She let herself into the house quietly; Liz was in bed and, when Nell checked, fast asleep. Then Nell took a bath, scrubbing herself with a loofah until her skin glowed pink.

To Liz she merely said, next day: 'That referral was a no-no. The client's fantasy was paedophilic.' She did not say that she was also sure that its mainstay was his own daughter. His name was taken off her client list.

For the most part, she fitted into the niche Liz had carved with only the most minor adjustments – and the occasional mistake. Like the 'client' who turned out to be a whole houseful of men all expecting to avail themselves of her services for the one fee; or the one who, when she was delivered to his house, turned out to be a swinger, and whose pool, jacuzzi and even his shower were full of copulating couples high on either drugs or booze.

She acquired another whose fantasy was the seduction of his best friend's wife. Evidently she was a woman who had eyes only for her husband, but the fantasy was that when her husband's best friend made known his desire for her, the ice-cap melted and a sexually voracious volcano erupted. It called for all Nell's acting talent for the client demanded sexual skills of a very high order; she had to come on like a woman consumed by lust and prepared to do whatever it took to leave the client drained to the last drop. Since he was both attractive and relatively young – about forty-five – this was not too hard, and since they consumed a bottle of vintage champagne prior to the encounter, the wheels were well oiled. The trouble was he had the smallest penis she had ever seen. He was at least six feet tall but when detumescent his penis was an acorn, when fully erect it was a bottle-cork. No woman was going to get any pleasure out of it. Nell told him it was *his* pleasure he was paying for, and small or not she would see that he got his money's worth. And she did.

She gave the performance of her life, initiating a seduction that took ten times as long as anything he had ever known and primed him to an eventual orgasm that afterwards had him almost pathetic with gratitude. Her tip was very large and he became a regular client whom she saw on almost a weekly basis.

He was satisfied, eminently so, and the fact that Nell was not was of no consequence. After all, he had *paid* her, hadn't he? Nell neither expected or ever pretended to climax unless the fantasy called for it. Some clients wanted it, some could not care less. But even those who wanted it never had any idea that the quiverings, the gasps, the indrawn breaths, the rigidity, were not real. They had no idea that Nell had withdrawn inside herself; that she was functioning through her brain rather than her feelings; that she felt nothing and that every movement was calculated, every flinch simulated. Every act of sexual intercourse was exactly that: an act. For which, she used to think as she either drove or was driven home, she should be given an Oscar. What she did was a job. And it was amazing how many men did not want sex anyway. They wanted the fulfilment of a fantasy. Like the man who wanted a private strip-tease, except the clothes she had to take off were the gym-slip, black stockings, white shirt and tie of a school uniform. Afterwards, she had to pretend to strangle him with the tie. At which point he would orgasm.

Or the man who liked to bath her. She had to do absolutely nothing. He ran the bath, tested the water with a thermometer, removed her clothes, hung them away carefully; he used the sponge and soap, spending a long time on her breasts. He would rinse her off with a hand shower and then, when he had dried her, powdered her, he would trim her pubic hair. And he never said a word. The ones she did not like were the ones who wanted to be humiliated. She found the sight of men crawling abjectly and calling her 'mistress' distasteful; those who wanted to be beaten aroused only her contempt, but if she looked on it as yet another performance she was able to do it – and well. Her reputation took root that first year; and as Liz gradually withdrew so did Nell take over – in more ways than one.

'What a remarkably accomplished little thing you are to be sure,' was Philip's comment when he discovered her busily whipping up a frothy zabaglione, one of Liz's favourites.

'A client's recipe,' Nell informed him. 'His hobby is cooking.'

Philip picked up a spoon and sampled. 'Mmmmm . . . I trust he is as delicious in other respects.'

Nell was aware by now that Philip did not like her independence. That he would have preferred her to be like Liz; not dependent, exactly, but needful. Unlike Liz, Nell did not discuss her clients with him, even the early ones obtained through his good offices, and he resented what he termed her 'secretiveness'. 'We are only all whores together,' he told her acidly. 'Let us not forget what it is we do to earn our crust.' But there was no cosy confiding in him of what had been done, said, partaken of, enjoyed or endured where Nell was concerned, and when she began acquiring her own clients Philip resented that too. It was fine while Nell was the pupil, under instruction, with a lot to learn and a teacher who knew everything. What Philip did not like was the speed with which she did learn, and the use to which she put that learning. When she acquired a client through her own sources Philip was quick to warn that he would have to vet him first. He was thoroughly put out when Nell told him that she had instituted her own check – 'but any additional information will be very welcome, Philip. I do appreciate that there are circles I cannot penetrate.'

'I am not so much of a penetrator myself,' Philip allowed graciously, with a feline swipe, 'but I do have the entrée, so to speak . . .' His glance was baleful.

'Really, one would think she had been on the game for years,' he observed acidly to Liz. 'I must warn her not to become too full of herself; that way she will never have room for anyone else and then how will she earn her living?'

Had he but known, Nell was not one self but several, and it was from the performance of the woman she created that she got her satisfaction. Her triumph was the result her perform-ance achieved in the client, and the referrals this brought her as *Cleo Mondaine*. Like Elly Little, the name was a paraphrase: Cleo from Cleo de Mérode, that legendary *grande horizontale*: Mondaine meaning worldly, as well as from *demi-mondaine*, and to Nell, the name personified a call-girl.

Cleo was *nothing* like Nell. Cleo was self-assured, knew her worth – and her power, always travelled first class, bought only the best, accepted only the very best. Cleo could come on like an untouched virgin or fuck like a whore. Through Cleo, Nell could give full rein to her talents as an actress, and she revelled in her performances, giving Liz cause to wonder whether, in re-making Nell, she had inadvertently created a person she did not know, for it was evident that 'Cleo's' imagination knew no bounds.

'Always remember only one thing remains constant,' Liz reminded. 'The male organ. That is what is responsible for Cleo; that remains unchanged as long as it can maintain an erection and it is what you can provide in the way of necessary friction to relieve that aching swelling that is the reason for the whole ball-game. Fantasies may come and fantasies may go, but there is only one way a man can achieve orgasm. Never forget that.'

And Nell/Cleo didn't. She fined and refined and re-defined her act until it became as natural as breathing. When playing Cleo she *was* Cleo; she thought, acted, spoke, walked, serviced her clients as Cleo. But always, once an assignment was over, once the wig and the make-up were off, so was the performance. Cleo was, on stage, a living, breathing creature. She was also nothing more than a prop.

10

Nell met the Brigadier at Paddington.

'How nice to see you again, my dear,' Brigadier Harvill said fondly. 'Prettier than ever.'

'Thank you. Hello Tiger, how are you?' Nell patted the dog's grizzled head and the tail showed its appreciation.

'Can we get him in there?' the Brigadier asked doubtfully when he saw the Mercedes Sports.

'It will be a tight squeeze but I think we might manage it,' Nell responded.

'He's getting awfully thin poor old boy; nothing but skin and bone and all due to old age. Can't think what I'll do when he finally sends in his papers. Had him seventeen years.'

Tiger finally sat on his master's lap, or as much of him as could be managed; hindquarters in the seat well, forequarters and head on his master's knees.

'How are things?' the Brigadier asked, as they left the station car park.

'She was as bright as a button when I left the house. Looking forward to seeing you.'

The old man brightened. 'Good, good . . . I've brought a brace of pheasants I managed to bag a few days ago. Need to be hung, but good eating nevertheless. I suppose that large West Indian lady knows how to prepare pheasant?'

'I've no idea, but she knows most things and if she doesn't she can soon learn – or I can come to that.'

The Brigadier was silent for a while, his hand smoothing Tiger's grizzled forehead. 'Haven't said it before, but I have to say that I'm indebted to you for all you are doing for m'daughter. Not as though you were family or anything – not that they always turn up trumps. Good friends – such as you, m'dear – are often worth much more than one's own flesh and blood. Old Tiger, here, is a dear old friend, as is Mercer. Only wish we all weren't so old. Makes you feel so helpless.'

The old man's veined and liver-spotted hand convulsively stroked his dog's head, and sensing his master's distress Tiger whined sympathetically. How very different from the home life of our own, dear Eleanor, Nell thought mordantly. I have no doubt my own father – had I been the one with a brain tumour – would have sat me down and explained in great detail, what I could expect and then seen to it that I was packed off to the right kind of hospital to let it take its course. And I'll bet he would not have come to see me, either. He hardly ever saw my mother in the last stages of her illness except as her doctor. Nobody could distance himself from anything or anybody like my father. This poor old man is distressed because he can't do more. My father would have done exactly what was expected of him – he was so keen on one doing one's duty, after all – but no more. Yet Liz thinks that she and her father aren't close! Nell wanted to laugh. Five minutes with *my* father and she would have known what distance is. My father kept light years between us even when – No! Now is not the time to go into *that*. Never is the time to go into *that*.

It's over.

It's done with.

You could not have done any different.

Why *will* you keep wondering if you could. Or should. Margaret is safe and well. And soon, now, you will be able to go and see her. Once you start earning money and have some of your own you can go and see her instead of ringing to find out how she is. Then you can explain; make her understand why she is where she is and why you are not there with her.

For now, Liz is the one in need of care and attention and for what she has done for you, saved you from, she deserves all you can give.

Nell could see the Brigadier nerving himself as they neared their destination. He seemed to blank out his feelings, put his emotions on hold and concentrate only on getting through the first few minutes when he would see the changes in his daughter since the last time he had seen her; the deterioration, the loss of weight, the creeping immobility of her limbs. Once Nell had helped him out of the car she saw him square his shoulders, set his head straight on them before stumping inside on his walking stick to greet his daughter, which he did as though the shock of her changed appearance affected him not in the least.

It was only when Nell put a glass of whisky into his hand that she saw how much it was trembling.

Dinner that night was gay and laughter-filled, and not just because Philip made a fourth. He set himself out to charm and amuse, giving Nell a glimpse of what he must have been like in his heyday. But I still don't see why the rest of us should pay just because it is over, Nell thought.

Some old friends, who knew both Liz and the Brigadier, came to lunch on the Saturday, which Lulu did as a special favour. That night, Nell cooked dinner, for six because Boy and his hard-faced harridan wife actually accepted Liz's invitation.

Susan Harvill ran her husband like clockwork, and woe betide him if he lost so much as a second. She did not approve of Liz, was suspicious of Nell, abhorred Philip and was bored by her father-in-law. She left most of her sorrel soup, picked at her shoulder of lamb à la turque and refused the Gâteau Margot, but she emptied her glass each time it was filled and, since Philip had chosen the wines, each glassful was superlative.

They drank one cup of coffee, refusing brandy or a liqueur, and when they made their move to go no protests were made. Only when they had gone did Philip bring out the Glenmorangie, and with Nell a newly taught fourth they settled down to some serious bridge. Philip partnered Nell since he was by far the most skilful player, but Liz and her father were too good for them and ended up winning. It was one in the morning by the time the Brigadier went up to bed, in a glow of whisky and well-being.

Next day, Sunday, Nell cooked lunch – roast beef with all the trimmings accompanied by an excellent bottle of claret, after which he napped for an hour or so. At four they had tea and then Philip, who had come by specially for the purpose, drove the Brigadier back to Paddington for his train, which Mercer would meet at the other end with the ancient Daimler with which the Brigadier staunchly refused to part. Before they left, Nell presented Tiger with the rib from the beef. 'Keep him happy for hours,' the Brigadier said, touched, 'only got half his teeth nowadays.' To his daughter he said: 'Lovely weekend, darling. Look forward to the next one.'

'Soon,' Liz said, with a dazzling yet loving smile. 'Very soon . . .' As they watched Philip's beautifully kept Bentley driving off; 'Not that he did much, poor old sod. But at least it's company for him.'

'He thoroughly enjoyed himself,' Nell protested.

'But he hates seeing me. He tries, poor old love, but my old man never was much of a dissembler. It's his eyes . . .' Liz turned her wheelchair with a savage sweep. 'Let's have some music . . .'

Later, as Liz was sitting listening to Herb Alpert and Nell was catching up on the *Sunday Times*, Liz suddenly turned down the sound to say: 'I don't want him to see me when it gets to the stage where I won't recognise him.' Her gaze was fierce. 'Promise you won't let him see that.'

'Of course I promise.'

'And keep him in happy ignorance of what I did for a living. He has his suspicions, but he's of the generation that would not dream of confronting me with them. If it came to the point where I was sullying the family name . . . but there has never been a breath of scandal.'

She looked at Nell, who said: 'And there never will be.'

Liz nodded, satisfied. 'You're a good girl . . . life dealt me one, last good hand in putting you in my path.' Her smile was twisted. 'Maybe it felt I'd had enough of the bad ones.' A long, indrawn sigh. 'But I can't really complain, you know. As Pa would say, I've had a good innings, achieved some pretty high scores.' Her smile was wryly humorous. 'I never expected to be bowled out so soon . . .' She used her remote control to switch off the record player. 'Now I think I'll go up to bed. It's been a busy weekend and I feel rather tired.'

Nell pushed the wheelchair to the specially constructed lift at the side of the stairs, lowering the platform to the ground and locking the wheels before pressing the button. The chair rose, carrying Liz with it, while Nell walked up. At the top she unlocked the chair and pushed it into Liz's bedroom, where she helped her undress and get into her nightgown before wheeling her into the bathroom. Then she helped her into bed.

Once she was settled, Liz caught hold of Nell's hand as she made to leave.

'Something you want?' Nell asked.

'Only to say thank you.'

'That works both ways.'

Satisfied, Liz released her grip, though these days that was not very strong.

'You're a good girl,' she said, emotion thickening her voice.

'Only at what I do,' Nell said mischievously.

Liz's laughter was what she liked to hear when she left her at night.

Liz began to fail rapidly over the next few months, becoming bed-fast before sinking into the coma from which she would never awake. The Brigadier, who had been so steadfast, could not take the sight of the bright butterfly that had been his daughter fading into the greyness of death. After the last time, when she tried, with her sunken eyes and colourless face to smile at him he had not come again.

'I would rather fight Arnhem all over again,' he wept.

'Typical,' was Philip's merciless comment. 'As he failed her in life so he failed her in death. He and his wife were so wrapped up in each other they never saw their children. Is it any wonder Elizabeth lived for the moment?'

He *did* love her, Nell thought angrily. He did! We aren't all armoured like you, you know. I only wish my father had loved me as much. The Brigadier would have changed places with his daughter willingly. He told me that. Would you? You who profess to love Liz so much. If my father had wept for my mother just *once* . . .

Boy, who emerged from his sister's room looking as if he wanted to do a bunk, she could understand. He was a moral coward. Liz had known her brother very well. From then on he sent flowers his sister could neither see or smell. His wife made no pretence and did not even bother to come. By then the full-time nurse was in attendance, but Nell had to admit that Philip came up trumps, spending hours sitting by Liz's bed in case she should come to. When he was not there, Nell was, so that with the nurse taking her shift Liz was never alone.

When Liz did die, slipping away quietly in the small hours, neither Philip nor Nell were in the house.

One of the most regular clients had asked her to fly to Paris to meet him on his way to the Middle East, while Philip had answered a call of distress from a former lover whose partner of twenty years had succumbed to a coronary.

Only the nurse was present to summon the doctor to certify death.

By the time Nell got back Philip was already carrying out the instructions Liz had left concerning her cremation.

'No misery. I had a good life, I lived it up in every sense of the word,' she had told them months before. 'And I want the clean, bright fire. No dirges. Bright, happy music – the kind I like. And lots of flowers . . . colourful, bright, perfumed flowers. And scatter my ashes wherever the hell you like. It is – they will be of no matter.' She had laughed. 'Literally of no matter . . .' She had held out a hand to each. 'I can't really complain, except that I could have done with a while longer. But I enjoyed the time I had.' She had turned to Philip. 'Remember Henry Miller?'

Philip had nodded. 'The aim of life is to live, and to live means to be aware; joyously, drunkenly, serenely, divinely, aware.'

'And have I not done that?'

'In spades.'

'Right. So say those words if you have to say anything. No platitudes please.'

'How about: "'Tis not a Pity she was a Whore?"' Nell asked.

Philip had looked surprised and somewhat peeved that he had not said it, but Liz had chortled delightedly, repeated it over and over again. 'That is exactly the sort of thing I mean.'

Her funeral was, accordingly, anything but solemn. The little church was crowded with those who had known her, and bright with flowers she had loved, whilst the music was equally up-beat. Liz not being religious there was no service as such.

Philip was the only one who spoke, and he did so eloquently, pithily and with much wit. As the coffin, completely hidden by flowers, moved slowly beyond the bronze velvet curtains, Ella Fitzgerald sang Cole Porter's 'Every Time We Say Goodbye.'

Afterwards there was champagne, more music, much talk, a great many remember whens and, as the bottles emptied, some maudlin tears.

Nell was bringing up champagne reinforcements when the kitchen doors swung and a woman came through them. Very striking, expensively dressed but in the hard, power-dressing way of a TV soap.

'Can I help you?' Nell asked politely.

'Only to five minutes peace and quiet.' Her accent was British overlaid with Aussie. 'We haven't met. My name's Delia Dupré, though when I knew Liz it was Davina Dawson. The name I used in the Life.' She waited for Nell's recognition. When there was none: 'I was the one Liz came to for advice when she decided to change her amateur status.'

Since it was obviously expected: 'Of course,' Nell lied. 'Liz told me about you.'

'Without rancour, I trust.'

'I don't recall any.' Liz had never so much as mentioned a Davina Dawson.

'Liz never bore grudges, I will say.'

'Should she have?'

'We had a – falling out. I asked her to pinch-hit for me with a client and she went and pinched him!' A thin smile. 'But I reckon she did me a favour because I caught an even bigger fish, and that one I married.' The woman looked Nell up and down. 'I take it you are a member of the Sisterhood?'

'Yes.'

'Are you the protégée I heard Liz had taken on?'

'Yes.'

'I resigned my membership when I married. My husband has no idea I ever belonged, but since we live in Australia there is little likelihood of him finding out. He thinks I'm in Switzerland having my face done. I read about Liz in *The Times* – I don't keep in touch with anyone any more, so I thought I'd come and refresh a few memories, though from the looks of some of the faces out there it is not so much refreshment they need as renewal. I hear occasionally from one good friend I can trust; usually in the broadest of terms, but she did say that Liz was ill. A brain tumour, she said.'

'Yes.'

'Was she ill for very long?'

'The last few months were the worst.'

The woman sipped champagne from the glass she was carrying. 'Liz was three years younger than me.'

The swing doors opened again revealing Philip. 'Where's the champagne, Nell? Glasses are empty out here . . . Good God! It *is* you!' he said to Delia Dupré. 'I spotted you in the church and then lost you in the mob next door. Slumming are we, since we joined the ranks of the SuperRich all those years ago?'

'Hello, Philip.' Delia Dupré was totally unmoved.

Nell had opened two more bottles of champagne as they talked, now she put them on the tray which Philip picked up, before delving into the cooler for two more.

'Don't go away,' he said to Mrs Dupré. 'I'd love a chat . . . let me help a few more guests on their way to being drunk and disorderly and then we'll talk.' He went out.

'Not if I can help it,' Mrs Dupré said. 'It is when you are drunk and/or disorderly that Philip Faulkner picks your mind and then keeps the contents as insurance.'

She nodded at Nell. 'Be careful around Philip Faulkner. He may have been uncharacteristically decent where Liz was concerned but that's probably because she knew just as much about him as he did about her. They'd known each other since puberty or something.' She moved to the door, turned as she got there. 'How are things in the Life nowadays? I suppose it has changed as much as life has in the past twenty years.'

'There is no lack of clients,' Nell replied non-committally.

Delia Dupré laughed. 'No. Nor ever will be. Good luck,' she said, as she went out.

Philip was annoyed when he found his quarry had eluded him. 'Why on earth couldn't you have kept her talking?'

'About what? She is a total stranger.'

'Only because when she left the Life she had herself made-over.'

His sniff was a snort. 'She had this yen for respectability. But the S&M specialists always do.'

'Is that what she did?'

'Nothing else – well, she did have one client who didn't go in for any of the murkier pain-giving routines; all he liked was to have his backside paddled with a ping-pong bat. Half a dozen really hard thwacks and he'd spout like a geyser. Public schoolboy, obviously. She asked Liz to stand in for her once when she'd double-booked or something and the client took a shine to Liz and switched allegiance. Deedee was furious. Turned out she had matrimonial plans, which included black-mail, of course. There's no other way she could have got him to marry her.' Philip smiled. 'I had a quiet word with him and told him a few unsuspected details about his ladyfriend. Apart from his personal peccadillo he was frightfully proper and when he learned what she did to other men . . .' Creamy with satisfaction: 'He refused to have anything to do with her after that.'

'In that case why are you so interested?'

'I am always interested in the ones that got away. Especially when they go to such lengths to alter their appearance – except it was shorten in her case; she used to have a nose down to her knees. She's had a jaw implant because she never had one before, not to mention an eye-restructuring.'

'Is that why you were not sure who she was?'

'Of course! There was something about her . . . but I never got up close until I found her in here with you. Then I knew at once. What did she want, anyway?'

'To ask about Liz; what had happened, why she died. She told me they had been friends.'

'Liz friends with that piece of dross? Never in a million years. The S&M brigade are a class apart – every one of them in need of extra coaching. What they do is, even to me and I have a mind as broad as the Champs Élysées – of a sleaziness and unpleasantness that is beyond belief. Only the fact that there are absolutely no limits to human depravity makes it believable. Deedee's equipment was ramps and clamps and padlocks and bolts and wires which she used to attach to various male genitals; she used to shave pubic hair so close she was within a millimetre of taking off the top layer of skin; she

used to attach saw-tooth clamps to foreskins and then mastur-
bate its owner until he was shrieking for mercy. She made a
fortune, of course. You can charge the earth for S&M. But a
friend of Liz she was *never*, though it was what she wanted to
be. I wonder what brought her here today? It's years since she
had anything to do with her former circle. She sloughed that
off with her name. She was hot stuff then. Now she likes to
give the impression that butter wouldn't melt.' His smile was
feline. 'Like you.'

Nell rode the swell of bitchery for it was something she had
prepared for. Now that Liz's conciliatory presence no longer
stood between them she knew Philip would show her no
mercy, and her strict sense of fair play made her make
allowances for the fact that it was probably his way of showing
grief.

There were storms ahead and no way in which she could
evade them while Liz's estate went through probate. Philip had
been appointed executor, something he had long known. What
he did not know, for Liz had not told him, was that she had
appointed Nell as co-executrix, and it was Nell who got the
bulk of her estate.

Lulu had been left a generous bequest – 'She's been a damned
good friend to me over the years, and she's stuck with that shit
of a husband who shafts every skirt in sight and lives off his
hard-working wife. He won't get this, though. I've made
damned sure of that. It goes to her and only her. I've warned
her to see he gets not so much as a bent penny!' Liz had
giggled. 'I've left Philip all the things he has had his eye on.
The T'ang horse and the Meissen milkmaid and the Italian
gesso mirror. He's been hinting – in his own inimitable way –
that I should leave them to him in my will so I have. Something
to remember me by . . .'

At the expression on Nell's face: 'I know, I know . . . that
flat of his is choc-a-bloc with objets d'art and I am well aware
that he has an acquisitive streak a mile wide, but he is my
oldest and closest friend and we have been through many ups
and downs together. He's always coveted that small Fantin
Latour above the sideboard so he can have that too. The
sideboard – and I would have you know it is Sheraton – is
yours along with the rest of the house's contents and the house

itself. Thanks to you the mortgage is all but paid – no, don't deny me this last luxury; pleasure, even. This house is mine; bought and almost paid for. I leave it to you to do with as you like. Go on living here, sell it or what you will. With my thanks.'

'But I'm not family – '

'Pa has that great barn in Wiltshire and Boy has his London house *and* the converted farmhouse in Sussex. He also has more money than I ever had. And I wouldn't leave that bitch his wife so much as a fare-thee-well. She has seen to it that I don't know my nephews so that's another no-no. For the past sixteen months you have been my family, while Philip was always more of a brother than Boy ever was. You've come to mean a lot to me, Nell. We were in synch from the first time we set eyes on each other and the rhythm has been steady ever since. You were a marvellous pupil and are now a natural at our job. You've brought more money in over the past months than I could have hoped for even in my wildest fantasies; made me solvent, enabled me to pay my debts – I owe you, as the Americans put it. I was desperate when I decided on my last gamble, and I was in luck, for my number came up. Nineteen – your age at the time. Which reminds me, if I'm still around come your twenty-first we'll have a celebration the like of which has not been seen these many years.'

But Nell's twenty-first was still two months away. I'll still make a celebration of it, Nell said silently now. As though you were there.

Lulu came into the kitchen carrying a tray of empty glasses. 'People leavin',' she announced.

'Coming . . .' Nell drained her glass.

'Soon as they gone we hold our own 'membrance,' Lulu said. 'How many these people come here when she sick? Not many. Fair weather friends.'

'Not all, Lulu. Liz knew lots of people but she had few real friends, and they came; then and now.'

Lulu's grim expression did not relax, and her broad back was eloquent as she began to wash glasses.

Nell saw that the wake was winding down. Philip was speeding people on their way with his practised handshake which acted like a lever in that even as it clasped yours it was also propelling you on your way, giving no opportunity to linger. Nell helped by steering people to him; people she doubted she would ever see again, for she did not, even, now, know any of them in any sense of the word. Except the Brigadier. He had looked very old, very shaken, leaned heavily on the arm of Mercer, who was small, wizened, wrinkled as a walnut, and as forthright as became a Yorkshireman.

'E's taken it hard, Miss,' he'd said to Nell. 'E's a right softy, is the Brigadier. But she were a good lass, Miss Elizabeth.' Here Mercer had fixed Nell with eyes that were still surprisingly blue. 'I reckon she were right lucky to have such a friend as you – and Mr Faulkner, of course. E's what you might call an acquired taste and one I never managed to acquire, but he were the best of friends to Miss Elizabeth, as were you. Just wanted you to know, Miss, the Brigadier and me, we appreciate all you did.'

The Brigadier had tried to say something along the same lines but he had not been able to speak, not been able to do more than press Nell's hands and, for a moment gaze speakingly into her eyes before his own filled. His son and his daughter-in-law took him away as soon as they decently could. He and Mercer was staying in Thurloe Square since the Brigadier was now no longer able to function on his own. Tiger had died in his sleep not two months before and that had been devastating enough. Liz following on so soon had been a blow he had not possessed the reserves to withstand.

Boy, on the other hand, acting on his wife's instructions, had made it plain that all further communication between Nell and his father was now at an end. It was obvious that to Susan Harvill, Nell was a bad influence. Nell forebore to say that Liz had asked her to keep an eye on the old man; it would have been a waste of time. They could do with him as they liked now that Liz was out of the way, and would brook no interference. Even Mercer's days were probably numbered. Nell was sorry, for she had liked the Brigadier and would have kept in touch, visited now and again, perhaps even written occasionally. It was what Liz had wanted. Oh, well, Liz proposes, Boy disposes, she thought, as she saw them go.

Once the door was closed on the last mourner Philip, Lulu and Nell sat down to remember Liz as she would want to be remembered: with fresh champagne and the music she had loved. For the most part Nell sat and listened to Philip and Lulu 'remembering when', but now and again, when a particular song took hold of her mind, she retreated into her own memories.

Fate had indeed been kind to her when it had put her in the way of Elizabeth Waring, for she had been a good friend, though apart from the difference in age they had also been possessed of totally disparate characters. Well, don't they say opposites attract? she thought, listening to Herb Alpert's trumpet laying down a seductive beat and seeing, in her memory, Liz's rigorously well-kept body gyrating hips that seemed to be mounted on ball-bearings. How she had *loved* to dance! While she was able, she and Philip – who was every bit as good – had often gone dancing, and not to Annabel's, where both were members, but to dance-halls, discos, places where they were regarded by the teenagers who frequented them with amused contempt – until they got on the dance floor. Nell had been envious.

'You mean you've never actually been to a dance!' Liz had exclaimed in astonishment when Nell had admitted that fact.

'I was not allowed to. I told you. My father – '

'Was very strict. My God, Nell . . . this is 1980; he sounds like he was born in 1880.'

'No; only his attitudes and beliefs.'

'You poor kid.' Liz had been so compassionate that Nell had had to swallow the lump which suddenly blocked her throat. 'We've got a lot of catching up to do, then. All the things he said no to I say yes to. Agreed?'

'Oh, yes please . . .'

And she had kept her promise, Nell thought now. From her I learned how to laugh and be light-hearted. How to enjoy myself; how to accept pleasure for what it was and not feel guilty.

'Was your father strictly religious?' Liz had asked once.

'No way. He had no use for religion at all. He said it was man-made and therefore suspect. He said he needed no fifth-hand apocrypha to instruct him as to morality or anything else. My father made his own rules as they were the only ones he obeyed – and expected me to obey also.'

'What about your sister?'

'Margaret was a different case. She did not know anything but the very simplest rules. Not to touch the fire, not to go into the kitchen when things were cooking, not to cross roads on her own. She went to a special school during the day. Father explained to me what had gone wrong genetically in the womb.'

'How old were you when she was born?'

'Seven'.

'A bit young for that kind of explanation, surely.'

'Father did not believe in shying from truth and he said I was old enough and intelligent enough to understand.'

'Sounds like a monster,' had been Liz's pithy comment.

'He would have been shocked to know you thought so. He always saw himself as the most rational of men. He set great store by common sense.'

'It still drove you to leave his bed and board at seventeen.'

'I had had enough,' was all Nell said.

More than enough, she thought now. You did not know the half of it, Liz. She set down her glass. And I have had enough champagne.

She stood up, swaying slightly.

'Giving up?' Philip asked.

'If I don't do it here I shall have to make a dash for the loo and do it there.' Nell turned to Lulu. 'Philip will order you a taxi when you want to go,' she said, conscious that the dark face was blurred at the edges.

'I sure ain't walkin' or gettin' no night bus.' Lulu too was feeling no pain.

'See you tomorrow,' Nell said to Philip, who flipped a hand before burying his nose in his glass.

And when Nell got downstairs next morning she found them both where she had left them. Philip in the big chair, Lulu on the sofa, empty bottles all around. Her own head felt as if someone was tightening a steel band around it, but she had taken two Alka Seltzer. Now she went into the kitchen to make strong black coffee. Philip opened one eye, winced and shut it again. Lulu was still out for the count.

'Here . . .' Nell handed Philip a glass of water that fizzed softly.

He closed his eyes and moaned at the noise but drank it down.

'I should *not* have opened that last bottle of champagne . . . but how often does one drink a Taittinger Comte de Comtes?'

'Liz ordered it months ago for this very occasion.'

'Thoughtful to the last. Dear Liz . . . *how* I shall miss her.' He sounded so desolate that Nell believed him.

Lulu came to with many groans and imprecations, refused Alka Seltzer but staggered into the kitchen to make what she said would put the most hideous hangover to flight. It was red, smelled disgusting and, Philip said once he had downed his, tasted the same way. 'Do not, I beg of you, tell me what it contained,' he shuddered. 'It is enough that I must keep it down.'

'That a sovereign remedy for somebody been at the black rum,' Lulu told him. 'Champagne give it no trouble. You'll see.'

Half an hour and two cups of strong black coffee later he allowed that the potion had worked its magic, and went upstairs to shower, shave and change, leaving Lulu and Nell to clear away the debris. Surveying the once-more-immaculate kitchen Lulu said: 'Right. That's me done.' She turned to Nell. 'I won't be comin' back.'

'Why not?' Nell was taken by surprise.

'Miss Liz, she need me. You don't. You organised. She pushin' fifty but she the child. Not you. You don't need me. You don't need nobody.' Lulu shrugged. 'Some folk don't. So I got me a job nearer home. This is long way to come and I only did it for her.'

Nell was silent a moment than said: 'All right. If that's what you want. You could have stayed on, you know.'

'To do what? You cook, you clean, you mend. You used to it. Miss Liz always had somebody do these things for her. You don't need me. You self-sufficient.'

'Miss Liz told me to give you all her clothes. She said you could sell them.'

'I'll do that.'

'She said to take everything. I emptied all her drawers and the big cupboard. If you need a case you can borrow one.'

'I got some big black bags. They'll do. But I'll take that taxi you offer last night. Too much to carry even for me.'

'Shall I order it now?'

'Tell it to come in half an hour. I'll go and get the bags.'

Lulu stuffed three of them with suits, dresses, coats and underwear, and stacked them beside the front door. When Philip came down, trailing *Eau Sauvage* and a distrait air he saw them and said: 'Don't tell me the vultures are here already.'

'Liz told me to tell Lulu she could have all her clothes if she wanted them.'

'They won't go near her!'

'To sell. Lulu knows where to get the top price.'

'In that case, I will gather up what small things she left to me.'

'Did she tell you?'

'Of course she did. She said it would be in her will. Don't tell me *you* don't know.'

'I'm not, but surely it is best to wait until the will is officially read.'

'Lulu is taking the clothes.'

'They are not in the will; not as an official bequest. I would prefer you to wait, Philip.'

'My dear girl, I would remind you that *I* am executor.'

'Even so.'

Eyes met, locked. 'Do not take me on,' Philip said softly. 'You will be out of your league.'

'So sue me,' Nell said flatly. 'The clothes are nothing to do with the will. Lulu knew to expect them as a perk, not a bequest. What Liz left you are valuable antiques and I want everything done in accordance with her will. We have an appointment with her solicitor this afternoon.'

'We?'

'I am your co-executor.'

Philip's eyes flared for a moment, the quicksilver becoming molten, then he shrugged. 'I might have known. There is always a worm in the bud. Come, Lulu, no need for that taxi. I'll give you a lift.'

'Half past three in Theobalds Road,' Nell called after him. He did not look back.

'Don't you pay no heed to him,' Lulu advised, as she hefted the bags Philip had left her to load. 'He always like to think *he* run Miss Liz, but he gonna be the one to feel the cold.'

Nevertheless the breath Nell let out as she shut the front door was a shaky one and her legs felt as if they had been boned. She was not stroppy by nature, though she did have a rebellious streak which her father, by his insistence on *his* way, had unwittingly over-fed, but she was not one to look for trouble unless it was to circumvent a greater pile of it.

Liz had warned her that Philip would attempt a take-over. 'Which is why I have made you his co-executor. No, don't look like that. I'd not have done so had I not thought he'd steamroller over you first chance he got. Philip has to be top dog; it's his nature, but you're by no means as meek and mild as you look and I know you'll see that *my* wishes are carried out rather than embellished with Philip's frills and flourishes. Also, there are things I don't want him to know. Here . . .' she had handed Nell a key. 'It opens a safe deposit box at my branch of Coutts. There's a letter authorising you to open it and I've had a word with the manager, who is an old friend – all those overdrafts . . . I want you to destroy the contents. Philip would read everything first; that's why I want you to do it.'

Nell nodded, throat thick. Liz's trust was an unexpected accolade.

'You know me,' Liz had said with a self-mocking smile. 'As sentimental as they come. They are mostly letters in the box; letters that I could not bear to part with even though the man who wrote them did me as wrong as any man did Billy Holiday. He was a shit but I loved him. The years I spent with him were like the little girl with the curl on her forehead; when they were good they were very, very good. When they were bad they were horrid. Go and get them for me, let me have one last read and then consign them to the flames. We'll go the same route together.'

Nell had emptied the box, put everything into a carrier bag and brought it home to Liz before leaving her alone with her memories.

What she consigned to the Aga later was a pile of confetti.

Thinking of it now stiffened her resolve to stand her ground against Philip's irresistible force.

Slowly she went upstairs and into Liz's bedroom. Empty now, oh, so empty, yet still carrying her signature fragrance. Ma Griffe. All the medical equipment was gone, the jars, the bottles, the covered bedpans, the kidney dishes. The big wardrobes were empty, but on the cleared glass top of the dressing table was her jewel box; originally a three-tier box of Charbonnel and Walker fondant creams. In her will Liz had left it all to Nell.

'Not all of it is first water but there are a couple of very good pieces; the diamond chandeliers – I always kept them in reserve for hocking purposes but it never quite came to that; the pearls are real too; a twenty-first birthday present, and the hideous knuckle-duster Michael gave me on our engagement, along with the sapphire flower brooch. The rest is a collection of obvious junk and first-class fakes. I've left Philip the Rolex Oyster I bought for Jose-Luis and made him give me back. It cost me a fortune and he'd only have sold it. Philip always said it was the most vulgar thing but I know he coveted it as a status symbol, and these days status is all important to him, poor love, since he knows it is only a matter of time.'

Nell went across to the box, lifted the lid. Lying on their satin base the diamonds flared as the sun from the window struck them. She lifted one of them, held it to her ear. It swung lazily, fully aware of its worth. 'And you?' Nell said aloud to her reflection. 'You realise that you are worth quite a lot now? These diamonds and pearls, this house.' She put the ear-ring back, sat staring sightlessly at her reflection. I'd give it all back in return for Liz,' she said to it. Then she put down her head and wept inconsolably.

When she met Philip later that day at the offices of Liz's solicitors, she was her normal calm composed self. She knew by now what Philip's serrated tongue would make of any signs of grief. He would not believe it, for a start. For some reason he persisted in regarding her as what he had first taken her for; on the make: coolly, even coldly calculating as to what the traffic would bear by way of making a killing. He affected not to see or believe in her gratitude and devotion to a woman she regarded as her benefactress and had come, in spite of their totally different personalities and outlook, to love as she had never loved anyone, except her mother and her sister.

Liz had seen behind the seemingly unemotional façade to the vulnerable girl who hid behind it because she had been hurt too much and too soon. To Liz, Nell had talked about her adored mother, whose memory she kept burnished bright and about whom she had never been able to talk to anyone else, especially her father. To Liz she had revealed – even if only in glimpses and then not the whole, painful truth – her early life with Father. She had been able to do this because Liz let her know and see she cared, and the warmth of it had penetrated the ice in which Nell had been encased for so long. Philip saw only what he was prepared to see in order to fit the view to his prejudices, and it had not taken Nell long to perceive that where she was concerned, Philip saw nothing else.

Lulu had put it bluntly: 'He jealous, that one. He so jealous he don't see straight. He always been number one with Miss Liz, and he don't like sharin' first place. He say he love her – and maybe he do – but he thinks lovin' means ownin'. He don't like it when somebody go off and do their own thing – like Miss Liz done with you. *He* should have found you; *he* should have made you over, *he* should be reapin' the benefit. Makes him pea-green with envy that he didn't – worse – that Miss Liz come up smellin' like a rose. You stick up for yourself, honey. That really gets under his skin.'

It seemed Lulu had him dead to rights for when they left the solicitors, where Philip had concealed any shock he felt at the revelation that he did not have a free hand where Liz's will was concerned, they adjourned to a nearby pub. When they each had a gin and tonic, Philip raised his glass to observe silkily: 'Not bad for sixteen months work, hmmm?'

Nell controlled her tongue (it will be your downfall one day, Eleanor, her father used to say sonorously before proceeding to punish her for its misuse) to counter levelly: 'Work which provided most of the income Liz received during the past year, while she was unable to earn. I have repaid everything she spent on me. I am good at arithmetic. I had to learn at an early age how to run a house and juggle its expenses. My father expected every penny to be accounted for, and I could do the same with you should you require it.'

'Oh, I am sure you could. Such a mass of virtues, aren't you? Liz, of course, was hopeless with money, but there had always been someone to look after it for her, you see. Unlike you she was – shall we say gently reared?'

His tongue had lost none of its edge yet to Nell his sigh, which proceeded a deeply felt: '*How* I shall miss her . . .' sounded genuine.

His one redeeming feature was his love for Liz. Had it not been there Nell would not have bothered with him again. It was not as though they would ever be friends. Now he set down his glass preparatory to saying: 'Normally I never bother with people I despise, but in your case I am willing to make an exception because Liz asked me to. I have done just about everything in the book but I have yet to break a promise.'

Nell opened her mouth to say: You surprise me, but thought better of it. If Liz had gone that far . . .

'I am well aware that you think me too clever by half,' Philip went on, 'but you should also know that I never do anything that way. All or nothing at all is my way.'

Nell burst out laughing. 'Only you, Philip . . .'

Suddenly they were in perfect charity with one another. His saving grace would always be his witty sense of humour, Nell thought.

'I think, if we put down our foils, that we may arrive at a *modus vivendi* satisfactory to us both; one that does not involve our seeing each other more than is necessary,' he pronounced.

'To do what?'

'Act as Liz asked me to: *in loco parentis*.'

'I should have thought that beyond even you,' Nell said gently.

The quicksilver eyes shimmered with genuine amusement overlaying appreciation. 'I was thinking in terms of my own – and Liz's education. Parental duties, in our cases, involved no more than occasional visits to school. Why, I sometimes went a whole year without seeing my mother or, indeed, *any* of my step fathers. Likewise Liz, because hers were abroad.'

'I don't need a fatherly eye, Philip. I don't need any kind of eye.'

'Liz thought you did.'

'Since when have you cared what people thought – even Liz?'

Philip was silent for a moment then said in a voice that was new to her. 'I always cared for whatever Liz thought. I have known – still know – very many people, but my *friends* I can count on the fingers of one hand, and Liz was my thumb. Have you ever considered how helpless one is without a thumb?'

Nell was silent, remembering what Liz had said not long before her death.

'I know Philip is not your favourite person but don't lose touch with him. You might need him one day. I did.' She had paused. 'There is also the possibility that he might need you. No, don't look so scathing. Philip needs to be needed, but the older he gets the fewer there are to feed that need. When I'm gone . . . He would be mortified if he thought you understood so for God's sake don't let on. Just – avail yourself of his knowledge and experience now and again.'

'And pay for it?'

But Liz had not shared the joke. 'He charges on the assumption that if you are willing to pay your need is genuine.'

Nell had sighed. It was not what she wanted. What she wanted was to cut herself loose from all strings. She wanted to be in sole control of her own life, feel the power of her own wings. Nobody, she had vowed, would ever control her again. And the last thing I either need or want is a surrogate father. The one I had was one too many.

'It is human nature to disregard good advice, even when offered in genuine goodwill, and in you, I have no doubt we have a prime example,' he said in his best Pontifical. 'Liz made me promise that I would not drop you from my mailing list but it is obvious that whenever you see my handwriting in future you will dump the missive in the bin, un-read. That being so, there is no more to be said.' He rose to his feet. 'Goodbye, my dear Nell, and good luck.'

Nell felt as if she had been briskly dusted off, but it was what she had wanted, wasn't it? Now she really was on her own. Nobody to say *no you can't* or *no you won't* or *I wouldn't do that if I were you* or *you don't run things around here*. She had her own house, money in the bank, a secure future. How far she had come, how much further she would yet go! She picked up her glass, drained it, but her intoxication came from euphoria. I'm free, she thought deliriously. I can do as *I* like. I'm free . . . I'm free . . . I'm free . . .'

11

When the new client was recommended to her Nell thought fleetingly of calling Philip but decided against it. She had not seen him for nine weeks and her life was running like a perfectly maintained engine. She had rearranged the little house to her own taste; re-siting furniture, re-hanging pictures and mirrors, placing a large, silver framed portrait of Liz as a bride, taken by Dorothy Wilding, on the table by the fire, next to a porcelain câche-pot containing a vividly shocking pink azalea – Liz's favourite. Otherwise the only difference was that she no longer lived alone. She shared. First with a British Blue, whose kennel name being one of those ridiculously pretentious pieces of idiocy Nell soon changed to Blossom since as a four-month-old kitten she had been a small piece of grey fluff with eyes like great golden asters. These eyes, almond shaped and set aslant, had led the vet who inoculated her against all the cat diseases to call her 'your little Chinese pussy cat' which in turn had led to Nell occasionally addressing Blossom as 'my little Empress of China', usually shortened to Empress, which she was.

All her life Nell had longed for a cat for she adored them, but her father had never allowed any animal across the threshold. Dogs smelled and cats clawed the furniture. Nell had begged and pleaded to no avail. She had once dared to bring home a stray which her father ordered her at once to take to the RSPCA.

'But they'll only put it down,' Nell had sobbed pleadingly. 'Please, please let me keep it. I'll be responsible for it, it won't bother you at all, I promise. It is only a poor little stray.'

'Of which there are far too many. Uncontrolled breeding is as reprehensible in animals as it is in humans. It is a kindness to remove it from a life whose harshness you do not begin to comprehend.'

Nell had never been able to comprehend her father. She had cried herself to sleep that night and made a vow that one day – *one day* she would have a cat of her very own. Blossom had cost sixty guineas and been worth every penny, so when she had a call from the cattery a couple of weeks after buying her to ask if she would be interested in Blossom's brother, who was not settling down since the departure of his sister, Nell agreed at once and promptly named him Bundle because, according to his breeder, he was a bundle of mischief. Blossom hid under the bed for the first few days after his arrival, and when she finally did venture out Bundle tended to push her around because he was bigger, but Blossom had a temper, and a couple of clouts soon taught him respect. After that they settled down amicably, sharing the same big basket – though at night they slept on the bottom of Nell's bed, played with, washed and groomed each other, and were company for each other when Nell was away. If that was for more than twenty-four hours she used a lady recommended by the breeder to visit and see that they were fed. They could enter and leave the house because Nell had a cat-flap fitted. Always, when she came home from an assignment, she would hear the jingle of their collar bells as they leapt off her bed – where they spent their time while she was away – and raced down the stairs to welcome her home. More than once, sitting in the big chair by the fire, both cats sharing her lap or on the rug in front of the flames, Nell would look round and sigh disbelievingly. Truly, she thought, she wanted for nothing. Work was steady, money was mounting up, she had a comfortable home. She was so *very* lucky. Never once, when she opened a bottle of wine and sipped it while either reading or watching television, did she fail to raise it in salute to Liz.

When the name was recommended to her it was not one she knew or had ever heard before, and in her circle, it was not unusual for her clients to be aware of, if not actually acquainted with, one another. But the recommendation was made by a client who had stayed on after Liz; one of long standing and considerable means whose fantasy was a gentle perversion in that he liked to be beaten, always on the bottom, always with a hairbrush – bristles down. Nell asked for details of the prospective client's sexual tastes and was told that he too liked to be beaten – but nothing untoward. There was nothing here to indicate a taste for S&M. He was young, very presentable as well as very rich, and married to a woman who regarded such a minor vice as a mortal sin and thus was of no use in affording him the kind of sexual release he needed every so often. Nell was to dress as a nursemaid – my God, she thought, what *is* it with the British upper classes – and be strict. Dinner would be served but during it she would constantly have to remind him to sit up, tuck in this elbows and refuse him pudding if he did not clean his plate. Needless to say he would not, and punishment would be called for. Well, Nell thought, an easy thousand pounds and a scenario I have done before, with variations. So she agreed. As she was dressing in pale blue uniform, white apron, black stockings (stockings had been strictly specified, – fifteen denier and with seams, as well as stiletto heels) some nurse, she thought amusedly, as she surveyed herself in her pierglass. The uniform was at least eight inches above the knees and if she bent it revealed the white expanse of thigh above the suspendered stocking. Men are so predictable, she thought, feeling a moment's bored impatience until she reminded herself what she would be paid for this particular charade. She had swept her hair up into a top-knot and the cap, white, starched with a frill, went on top of it. To confirm the illusion she wore the glasses she had bought; round, owlish, somewhat severe, but with plain glass in the lenses.

She turned from the glass, saw the cats regarding her from her bed: 'This should not take long,' she told them cheerfully. 'And you shall have your share in the shape of chicken liver.' She dropped a kiss on each head, heard them purr and then went downstairs to wait for her taxi.

It took her to a big house in a Kensington Square, where she had it drop her on the other side of the street as instructed. Only when it had driven off did she cross it and walk back some fifty yards to the number she had memorised. She had been given a key, and once inside she put the latch on the door – again following instructions – and went up three flights until she saw a thread of light under a closed door. Knocking, she went in. A man was standing in front of a fire behind a wire-mesh guard and behind him a table was set for two, with a trolley to one side, of the kind that contained heated dishes. The man turned and it was only because (a) Nell was already in character, since she had begun to immerse herself in it from the moment she left her own house (b) she was by now too well trained to display her feelings, that she did not gasp for the face was well known to her. She wondered if she ought to drop a curtsey but knew that would be fatal even as she squashed an instinctive urge to do so.

'Good evening,' she said, instead.

'Hello, Nanny.'

'Are you ready for your supper? Have you washed your hands?'

'Yes, Nanny.' Obediently he held them out to her. Unfastening her cloak, Nell dropped it on to a chair by the door and came forward, straightening the cap she had donned as she ascended the stairs. She inspected the well-shaped and beautifully kept hands held out to her, turned them both ways to examine the well-manicured nails. He was wearing striped flannel pyjamas and a traditional school dressing gown, dark grey with a red and white scrolled braid trim, tasselled cord to match tied at his waist. He smelled familiar and in a moment Nell knew what it was because memory supplied the clue. Wrights Coal Tar Soap; the kind her father had used in his surgery.

For a moment her concentration wavered then she forced the memory back and said as briskly as she could: 'Yes, they will do. Now come along and eat your supper. If you do – and I mean every bit – you shall have a story. If you don't . . .'

She saw his eyes, pale blue and somewhat bloodshot, burn fiercely but all he said was: 'I will eat it all, Nanny. I promise.'

'Not a piecrust promise, I hope. You know what I think of them.'

Her voice was sharp and for a moment she saw surprise flicker. She changed it to briskness as she said: 'Come along, then. We don't want it to get cold, do we?'

'Yes, Nanny.' He took one chair, leaving Nell to take the one nearest to the trolley. It was obvious she had to serve. Lifting lids she saw standard nursery fare: some kind of casseroled meat, she could not tell if it was lamb or beef, mashed potatoes, carrots, green peas. She took a plate from the hot cupboard – it too was nursery china, decorated with nursery rhymes – and ladled out a child-sized helping of each. How old was he supposed to be, she wondered; decided that eight was about right; old enough to know his table manners yet young enough to be still in the nursery. There was a glass jug filled with water and she poured him a glass, placed plate and glass in front of him. 'Now then, eat up like a good boy'.

'Yes, Nanny.'

He began well, even enthusiastically, but it did not last. He began pushing the food around his plate, and soon she heard the steady thump thump of his feet on the cross bars of the table. 'Stop that!'

'I'm not doing anything, Nanny.'

'Don't tell lies. Boys who tell lies are punished for it. And eat up; no dinner, no pudding.'

She leaned across to push the plate he had shoved away from him back in front of him again, and the smell of the familiar soap overwhelmed her again.

'Don't want any more.'

'Don't want doesn't get!' Nell's voice threatened. She saw the eyes flare again. He liked her anger. But he still did not eat; he began to push the food from his plate on to the clean, plain white tablecloth. 'Stop that!'

It was such an order that he did stop, mouth open slightly. The pale blue eyes had deepened in colour and the pupils enlarged. She saw a hand lay down his fork and drop to his lap.

'And you can just stop *that*! What have I told you about boys who play with themselves?'

In a small voice: 'Their hands fall off.'

'Exactly.' Firm of voice and manner: 'Now eat up like a good boy.'

Smaller voice but underpinned by defiance. 'Don't want it.'

'I shall count to three. If you are not eating by three then I shall have no alternative but to punish you.'

'Don't care.' He was mutinous, now, and the hand had dropped to the lap again.

'Nell pushed back her chair. 'Very well. Go into your bedroom.'

Head down, a sidelong look, he went, eagerly. Nell took off her cap, unpinned her hair, shook it free. Now for the pay-off. She had learned to play the preliminaries by ear; to follow the lead given by the client and if it was strong enough, take it from him. If he approved he would follow; if he did not he would take the lead again. So far, she thought, so good. It was standard childhood fantasy-fetish and nothing new. She would no doubt find him, dressing gown folded neatly on the bottom of the bed, pyjama pants around his ankles, back turned, waiting with anticipatory dread, his hands on his erection and rarin' to go.

She dawdled, stretching his anticipation to the point where what was to follow would be brief but intense. When she thought he had waited long enough she went in to the bedroom and all was as she had anticipated. He did not look round as she came in, but the brush was lying ready to hand, and as she picked it up – it was silver-backed, heavy, the bristles stiff and harsh – she resolved to go carefully; such bristles tore tender skin with ease.

'Bend over,' she ordered in her best stern nanny tones. He did so with alacrity but Nell paused: 'If you are ready to say you are sorry I will accept your apology.'

'Not sorry.'

It was gleefully defiant.

'Very well.' She laid on, but held back from using her full strength, reasoning that he was so near the edge it would not take more than four or five strokes, but although she could see his hand working strenuously, as she reached her seventh stroke there had been no release. She increased the force behind her blows but she had soon administered twelve strokes without the desired end-result. My God, she thought, he must be inured to this sort of thing, and hit him with all her strength. She heard him grunt, as if in satisfaction, but he was still masturbating furiously. Nell felt her competence was being threatened and leaned slightly to the left so as to catch a glimpse of his face; it was red and shiny and his mouth was open but

191

his erection was still rock hard. 'He must have been doing this for years,' she muttered to herself silently. Her arm was tiring and she had not counted on twenty strokes with a heavy brush. His buttocks were red and in several places showing a rash of tiny blood-filled pin pricks. He must have felt her falter for he straightened and turned to yell: 'Harder, damn you . . . what the hell am I paying you for?' Which was when she understood why he was having trouble reaching his climax. Between leaving her and being ready for her he had taken something; it was obvious from the glazed-cotton shine to his cheeks, the wild brilliance of his eyes with their huge pupils. Nell dropped the brush, stepped away from him.

'Not to waste my time, and that is what I am doing. If you have snorted or injected a drug – '

'Who the hell are you accusing of taking drugs! Don't you know who I am? I'll have your guts for garters if you don't do as you're told and what I am paying you for. Now get to it!'

Nell shook her head. He'd be flogging himself to death and she'd be flogging a man whose sexual response had been depressed by the drug he had taken, whatever it was. Probably cocaine, she thought. Wasn't it the rich man's pleasure-powder? She would have to beat him red raw before he got off.

'Insolent bitch!' Before she knew what he was about he had plucked the brush from her hand and was belabouring her with it, thwacking her with the force and rage of a man not used to being thwarted. She raised her arms to shield herself but not before he had caught her on the cheek, on the forehead and the crown of her head. The blows were delivered with the gathered strength of a well-built man and they hurt. As her face and head were protected he began beating her about the body, and when she twisted and turned to avoid them she caught her foot in the rug by the bed and fell to the floor. Instantly he bent down, not pausing for a second, and beat the bare flesh revealed by the gap between stocking and briefs. That hurt even more, and before she knew what she was doing, smarting from the effect of the blows and sickeningly angered by the smell of the soap, she reached up for that part of him which offered itself – his still rock-hard penis – and executed a manoeuvre taught her by the girls before she first went on the streets. She gripped it hard, twisted it first one way then the other and then jerked downwards, hard. 'It's a killer,' Paula had told her. Truthfully. His scream was agonised, and his delayed orgasm erupted, spraying wildly and continuing to dribble though his fingers as he clutched himself before falling to the floor where he curled up in the foetal position, moaning piteously. Nell scrabbled backwards, her thighs beginning to show red weals where he had hit her, her face smarting and her forehead sore, not to mention her head itself. She felt dizzy, sick from the smell of the soap, and the dull beginnings of a humiliated anger. Sod this for a lark, she thought, as she got to her feet. I don't care who the hell he is he has no right to do me grievous bodily harm. She limped for the door, for one of his blows had missed her thigh, hit her ankle bone and really did hurt, but before she could get there it opened and two men came in. The one in front she recognised for he was her contact; the other she had never seen before. The first motioned the second forward before jerking his head at Nell in the direction of the day nursery.

'What happened?' he asked coldly.

'You never told me the client was a junkie, that's what happened! He had either injected or snorted something and when I objected he got stroppy and began beating me!' Nell rubbed at her reddened thighs. 'So I stopped him the only way I knew how.'

His glance raked her. 'You will be seen to before you leave. Until then I must ask you to remain here.'

He asked, but he was telling. As the door shut behind him Nell sat down gingerly, wincing as the edge of the chair dug into a painful spot. Now what? she thought uneasily. The Tower? For dealing with someone in anything but the manner to which they are accustomed? Anxious dread was beginning to make her stomach flutter. Wasn't laying hands on someone of his eminence some sort of lèse-majesté? True, he was a very minor member of his family but minor or not, still a member. She put a hand to her aching forehead. A nursery fantasy, they said. A harshly strict nursemaid followed by some minor chastisement. Nothing untoward. Untoward! Nell thought aggrievedly. I could have ended up with a useless arm trying to help *him* reach orgasm.

She lay back in her chair and closed her eyes. Now I've done it, she thought. Probably ruined everything. Including my business. But how was I to know he was on drugs? Because I should have checked, that's why. Didn't Liz tell you *always* to check? But this recommendation was pukka; from a good client. So where did I go wrong? You should have known what you were getting into the minute they made you sign that undertaking, she answered herself. That always means a very important person. You should have acted on your instinct, which was to tell them you had changed your mind. Or you should have gone to Philip and asked his advice. But you didn't do that either, did you? The thought of a thousand pounds for a maximum of thirty minutes' work was all you could see. The man has *minders* for God's sake! The house wasn't empty at all. For all you know the whole thing was videotaped. She sat up in alarm, but a swift sharp sweep of the room showed her nothing that could be identified as a lens. Was there a mirror next door? She chewed a nail, closed her eyes, brought the room into focus. Yes, there was a small one above a chest of drawers to the right. Oh, my God. She was all of a sudden very afraid. A twenty-one-year-old out of her depth in waters where all the sharks were Great Whites. What have I got myself into here? Her mind chuntered. It was not meant to be like this.

Well, you wanted to be on your own, didn't you? Her mind sniffed. Miss Independent.

All right, Nell admitted wearily. I made a mistake. *Mea culpa.* I'm sorry. I've learned my lesson. It won't happen again.

Your desire to be in control got the better of your judgement, her mind lectured.

All I wanted was to be free at last. It felt so good.

Of course it did! Which is why danger always lurks behind it. Twenty months at this level and already you have come a cropper.

Too late she saw how arrogant she had been in believing herself to be ready to swim in shark infested waters without bothering to check with the lifeguards.

Fool! she raged at herself. How well Liz knew you. *Now* do you see why she asked Philip to keep an eye on you? She knew your 'freedom at any price' banner would cost you more than you could afford.

Nell shivered. The fire had burned low but the coldness she felt came from within. For the first time since escaping from the clutches of Mickey Shaugnessy, when she faced an uncertain future alone, she felt afraid, only this time was much worse. She was caught up, through her own folly, in something more more dangerous and powerful than a street pimp.

She put her face in her hands. Just get me out of this and I'll consult Philip at every turn, she prayed. I won't take a step unless he okays it. Please, just get me out of this.

She took her hands away, straightened quickly as the door opened.

Her broker came out of the night nursery, but paid her no attention and left her alone again. When he came back he had a third man with him. From the bag he was carrying he was a doctor.

Once more Nell was left alone to wait. Feeling cold she moved nearer to the fire. Once before she had felt like this; her against the world, but she had stuck to her guns in spite of the opposition and she had won. She still had the rights she had then. And – if he would take her back – there was still Philip. If he would overlook her arrogance she would take whatever advice he had to offer.

The door to the bedroom opened after a while and both men came back into the day nursery. In silence the doctor examined Nell's injuries. 'Superficial bruising,' he said, not to Nell but the broker. 'No real damage done.'

Like the broker, there was absolutely nothing to be deduced from either his face or his voice. Both were totally devoid of anything resembling feelings.

'Here . . .' the doctor took a tube of ointment from his bag. 'Apply this wherever you feel sore. It will help with the bruising.' He applied some in good faith. Nell winced as he smoothed it into her cheek. 'Hurt?' the doctor asked.

'A little.' She did not tell him that another man had hit her there and broken her cheekbone.

'It will probably be tender for a day or two, but there will be no trace once the bruising fades.' He nodded, shut his bag and the two men went to the door where they had a low-voiced conversation then the doctor left.

'Can I go now?' Nell requested politely.

'Once you have signed this.'

'I don't give receipts,' Nell said.

'This is not a receipt. It is an undertaking that you will not reveal to anyone – I repeat *anyone*, now or at any time in the future, what has happened here tonight.' His voice, his demeanour, were unchanged. Her little joke had not even been noticed.

'I never talk about my clients,' Nell said frostily.

'I am glad to hear it, Nevertheless, you will still sign this.'

Nell read it, saw it was typewritten and realised at once that this was not the first time someone like her had had to sign it. They are not minders, she thought, as she scrawled her fake signature 'Cleo Mondaine': they are keepers.

The broker glanced at it, returned it to her. 'Your real name,' he said. His voice and eyes made her skin crawl. She signed it Nell Jordan. They still did not have her true identity. A small triumph, but mine own, she thought. He took it, folded it and tucked it away in an inside pocket before laying in front of her a thick white envelope.

'In view of – developments, which I must tell you were quite unforeseen – your fee has been doubled to take account of your – er – injuries and distress. There will be no further contact.'

Nell concealed her elated relief, managing to say: 'I am delighted to hear it.'

He stood. 'No doubt you can find your own way home.'

Nell got her cloak and left. It was only in the cab that she began to shiver. Back home the cats came to greet her and she picked them up, buried her face in their fur, felt the throb of the little engines that produced their purr.

'You never judge, do you,' she said to them her voice all wobbly. 'Only love, and unconditionally. That man tonight looked at me as though I had been fished out from the bottom of a sewer, whilst minding a sick pervert who just happens to be a Somebody. What does that make *him*? I at least have no illusions as to what I do. How would he explain *his* occupation?'

She ran a hot bath, filled it with silky bubbles smelling of 'Y' and scrubbed herself pink. She had never come back from an assignment feeling this way; dirty, sub-human, unfit for human consumption. She could not rid herself of the contempt in – she thought of him as The Minder – the pale blue eyes that had left her with a residue she could not seem to scrub away.

Well, she thought, as she pulled the plug, look on it as the end of your running in period, and don't let it put you off course. What you do is no worse than what he does; clearing away other people's messes just so he can appear in some future Honours List. *That* makes him better than you? Everyone has their own level beneath which they regard everything as untouchable. I was his. He was mine. I'd rather do what I do than be the paid-lackey he is. What right has he to look down on me? He's pandering, isn't he? But just because that perverted little creep belongs to Snob Heaven whatever he does is 'amusement' while what I do is despicable.

By the time she was in bed, the heavy cats acting as hot water bottles against her feet, her anger had cooled and she was able to look at the situation without wanting to take an axe to it. There really was only one course to take. She must call Philip, eat humble pie, explain what had happened and ask to be forgiven and reinstated in his good graces. He would exploit her humiliation, of course, but she could cope with that because what she would get for it was not only invaluable it was essential. She just did not know enough or know the right people as yet. That would come with time and experience. Until then, Philip was a necessary evil.

If he was surprised to hear from her it did not show, nor did he display any enthusiasm, just his usual silky sarcasm: 'To what do you owe the pleasure?'

She had rehearsed a speech designed to leave her with as much credibility as she could manage but discarded it in the face of his obvious amusement. She gave it to him straight. 'I have got myself into an awkward situation, through my own fault. I'd like to talk to you about it but not over the telephone. Will you come round?'

As always his osmosis picked up every last vibe. 'Twenty minutes,' he said. When he arrived Nell apologised nicely and sincerely, making no bones about her own stupidity. 'I should have checked with you', she finished, 'And I am very sorry I didn't. Liz was right; I do still need guidance in certain matters. Will you forgive me and continue to supply yours?'

'Just so long as you *never* refer to me as Daddy.'

Nell giggled and she was so relieved she did what she had never done before. Hugged him.

'I see you *have* landed yourself in the mire,' was his only comment. 'Now tell me all.'

When she had done so he sighed. 'Your first mistake has to be what an American lover of mine used to call "a doozy".' This particular man is a no-no. I thought he was still incarcerated in the depths of the Highlands in what is euphemistically referred to as a clinic but is in reality a very expensive prison for troublesome members of our so-called better families.'

'What worries me is if he still has the power to see me off.'

'Not in this day and age, and he is a minor in the scheme of things since he descends on the distaff side. Tell me, how did they get on to you?' She explained. He nodded. 'Yes, a very up-market firm of solicitors who act for the family. Describe this – minder.' Again Nell did so. 'He looked and spoke to me as though I was dirt beneath his feet.'

Philip's smile boded ill. 'Not surprising since his job is to sweep up the manure; he is a payer off of people bought and paid for, such as you. I would still like to know where he learned about you. Normally, it is the experienced S&M practitioners who are allowed to go and play, and you are hardly that.'

'They told me he liked the nursery fantasy and to be beaten with a brush, but not for too long. That it was child's play – literally.'

'They? Who else did you see?'

'Another man; younger, very smooth, very – polished. He said it was only an occasional thing but that a professional was called for. And I was to keep my mouth shut afterwards. They made more fuss about that than anything else.'

'Naturally.' Philip was pursing his lips as he always did when deep in thought. 'Leave it with me. There is something not quite kosher about this. I will make further enquiries.'

In the face of Nell's instant unease: 'Trust me,' he said, to which Nell replied: 'In all honesty, I should have done so in the first place.'

'Well, you have learned your lesson, haven't you?' It was in no way sympathetic.

Nell nodded. 'I won't make *that* mistake again.'

A week later Philip came again. 'You were set up,' he announced.

Nell stared.

'Do you remember, at Liz's funeral, my finding you talking to a woman I told you was an S&M specialist.'

'Deedee somebody. Yes, I remember her. You told me she had given up the Life on making a spectacular marriage.'

'Insofar as she does not service clients herself she has. What she has not done, however, is relinquish her interest – fifty per cent they tell me – in an agency which specialises in supplying S&M practitioners. She comes back from Australia twice a year to check up on her investment. The gentleman who engaged you has it seems, been using her agency for some years now. They recommended you.'

'But – I'm not with any agency – and it was an existing client who – '

'No matter. He took the bait and so did you. Evidently the client has been for some time becoming much more difficult to satisfy.

'Naturally. A man on drugs has great difficulty – '

'I am aware of the sexual dysfunction caused by drugs. Which he has, of course.'

'Then why don't they stop him!'

'In whose interest?'

Nell's jaw fell slightly.

'Exactly. He is of no use to anyone and when he eventually does overdose the only reaction will be a sigh of relief. He is sequestered for most of the time but every now and again – to show he is still capable of being part of the scheme of things, he is brought down to London and put on show. As a treat they allow him to indulge his fantasy.'

'But – ' Nell was still puzzled, 'Why me?'

'Why not you? Liz's protégée.'

'Liz is dead!'

'But you are not.'

'Oh, now, Philip . . .'

'Just because *you* do not bear grudges does not mean that everyone else does not either. That woman hated Liz – and I mean *hated*. Resented. Envied. You name it and she felt it. She could not do anything to Liz, poor darling, but you were

199

handy and obviously oh, so new. It was revenge at the remove, so to speak, but it must have afforded her some satisfaction, even if from a distance. She is back Down Under. And long may she stay there. But you see what I mean about the importance of checking what you are told?'

Nell nodded. Her voice was flat when she said: 'You just never have any idea when somebody is out to get you, do you? I mean – it never entered my mind.'

'The title of one of Liz's favourite songs, if you remember.'

Nell's smile was soft. 'Yes.' She sat back, drank deep of her drink. 'How well she knew me . . .'

Philip shook his head. 'Lamb to the Slaughter.' That he had heard nothing, not even a whisper that the man concerned was in town, was something he kept to himself. It would not do to allow Nell to realise that this net of informants was now showing the occasional tear, allowing juicy morsels to slip through and escape. He now needed the kudos he received from each piece of information supplied. He had kept track of her these past weeks, prepared to wait her out until such time as she made the inevitable mistake. The nine weeks it had taken had been longer than he might have expected for someone so relatively inexperienced and young enough to think she knew it all. But better late than never. And it had given her a nasty fright. He decided to let her stew for a while in its unpleasant juices. The retarded creep she had been sent to service was not important enough in the scheme of things to cause the kind of retribution she obviously feared. He decided not to explain that the business of signing an undertaking not worth the paper it was written on was all front. The days when such a minor infringement of their rules resulted in two Scotland Yard detectives escorting you out of the country were long gone. The power of the tabloids had done for that. The power conferred by the people who read them. But he was not about to tell Nell that. She had to learn her lesson in a way that she would never forget.

'What about the drugs?' Nell asked, revealing another source of concern.

'Nothing to do with you. A separate matter entirely.'

It was as though he had lifted a millstone.

'Thank you,' she said, offering him her gratitude polished to a shine. 'In future, *all* new referrals will in turn be referred to you. Now, can you stay to lunch? I've got some thick lamb cutlets . . .'

That had been her first mistake, filed under the heading of youthful arrogance. She could not have filed her second in the same place, so she put it down to the fact that she had allowed her heart to rule her head and failed to follow her motto: DON'T TRUST NOBODY.

She had been coming back from visiting a client for the last time. He had not been a young man when she had acquired him; now he was crippled with arthritis and he had told her he would not see her again since he was no longer able to do what he liked with her body, which was to sketch then paint it. The sex had been minimal once he had seen her nude; from then on she spent her visits posing. This time he had been forced to accept that his twisted fingers could no longer hold a piece of charcoal. It had been melancholy, and Nell was feeling depressed as she got off the train at Paddington to look for a taxi. Searching the traffic she did not register the young girl struggling with the big, tattooed man, until the girl called desperately: 'Somebody help me, please . . . help me . . .'

When Nell looked she was the only one who did so except those at a safe distance. Everybody else averted their eyes and removed their person from the danger. The man was very big, with shoulders like a scrum-half and a shaven head like a bullet. In one ear he wore three gold rings.

Nell knew what the girl was at first glance. It was all in the thin wrist clamped in one huge fist, the fear on the childish face, the panic in the reedy voice. She saw herself, only a few short years ago, in the clutches of Mickey Shaughnessy, heard her own voice pleading: 'Don't, Mickey . . . please, don't hit me,' which brought back echoes of a still younger Nell begging her father: 'Don't put me down there, Father, please . . . don't put me down there . . . there are rats, I know there are . . . *please*, Father, *please* . . .' Nobody had answered *her* pleas. She had been punished. Again and again and again.

Without consciously making the decision, for a swamping

rush of anger took over her mind, drowning her rigorously exercised and relentlessly maintained rationality, she found herself heading straight for them, where she said in the voice of authority: 'Let that girl go at once before I call the police!'

The man did not even bother to look at her. 'Fuck off,' he said.

'I most certainly will not, but if you know what is good for you you will!'

This time he turned his head to look at her, looked her up, looked her down and then laughed.

Nell gritted her teeth. The girl threw her a look of frantic appeal, all the while struggling to free herself. She could not have been more than fifteen; her body was still that of a child, her budding breasts, still pubescent, and scrawny thighs were not shown off to advantage by the skin-tight black lycra cut-off top and leggings she was wearing. There was a five inch gap between the end of the leggings and her grubby white plastic stiletto heels, while around one bony ankle she had a thin gold chain. Her badly bitten nails were painted and so was her immature face under straw-yellow hair with an inch-wide black parting. Plastic multi-coloured ear-rings dangled to shoulders that were skin and bone. She looked as if a good meal was something she had never been introduced to.

'I will not warn you again,' Nell said crisply but in tones which had him, as she had intended, turning to face her, whereupon she brought up the hand-bag size spray of Mace she had bought last time she was in New York and gave it a short, sharp but devastating burst. He let out a howl of agony as he let go of the girl's hand and clapped both hands over his eyes.

Nell seized the girl's hand. 'Run!' she commanded. 'Come on . . . to that cab there . . . the one by the poster . . . *come on.*' She bundled the girl into the taxi, gave an address in West Kensington and then turned to peer out of the back window. The man was bent double, obviously in agony, but nobody was taking any notice. There was a wide circle around him as though he was surrounded by an impenetrable force-field. By the time the police got there – and there was no sign of so much as a single constable – Nell and the girl would be long gone. Just as well, for the use of Mace was illegal in England.

Never had she expected to have to use it outside the USA, and not in broad daylight, for it was only five o'clock on a Sunday afternoon. The girl was weeping noisily, so Nell handed her a tissue. 'It's all right,' she said consolingly, 'we are safe now. He won't be coming after you.'

The girl only blubbered all the more, wailing something about how he would kill her when he got hold of her and it hadn't been her fault that business was slow. Sunday afternoon always was a dead spot on account of all the punters being at home sleeping off their lunch. She'd told him and told him but he wouldn't have it and she didn't know what she was going to do now because she daren't go back to him.

'I should hope not,' Nell said warmly. 'You are far too young to be on the streets. How old are you, anyway?'

'Eighteen . . .' China blue eyes attempted to stare Nell down and failed. 'Fifteen,' she admitted sullenly.

'And how did you get started? By running away from home?'

Round-eyed: 'How did you know?'

'You've got a Liverpool accent and running away is how many girls get started on the game.'

'I didn't have no home to run from,' the girl sniffed. 'I been in care since I was eight. Anybody with any sense gets away from there soon as they can.'

She wiped her eyes, looked out of the window. 'Here . . . where're you takin' me?'

'Home with me.'

The girl stared.

'It's all right,' Nell soothed reassuringly. 'I only want to help. You can stay with me tonight and then tomorrow we'll go and see some people who will help you get away from men like your pimp.'

She told the cab driver to stop at Lancaster Gate, and after paying him flagged down another which she told to take them home. That way, there would be no easy way of tracing her should somebody decide to press charges.

The most important thing was to get this stick-insect of a girl back home, give her a bath, feed her up and then see she ended up in the hands of one of the many charitable bodies Liz had been involved with as part of her 'get a little, give a little' policy. Liz saved my life, she thought to herself. Maybe I can give my little by saving this one. Fifteen! she thought. I thought I was bad enough at seventeen, but fifteen! Dear God . . . that's just about Margaret's age. Pain spurted, as it always did at that name, like biting down on a bad tooth. Maybe this is for you too, Margaret, she thought. There is little enough I can do for you, try as I might, and I can't go on for ever thinking 'if only things had been different'. They weren't and there was nothing I could do about it then anyway. We would not even have had what little time we did have, and I promised our mother . . .

'Where're we goin'?' whined the girl, growing more suspicious.

'I told you, my house.'

'But I don't know you . . . what you goin' to do with me?'

At the fearful note in the girl's voice Nell said cheerfully: 'Give you a bath and a good meal first of all. Then after a good night's sleep we'll see what is best for you.'

'I ain't goin' back into care!'

'I have no power to see that you do. I am not a social worker.'

'What do you want with me, then?'

'I told you – to help.'

The girl was flummoxed. Help was something she was obviously not used to. Wasn't I suspicious where Elizabeth was concerned? Nell remembered. I too was sure there was a catch somewhere.

When they got home the girl was silent; awe-stricken if her expression was anything to go by. While she was in the bath Nell put her clothes in the washer, for they had not seen soap and water for a long time. She gave Kim – for that was the name the girl gave her though she refused to give any more than that – a towelling robe to wear while Nell cooked her what she had asked for: bacon, egg and chips, which she demolished on the double along with two mugs of well-sugared tea.

'With an appetite like yours how on earth are you so thin?' Nell asked in astonishment.

'Dunno . . . I never been fat, but I was always hungry at

home. Me mum didn't like cookin' so we was brought up on crisps an' things like that.'

She pushed her plate away. 'Gotta fag?'

'I don't smoke.'

'Where's me clothes. I 'ad a packet . . .'

'I washed them. The cigarettes are over there, on the worktop.'

'Oh . . . ta . . . What you wash me clothes for? They wasn't dirty.'

'Habit, I suppose,' lied Nell. 'I always wash mine when I've had a bath.' The clothes had been filthy, especially the underwear. What ought to have been white was grey and the black stretch top and pants were stained with food and God knew what else.

The girl lit up, dragged smoke deep into her lungs with the expertise of one who had been hooked on nicotine for years, and then blew it out on a sigh of satisfaction. 'That's better.'

'So tell me, how did you get started on the game?' Nell asked.

'I told yer. I ran away. 'Ow else was I supposed to earn a livin'?'

At Nell's look: 'I 'ad a friend and she was already doin' the business so I teamed up with 'er. She knew this man who was bein' sent down to the Scrubs for GBH and she said we could stay in 'is flat in Lambeth. While 'e was in jail she used to go and see 'im and she took me. When 'e come out he said I could be one of 'is girls . . . and he was out sooner than I expected on account of the charge of GBH was dropped 'cos the victim wouldn't press charges.'

'Was it a woman?'

''ow d'yer know that?'

'I know someone who worked with prostitutes and their pimps.'

Nell had heard that story dozens of times; had known girls who, even though beaten almost to a pulp by their pimp, refused to press charges because they had persuaded themselves that once the beating was over it was a matter of regret on his part and he was filled with remorse. She had never understood the attitude of so many girls to their pimps, which was that it was better to be beaten than to be ignored. Perhaps because she had had years of experience of the latter. When her father had been in one of his moods a whole week or more could go by without him so much as looking at her, never mind speaking to her.

'Why do you stay with him if he beats you?' she asked Kim.

''Cos there's a lot as is far worse. An' 'e don't allow nobody to get away with nothin'. Some punters'll try and do the business without comin' across with the readies. They only do it once, with Eddie . . .'

'Why was he beating you this afternoon?'

''E said I was lyin' to 'im . . . that I'd earned more than I told 'im I 'ad . . .' Kim's grin was slyly triumphant. ''N I 'ad, an'all . . .' She giggled at her bit of one upmanship.

'How long have you been on the streets?' Nell asked slowly, perceiving that instead of a younger edition of herself, she had picked up another Jenny.

'Since I was thirteen.'

'I can help you if you want to leave them.'

'To do wot? I 'ated school and never went unless I was made to. I got no qualifications, no trainin' and the first thing they'll do is send me back into care.' Kim shook her head. 'No way! I ain't *never* goin' back into another 'ome. Nobody who ain't been in one knows what it's like.'

I do, thought Nell, who remembered how much she too had hated it.

'Well, you can stay here tonight and we'll decide what to do in the morning, what is best for you,' she said.

'An' what's in it for you?'

Nell met the knowing eyes. Yes, definitely another Jenny. It would be as well, tonight, to lock up anything of value.

'Only the knowledge of a good deed well done,' she answered.

'What's a good deed?' Kim asked innocently. 'I ain't never seen one o'them.'

Which she proved by leaving early the next morning, before Nell was awake, and taking with her the little carriage clock which stood on the mantel, as well as the silver cigarette box which had belonged to Liz, and the small silver sugar bowl in which Nell had kept her spare keys.

She had also had the cheek to make herself a pot of tea and a couple of slices of toast. Needless to say there was no sign of a thank-you note.

'So much for my good deed for the day,' Nell said to the cats, as she washed Kim's dirty dishes in plenty of scalding water. 'Philip has told me time and time again that I am wrong in judging people by my own standards. Just because I was desperate to leave the streets and grab the first decent chance offered does not mean that every other girl in my position wanted to do the same. In your own experience you have known girls who have managed to escape from the most vicious of pimps only to be back again within a month or two. You have to accept that there are some girls who actually *like* it. And let's face it, what is it that you do which makes you any better than that little girl who must have thought she'd got hold of a real downy one? I was only trying to help, she told herself aggrievedly.

Someone who obviously did not either want or need it. Your clock and silver will end up in some pawn shop and the money go to placate her pimp, the one she seemed to be so afraid of. The same one she has without doubt gone back to.

Nell scrubbed viciously at the cup Kim had used. There had been a heavy lipstick imprint on it. In a sudden spasm of rage at her own still lingering naïveté she smashed it against the side of the sink, threw the pieces in her waste-bin. She was not angry with Kim. She was angry with herself for being taken in yet again.

She could hear her father's voice saying icily: 'You simply will never let well enough alone, will you, Eleanor?'

'Like you did?' she asked him savagely. 'You and your week-long silences and curt dismissals of me when I had no one and nowhere else to turn to. You and your strictures. I wasn't even allowed to bring a friend back home for tea. When you finally allowed me to, you frightened her so much she spread the story and nobody would so much as come near me after that. The most trivial annoyance would result in your silent treatment. Is it any wonder I feel a need to help since never once did it ever occur to you that I needed any?'

Oh, what's the use, she thought, drying her hands and surveying her once more immaculate kitchen. I picked a wrong'un, that's all.

That fifteen-year-old is harder than you will ever be, but you still assumed that she was what she seemed to be: in need of help. And one of the first things you must do before she or her pimp get the chance to help themselves is change all your locks.

As she dried her hands, massaged them with emollient cream she said to her beloved cats: 'It seems I am a lousy judge of character. Either that or I project my feelings on to other people. Whatever, that is the last time I ever intervene in anybody else's business. From now on I mind nobody's but my own.'

BOOK THREE

1990

12

When the alarm went off Nell groped for the button to turn it off and at once the buzzer became a voice intoning the weather forecast. She yawned, stretched, realised that there was no heavy weight on her legs because the cats, with their usual courtesy, had silently left her and gone downstairs and out into the garden to do their necessaries. Now, as they heard the buzzer, Nell heard their collar bells as they came upstairs to say good morning, and how much they would appreciate breakfast. They were well-trained and their manners were perfect. When they came in from the garden they washed and groomed themselves and each other and then sat on the bottom stair until the buzzer told them Nell was awake.

'Good morning, my loves,' she said to them, giving each a scratch behind the ears and under the throat. 'Let's see what we've got today.' She put on her dressing gown and slid her feet into fluffy scuffs. By the time she got into the kitchen both cats were sitting expectantly by their bowls, but first Nell put the kettle on before getting out the diced kidney she had prepared the night before, filling their china bowls, putting last night's dirty ones in the sink to soak. When she raised the kitchen blinds she saw it was raining, and heavily.

'Oh, damn! Just as well I don't have far to go.' She made herself a pot of tea, covered it with a quilted cosy and then went back upstairs to shower and dress. By 8.15 a.m. she was back downstairs again wearing an unfashionably long heather mixture tweed skirt and a plain lambswool sweater the colour of peat. Her hair was scraped back from her face and coiled into a netted bun. She looked at least ten years older than her current thirty-one, aided and abetted by her far from sheer stockings – of a dull verging-on-grey shade and her 'sensible' shoes. She made herself a couple of slices of wholemeal toast, spread them with butter and Frank Cooper Oxford marmalade, and ate her breakfast while reading the paper – the *Daily Telegraph*, as befitted the day-time life she now lived.

Ten years ago, some five months after Liz had died, she had moved house, selling the converted coach-house for another, smaller mews house in a quiet cul-de-sac behind Wigmore Street. She had bought it because in trying to sell it, the agent had emphasised how quiet it was, especially her house, since those on either side rarely saw their owners, the one being an internationally known fashion model and the other an actor who spent most of his time abroad making films. The other side of the cobbled court was the back of houses. It was very much like Liz's little house except that it had only the one bedroom, but it had a cellar, dry and roomy, and Philip – who had no suitable room in his flat, huge as it was, to store wine, kept his there, paying to have racks fitted to two walls.

In the years Nell had lived there the model had long gone, but the new tenant, a photographer, was another rarely-seen neighbour, while the actor still made his living abroad. There were only the five houses; the bottom half of the mews was occupied by a storage warehouse. Now and then big vans came either to load or unload cardboard boxes. It suited Nell admirably, since there was no one to peep through curtains and see her leaving on an assignment at night, and her day-time cover was that of a single lady (the polite term for a spinster) who lived alone and worked part-time as a doctor's receptionist. She had seen the job advertised in the window of an employment agency in Wigmore Street. A part-time receptionist, three days a week – Tuesday, Wednesday and Thursday – for a Wimpole Street surgeon, 9.30 a.m. to 5 p.m. Experience in the keeping of medical records essential. Salary commensurate with experience.

She had taken to walking around those parts of London where she had decided it would be convenient to live; somewhere in the centre since she did not want to have to travel too far. She took a lot of taxis and if she lived as far as out

Hampstead, say, it would cost her a fortune since she never drove her own car to assignments. The little mews house also attracted her in that, unlike Liz's, where one had to park outside the house, this one had a garage. She had been coming from the estate agent when she saw the job advertised, and since she had come to believe that her meeting Liz had been engineered by fate, she likewise so labelled these two events and looked no further.

It had been in her mind for some time to get a part-time job; something to do in the day-time. Liz had always slept late, but she had been much older. Unless she was very late back from an assignment, which was rare unless it was an all-nighter, Nell was usually up by nine o'clock, and after doing the housework and any other chores had found herself with a lot of time to fill, not all of which could be spent on either shopping, afternoon visits to the movies, or perambulations around museums, etc. Three days a week was an ideal solution; it was work she knew since as soon as she was old enough her father had co-opted her to keep his records and his files in order. One look at the consultant with the vacancy and she knew it would be a doddle. His practice was all private, his clientele the kind who spent Friday to Monday in the country, thus allowing him to do his NHS stint on those days, which was why he did not need a receptionist more than three days a week. Nell created the Eleanor Jordan who applied for the job from the inside out. She added years to her age by wearing the sort of clothes a quiet, introverted late-thirties spinster would wear, co-opting the clear-glass spectacles she wore whenever a fantasy called for them. Coupled with the unflattering hairstyle and the quiet but competent manner she adopted, together with the much-expanded experience she claimed to have acquired working for her father – and here she said that since he had died, some ten months before, she had found herself at a loose end; it was not that she needed to work rather that she needed to occupy her time – she made a convincing case.

The consultant, early fifties, urbane, sleek, took one look and leapt at his chance. She was exactly what he was looking for. Neat, tidy, probably effortlessly efficient and, best of all, no longer young and no head-turner. Neat little figure, but her clothes did nothing to advertise the fact. She would in no way put up the backs of his clients, women for the most part and of an age that regarded younger women (like his last receptionist, for instance, who had been twenty-six, blonde, good-looking and seen as a threat by his patients who were sure he was in sexual thrall to her and thereby jealous) as emphasising the reason for their visit to her employer, since his field was plastic surgery. This quiet mouse would be most reassuring, and after the mess he had almost ended up in with the blonde, who had grown greedy and grasping, it would be a relief to be able to go back to a strictly working-relationship. To be sure, he suggested a month's trial.

By the end of it Nell had established her credibility to such an extent that the good doctor could not wait to make the arrangement permanent, and she had been with him ever since. She was 'Eleanor' to him, but he was never anything other than 'Mr' to her. Both were admirably suited. The clients were reassured by her, she was never late, never absent, and she was every bit as efficient as he had somehow known she would be. His records were in perfect order, his files scrupulously maintained, she even sent his bills out on time and his trust was such that he let her do his office accounts: his accountant did the rest.

Best of all, she was so self-effacing that once out of sight she was invariably out of mind. He had no idea where she lived, except that it was alone but for two cats. He knew she had independent means but no idea what they might be. Nor did he care. Eleanor Jordan impinged on his consciousness only in his consulting rooms, though he was not above boasting about his 'treasure' when he heard colleagues bemoaning the inferior quality of the receptionists they had to employ. He neither knew nor cared what her life was outside the three days she worked for him – or indeed if she had one. As long as she ran his consultancy like a beautifully maintained engine he was content. At Christmas he bought her a pot plant or a box of chocolates or both, and where she went on her annual holidays he could not have said, though he always heartily enquired. Vaguely he would remember something about a quiet hotel in Eastbourne or Torquay or some deadly dull place like that: the sort of place a middle-aged spinster would go. He so rarely looked at Nell with any sort of interest that it never occurred to him that had he seen her under the magnifying mirror in his surgery, he would have seen the unlined skin of a woman much, much younger than he believed her to be. But her unobtrusiveness meant that she became part of the furniture and thus taken for granted, exactly as Nell wanted. She knew that appearance mattered and that people took you for what they saw, which was why her clothes were drab, her spectacle frames unflattering, her hair likewise. And she never wore makeup to the office. As the years went by she creatively added to Eleanor, spraying grey streaks in her hair and pencilling in faint lines at the side of her eyes. Both were easily washed away when it was time to change roles and play Cleo. And here too, she created a whole new persona.

Cleo had jet black hair, short, glossy as a raven's plumage and cut as Liz's had been, so that a shake of the head was all it needed to fall effortlessly into place. An Italian wigmaker made the wig from real hair provided by a newly professed nun, and it had cost a fortune, but when worn, changed Nell into Cleo in such a way that never in a million years would anybody have suspected that they were the same woman. She aided and abetted the transformation by wearing contact lenses which changed her eyes to the deep green of pond depths, and with the black hair and green eyes she made up her face to bring out the best of both.

At first she was the new Cleo only to new clients, but as time went on and new clients became old clients, there came a time when none of them had ever known her as anything else. She had grown into the part, even as the money deposited at regular intervals in a numbered bank account held by a bank in Zurich had grown. Both were considerable performers.

Her income from her job was taxed (she did the PAYE herself) at source, and to account for her house she had put a sum into a unit trust which provided an income from which she paid her mortgage. The Mercedes Sports had gone (too expensive a luxury). Cleo now drove a Golf GTi. Not so Miss Jordan. She was never seen at the wheel of a car. She took the bus or tube or walked. To work, for instance, only ten brisk minutes away.

She had, as Liz had advised long ago, never taken her client list to extreme numbers. That way she could juggle their appearances in her life with the minimum of difficulty. She could also afford it, since some time before she had come to an arrangement with an American client, among whose interests was a Madison Avenue art gallery which he had gone into on the advice of his accountants as he needed a tax loss. Unfortunately, the so-called 'critics' had decided to take up the first artist the gallery showed – a pretentious shit, according to the client, who produced indecipherable messes acclaimed as 'great art' but was quite unable to use a pencil and sketch a likeness of anything except a dollar bill.

'He's a con artist,' the client told Cleo as they rode downtown in his limousine to the Friday night opening. She had arrived on Concorde earlier that day. 'The whole damned thing is another case of the Emperor's new clothes. My only consolation is that it won't last. They never do. This town eats up five-minute wonders by the shovelful. I only have to stop in, you understand – it wouldn't look right if I didn't and that would start the questions rather than me turning up with you. Your cover is an English gallery owner interested in – *maybe* – bringing the artist to London. Just mix and mingle and don't say much, just look thoughtful. OK?'

'All right.'

'Thirty minutes tops then we'll be on our way . . .'

Fortunately she was dressed for the occasion in an ivory silk Valentino dress spotted in a window last time she was in Milan and bought there and then. She had a client whose thing was white or ivory – his fantasy was deflowering virgins – and he would bear its outrageous cost. But it was just right for a gallery opening, so were Liz's eighteen inches of pearls, obviously the real thing, as were those in her ears. And she smelled of Balmain's *Ivoire*.

'Classy . . . very classy . . .' the client had said admiringly, being a self-made man who had come up the hard way but now, after thirty years had it easy, except his wife would have been horrified to learn about his penchant for cross-dressing. She was a straight up, lying back, missionary-position-only woman who, like a good Catholic, believed sex was for procreation only and so did not seem to see her husband's forays into the sexual jungle, although she knew of them. 'Men,' she would grimace, and leave it at that. She was his wife, would always be his wife and had produced five children to prove it.

The gallery was crowded with the kind of people who read *Vanity Fair* and would not have been seen dead in anything not sporting the right label because otherwise who would recognise them? The women were clothes hangers and the men custom-made. Except for one. Cleo was conscious of his stare from the moment, looking round the dazzlingly white room – 'white lets the pictures blaze forth' the artist had gushed modestly – she had encountered his eyes. Black as obsidian and shiny as varnish. And steady. Admiringly steady.

She never *ever* accepted overtures from men when out with a client. *He* was paying for her time and he got it. But no matter where she went, gazing at the talentless daubs on the walls or trying to make sense of a scramble of copper which the tiny card it bore said was entitled *Passion*, she was conscious of those hard, shiny eyes, though she never looked his way again. She held one glass of inferior champagne – she never drank while working – and after discreetly checking the time by the watch of a man standing nearby whose raised arm bared it, began to drift in the direction of her client. He was in a group of men with their heads together, which she did not approach, just passed by in such a way that he became aware of her perfume, looked up instantly and caught her eye. He nodded slightly then dipped his head equally slightly towards the door. She left as she had entered, without speaking to a soul, though she had been conscious of interest. The client had vaguely muttered something about 'a London art gallery . . . maybe a spring showing . . .' but never actually introduced her, which was the way she preferred it. People could surmise all they liked as long as they did not actually know. Her other New York client was much more discreet, never being seen in public with her, since it was his wife who held the purse strings. One hint of what he did with Cleo and he would be strangled with them. Which was why the concentrated stare made her uneasy. Did he know her? Had he heard of her? Recognise her, perhaps? Seen her with another client – one he perhaps knew. Her ability to charge highly for her services depended as much on her discretion as her talents; it would be fatal to become a *known* whore, for that would mean any man she saw would be tagged – in some cases fatally. So she left the gallery and waited under the awning for the client's limo to be brought. By the time it came he had joined her, and as they drove away there was no sign of the Man with the Penetrating Eyes, though Nell took a discreet look through the back window to be absolutely sure. They drove to a small, secluded house in the Village; the client's hideaway, where he kept his cross-dressing clothes and a mirrored room wherein his fantasies were enacted.

They went straight upstairs to it, but while she kept her clothes on, he stripped naked before going into the bathroom to shower. Once that was done Cleo, using an old-fashioned cut-throat razor as Philip had carefully taught her how, shaved him as close as was possible without taking off his top layer of skin. There had to be no blueness showing once the foundation was applied. This was done while he sat naked in front of the theatrical-type dressing table, every bulb lit and a large magnifying mirror placed over his face so that she could work on it. First of all a thick yet light cream under the eyes to blank out the deep shadows there.

Once that was done to her satisfaction she did the rest of his face; first foundation, then a transluscent powder with a hint of sparkle, a delicate flush of colour highlighting the cheekbones. The foundation and the powder were taken right down his throat, shoulders and body to where the false breasts began, and Nell carefully applied extra glitter to his cleavage. Then she did his eyes: base, shadow – three colours – eyeliner and a very real pair of false eyelashes top and bottom which she then emphasised with two coats of mascara. Finally she did his mouth, using a brush she had searched every cosmetics hall in New York for, finally finding it in a Third Avenue speciality store which sold theatrical makeup. It had a sharply chiselled edge and enabled her to invent a pair of bee-stung lips; though his own were quite full they lacked definition and he liked a cupid's bow. Finished, she turned him to the mirror and he admired himself, making little *moues* with his lips and flirting with his eyes. Already they had taken on a coquettish sparkle. Then she brought his 'clothes'. A boned silk basque, strapless and hooking up down the front, edged in black lace frills and bearing eight-inch long suspenders. It was the vivid scarlet of blood. With this he wore black nylons and specially made fetish shoes with incredibly high heels and ankle straps. Fuck-me shoes. They were – as were all the clothes he wore for his fantasies – specially made to order. The last item was the wig; blonde, bouffant and stiff with lacquer. Nell helped him into each of them, while he pursed his lips, arched his neck, smoothed his body, put his hands under the cushions of his false, latex breasts, complete down to large brown nipples, posed, hip-sprung, feet in model-stance as he paraded up and down, the final accessory being a cigarette in a long jewelled holder and a chiffon scarf. Nell thought he looked so grotesque as to be a total turn-off but as he flirted with his image in the mirror it became obvious from the way he kept having to ease his panties, that he was becoming aroused. Once Nell saw his erection protruding it was the signal for her to go into her act. She left the room silently, he so intent on his mirror image he did not see her go, but when she returned it was noisily, flinging open the door and erupting like a geyser after fifteen seconds of shocked silence. Then she proceeded to flay him verbally, laughing at him, jeering at his feminine pretensions, laughing at the gargoyle he was, her voice gradually changing from mockery to savagery. This latter would have the effect of turning him on even more, so that his erection would be so hard it would be purple with effort. Which was her cue to taunt: 'You are about as much like a real woman as a wax model, and you are probably not much of a man, either. I'll bet you don't have any idea what to do with *that*, for instance,' pointing to his bobbing penis.

'Don't I!' he would bellow, and leap on her. It was always tumultuous, always brief, for he was so aroused that no sooner did he get inside her than he climaxed. She obviously satisfied him, though, for his orgasm was such that he collapsed, totally deflated, before rolling off her. When his breathing had quietened he said appreciatively: 'Jesus, Cleo. You certainly know how to get a guy going and then get him off in no uncertain fashion! I'll not be able to use my dick for a month except to pee!' He turned his head to look at her. 'You play my game better than anybody I've ever played with. I'd like to put you on my payroll. Whaddya say?'

'I deal only in cash, you know that.'

'Sure . . . goes without saying. I mean I pay you a retainer up front then I get first call on your services.'

'How much?' Nell asked shrewdly.

'Hundred thou a year?'

Nell concealed her elation, seemed to think it over. 'All right,' she said finally. 'I'm prepared to give it a try.'

'That's my girl. I'll send the money round to you tomorrow morning. But I get first dibs for it, understand?'

'Yes.'

He nodded, satisfied. 'I like the best and I don't mind what I pay for it and in my book you're the best I've had.' He checked his Patek-Philippe, lying on the nightstand by the bed. 'Shit! I gotta go. We're goin' to the country for the weekend and if I'm late there'll be an inquest. I'll be in touch, OK?'

'All right.'

She helped him out of his bustier and stockings, cleaned his face first with cream then with a mild tonic, putting the eyelashes back in their little box and the wig on its block in a cupboard behind the mirrors. Then he showered and dressed. He left first, and after rinsing out the stockings and hanging them over the hot towel rail – being specially made to his size they cost fifty dollars a pair – Nell left the place as tidily anonymous as it had been when they arrived before taking a cab back to her hotel, where her suite was booked for the weekend. There, she became Nell Jordan again.

She took a bath, performed her usual hygienics and put on a favourite pair of jade green silk pyjamas, old as the hills since they had been bought by Liz who did not suit the colour, and passed on as unwanted. But Nell loved them, not only the feel of the silk against her skin but the link with someone who, even now, she missed. Her suite had a kitchen so she made herself a cup of coffee and took out the roast beef sandwich she had thoughtfully bought from Woolf's on Lexington Avenue, earlier that evening. It was six inches of sliced beef on rye and it had coleslaw, tomato and pickles. She curled up in front of the television and watched an episode from an umpteenth rerun of 'M.A.S.H.' while she ate, licking her fingers beatifically. New York deli sandwiches were an art form and one she adored. She followed hers with a slice of New York Cheesecake, which clung to the roof of her mouth and went down a treat with the coffee. As she went to rinse her cup and plate she saw it had begun to rain. Let it, she thought luxuriously. I am not going anywhere . . . The thought of the hundred thousand dollar retainer she had just clinched warmed her through and through. He was not a demanding client. Truth to tell she rather liked him in spite of what he did to himself, but for the life of her she would never be able to understand why. He was a self-made man from some small industrial town in New Jersey; he now had fingers in several lucrative pies and dabbled in whatever took his fancy. He owned a trucking company, a whole raft of radio stations, several small newspapers, ditto television stations in various states; he had a fifty per cent investment in a musical that had been standing room only for the last six months. And he liked to dress up as a tart. Still, when it came down to it he played the man, whereas another of her clients took the fantasy to the ultimate by having her use a startlingly lifelike dildo on him. For which he paid extra.

There is no accounting for tastes, Nell thought, staring out at the starscape of night-time New York through the rain-streaked window. But as long as I can keep on satisfying them . . .

She left the kitchen, switching off the lights, and decided to have an early night. She had been up at the crack of dawn in order to make the morning Concorde, and there was nothing in the TV Guide that made her want to stay up and watch it. No; an early night and her book, she decided. Tomorrow she would be up bright and early to make the most of her free day by indulging in an orgy of shopping before catching her night flight back to London. She always exchanged her Concorde return for a Business Class seat and spent the difference on her shopping spree. Since she had no work on a Monday she could catch up on any jet lag.

All in all, she thought, as she got ready for bed, she had her life beautifully organised – her lives, rather, for she had two, back to back. A Double Life. By day she was Eleanor Jordan, spinster of this or any other parish, who, once seen, was instantly forgotten. By night, she was Cleo Mondaine, high-priced call girl, with a face and body – always displayed to best advantage – matched only by her sexual skills.

She had learned from her early mistakes, throttled back on her tendency to follow her own devices and desires, learned to be very cautious and do a thorough check now that she knew how easy it was to be set up. Her days were full – for on the days when she was not typing or filing or doing accounts – she did her housework, shopped, maintained her wardrobe and, even more important, her body, by spending one day a week at a private establishment where she was massaged, steamed, manicured, pedicured and generally toned up. Her days – and most of her nights, were pleasantly full, which suited her, for she hated to be idle, and she had learned to balance her two lives so that on the scales, they matched perfectly.

Best of all, she had a perfectly balanced ledger, and one day a week she brought that up to date by adding her earnings for the previous seven days, subtracting her expenses and invariably smiling beatifically at the steadily increasing black total. She lived well within her income, for her intention was to leave the Life when she was thirty-five; to have enough to live on while she did a university course as a mature student. Armed with a degree there was no telling what she could go on to – perhaps take a second one! Whatever, the first thing was to put enough away so that when the time came she had enough to give her an income for the rest of her life.

She was about to switch off her lamp when she heard the buzzer to the door of her suite. Sitting bolt upright she frowned. Who on earth could it be at this time of night? For anyone to call was unusual; for anyone to call so late was *most* unusual.

Nobody knew she was here; she had not asked for any room service. It was highly unlikely that the client wanted anything more – of course! she thought relievedly: the money! Getting out of bed she went into the bathroom and wound one of the small towels around her head; she did not sleep in her wig and it would not do to answer the door in her own long brown hair. Peering through the security spyhole she saw what looked like flowers. Flowers!

'What is it?' she called.

'Special Delivery, Miss Mondaine.'

The money *and* flowers, she thought, undecided between amusement and surprise. This particular client had never sent her anything before. Still, a hundred thousand dollars . . . perhaps he liked to do this sort of thing with a flourish. She opened the door.

The bouquet was so large she could hardly see it, but she held out the two dollar bills she had picked up and felt them taken from her.

As the bellman turned to go: 'Is that all?' Nell asked sharp with surprise. 'No – package?'

'No, ma'am. The flowers is all.'

'Thank you.' Frowning in puzzlement Nell backed into the hallway of her suite, kicked the door shut, heard the security bolt click back into place. In the sitting room she put the flowers – fresh and wrapped in tissue paper, not cellophane – on the table. They were a mixture of long-stemmed American Beauty roses, pink and white carnations and white orchids. She stared at them, nonplussed.

Receiving flowers was not something to which she was accustomed. In fact, whilst by now an accomplished courtesan, widely experienced in the sexual arts, Nell was an emotional virgin. Romance was a country she had never visited. Her life was full of men, but every single one was a client. There was – never had been – a man. One who was special. One who was not just a client. One who was important. Not just another penis, for Nell never either 'saw' or 'felt' the men behind the erection she serviced. Her activities, though of a deeply personal nature, she experienced in a wholly impersonal way. There was never any emotional content in her encounters; it was because of its absence that she was so successful. Her clients did not want emotion; they could get plenty of that for free at home with their wives and/or mistresses; what they wanted from Nell was uninvolved, unemotional, uncommitted sex, and that was what they got. That she got nothing from these men but money was something she gave no thought to. It was the way things were and the way they always had been. Where she was concerned, anyway.

Whilst Cindy had been crazy about Mickey – something Nell had never been able to understand since her own hatred of him was so strong – Paula had had a regular client with whom her relationship was more than just business; even Maureen had had a whole string of 'boy friends' none of whom

223

lasted very long, but Nell had never had a relationship with a man that was other than highly sexual and totally void of emotional content.

Her own emotions had long been atrophied by the total lack of them in her life once her mother had died. For a long time she had treasured those memories, for they were all she had of her relationship with her mother, but like all memories they had dimmed over the years. Sometimes Nell had difficulty in bringing her mother's faded face to mind, but she only had to close her eyes to see her father, hear his voice. It was his coldness, his domination, his arid detachment which had served to deaden her own emotional responses, though had she been told so, she would have hotly denied it, since she had long since come to accept her abnormality as normal. And in her profession, emotions were best left behind once you left home on an 'assignment'. Nell was a perfect example of the old saying: 'How can you miss what you have never had?'

Now, she regarded the flowers with some puzzlement. What a mixture, she thought. And from whom? She felt inside the foliage, found the square card and drew it out. Plain white envelope, plain white card. And on it a pair of eyes . . . black eyes. No message. Nell dropped the card as if she had been stung. He knew she was here! How? Who had told him? And what did he want? There was a correct procedure when it came to new clients. They were referred by an existing one. Nothing had been said about the owner of the insistent black eyes. Then how had he found out where she was staying? Nell felt something like panic because she also felt instinctively that something was not right here; that this man was outside the scope of her frame of reference. Why had he sent flowers? And why the cryptic message? Perhaps he doesn't know *what* you are, she told herself, only who you are . . . Yes, and how did he find *that* out? The discretion on which her clients relied and on which she prided herself felt threatened. Nothing like this had ever happened before. Her visits to New York – and Chicago and San Francisco and Los Angeles – had hitherto been very low key. That was the worst of letting a client take you out in public; Nell had always thought it risky; now she knew it was positively dangerous. Never again, she decided. Never! If what I do here comes out I'm finished and there goes a one hundred thousand dollar a year retainer. Damn! she thought furiously. Whoever you are, damn you to hell and back!

The buzzer went again. Now that *had* to be the money . . . It was difficult to make out the figure standing in the hallway because it was standing to one side, but she thought she saw the gleam of braid . . . another bellman. She opened the door and stared straight into the shiny black eyes of the mystery man. The gleam she had taken for braid through the spyhole was the glitter of raindrops on the shoulders of his black cashmere coat and the jetty sweep of hair above a face that was wearing a smile and a hopeful expression which faded under the withering fury of Nell's glare, but: 'Hello again,' he said confidently, mustering the resources of that face which had been launched a thousand times and never sunk once.

Nell looked him up then she looked him down. 'I don't think we've met before.' Her voice was as cold as her face but inside she was a churning mass. First the flowers, now him. How had he tracked her down? Who had he asked – more important, who had told him? And why? Added together it meant that her much-vaunted security was blown. The last thing she needed – in this hotel in this city in this country – was to be approached directly by someone wanting to buy what she sold. Selling sex was against the law here, whether solicited or not. What was not regarded as illegal in England was seen as a crime in the United States, punishable by jail and/or a fine. And a record. Nell's panic-stricken thoughts skittered about in her mind like drops of water on a hot griddle. As casually as she could she checked the corridor both ways. Empty. But who knew what policeman or house detective lurked behind that slightly open door?

'I asked for you at the desk,' her caller said quickly, sensing her unease. 'And I sent you flowers first.'

'I am not interested in them either!' Nell snapped, wanting only to be rid of him. She had heard stories about entrapment from Liz and Philip. Again, what was not permissible in English law was permitted in America in that policemen often masqueraded as punters in order to make arrests as soon as money changed hands. Nell found her panic building, her heart thundering in her ears and her whole body trembling. 'In fact,'

225

she said, her voice cracking with rage at his idiocy in exposing her like this, 'You can have the damned things back because *I* don't want them!'

Retreating inside her suite she slammed the door shut, ran for the flowers, opened up again and shoved them at him. 'Now kindly take them and yourself off and don't bother me again!'

She made a great business of noisily bolting the security locks, after which she leaned against the door gulping air.

'Hey . . . don't be like that . . . I don't mean to cause a major disturbance . . .' He sounded disbelieving. 'I only want for us to get to know each other. The minute I spotted you at that boring opening I couldn't see anyone else. Next thing I know you're leaving so I did the only thing I could – I followed you . . .'

Nell closed her eyes and moaned. It got worse by the minute.

'I don't make a habit of this. Honest. But well, we sort of collided back there . . . our eyes did, anyway. You had an effect on me like a thunderbolt. Look, if I've upset you I apologise. Just let me in and I can straighten everything out. I promise my intentions are strictly honourable.'

But Nell was at the telephone, stabbing the buttons that would get her the front desk. When they answered she said in tones of affronted outrage: 'This is Miss Mondaine in Penthouse D. There is a man outside my door – a total stranger – making a nuisance of himself. He actually followed me here tonight, and I want to know why you allowed him to come upstairs and molest me. Kindly have him removed at once!'

She slammed down the receiver. Then she closed her eyes and took deep breaths. Calm, she told herself. Calm . . . before stalking back to the door only to hear him still talking. ' . . . show you New York. I can tell by your accent that you're English. I hope to go to London soon and maybe we could get together there too. I don't mean to come on heavy but a guy has to take his chances whenever they come his way . . .'

Chances! Nell thought, clenching her fists and wishing fiercely that she could use them to box his ears. Stupid young idiot – for he was much younger than she had at first thought; her own age or even less. A bit young for a Vice Squad member – or perhaps that was why he was one in the first place, because he was attractive.

He was also suddenly sounding angry. 'Hey . . . take your hands off me . . . I'm no street-bum. I have identification . . . if you'll just let me get at it . . . hey, watch it buster, that's real cashmere . . . now wait a minute, I'm a legitimate visitor to this hotel . . .'

The voices faded and Nell heaved a sigh of relief. When someone else knocked and said: 'This is the night manager, Miss Mondaine,' she opened up again to a middle-aged man in regulation black jacket and striped trousers who smiled at her ingratiatingly and bowed before saying: 'Our most profound and sincere apologies, Miss Mondaine. This should not have happened.'

'Not in this hotel it shouldn't,' Nell agreed angrily. 'I thought all visitors had to be announced?'

'They do; the employee who failed to do so this time will be dealt with. However, I thought I would reassure you that the young man is a well-known actor, known for his – shall we say impulsive – behaviour.'

'I am not used to men following me to my hotel and then coming up and expecting to be entertained,' Nell said glacially. Which was nothing more than the plain truth. She never ever did business in hotels unless the client was such that whatever he did he was perfectly all right with the management and the suite was his, not hers.

'He is a young man, very . . . American.' His shrug – as European as his accent, said it all.

'Even so. I was assured this hotel was absolutely safe. What has happened tonight proves that it is not, but as I am checking out in the morning I trust that my last night will be undisturbed for the rest of it.'

'I will personally see that you are not bothered further.'

'Thank you – oh, I am expecting a package tomorrow morning – early. By messenger service. A very important package. That *will* be genuine. Apart from that I do not wish to be disturbed – by anyone – until it arrives.'

Another bow. 'It shall be as you wish, Madame. Once again, please accept our apologies. It will not happen again.'

You bet it won't, Nell thought, as she rebolted her door.

She felt so shaky that she went to the well-stocked fridge and poured herself a stiff gin and tonic. That had been a shave too close. An actor! She had not recognised him. Perhaps in the theatre, but his looks had been the sort one saw on television. Anyway, he had not been a policeman, thank God. But he had given her a fright. She gulped her gin. I never heard of anything so stupid in all my life, she thought furiously. Following a total stranger and expecting a bunch of flowers to soften her up for the kill. I'd have killed *him* if I'd got my hands on him!

I should never have gone to that gallery. Last time I make *that* mistake. And as for following me to the Village. She chewed her lip. She did not know whether to warn the client or not. If she did she might alarm him to the point where he would decide the retainer was not worth the aggro. If she didn't . . . No, she reasoned. That young idiot would not be so stupid. He wouldn't know I was in New York anyway. No, but he knows my name. And he knows I know the client. That I spent more than an hour with him.

She paced back and forth, chewing at it for a good half hour, finally came to the decision that it was best to leave well alone. It was a sleeping dog that might bite if it was disturbed. She would not use this hotel again; she would never accompany any client – in America anyway – anywhere in public, and she would never go direct to a client but take the extra time to make sure she was not being followed before using a circuitous route. Damned nuisance, she muttered irritably, as she emptied her glass. He hasn't any idea of the trouble he has caused me . . .

The package came next morning. Wrapped in plain brown paper; thick wedges of one hundred dollar notes. Nell tipped the messenger five dollars and when he had gone repacked the wedges in her bags – a week-ender and matching vanity case, wrapping them in underwear. She always went through the green channel at Heathrow because she was careful never to exceed the customs allowances and carried the duty free bag for all to see.

When she was ready to go she rang for a bellman and after him spoke to the day manager who said that yes, it would be possible for her to leave by a service entrance if that was what she wanted. It was. As added protection she wore a scarf and dark glasses à la Jackie Kennedy, removing the latter once the cab turned into Madison Avenue, revealing her own brown hair styled à la Eleanor Jordan. To make absolutely sure she also put on her glasses. Neither really went with the Versace dress and jacket, but she had not put on the ear-rings she normally wore with it and instead of leaving the jacket open, as it was meant to be worn, she fastened it, which ruined the look altogether. Now let him recognise me, she thought, as the cab dropped her off at Bloomingdale's.

But she did not enjoy her day's shopping as much as usual, though she spent her money as carefully and sensibly as ever, and instead of lunching in the store where she was shopping, went to a coffee shop. When she got to JFK late that afternoon she went into the nearest restroom where she became the Cleo Mondaine of her passport, and she was lucky enough to have no seat companion on the 747. Only when the big plane took off did she feel safe, unbuckling her seat belt and picking up the copy of the glossy she had bought to read until dinner was over and she could sleep. But as she leafed through it her stomach staggered as the black eyes that had stared so hard and so hungrily last night now met hers from the printed page. FROM SOAP TO SUPERSTAR IN NO TIME (AND NO TALENT). He was an actor in a prime-time soap who, given a small walk-on, had so seized the imaginations and libidos of the women who watched it that he had been all but buried in the avalanche of mail which resulted. His part had hastily been expanded – and expanded and expanded until now, eight short months later, he *was* the soap, with his name and his name only above the title. Now, he had been signed for an unheard of – hence still speculative – amount of dollars to play the lead in the new Lorimar prime-time due to start shooting in the next two weeks. The gist of the article was that 'actor' was not the right word to describe him; the one that did could not be used by the magazine for fear of prosecution. All he did was turn women on merely by looking their way. And all at a mere twenty-six. Cleo's main feeling was one of euphoric relief that he had not, after all, been a member of the Vice Squad, and once that took the lid off her pressurised emotions, anger at having been caused so much needless anxiety.

Zack Gentry! Cleo thought contemptuously. His name is as

fake as the rest of him. All I was, was a notch on a gun. Arrogant twit! But she still felt boneless with relief, so much so that she accepted the drink her flight attendant offered. She found she had also recovered her appetite. Not having been able to face breakfast she did full justice to the Sole Amandine she chose, along with a half bottle of wine. Once the lights went out she snuggled into her blanket, sighed happily and slept the rest of the way across the Atlantic until she was awoken by the offer of cold orange juice and a hot towel.

Philip would appreciate her little escapade, she thought, gazing down at rain sodden Middlesex. Especially the retainer, and these days, Philip needed all the appreciation he could find.

Six years before, in 1984, he had been diagnosed HIV positive. Twenty months ago that had become full blown Aids with a prognosis of three years. What had triggered the virus was as yet unknown in spite of all the research. What was known was that like Liz, Philip was under sentence of death, and like Liz, he was not letting it kill him now.

'I have three years, and every one of them does not detract one whit from the previous thirty years – or the twenty before that. I am and always have been a practising homosexual' (Philip never used the word 'gay' because he said that its original connotation was good enough for him and besides, it was totally the wrong word to use for a group of people whose lives were anything but) 'and it is a fact of life that there is a price to pay for everything. At least life allowed me fifty years of an active, pleasurable – and profitable – sex life before it called in my loan. The tragedy is that of the young men, pitiably young men.' He had fixed Nell to the wall with one of his pushpin stares. 'And the young women.'

'I take care, Philip, I always take precautions and I buy my condoms by the gross.'

'And your last check-up?'

'Was negative.'

'Well, for the time I am around to do it I will continue to vet all prospective clients.'

At the time Philip learned he was HIV positive, Nell had decided not to take on any more bi-sexual clients and she dropped the one she had, on Philip's advice.

'We are living amidst the twentieth century's version of the Black Death,' he said. 'Just punishment according to the self-righteous, but while I have been called upon to pay my forfeit there is no reason why you should not get through the game without having to pay yours. It is only a matter of time before the plague reaches the heterosexual population but it will take longer because there are more of you and not the – shall we say repeat performances one finds in the homosexual world.'

'I know my clients, Philip. Most of them are of long standing and with just as much determination to stay healthy as I have. And I have told the one bi-sexual not to call me any more. I shall do all that is necessary to ensure sex at its safest.'

'I hope so. You are a member of a group where the rate of infection is very high.'

'Not on my level.'

'Perhaps not, but that gives no cause for laxity.'

Nell had smiled at him with something like affection. Though being who and what she was he would never be to her what he had been to Liz, he had still become involved in her life, for since her debacle with the VIP she had never taken on a client without asking Philip to vet him first. He had former lovers strategically placed just about everywhere, all over the world, and to Nell the miracle was that they remembered him with affection, even love, and were only too happy to put themselves out for him, and thus indirectly, benefit her. Now, having invited him to dinner and cooked him one of his favourites, a casserole of venison in red wine, she told him about her encounter with the actor.

'Do you wish me to investigate him?'

'Why?'

'I did not mean as a prospective client.' Pause. 'I meant as a prospective lover. Purely for pleasure rather than profit.' His tone was silky smooth and Nell met his probing eyes head on.

'No.'

'According to the article you showed me he has a reputation as a stud.'

'Then perhaps Tattersalls might be interested. I am not.'

'Were you not flattered by his – quite blatant – pursuit?'

'Hardly! I was furious. *He actually followed me to a client's house!* Think what *that* breach of confidentiality could do to my reputation.'

'A somewhat brash young man, I will agree, who has obviously let his success go to his head – via his groin, but I still do not see why you automatically jumped to the conclusion that he was a threat rather than a promise. Did it not occur to you that it was not the courtesan he was pursuing but the woman?'

'No,' Nell answered shortly. 'It didn't. When I am working, my mind is on the job. All I could think of was that I stood to lose a valuable retainer almost as soon as I'd found it.'

'Why is it that with you, money has the power to excite where men do not?'

'Flattery pays no bills.'

'Are you telling me that the thought of sex purely for pleasure rather than money holds no appeal to you?'

'I get more sex than any dozen average women. I have no need for more.' Yes, Philip thought, sex for sale you can handle. What I would like to know is why you are very careful to distance yourself from any other kind.

Long study and careful thought had confirmed his initial theory that Nell, like Madame de Pompadour before her, was not a passionate woman. Cleo *appeared* to be deeply sensual, but it was all technique and Nell's consummate acting skills. He had watched, fascinated, as Cleo was created – and from the inside. Cleo Mondaine was alive and well and living outside Nell Jordan. The person, the eyes, the voice, were a separate entity, even though what it experienced, saw, said, were directed by Nell. It was as complex a bundle as he had ever encountered and he was still, after eleven years, trying to untie it.

Even now he still had no idea where she came from; where she had lived for her first seventeen years. All he knew was that those years had been such as to make her bury them deep in a past she then proceeded to lose; that they held memories too painful to dwell on, even now.

He knew she went to visit her sister; Liz had told him that one of the first things Nell did once she could afford it was make the journey to the special home where Margaret was now living, but that she had come back both shocked and depressed, for it seemed her sister was not just mentally damaged; she was autistic.

Liz had said that all Nell could say, in a shocked, disbelieving voice was: 'Margaret didn't seem to know me. She never spoke, never looked at me. It was as though I was a stranger.' And then she had raged at herself: 'It is all my fault. I left her alone all this time. I should have begged borrowed or stolen the money but I should have gone to see her . . . I should have. Is it any wonder she doesn't remember me? It is three whole years after all. I shall never forgive myself, never!'

Which meant, Philip had thought at the time, that she was toting a heavy load of guilt. But with an autistic child what sort of a relationship could one have? Philip had wondered. Come to that, Nell herself was no dab hand at relationships. The one she had with Liz was her only close one; Philip she had always circled, and at a distance. She did not seem to feel the lack of friends. The life she now lived was, to all intents and purposes a solitary one, though one could not say truthfully that she lacked for social life: Cleo had a full appointment book at all times. Eleanor's job was also a solitary one in that she had no co-workers. Philip was of the opinion that Eleanor had taken the job precisely because of that. Nell was obviously perfectly happy with her own company; unlike most people she did not regard that as some sign of a character defect. But what he found most intriguing was that she should not for one minute have thought that a man had followed her not because he wanted (a) to entrap her or (b) to employ her, but simply because he was powerfully attracted to her.

Cleo is a sex-pot, Eleanor is neuter, which leaves Nell where? Why is sex a closed book to her – though God knows she has read just about everything else? Why is Nell not allowed a life of her own? Her only existence is as the puppet master, for make no mistake, she pulls the strings. What I would like to know is . . . what or who runs Nell?

'You are staring at me like something under a microscope,' Nell protested.

'Was I? Probably because I was wondering why you feel the necessity to live two entirely different lives? Why one is not enough for you as it is everyone else?'

A lift of the shoulder. 'Probably it is the actress in me.'

'Is it?'

'No psychoanalysing tonight, if you please. I am not in the mood for it. I would rather you cast your eye over these two names and advised me as to their suitability as clients.'

Getting too close, was I? Philip mused. I thought I might. Why you found it necessary not only to create a new persona but to *become* her is a question I find endlessly fascinating. And I shall find out, my pretty. Devious minds are no challenge to me since I hold the patent.

He put on his half-frames before inspecting the sheet of paper Nell slid across the table to him.

'I do not know the first name . . . what is he?'

'Argentinian, but based on the Riviera. An industrialist.'

'Aren't they all? I will investigate. The other is a definite no-no.'

'Why? You do know him?'

'Of him. He is a politician. Languishing on the back benches just now, to be sure, but destined, if what I hear is the truth, for higher things. That means minders. Special Branch and all the paraphernalia of political life. Have you forgotten Lord Lambton and Norma Levy? Politicians are best left to their constituents, otherwise they are more trouble than they are worth, even at a thousand pounds a time.' He laid a finger against his nose. 'Plots, cabals, assassinations.' He struck the name through with his fountain-pen. 'A definite no-no, I think.' The name of the Argentinian he wrote – in his own special, self-invented code – in his pocket diary. His memory – though he would never admit it to anyone but Nell – was not the flawless thing it once had been. He then folded the paper into a spill which he held to one of the dinner-table candles, before dropping it into a heavy cut-glass ashtray and watching it burn to black ash. 'Nothing in writing,' had been one of his very first admonitions. 'Always remember the Germans. They kept meticulous records of every last thing – such a passion for efficiency – and when they fell into the wrong hands they were done for.'

Chin in hand: 'How *do* you know all this?' Nell had asked fascinatedly.

'Because I make it my business to find out. Human beings are endlessly of interest in one way or another. Even when they are boring. But all have one thing in common. They *love* to be listened to.'

'And nobody listens better than you?'

Philip smiled.

13

Some weeks later, on a Saturday morning, Nell put her weekend case into the boot of the Golf, donned her Ray-Bans, for it was a brilliantly sunny May morning, and set off to drive to deepest Wiltshire. The client was fairly new; this was only their fifth assignation and the others had all been in his London flat. He had been recommended by an existing client, who did business with him, and Philip had checked him out, reporting him to be whiter-than-white. Since all he wanted was straight sex, no hang-ups, no idiosyncracies, Nell accepted with alacrity.

He was about fifty; short, quite plump, with penetrating brown velvet eyes behind thick horn-rims, and a powerful sex-drive. He enjoyed going at it for a length of time that would have been impressive in a much younger man, which was why he wanted someone who could stay the course. It was obvious to Nell, after the first time, that he was adept at the ancient art of Imshak, or the withholding of his own orgasm until the woman had been satisfied again and again, which confirmed her initial belief that he was of Eastern origin, (though his name was Armenian) since she had learned from Liz that Imshak was also from the East. For his part he was eminently satisfied with her stamina, though there was an element of cruelty in his testing that to its limits at their subsequent encounters. It had become something of a battle of wills, and she had the feeling that he had invited her to his country house that weekend for the express purpose of breaking his record. His excuse was that pressure of business prevented him from returning to London merely for the purposes of sex. It would have to go to him. He suggested she arrive in time for tea. Afterwards he would give her a guided tour of his house and the restoration that had been going on for the past two years. He would give her a splendid dinner, after which they would conduct their business. She could return to London after breakfast on the Sunday morning.

It was a pleasure to be out of London, and she had so arranged her departure to allow a no-haste, meandering detour of minor roads and pretty countryside once she left the last suburb behind. That would give her time to stop off at a small pub somewhere for a drink and a sandwich. He had been particular as to the time of her arrival. Not before four o'clock, he had said. I shall not be free until then. It was no skin off her nose; for the fee he was paying she would have arrived at 4 a.m. if that was what he wanted.

He had given her explicit instructions – he was meticulous in everything, not only sex, and she found her way without difficulty, but it did occur to her, over the last few miles, that she seemed to have left the twentieth century some way behind. The house itself was hidden in a fold of the Wiltshire Downs which made a natural amphitheatre, as if someone had pressed firmly with the back of a spoon. The village lay some five miles away down a very minor road, and when she turned off that down a narrow but well-maintained track, she plunged into the silence of thickly mysterious trees, so crowded overhead they shut out the sunlight. Eventually she came to a high wall, obviously newly built, broken by a pair of elaborate iron gates surmounted by television cameras. Security was patently important. A metallic voice issuing from a grille asked her to state her name and business and when she did so opened the gates with a click to allow her through and on to a wide and handsome drive which descended into the valley proper, curving to the right as it did so. Not until she rounded it did she catch her first sight of the house; an exquisite William and Mary gem of faded pink brick with a creamy pediment and a balustraded terrace falling to weedless lawns ending in stands of ancient trees. Above and behind the hills stood guard, protecting it from wind and weather.

Well! thought Nell, quite taken aback. It may be at the back of beyond but it certainly is worth it. She would not have taken this client, who always struck her as a man who was more at home in cities than the countryside, for a man who liked such solitude. The village was in no way near-at-hand, and there were no other houses in the vicinity. As she slowed the car she caught sight of scaffolding to one side, and at the back of the house glimpsed a large skip discreetly tucked away under a low hanging tree. Obviously restoration – for the client had told her the house, having been neglected for many years, was now being brought back to its original beauty – was still going on. As she stopped the car before the front door it opened and a manservant in white jacket and black trousers came out of it. He wished her a good afternoon in an accent she could not identify and asking for her keys, opened the trunk and took out her single case, which he then carried into the house for her. Her host was just descending the stairs.

He was evidently pleased to see her, but she sensed a preoccupation behind the good manners. He carried a British passport but she knew he had been born elsewhere, though where she had no idea. His English was all but accentless. She had also heard him speak both French, Italian, German and some Arabic-sounding language with lots of gutturals and Spanish sounding harsh h's. Now, he asked her if she would like to have a look around before tea, or would she prefer to go straight to her room?

'No, I should love to see the house . . .'

'It is my retreat. Strictly private. That is why I bought it.'

'It is rather remote.'

'That is what I was looking for. I come down here to get away from things – the pressures which squeeze one every day. Here, there are none. Only peace, quiet and tranquillity.'

'It restoreth your soul?'

His frown was that of one not familiar with the quotation. Not a Christian, Nell realised. He was a great deal more foreign than he admitted to.

'When was it built?' she asked.

'In 1692. When I found it, it had been allowed to lapse into shocking decay. The previous owner had not been able to afford its upkeep. When he died his son did not want it. So I bought it. That was two years ago.'

Nell felt a chill. 'What was the name of the previous owner?'

'Harvill. I understand the family had lived here for centuries. I am re-creating it as it would have looked when it was built.'

My God! Nell thought numbly. Talk about full circle . . . She had seen the notice in *The Times* about the Brigadier's death in 1984 at the age of 83, and had written to Boy, who had not bothered to reply. Oh, Liz, Nell thought, wanting to laugh. How you would have appreciated this . . . You had your brother dead to rights.

Inside, work was going on just about everywhere, though some of the downstairs rooms were finished and several of the bedrooms. But as they left one wing Nell looked across the central staircase to where the other one was festooned in scaffolding.

'I must ask you to excuse me in not showing you that part of the house; it has some beautiful rooms and a particularly fine scrolled ceiling but also dry rot. The floors are up and therefore dangerous. I would not want you falling through the holes that are left.'

He gave her tea in an exquisite little drawing room hung with silk the colour of just ripened apricots, then took her for a stroll in the grounds. It really was isolated. From the hill behind the house Nell could see the smoke from other chimneys, but no sign of the houses. They dined *à deux* in a panelled dining room served by the silent servant. There was no sign of any other servants, yet someone must be in the kitchen because the food was superb. Afterwards, they drank coffee and listened to music – he always liked a very formal preliminary before getting down to business, as though he was entertaining an honoured guest rather than a high-priced courtesan, and nothing loath, Nell went along with him. Luxury was something she never refused.

She went up first to shower and prepare herself; (he liked her squeaky clean and smelling of a particular perfume he specifically asked that she wear. Obviously he did the same thing, for he always smelled of the aftershave and bodysplash that only he used; a mixture of sandalwood and citrus that she had never smelled on anyone but him) anointing her body with handfuls of silky lotion that also had an eastern connotation, before donning a nightgown and peignoir – both provided by him –

in pale lavender, not a colour she either liked or ever wore herself but he was paying for it, and both were of pure silk crêpe-de-Chine much adorned with blonde lace. Then she let down her hair. With him, she always wore a black wig of real, shiny, silk-soft hair which she wore pinned up until it was time to earn her fee, when she let it down, brushed it and let it hang down her back, rippling almost to her waist. It had cost her a lot of money and was so fitted that it would not come off even during the most energetic sex. He liked to play with it, wind it around her throat once she was naked, and to complete the illusion she tinted her pubic hair to match. He had once asked her to shave it but when she pointed out that she had other clients who would have been put off by her lack of it, he had shrugged, smiled and said: 'In that case . . .' Finally, she sprayed herself with the perfume which matched the body lotion, paying particular attention to her hair, even though she knew that until she could take another shower and wash it off, its cloying sickliness would give her a headache.

Then she waited. She waited for longer than usual, which was most unusual. Time was money, he said. Often. Then she heard what sounded like raised voices.

She went to her door, peered out. Nobody. Nothing. What *could* have happened? Had he been taken ill suddenly? It had to be something serious for he was a man who expected full value for money.

She was hovering there undecidedly when she saw the carved door behind the scaffolding on the other side of the stairs open, and her client come through it, pausing as he did so to speak to the man waiting to shut it behind him. It was the sight of that man which had Nell instinctively whisking herself back into her bedroom, shocked and disbelieving, for the face was one she had once had nightmares about. Tony Panacoulis. Back against her bedroom door she thought she had been quick enough to escape detection. The last thing she wanted was to be seen by that loathsome man. Even now he made her flesh crawl.

What on earth was Tony Panacoulis doing here, of all places? And how did he come to know Reza Dominitian, for that was the name of her client? What was a wealthy, eminently respectable business man doing with one of the biggest porn merchants in the business?

Could it be that Tony Panacoulis was no longer involved in what Nell considered to be a filthy, if lucrative, trade? Or – and this horrified her – was Reza Dominitian not all that he seemed to be? Had he somehow fooled Philip, whose checks were always very thorough?

Perhaps I was mistaken, she told herself. Perhaps it was someone who only looked like Tony Panacoulis. But she knew she was clutching at straws. There was no mistaking that pulpy face with its melon-rind mouth and black-olive eyes. As soon as she saw it, behind Reza Dominitian's plump, well-tailored shoulder, she had known. It was a face she had never forgotten because it belonged to a man she had instinctively disliked on sight the very first time she met him. Once she knew how he earned his money that dislike had turned to loathing. She was not usually one to form an instant, irrevocable opinion, though she had found she was usually right when she did, but something about that doughy face, the look in the dead eyes, had given her the creeps. Now he had turned up in her life again.

What was *really* going on in that forbidden wing? Was it a studio? Was that where Tony now made his hard-porn movies? It was isolated enough, secure enough. But where, then, were the 'actors and actresses'? She had not seen or heard a soul. It was sheer fluke that she had happened to be standing at her door when the other one had opened. None of your business, she reminded herself. But when she checked the time she saw the client was now thirty minutes overdue. Was Tony Panacoulis the reason he could not get up to town? Some hitch in the making of a movie? Whatever, she would not see this client again, purely because he did business with a man Nell had always given a wide berth to, who was bad news. There was also the possibility – remote but still dangerous – that he would recognise Nell, though it was eleven years and a partly-new face later. There was nothing he could do even if he did, she told herself resolutely. She was no longer the nineteen-year-old caught in a trap from which she longed to escape. He had been Mr Big then, and if he was running with Reza Dominitian he was probably Mr Bigger by now, but these days she had her own power and influence. Not in the least Philip Faulkner.

Leave it, she commanded herself. If the client has a financial interest – or any kind of interest in the making of pornographic movies it is nothing to do with you. Just see that in future you have nothing to do with him.

Just then the door opened and the object of her thoughts entered. 'My dear, please allow me to apologise . . . a lengthy phone call and of such importance I had to take it. I have kept you waiting far too long. Please, may I ask you to wait a few moments longer? I will be with you as soon as I can.' His lying, like the rest of him, was very assured.

I would love to say no, Nell thought, knowing it would be the worst thing she could do. The thought of sex with this man she now found distasteful, but now was not the time to show it. And remember what Liz told you: What the client does when he is not with you is none of your business, remember? Absolutely *none* of your business!

By the time the client returned she was ready for him; languorous, perfumed, subtly skilful yet strong enough to withstand his prolonged assault. For he went at it with all the determination and enthusiasm – if considerably more skill – of an insatiable eighteen-year-old. For a man of his age – whatever that was but she was willing to bet he would never see fifty again – his stamina was unbelievable. She blessed Liz for teaching her various pelvic exercises which, she said, had been taught her by one of the wives of an Arab client. 'Keeps you from becoming too sore when you've got a man who is capable of the hundred and one thrusts.'

By the time he finally allowed himself to orgasm Nell wearily conceded that had she been able to count it would have been a thousand and one. But he was obviously both pleased and gratified, and his smile, once he was back in his gorgeously brocaded dressing gown and Eastern Promise slippers, was that of a man who was very well pleased with himself and gratefully admiring of her.

'As always, the consummate professional,' he complimented. He laid down his long white envelope. 'And worth every penny.' The proceedings closed he became brisk and businesslike. 'I will be in touch, but I shall not see you at breakfast. I have to leave very early.'

He bowed, picked up a hand, kissed it, then left her. Cleo threw the covers back, stripped off the wig, picked up the discarded nightwear and went into the bathroom where she ran a hot bath. The cloying perfume had, as usual, given her a headache, and when she eventually went back into the bedroom found it still lingered there. She would have to open a window; let the fresh air blow it away.

Parting the curtains preparatory to opening one of the casement windows she paused; a man was coming round the corner of the house carrying a roll of carpet over his shoulder. Somebody's working late and no mistake, she thought, just as he looked up to scan the windows. Instinct made her let the curtain − heavy, crimson silk-damask − fall back into place, though there remained a slit through which she could see − with one eye − that it was no casual look. It was a making sure look. Evidently satisfied he made for a van, parked on the grass not the gravel drive, which stood, lights out, rear doors open, facing the way out via the long curving drive. He dropped his shoulder, let the carpet fall into the van, used his foot to push the end over the tailgate then shut and locked the doors before going round to the driver's seat. But he did not start the engine. Instead, he released the handbrake, allowing the van silently to roll down the slight slope. Nor did he switch on his headlights, only his sidelights, and it was as the van rolled away that Nell noticed its right-hand side rear-light was not lit: only the left rear-light showed red. The van rolled silently round the bend and disappeared, and only after a moment or two did she hear the faint throb of its engine as it was started up. Well! she thought, preparing to lift the window, that was tactful, I must say. He must have them working round the clock. Ah, well, he can afford it if anyone can.

The window refused to open. Either it had been closed on paint that was not dry or it was not meant to open in the first place. She went to the other side of the room where there was a smaller one, and this she managed to raise about six inches, allowing fresh air to blow away the sickly smell.

She did not sleep well. Her dreams were disturbing. She was

awake long before the silent houseman brought her breakfast tray at nine o'clock, nor did she have any appetite for the oven-warm, morning fresh croissants with butter and apricot jam. She contented herself with two cups of delicious coffee. She could not keep her mind from worrying about the events of the night before but – leave it! she told herself. You don't want to know. What niggled at her was that this lovely old house was where Liz had been born. If it had become a pornographic centre it was a desecration, but she had no proof that it was. Only instinct confirmed by a certain face. She wondered if she should say anthing to Philip. He had stayed here many a time. And he would be able to make discreet enquiries. But the thought of having *anything* to do with Tony Panacoulis made her retreat. Forget it, she decided.

By ten-thirty she was ready to leave, double-checked she had left nothing, opened the curtains the manservant had not drawn and closed the window she had opened. He came for her case, took it down to her car. She slipped him a five-pound note. As promised, there was no sign of her host. No sign of anybody. It might almost have been a dream, she thought. A nightmare.

As it was Sunday, traffic was light, but she did not dawdle as she had coming down. She wanted to put as much distance between her and that house as possible. It was a lovely place and had the Brigadier still been its owner she would have been happy to return. But Boy Harvill and his self-serving wife had sold it to a man who, if Nell's suspicions were correct, provided financial backing to another who made hard-core pornographich movies. Poor Brigadier! He must be spinning in his grave. Liz would be laughing her head off wherever she was. 'What a turn up for the books!' Nell could hear her saying.

Familiar surroundings reduced her unease. The cats came to greet her. The Sunday papers were waiting to be read. Best of all she had a nice, fat envelope. As always, money for her 'Fund' lit everything with its rosy glow. If you had been seen you would not have been recognised, she told herself, applying reassurance with a trowel. What you are now and what you were then are two entirely different women. No . . . put it and him behind you. Take Reza Dominitian off your client list; be 'unavailable' next time he calls, and the time after that until he gets the message, but have a good story ready. Philip spins the perfect ones . . .

Again she wondered if she should mention this to him. She knew – as did he – that one or two members of the Inner Circle had, though the fact was never discussed – begun their illustrious careers by making pornographic films, and had no doubt that if she made the right approaches – again through Philip – she could discover just exactly what Tony Panacoulis was up to; how big he was nowadays, how what he did tied in with Reza Dominitian – if there was a tie. You know damn fine there is, she told herself derisively. What would bring those two together?

Money?

Exactly . . . the one thing they are both passionately devoted to. But it was instinct, pure and simple, that decided her on a policy of non-involvement.

After a week she wondered what on earth she had been so worried about. After two it had dwindled to a minor matter. After three she had forgotten it. After four she had forgotten Tony Panacoulis again. It was a whole two months later that she settled down one evening to watch the late movie – Alfred Hitchcock's *Spellbound*, piling the cushions behind her, coffee and chocolate biscuits to hand, the cats ensconced in the hollow of her lap. The previous programme had some time yet to run; one of the Crime Assistance appeals to the public made with the co-operation of the police who needed the viewers' help in identifying either people, property – stolen usually – cars – ditto, and clothing, usually worn in crimes of one type or another. Nell did not at first pay attention, but as she picked up her chocolate digestive the announcer was saying, 'the body of a thirteen-year-old boy buried in what appears to be a hastily dug grave in Wareham Forest, Dorset, not far from the B3075. The spot is a well guarded secret as it contains a badger sett over which a twenty-four watch had been mounted for the previous two days, following evidence that badger hunting had been taking place. It is known that there is a badger-baiting ring working in the area. The police say that it was probably the digging of the badgers and foxes that uncovered the grave, which was otherwise well concealed with brush and leaves.

They also say that the boy had been savagely sexually assaulted before being asphyxiated. Where they need *your* help is in tracing a van seen near the badger sett early in the morning – about half-past one – of Sunday, May 22nd. According to the badger watchers, who were also parked there but well out of sight and well concealed, the van was parked without lights for at least half an hour, but when the watchers grew suspicious and approached, the van drove off. However as it did so, they noticed that only one of its rear lights was working – that on the left. The one on the right was not lit at all. The Dorset Police would like anyone who was in the vicinity of Wareham Forest or the B3075 in the early hours of that Sunday, May 22nd, to telephone them at this number . . .' A telephone number was flashed up in front of Nell's wide, disbelieving eyes. 'The van was a minivan, dark in colour, of the type shown in this picture. It was unmarked.' The telephone number was replaced by a van identical to the one Nell had seen loaded with the roll of carpet.

'The Dorset Police have asked us to say that this is a crime of unparalleled savagery and that any information, no matter how slight, will be of enormous assistance to them in finding the perpetrators. So, if anyone out there can be of any assistance, no matter how small, please telephone. As usual, we will be back at 11.15 p.m. with details of your response to our appeals.'

Nell felt a scalding sensation on her thighs and looked down to see that her coffee cup had slid from her stupefied grasp, tilting to allow the hot liquid to cascade everywhere, including the cats, who leapt away with a howl, retreating to the door, where they licked themselves vigorously. Nell jumped up, shaking liquid from the soaked material of her lounging pyjamas. 'Damn . . .' She took them off; her thighs were bright red, but her mind was too numbed by what she had seen to register any pain.

'No . . .' she thought, out loud, refusing to accept the logical conclusion. 'No!' she repeated, her voice rising, making the cats bolt behind the curtains. 'It can't be . . . It's coincidence, that's all . . .' But she still found herself making for the drawer where she kept her road atlas, measuring with a ruler the distance between the place where she had seen the van and the wood in Dorset where it had been parked near the badger-watchers. Forty miles, she thought. Which would allow for the time difference.

She stared blindly at the map, but all she saw was the van, rear doors agape, a man shrugging a rolled up carpet from his shoulder into its interior, locking it up, rolling silently away. Not starting up the engine out of consideration, as she had thought. But out of caution. Her knees went and she sat down suddenly in the chair by her desk. *Think*, she told herself desperately. Don't go off half-cocked. There are thousands of mini-vans like the one they just showed. With a broken rear light – a right-hand rear light? When she compared what she had seen (and heard) with what she had just been shown, the total had her biting hard on a forefinger. She had always been one to trust her instincts, and her unease, that particular Sunday, had just been proved spot on.

You *have* to tell them, she argued with herself. It is your bounden duty. Oh, yes? And just what *do* I tell them? 'I was at a remote country house in Wiltshire that weekend visiting a client – my business? Oh, I'm a high class call girl, and at 12.40 a.m. I saw this mini-van parked on the lawn in front of the house and a man loading a roll of carpet into it and when it drove off – with great stealth, I might add – I noticed that its right-hand light was broken. Oh, and another thing, I saw a man I know to be a porn merchant in that same house, in a part of it I was warned to keep away from. How about that for starters?'

It *is* a start, that's what matters.

'And when they ask if I would be prepared to give evidence should it come to court? What do I say then? Fine? I don't mind ruining my business, ruining my life.'

She came to her feet in alarm.

I can't . . . I daren't! It will destroy everything! What about my own life! If I blow the gaff on this I'm blowing up my nice, safe comfortable existence! I'm exposing a client, which means all the others will run for the hills. I am destroying myself! All I've worked for, saved hard to provide, kept my mouth shut about, striven to attain. Another five years and I am home and dry; I can retire, leave the Life and everything to do with it. This has nothing to do with me! I have absolutely no definite proof that there was a body in the roll of carpet. Conjecture is what I have. Plus some surmise. And my instincts. And that bloody Tony Panacoulis. *Why* did I have to open that door? *Why* couldn't I have minded my own business? Damn it all to hell, she thought despairingly. It's not fair! It's just not *fair* . . .

She switched the television set off – there was no way that she could watch that movie. No way she could sleep, either. This would agitate and revolve and pace the bars of its cage until she managed to resolve it one way or the other. Because it had to be resolved. She would be fit for nothing until it was. She kept seeing that roll of carpet and visualising the lonely grave; the badgers and the foxes sniffing round it, scratching, then digging, uncovering the thirteen-year-old . . . She caught her breath on a sob. Why did it have to be a child . . . a thirteen-year-old boy? Was he a runaway too? Or kidnapped from somewhere, a child from a loving home. *Stop this!* she told herself. You know where that road leads.

She went to the drinks tray, poured herself a stiff gin, added less tonic than usual. Two gulps and it was gone. She made herself another. I have to have a plan, she thought. I have to decide what I do about this. Do I accept that I could well be making a mountain out of a molehill and salve my conscience by admitting that I have no real evidence except the purely circumstantial, or do I obey my first instincts and tell the police what I know – only not the Dorset police. I have to stay away from that part of the country. Scotland Yard, then? The Vice Squad? Or isn't there one that deals with pornography and obscene publications? She put her head in her hands. She had to make a decision but could not bring herself to do so. Don't force it, she counselled herself. Sleep on it. Think about it. Especially about what is at stake.

She made peace with the cats, apologising to them, kissing and stroking them until they purred and head-butted her indicating all was forgiven, accepting the dish of crème fraîche she offered with good grace, as perfect amends.

Then she went upstairs to attend to her scalded thighs, applying a liberal coating of Savlon to their scarlet soreness before putting on a mini-nightshirt which would not chafe them. Then she went back downstairs where she mopped up the mess and did her best to scrub away the coffee stain on the lemon-yellow slubbed silk which covered her big sofa. When it was done to her satisfaction she made herself a fresh cup of coffee, added a slug of brandy and then sat down to think.

It all came down to a single choice. Either she put herself first – her life, her business, her deep-cover activities – or she allowed her conscience priority and told the police what she had seen added to what she knew. With a rider to the second course of action. That nobody else must know. Either what she saw or who it was had seen it. She would have to rely on their promise of total confidentiality. What worried her was that they might want more than she was prepared to give. Like appear as a witness, which was absolutely unthinkable because she would be cutting her own throat.

Her experience of the police was limited to the times she had been cautioned; once by the motherly WPS and twice – though by rights he should have arrested her that second time – by the tall, blond Inspector. He'd just been transferred to the CID on the occasion of their last meeting, and been somewhat the worse for wine, but she'd also sensed a kindness in him. And what she had never forgotten was that he was the only person ever to have understood the meaning behind the name Elly Little. The police in Dorset might be very different, and she could not afford to be connected with that part of the country anyway. Surely, she thought, somebody else saw the van with the broken rear-light during the early hours of that Sunday. There were other people in the vicinity, other houses, a village five miles away. There must also, then, be hotels, pubs, shops, maybe even restaurants. People went out on Saturday nights, and stayed out late because they didn't have to get up for work next morning. There *must* have been traffic on the roads. And a broken rear light was an attention catcher if ever there was one. There must have been other cars going home, travelling behind the van, noticing the broken rear light. They would ring in, wouldn't they? After all, it is nothing more than a bit of excitement to them.

'Ooooh, George, we saw that van, remember? I said, didn't I, he's for it if the police catch him. Quick, ring them and tell exactly how we saw it . . . it was about one o'clock. I remember because I checked my watch when I heard that church clock strike.'

Yes, somebody will have rung in, she told herself encouragingly, feeling better already. But when the programme came back for the update, although there had been a good response from members of the public on their other enquiries, nobody, nobody at all, had called to report sighting the mini-van with the broken rear light. Another earnest appeal for help was made.

Oh, God, Nell thought again. She felt sick. I have to, she thought. I have to. I can't let it go. What if it had been Margaret. Almost without volition she got up, went to the telephone, dialled the number as it was flashed up on the screen, and when a voice answered 'Incident Room' she said in a rapid monotone and in the flat Geordie accent that was impossible to acquire by those not born on the banks of the River Tyne: 'I'm ringing about the mini-van. I saw it. Nearly did me in. It came out of a right-hand side turning halfway between Compton Amyas and Little Bourne, at a right speed I can tell you – I had to swerve else it would have smashed into me. He was going far too fast. I think it was a private drive he came out of because there was no road sign that I could see – oh, and it was at exactly twenty to one on the Sunday morning. I know because I checked my watch as I saw him speed away *and* I also noticed that he had only one rear light, on the left. He's a menace on the road and ought to be seen to.' She hung up, gasped the breath she was dying to take, for her last sentence had been spoken without any, and leaned, shaking and all but panting, against the wall, heart hammering. When she raised a hand to wipe her damp forehead it was palsied. She slid down the wall onto her bottom, put her head between her knees. If they recorded that they won't get anything from my voice, she thought. Nobody has any idea I'm a Geordie, nobody who knows me now has ever heard me speak in my native dialect, and if they wanted to trace the call they'd have a hard job because I wasn't on long enough. She was both astonished and pleased that the words had come so easily, until she realised that subconsciously she had been arranging and re-arranging them ever since she had first heard the appeal.

Well, I've done it, she thought. That ought to help. It gives as close a pointer to the house as I dare admit to, and I've given them the right time. It is now up to them. I can't do any more because I have to protect myself. I have my own life to think of.

At work next day she was so unwontedly abstracted that her employer asked her concernedly if she felt all right. He had never seen her so immersed in herself. Every time he came out of his office into hers she was sitting staring into space, and for the first time ever she gave him a wrong file; right surname but wrong initial and no title. Alarmed, he realised just how appallingly different things would be without the super-efficient Miss Jordan to run them, and when one of his best patients, a lady who had already had everything pinned, tucked, nipped and stretched, referred with her usual spiteful vagueness to 'Miss er . . .' he said coldly; 'Her name is Miss Jordan: Miss Eleanor Jordan,' and did not flatter her with his usual fulsomeness.

'I am concerned about you, Eleanor,' he said, telling her only half the truth as usual since he was much more concerned about himself and what sort of inept bimbo the agency would send if for some reason this treasure was to desert him. 'I can see that you are not yourself.' She looked the same; neat, tidy, drab, but something was obviously troubling her. He was pretty certain she lived alone – or was there an aged mother? Truth to tell he could not remember, so he asked tactfully: 'Is there something on your mind?'

He saw her settle her glasses more firmly before answering primly: 'Thank you, but I am quite all right. I should not have allowed my mind to wander like that. Please be assured it will not happen again.'

'Have you a headache? Perhaps an aspirin. I have some first class analgesics.'

'No, thank you. I *never* take patent medicines.'

Nonplussed: 'You are not a Christian Scientist, are you?'

'No, I am not, but nor do I believe in taking a pill or a tablet every time I feel out of sorts.'

'Cup of tea, then? Sovereign remedy, tea. Hot and strong. Why don't we both have one?'

He loathed the stuff and never muddied his insides with all that tannin, but he knew she drank it. Anything to get her back to normal. He had taken her for granted so long now that panic set in at the very thought of not having her there to be taken for anything. Poor bitch, he thought, really seeing her for the first time. What sort of a life must she have? If ever there was an archetypal spinster. A dying breed, though the Matron at his teaching hospital had been of similar if tougher ilk. Put the fear of God into the students, she had. Eleanor did not aspire to that but she could be very cool if she was not best pleased, fortunately something that rarely happened. She was far too respectful of authority. Now, she got up from her desk, saying: 'Yes, I think perhaps a cup of tea. And a chocolate ginger?'

'Yes, please.' He'd eat that, pour the tea away. As long as she was happy. Relievedly he went back into his office to write up his notes, resolving to take more notice of her in future, for upon her, as much as his patients, depended his own well-regulated, smoothly running professional life.

In the little cloakroom which served as kitchen as that was where the hotplate, kettle, cupboard and sink were, Nell looked at herself in the mirror. Normally, Eleanor never had much colour – she always wore a putty-coloured foundation that was neither flattering nor enhancing – but today, there were shadows under her eyes – the result of a wholly sleepless night – and the lines she was normally so careful to paint around her eyes and mouth corners had not been done with her usual light hand. She looked positively haggard. No wonder he had been concerned. And her mind was wholly in thrall to what was happening down in Wiltshire. Had the police acted on her information? Had they searched the house? If so, had they found anything? Had they indeed *found* the house? Had someone – that silent servant, perhaps, watched the same programme as she had and given warning? Had they dumped the van? Questions skittered and jumped around her brain, giving it no rest. This won't do, she scolded her reflection, smoothing the nut brown hair and securing her bun more firmly. He is not supposed to notice too much, remember? You have got him nicely in the rut you dug; he knows you are there but if anybody asked him to describe you, for the life of him he would not be able to remember the colour of your eyes. *You* are in control, remember? And you are *still* in control as Cleo. You have done nothing that will connect you to what you saw that weekend. And not a word from the client. Which is normal, since on average you see him every ten to twelve weeks. Everything is under control. Relax. Nothing untoward, remember? Nothing that could give your name – or is it games? – away.

She made the tea, took it in, her usual efficient yet prim self, and for the rest of the day forced her fears to the back of her mind. She had read the *Telegraph* from cover to cover but there was nothing in it about the murder, so at lunchtime, when she was alone, she had slipped out and bought every single tabloid and it was there, in all of them, on an inside page. As yet, it was just another murder.

That Saturday she had an appointment with a peer of the realm, a member of various august government bodies and director of half a dozen companies of vital importance to the economy of the country. He liked to be 'massaged' but was too well known to risk an open visit to a massage parlour. He paid Cleo, instead, and met her at the flat he kept for just such purposes. Ostensibly, it was a flat-cum-office, and Nell always turned up in civil servant type clothes, wearing her glasses and a brown wig, carrying a briefcase which contained 'Cleo's' equipment. There was no porter and she had a key. By the time the client arrived she was changed, ready and waiting: Cleo with her glossy black hair, black satin teddy, sheer black stockings and high heels. It was always in the afternoon, he was always primed and ready, and she noticed, in reading the evening paper afterwards, that invariably he had been involved in some business either in the House of Lords or some Government quango or high level discussions. After she had drained him dry his 'Massage' seemed also to have benefited his mind. 'I have heard some fluent and persuasive orators in my time, Cleo,' he said appreciatively afterwards, 'but there is no doubt about it; yours is the most golden tongue of them all. Can I book you a week Thursday? Same time, same place?'

When he'd gone, Cleo re-packed her things in the briefcase, then noticed that the client had left his newspaper lying on a chair. CHILD VICTIM OF PORN RING said the headline. The article below said that Dorset Police were hunting a pornographic ring of men who were abducting runaways, forcing them to perform obscene acts in pornographic films and then, finally, murdering them in their last role of all, as the lead in a 'snuff' movie, which captured their life being snuffed out.

The name of the latest victim was Darren Henry. He had disappeared from his home in Camden Town just nine weeks before, saying he was fed up with school and wanted to earn some money. His mother had three other children, all younger, and it was a one-parent family. It was thought that Darren had become involved with a paedophile/pornographic ring for he had been sexually abused before being asphyxiated. Beside the article was a picture. He had curly hair and a cocky smile.

Nell crumpled the paper violently, thanking her lucky stars she had seen it after rather than before, for it would have affected her performance and no mistake. She prided herself that 'Cleo' felt nothing but what she was expected to feel while on the job; that her professionalism was up to all situations, no matter how bizarre. Nell and 'Eleanor' were left behind when Cleo was on stage, but this – this was different because Nell *was* very much involved. Sex involving children was something about which she had very strong feelings – passionate feelings. It was those feelings which had compelled her to telephone Dorset police. Had she seen this, Cleo would have been undermined by Nell struggling in the background.

On the way home – she walked the long way because she wanted to think – she knew that she could not let it rest here. She knew enough to give the police a definite lead as to the men who had murdered that thirteen-year-old; she knew a name, a place – she had seen what was probably the body being taken away to be dumped in that unmarked grave. She could not sit *shtoom* and let them get away with it; perhaps entice and murder other children. But neither could she self-destruct her own carefully structured, firmly controlled life.

I've worked long and hard to get where I am, she argued with herself furiously; done things normally regarded as way beyond the pale; rented myself out – for high fees, yes, but nevertheless I've used my body as my stock-in-trade for years and I'm entitled to the right to further years of decent obscurity. If I go to the police I have to tell them *what* I am as well as who I am; why I was in that house in the first place, how I knew and was thus able to recognise the face of a man I know from past experience is heavily involved in the making of pornographic movies. I have to expose a life I have deliberately kept as private as possible. What will I be left with? My clients will run for the hills the moment it becomes known I blew the whistle on one of them. I'll be *done for!*

And if you don't go you will be damned, her inner self told her stonily. We are talking children's *lives* here. This is not just a case of pornographic movies; this is a case of adult men who get their kicks from having sex with children! For God's sake, Nell! What you do is considered morally reprehensible by most people, but what these men do is absolutely appalling! That poor boy was obviously sodomised again and again before being asphyxiated. This is as low as you can get! This is foul, aberrant, abhorrent – oh, you name it and it is what men raping children is. Dear God, if anyone should know it is you. Remember Margaret . . .

Her step quickened until she was almost running, as if being pursued by something from which she was in a panic to escape even while knowing there was none; that it would always be there, behind her, waiting to pounce. By the time she reached home she was out of breath and gulping air. This won't do, she told herself, as she went once more to the drinks trolley. One way or another you must settle this before you become an alcoholic.

Even though she went to bed half-cut she still lay, sleepless and wide-eyed. Four o'clock found her at the kitchen table drinking coffee and understanding, for the first time, what Scott Fitzgerald had meant when he described 4 a.m. as 'the dark night of the soul'. By eight o'clock she was downstairs again the moment she heard the thud of the Sunday papers and saw to her annoyance that though they had delivered the *Sunday Times* they had left the wrong tabloid. She always read both kinds of Sundays: one for news and the other for amusement. This one had her drawing in a startled breath as she saw the picture on the front page and the headline: MOTHER'S ANGUISHED PLEA – FIND THE MEN WHO MURDERED MY SON. The picture was the one she had already seen; the curly-haired, cheekily smiling thirteen-year-old boy, but the story was about his mother; her pain, her grief, her bewilderment, her plea for anyone who knew anything, no matter how insignificant, to come forward and give the police their help. The story – written by the crime reporters – said that Dorset police were playing this one close to their chest but that the word was out that Darren was the latest in a series of child murders. The bodies had been found miles apart, but there was a similarity to the killings: what it was they were not saying. What was obvious was that there was a well-organised paedophile ring which filmed their own activities. 'These men are dangerous,' the Chief Inspector in charge of the investigation said. 'They must be stopped before they can kill any more children. I am asking the public at large to be on their guard and at the same time to report anything suspicious in the area in which the body was found and for another seventy to a hundred miles beyond that. A mini-van was sighted near the spot and we have had a very helpful report that puts us a little more in the picture but if anybody knows anything more – anything at all – please call us. Your calls will be strictly confidential.' Once again the telephone number was given.

That was Nell's Sunday ruined. Normally she had a leisurely breakfast over the papers, then spent the rest of the morning pottering: doing chores, catching up on odd jobs. She always cooked herself a special lunch and the afternoon was spent on the sofa with the papers, finishing off with a leisurely bath after which she washed her hair. The evening was always spent on the sofa, watching television if it was worth while, with her current book or a video if she felt like it.

The story on the front page put paid to that. It drove her from the house to walk the streets, walking and walking and thinking and thinking. When she finally became conscious of her surroundings, because her feet had begun to ache and she felt like a sit-down, she realised that her subconscious had brought her back to a part of London she had not revisited since her time with Mickey Shaughnessy. She was on Queen's Drive, off Seven Sisters Road, one of her old stamping grounds. She had not walked it since, saw that in the intervening decade it had changed. There were metal gates at the entrance to Queen's Drive from Seven Sisters Road, preventing cars from driving round the block, which was what the punters had done back then, giving the girls the once over before making their choice.

Nell shuddered. How she had loathed that life. Queen's Drive had been a meat rack, no more. They had all been meat racks. Flesh for Sale. It had been cheap. She had been cheap. Felt cheap.

Liz rescued me from this place, she thought, as she searched for a taxi among the traffic. All right, so maybe it was enlightened self-interest as Philip says. It still saved my life. Thank God Liz did her voluntary work at the hospital; her way of giving something back, she said. Well, maybe you are now being offered your opportunity to give something back. Tell the police what you know. Help them. These are *children* they are murdering. You can't *not* do anything, you *can't*. If anyone has reason to loathe what men do with children sexually it is you. Remember Margaret . . . do it for her. God knows there is little else you can do for her. The only way you are going to purge your guilt is by doing something positive. Telling the police about what – and who – you saw is about as positive as you can get.

It will help put Tony Panacoulis away. That loathsome creature should be stopped from doing what he does. Paula told you years ago that he made pornographic films using children. You know he is involved in this present appalling business so *do* something about it!

Wracked with indecision and torn by doubts, she flagged down the first cab she saw and arrived back home in a tormented frame of mind as well as clobbered with tiredness. Not having slept at all and then having walked her feet off, she was too tired to eat and by the time she made her heavy way upstairs to fall on her bed she was already half asleep, but such was her still disturbed emotional state that her dreams were nightmares in which she felt as if she was being literally torn apart: the plump, motherly Sergeant held one of her arms above the elbow, the nice young Inspector held the other, but her legs were held by Philip and Mickey Shaughnessy. It was a tug of war, and she could feel herself coming apart. She woke up to find that she was twisted in the duvet, her legs wrapped tightly in it, while she had somehow worked one of her arms into a pillow case which had caught itself between the cotton satin of the bedhead and the mattress. She was soaked with sweat and her mouth felt thick and nasty, her eyes gritty.

Five minutes under a brisk shower and a session with the toothbrush followed by a mouthful of Listerine and she felt better. The cats, who had followed her to bed, padded downstairs after her, and she fed them both, after which she made herself a plateful of scrambled eggs which she ate with two slices of well-buttered wholewheat toast, washed down with not one but two cups of tea. Then she felt better, up to getting out the phone books to look up the number of the police station at Kings Cross.

She wrote it down on her pad, picked up her cup and sat sipping and staring at the number. If that nice young Inspector was still there she could tell him. It was doubtful that the Sergeant would still be around. She must be long retired by now; she'd had twenty years in back in 1979 and twenty-five was the norm. But the Inspector; he'd been young and firm – no nonsense about being sympathetic, but he had been understanding. If she told him, face to face, he could get the information back to Dorset, couldn't he? It was best and certainly safest. She could not afford to take chances with Dorset. Best she stayed away from there. Who knew what spies Tony had planted here and there.

The rumour, back in 1979, had been that he had a certain high ranking officer in the Vice Squad on his payroll, which was why he was never bothered. He was probably bigger and more powerful now, eleven years later. Who knew how long his reach was? No; better deal with the Met. They could pass her information on. And no names. She would insist – get it written in blood if necessary – that she be kept out of it. She would be – what did they call them – 'an anonymous informant.'

She would not say a word unless she had that promise. And she wasn't going to Kings Cross either. She had once known too many people in that area. No; they would meet in her part of town. And no uniform. Plain clothes. Either he met every single one of her conditions or he didn't meet her. Yes, she thought, as she dialled the number. Be firm. Philip always says – her finger stopped and she slammed the receiver down. She had dreamt that Philip did not want her to say anything. He had been aligned with Mickey Shaughnessy. Mickey she could understand, but Philip . . .? Philip's first concern was always himself. Once he was certain he was in no danger, then he acted.

She could see him in her mind's eye, lips pursed, that little frown knitting his exquisitely shaped brows, hear that judiciously considering voice saying: 'Tricky, very tricky. One has one's duty to assist if one is quite certain one can, but in your case . . . *You* must decide: do you have more to gain than lose by coming forward? If you can do it and still remain in deep cover then all well and good, but in these publicity ridden days there are spies simply *everywhere*. It's those wretched newspapers and the ridiculous sums of money they are willing to pay for the most insalubrious scandal, especially connected with sex. I applaud your public spirit, my dear, but I admire your courage even more.'

You wouldn't do it, would you, Philip? she asked him in her mind.

'Only if I could do it in such a way as to leave no trail whatsoever,' she heard him answer. 'You are dealing with dangerous men. What they do is held in utter opprobrium by all right-thinking people, yet they still do it because they are driven to it. I have always found that paedophiles are, for the most part, driven men. And driven men are dangerous. They have already murdered. Think on that before you decide to involve yourself in their nasty little world.'

I have, she told him silently. I've done nothing else but think, lately.

'Write an anonymous letter,' his voice suggested.

'No; I'd never know a moment's peace unless I knew *for sure* I was safe. If I do this I need protection. Besides, forensic science these days is an advanced art. I'd be worrying all the time that they'd trace the letter to me. If I do this I have to *tell* somebody, face to face.'

'Catharsis', she visualised Philip saying with grave authority. 'I always knew you had a bad case of conscience-ache.'

Nell sat rigid, then slowly she relaxed. Yes, she admitted, to herself as well as him.

'Paying for the erasure of a few black marks?' The snide tone she knew so well echoed in her mind. 'Bargaining for redemption?'

'I have my reasons,' Nell told him out loud.

'Oh, I know *that*', she imagined the clipped voice saying slowly. 'It is what they are I cannot seem to discover'.

And never will if I have anything to do with it, Nell thought. But she picked up the phone again, stabbed the number with firm conviction.

'Kings Cross Police Station'.

'Oh, I wonder if you can help me. I would like to speak to an Inspector Stevens.'

'Who?'

'Inspector Stevens.'

'No Inspector here by that name, Madam.'

'But he used to be there – I knew him when he was.'

'When was this, Madam?'

'Oh . . . some time ago. 1979.'

She heard a whistle. 'A lot of people have come and gone since then, Madam,' the voice said with exaggerated patience.

'Then could you tell me where he is stationed now, please?'

'Hang on a minute . . .'

Nell waited, finally another voice came on: 'You wanted Inspector Stevens, Madam?'

'Yes. He was – very helpful to me some years ago and I would like to get in touch with him again, if possible.'

'Then you'll have to try Scotland Yard, Madam. And he's not Inspector Stevens any more. He's Detective-Superintendent Stevens.'

'Oh!'

'If you ring 230 1212 and ask for Det Supt Stevens I think you'll find him,' the voice said. 'He hasn't been at Kings Cross for more than ten years now.'

'Thank you,' Nell said. 'I'll do as you suggest.' She hung up. Detective-Superintendent Stevens!

Her nice young Inspector had gone far.

So far as to have no memory of a young prostitute he had twice cautioned all those years ago? He had given her a fair deal, then. But a Superintendent . . .? She had not bargained for seeing the Headmaster when what she expected was her form mistress. This was not working out as she had hoped, which was to pay a quick visit to Kings Cross, tell her story to a policeman she felt comfortable with then retire while he lit the blue touchpaper.

I can't afford to be seen going into Scotland Yard. That would be absolutely fatal as far as my discretion is concerned. All it would take would be someone to see me doing so. He'll have to meet me, she decided. I'm the one with the information, after all. Somewhere on neutral ground. A bar? A hotel lounge, perhaps? The sort of place where I'd blend in with the background. He'd be in plain clothes. He is a *Detective* Superintendent after all . . .

She could not get over the fact, for some reason. Would he be the same? Would she recognise him? She remembered him very well. Had he not been half-cut that night she would have a police record. She had always felt she owed him one. So, now is your chance to pay the debt, she urged herself.

All very well, but what if he is anything but pleased to be looked up by an ex-tom he should by rights have arrested. All right, so it is because of him that you have no record, but he may not wish to be reminded of that. He did you a favour but he was going against his own regulations. You may be an episode he prefers to forget now that he is that much further up the ladder – and probably intent on climbing even higher.

In which case he'll seize the information you have got for him with cries of Alleluia! This murder is of sufficient importance to warrant the police asking for help on national television! In which case I could be involving myself in something from which I will have great difficulty in extricating myself. Oh, God, she thought tormentedly. I don't know . . . I just don't know . . .

She mulled it over for the rest of the evening, went to bed still undecided but so tired by her emotional karate that she fell asleep in minutes and knew nothing more till the rattle of the milkman's bottles woke her.

She did not get a morning paper, she always read the *Evening Standard*, but today she made a point of going out to buy a couple of tabloids. They had picked up on yesterday's story and the distraught mother's plea was featured on both front pages.

'It's no use,' she told the cats as she sat over a cup of coffee in the kitchen later. 'I am being pushed inexorably towards a certain course of action.' They both chirruped at her, blinking their liquid-gold eyes. Sensing her mood, they jumped up on to the worktop as she went to the phone on the wall and dialled the number for Scotland Yard.

When she asked for Superintendent Stevens and was asked: 'Who is calling, please?' she said: 'My name is Elly Little.' That name had produced a surprised quirk of the eyebrows then. What would it produce now? To spur slumbering memory she added: 'I knew Superintendent Stevens when he was an Inspector at Kings Cross.'

'What is it in connection with, please?'

'I have some information for him.'

'One moment please.'

She waited. Finally, a voice said: 'Stevens here.' Nell took a deep breath then said: 'I doubt if you will remember me but we did meet some years ago when you were an Inspector at Kings Cross.'

'I left Kings Cross at the end of 1979,' the voice – deep, crisp and even, as the carol says, Nell thought irreverently – said. 'Was it in connection with a particular case?'

'Well – mine, I suppose. You stopped me on York Way one night – accused me of soliciting, but you let me off with a caution.' She did not mention Park Lane. That could come – if anything at all came of this – later.

'I am no longer with the Vice Squad.' There was no change to the voice but Nell sensed he had lost interest.

'But you would be able to pass on such information as I have to the right quarters, wouldn't you?'

'Information about what?' He was still giving nothing away, not even curiosity.

'The body of the thirteen-year-old boy who was found in a shallow grave in Wareham forest, Dorset, near a badger sett.'

There was a hanging silence then he said in a different voice: 'Yes, I would be able to do that. What connection is there between you and that death?'

'I think I know where it took place, when – and perhaps why.'

'Why have you not contacted the Dorset Police? They are in charge of the case.'

'There are reasons – very good ones – why I don't want to have anything to do with them or that part of the country. If you want to know more I am willing to meet you somewhere and tell you.'

Without missing a beat the voice said smoothly: 'Where and when?' Nell named a fashionable watering hole in the Kings Road. 'This evening, six-thirty. I'll be at the bar.'

'How will I know you?' Still no surprise that a one-time tom should wish to meet him in a favourite Sloane rendezvous. 'My hair is black, short, with a fringe, my eyes are green and I will be wearing an ivory silk dress and a single row of pearls. Oh – and Giorgio. Do you know anything about perfumes?'

'I know that one.'

'At six-thirty then.' Nell rang off.

Mark Stevens leaned forward, switched off the tape recorder he had turned on as soon as his caller had mentioned the death of Darren Henry, wound it back and then replayed it. 'Listen to this,' he said to the man sitting across his desk.

When they had, Mark Stevens switched it off again.

'Well? Do you remember her?' Detective Sergeant Bill Ross asked.

'Haven't the faintest. I cautioned or arrested a hell of a lot of toms back then. Elly Little . . .' He cocked an eyebrow at his colleague. 'Did she sound like an Elly Little to you?'

'No. More of an Elaine. Nice voice, educated accent. I can't say I ever met anybody like her during my time on Vice, but for what its worth I'll check the Central Index for 1979 – maybe 1978 to be quite sure.'

'Thinking it over I doubt if she'll still be there. It's too far back.'

'But if she is?'

'I'll feel better, but I want you there in the background tonight. Get there about 6.15. See her come in and then sit where you can keep an eye on us both once you've checked the other customers.'

'Do you think it could be a set-up?'

'One never knows, but this Dorset body ties in with the ones found on five different Met patches in the last eighteen months. It's vice, it's organised and it's a similar modus operandi. She could be part of it, maybe a disgruntled part; somebody who feels she's not getting her fair share of the action. We know there's a paedophile ring and we're pretty sure they film or video their activities. Could be she's a performer. Or it could be that she has stumbled, quite by accident, on something she can't handle.'

'Is that why she wants to tell you, do you think?'

'I have no idea, but it is probably a case of The Devil You Know. You heard what she said about not being able to tell Dorset Constabulary.'

'You are sure you don't remember her?'

'For God's sake, Bill, there are more toms on the streets of the Cross than there are discarded fag-ends!'

'Yet she obviously remembers you.'

Only you, Bill Ross thought wryly, torn between admiration and envy. Mark Stevens had been brought up by a mother who thought the sun shone out of his aspect, and this had given him a confidence with women that he took for granted but had other men pea-green. He was a career-cop; at thirty-eight one of the youngest Superintendents in the Metropolitan Police. His father had been a successful barrister but his mother was the driving force. Her ambitions for her only son were limitless, even though she had not been pleased when, on coming down from Cambridge with a First in Law, the light of her life had opted to uphold the law rather than practise it.

He'd gone to Lewes for his three-day interview, been grabbed with delight and been a Sergeant in two years. They had then sent him to the Police College at Bramshill where he had studied under an accelerated promotion course. At twenty-five he had been an Inspector. For two years he was on Vice at Kings Cross then applied for the CID. After two more years at Vine Street he went for Det Chief Inspector and got it. This resulted in him being posted to Paddington for three years. By the time he was thirty-eight he was a Detective-Superintendent attached to the Serious Crime Squad (Paedophiles) at Scotland Yard.

He was regarded as upper echelon material and his QRs were songs of praise. His record as a detective was excellent because he had, as they said, 'a nose for it'; could read between lines that looked blank to everyone else and never took anything at face value. He could charm the birds off the trees one minute and blast them to a handful of feathers the next. He liked nothing better than taking what looked like a Gordian knot and patiently unpicking it, yet he could be corrosively cutting if a file he asked for was late in coming. He was generally liked but resented by some who called him 'the blue-eyed boy' because the Commissioner called him by his first name.

By the time he was forty, they said, he was expected to be Chief Superintendent and Commander by forty-five. That left only two more rungs to climb, 'and if by some miracle the Home Secretary is a woman he's an odds-on cert,' was the general opinion, 'because one look into those baby blues and he's home and dry.'

Except they weren't baby blue; they were a hot, fierce cobalt which could chill to a North Atlantic grey when displeased. They made a vivid contrast to his prematurely greying yet still blond hair – he'd begun to go grey at thirty – and he had the height – two inches above six feet – and the long legs which most women found made their libido distinctly itchy. Bill was not in the least surprised that this unknown would-be inform-ant had remembered the young Inspector of all those years ago. Women had a habit of retaining not only Mark Stevens's name but his face and personality in their minds. 'Once met, never forgotten' they used to say about him to his face. Now they said it behind his back. In any case involving a woman or women it was always Mark who got the come-on. Sometimes he took the hook, sometimes not, but there was no doubt as to the love of his life: his job. No woman had ever managed to push that from centre stage, though a few had tried. Most gave up because of the unsociable hours, his willingness to work them, his dedication, his absorption in something other than themselves, the hours spent waiting for him until they realised that they had been forgotten. His last affair had been with a Hollywood star making her latest blockbuster at Pinewood, who had been receiving sexually threatening letters from some nutter. She was Big News; powerful enough to rate something more than an overworked Inspector, so because she was creating merry hell and he was good with women, they sent

Mark Stevens. It had lasted as long as he had the time to spare and she realised, once he hadn't, that his mind was not on her even when he was in her. She had taken Five-Million-Bucks-a-Picture umbrage then taken up with a noble Lord who was only too happy to let her rent his stately home for five thousand dollars a day and follow through his family motto 'Service is Our Duty' at night. Since then – and it was more than six months now – the only woman who saw anything of Mark Stevens outside work was his mother.

'So,' Bill asked, 'how do we work this. Usual set up?'

'I think so. Until we get a look-see and good sniff at the atmosphere. She could be a plant, she could be something entirely different.'

'Like somebody whose old man you sent down?'

'Possibly. We treat it with caution. A possible informant but with you watching my back.'

'Do you know this bar?'

'Yes.' Mark grimaced. 'It's all flash and filigree; a place to be seen, but not at half past six in the evening. The people who go there aren't even out of bed at that time. It will be quiet, sparsely populated. Something she obviously knows.'

'Still on the game, do you think?'

'Not the one she would have been playing at Kings Cross. The Kings Road attracts a different kind of player.'

'So how will *you* play it?'

'By ear. Let her do the running. If she's progressed onwards and upwards to a club like this she will know the form,'

'And I'll check the Prostitutes Index meanwhile – just on the offchance.'

14

When Bill saw her come in – he had already been in place ten minutes, every inch the overworked businessman relaxing after a hard day – he had to do a double take. It was her; no doubt at all. She fitted the description perfectly. Short, glossy black hair framing a camellia-pale face with eyes so startlingly green he could see their colour from where he sat, at a table by the wall, and a lusciously red mouth. The ivory silk dress would have somebody's name on the label and those pearls had the glowing lustre of the real thing.

You're a long way from Kings Cross, love, he thought admiringly. I doubt if I could afford you myself these days – if you are still selling it, of course. You look as if you found yourself a rich punter and button-hooked him into marriage. It's been done before, after all.

He rustled the paper he had bought, watching her over the top of it; noticed she was in no way intimidated by being the only woman in the place; that the man behind the bar was there the moment she perched herself on a chrome and leather stool. Her smile was just right; friendly yet with the perfectly judged amount of distance. However, Bill doubted she was a regular. Had she been, the barman would have addressed her by name. That was always good for a bigger tip.

She ordered something which was shaken, not stirred, and poured into a glass rimmed with salt. Tequila, thought Bill. Probably a Margarita. He picked up his own Scotch and sipped carefully. The Department was coming down heavy on expenses incurred in these days of financial stringency.

As he sipped he saw Mark Stevens come through the swing doors – the bar was down a double flight of expensively carpeted stairs once you entered a lobby at street level – and stand there, looking around, every bit as confident as she was.

This ought to be interesting, Bill thought, as he saw their eyes meet in the mirrors that lined the wall behind the bar. Bingo! He thought as he watched the way they sized each other up.

In fascinated attention he saw her smile, swing round on her stool, slide from it in one easy movement and flow across to where Mark was standing, reach up to graze his cheek – just missing his mouth – with her lips. 'Right on time, as usual,' she said, in a voice which promised the best of all possible rewards for such punctuality. Then she slid her arm through his and walked him to a table by the wall, the one furthest away from where Bill was sitting, but which, if he faced the other way – which could be done after a trip to the bar for a second drink – gave him an unobstructed view. He saw Mark, without appearing to, give the bar's other occupants the once-over, satisfying himself, as Bill had done, that there was nobody there worth worrying about. They both remembered the case of a detective, some years before, who had gone to meet an informant alone in a pub when it was too early for it to be crowded, and been pinioned in his chair by one man while another cut his throat. They had been gone before their victim hit the floor and nobody in that pub was ever able to make a positive identification. Now, he saw Mark slide into the banquette beside her and nod at the hovering waiter. His hand had been in his jacket pocket, now he took it out and smoothed the flap in place. That meant his pocket recorder had been switched on. Bill waited until the waiter had brought her drink over as well as a Scotch for Mark, and then himself drifted to the bar for a refill. When he came back he sat so as to be able to see everything that went on in the corner.

'That was nicely done,' Mark Stevens complimented, and sincerely.

'This is the sort of place where couples meet. That's why I chose it.'

She was no one he had ever seen before. As her name had

rung no bells, nor did her face. She could not have looked like this, he decided. This was not a woman easily forgotten.

'You don't remember me, do you?' she asked, as if reading his mind. She was not put out, merely factual.

'No. But I met a lot of girls during my time at the Cross.'

He tensed as she reached for her small black patent clutch bag, but what she took from it was a photograph which she slid, face down, across the table towards him. 'This is what I looked like then.'

He looked at it, then at her, then at the photograph again. There was, he supposed, a certain likeness, but it was so vague that unless the direct comparison was made the connection would not be. The hair was a mass of back-combed frizz, the make-up was overdone and the cleavage was crude. And she was pathetically young. It evoked no memories whatsoever. He had seen so many young girls like that. In the years since then she had been re-made. Plastic surgery, he thought, of the very best kind. A new hairstyle or even a wig, and made up to look as if she is not. Or is she? He had never seen such a flawless skin, while the dark-green, exceptionally brilliant eyes were extraordinary. The fragrance of her – just enough, for Giorgio was a powerful perfume – eddied about him like a mist.

'I was Elly Little then,' she said, taking the photograph back and putting it away. 'Mickey Shaughnessy was my pimp.'

'Now I do remember *him*. He OD'd about five years ago.' He caught the echoes of her surprise. 'You didn't know?'

'I haven't been back to Kings Cross since the day I left it eleven years ago.'

'So Elly Little was not your real name.' None of them ever had given their real names; everyone had been known as somebody else.

'No. I was formerly known as Nell so I turned Dickens on his head.'

His cobalt blue eyes lit with appreciative laughter. 'Little Nell – Elly Little! I like it.'

'You seemed to at the time. Nobody else had ever twigged. I suppose that's why I remembered you – plus the fact that you only cautioned me.'

'It was not often I met – girls,' his tongue would not call this woman a tom, not yet, anyway – 'who read Dickens.'

And it still did not bring her to mind. It could all be as made up as the rest of her.

'I am known now as Cleo Mondaine, and what I have to tell you is what I came across in the course of an engagement with a client who owns a house in Wiltshire.'

There was nobody near enough to hear but she had lowered her voice just the same.

'An engagement?' He knew what she meant but he wanted her to say it so it could be on tape and no mistake.

'I am still in the same line of work only much further up-market. I don't walk the streets any more, I have an answering machine and a steady clientele. I go wherever my clients ask me to go, all expenses paid. That was how I found myself in Wiltshire.'

'Go on'. He never took his eyes from her face, and his voice was as low as hers. To anybody watching they would appear to be having an intimate lover's conversation.

She told him what she had seen that weekend in Wiltshire; what she had heard, what she had put together, what she had done about it.

'Now you see why I can't be associated with that part of the country. If one word of this gets out I'm done for; not only as far as my profession is concerned but maybe my life. Tony Panacoulis is a nasty customer – or was when I was with Mickey Shaughnessy. The only thing I could think to do was get in touch with you. For some reason I still thought of you as the Inspector who read Dickens. I ought to have realised that if I had gone up in the world there was no reason why you should not have done the same.'

There was dry amusement in her voice, and he found himself intensely curious as to how she had effected her own transformation. He had never known it happen before, though he had heard stories, of course. Normally, the gulf between the girls who walked the streets and the ones who entertained 'at home' was one that was impossible to cross unless you had either the talent, the brains or the sheer *nous* to do so. This woman, he thought, has all three. I'll bet she charges for what she trades in. And I'll bet she's worth it. As one who had never had to pay for it in his life, his attitude was more than somewhat patronising.

'So let's go through this again . . . give me dates, times and as much description as you can.'

She did so, answering his detailed questions to the best of her ability. When he was satisfied, he asked her if she would mind giving him her address and telephone number which at first she refused to do. 'I have to be careful,' was all she would say.

'And we will protect you; we always protect our sources of information.' She met his eyes and put the boot to his delicacy.

'A grass, you mean.' Her eyes challenged him. He lobbed it back.

'I mean we will protect your anonymity. All I can tell you right now is that the information you have given will be looked at and, if necessary, acted upon. I'll give you my pager number; that way you can get in touch with me any time you feel the need. In turn we need to know your address, telephone number and your date of birth.'

'Why that?'

'It's something we always ask. A means of verifying identification.'

She shook her head. 'This is not what I bargained for. All I wanted was for you to know what I saw, help to get whoever it was murdered that poor innocent boy. I can't afford to get involved beyond that. I am putting my livelihood on the line here.'

She was obdurate and he recognised a strong will; someone who would not be bullied. It was not that she was ashamed of what she did; he had no sense of prickly self-esteem or defiance. She was totally self-possessed and secure in her estimation of herself, which was that of a successful businesswoman, even if what she did peddle was her body. Something he had been conscious of since he saw her get up off her stool. The ivory silk crêpe dress was by no means tight fitting, but it clung lovingly where it touched, and when she crossed her legs his acute hearing caught the sensual rasp of silk against silk – that most female of sounds. When she raised her glass – and she made her one drink last and refused another – he saw the soft curve of her breast and, as the silk momentarily pulled taut, the outline of her nipple. Her sexuality was like the low hum of an electricity generator. He wondered what she charged.

Top whack, probably. If he could only find out where she lived, that would be a good indicator. High rent meant high earning.

Appearing to give up he sat back, raised his glass and glanced around the room. Catching his detective-sergeant's eye he put up a hand to straighten his tie. This was a pre-arranged signal and meant that he was to follow the informant when she left the bar. A pat of the re-arranged tie meant it would not be long now. He saw Bill fold his paper, empty his glass, check his watch and then heft his briefcase preparatory to going home to the wife.

'It is really no big deal to tell us where you live, you know,' he said, making one last try. 'Your information has to be checked. Should there be anything further we wish to know how do we get in touch with you?'

'I will get in touch with you,' she countered. What is she hiding? he thought, absolutely determined, now, to find out where she operated from but sensing that it paid to go carefully. If she was as high-powered as his instincts told him, it was likely that she had clients very well placed to offer her not only the very best legal advice but also very politic – even political – advice. She was certainly used to dealing with authority. As a senior police officer he was used to his rank producing both nervousness and unease. Except in her case.

She had come a very long way indeed from the young scrubber he had absolutely no memory of cautioning all those years ago. But she had been cheap then; to buy and to look at. The intervening years had refined and defined her. Only her own composedly candid admission had placed her position in the scheme of things. Had he not known what he was meeting he would never had guessed, but he was thankful that she had remembered him, thanks to his recognition of the back to front name she had given him then. He appreciated her sense of humour but he was angered by her obstinacy. If she persisted he would have her for obstructing the course of justice. She was a whore, a fully paid up member of Rent-a-Body. All right, so she was not what she had been but then, neither was he, though he had to give her the fact that she had recognised him right off. But that was because there had only been one of him.

'Am I to take it, then, that you are not prepared, to co-operate with us?' His voice suddenly lowered the temperature, but she was hot with certainty.

'I have taken an enormous risk in giving you the information I possess as it is. I am not prepared to become involved any more than I already am.'

'Yet you expect us to involve the Metropolitan Police in a murder that is not strictly within their jurisdiction; to involve us in the expense of checking a story that you refuse to back up with factual proof that you are not just making all this up. I came here in good faith but I am still waiting to see evidence of yours.'

Oh, he had changed. There had been a steely purpose to the young inspector but he had also been kind; it was with relief that she had recognised him; older naturally and with prematurely grey hair, but still good looking, still the man who had taken pity, done no more than caution and kept her from having a record. Now there was no softness at all, no sympathy, no understanding. The poster-paint eyes looked at her as if *she* was a suspect and his voice brought out gooseflesh. It also raised her hackles. Nobody bullied her. She didn't care if he was a Detective Superintendent. She had been driven to expose her carefully preserved anonymity to him by a conscience kept primed by memory; she was damned if she was going to let him treat her as if she were still the nineteen-year-old tom. She was worth a hell of a sight more than that!

'I am not prepared to say anything more,' she told him curtly. 'I am already beginning to regret having said anything at all! I *volunteered* this information. I could have kept my mouth shut and wiped my memory clean but I didn't. I got in touch with you because I remembered you as someone sympathetic, who would understand my situation and act accordingly. Don't bully me, Superintendent. I may be beyond your particular pale but I am no longer some pathetic tart to be pushed around by self-important policemen. I have friends in high places and I know enough about them to be absolutely confident of their help should I need it. I have told you all I am going to say, and I'm damned if where I live and how old I am have anything to do with it!' She rose to her feet. Her chair scraped and people looked, but only momentarily. A lover's quarrel. Big deal. They returned to their own concerns. 'If you want to take this further, Superintendent – ' the way she spoke his rank had red flagging his high cheekbones but he did not move as she bent towards him – 'then arrest me!'

Then she was walking – no, striding out of the bar, almost cannoning into Bill Ross who was also leaving but who stepped back with a a murmured apology, keeping his head down, before following her out, putting on his hat as he did so, leaving Mark Stevens seething.

Nell was conscious of having made not only a bad but a stupid mistake, but it was too late now. You and your hasty temper, she despaired of herself. The last thing you want is a mean policeman on your tail. Even if what you do is not against the law he can make it his business to make your life a misery. If he can find me, she told herself.

Oh, come on, Nell. He's in the Met! Of course he can find you. He's probably got you on file somewhere even if you don't have a record. He can use his authority to get your telephone number from British Telecom, you idiot. You gave him your professional name, didn't you? Yes, but my number is ex-directory. No matter. If he hasn't the clout he can go to someone who has. You don't talk to high-ranking policemen like they were errand boys. All he has to do is go to the Police National Computer, which is said to interface with all other ministry computers, and he will find you on one or the other. But not as Cleo Mondaine. The house is Eleanor's. I pay tax as Eleanor. Only my accountant knows I am also Cleo Mondaine and he won't say anything because he does the accounts for too many people who have absolutely no desire to have the police talking to the man who keeps their two sets of books. Yes, but if this no-longer sympathetic copper decides to go for me he can drop me in it with the Inland Revenue. He will know enough to know that my fees are always paid in cash – which I don't and never have declared. *Now* what about your precious privacy? You and your tender conscience, she raged at herself, walking so fast that Bill Ross had to move to keep up with her though careful to keep at least ten yards behind. He had thought she would take a cab, had not planned on having her walk all the way from the King's Road to Hyde Park Corner to the little mews behind Wigmore Street. He was out of practice and out of breath by the time he saw her unlock the door of the house next but one to the big double doors of the warehouse; the one painted sugar pink. He noted the address before making his way back to the Yard, where he checked it against the electoral rolls.

Mark Stevens found all the information there was about the little house and who lived there waiting on his desk when he returned to his office later that evening.

For a day or two, Nell's mood was rendered fretfully uneasy by the conviction that she had not done herself any good in contacting a man remembered for one small good deed which to him was so small he had absolutely no remembrance of it. But then, didn't she know only too well how two people's memory of a particular incident could differ so as to appear to be two completely different occurrences? Certainly the man she had met the other night and the one she remembered were not the same. He had been a smart copper, she remembered that; uniform immaculate, buttons and insignia shiny, but the elegant man in the Armani suit was not what she had expected at all. It was not that she was not used to elegant men; she dealt with them all the time. It was that she had frozen one small encounter in time; encapsulated it in treasured memory and got it all wrong. You should have known better, she told herself bitterly. You ought to know that the higher they climb the tougher they become. It's all that lack of oxygen; the competition is so fierce that only the strong survive, and your nice inspector is now a survivor. Remember that matronly sergeant at Stoke Newington? She'd been in the job for twenty years but had been a sergeant for only five. He's gone from inspector to detective superintendent in eleven years! Talk about accelerated promotion! I picked the wrong man, she thought. I should have tracked down the sergeant, asked her advice. Or kept my mouth shut. He won't let it rest there. I know he won't.

One day passed, then another and then another, and her fears subsided. I gave him the information, she thought relievedly. And that is what matters, surely. She scanned the newspapers back to front but nothing appeared in them concerning the body and the badger sett. Nor did she hear from the client. For her own part she kept her head down and her nose to the grindstone.

Which was why, when the doorbell rang one Thursday evening, not fifteen minutes after she had returned from work, she was shaken rigid, when she looked through the glass spyhole she had had installed, to see Superintendent Stevens standing outside. He *had* tracked her down! Fool! Fool! she berated herself, than catching sight of herself in the Regency mirror above the telephone table her eyes widened, she caught a breath and then smiled. Let him make what he could of this! She opened the door.

Mark Stevens's practised smile faded as he saw the middle-aged woman standing there.

'Yes?' Miss Eleanor Jordan enquired.

'I would like to speak to Miss Cleo Mondaine,' he said politely but firmly.

'Why?'

He held out his warrant card. 'I am Detective Superintendent Stevens. I met Miss Mondaine last week concerning enquiries we are making.'

'Well you won't be able to make any more because she's not here,' Eleanor lied innocently. 'She is in New York.'

'For how long?'

'I don't expect her back this week.'

'Are you her housekeeper? You live here?'

'No to both. I come to feed her cats.'

'Then perhaps you will be able to answer my questions.'

'I have strict orders not to allow strangers into the house.'

'I am a policeman, Miss – er?'

'Jordan. Eleanor Jordan.'

Holding the hot blue eyes she saw them flicker at the name and knew he recognised it, which meant that the enquiries now concerned her. Well, in for a penny, she thought, yet conscious of excitement sparkling along her nerve endings, adrenalin changing her blood into top gear.

She stood aside and motioned him through the front door. 'I was just making myself a cup of tea,' she told him, 'would you like one?'

'Yes, I would. Thank you.'

She led him into the bright kitchen, watched him appreciate

its designer luxury, then punctured his surmise by saying: 'Actually, I am not Miss Mondaine's housekeeper. She is *my* tenant. This is *my* house.' There: if he had been raking through electoral rolls and rates demands he would see she had nothing to hide. 'When she is away I come in to keep an eye on things and feed the cats.'

Which was when he saw two beautiful cats, the colour of smoke, sitting on the wide window sill, regarding him from twenty-two carat eyes.

'She travels a lot?'

'Oh, yes, All the time.'

'On business?'

'Yes. She is a public relations consultant, you know.' Since this was what Cleo Mondaine's passport said and there was no knowing if he had checked that too, it was as well to be honest – well, as near as dammit.

'How long has she been your tenant?'

'Oh, for some years now.' She poured tea into a breakfast-cup-size example of Villeroy & Bosch's *Geranium* pattern, which matched the decor, and set it in front of him. 'Help yourself to milk and sugar.'

'Is she a good tenant?'

'I could not ask for better. She is immaculate – as you can see – and her rent is always paid at least one quarter in advance.'

'Do you live in the district?'

'No.' Nell improvised wildly. 'I live near Westminster Cathedral.'

'But you work in this locality?'

He had been checking. 'Yes. Three days a week. I am receptionist to Mr Ronald Dysart, the plastic surgeon, in Wimpole Street, and have been for some years now.'

'How did Miss Mondaine come to be your tenant?'

'She saw my advertisement in the window of an estate agent. It was originally only to be for six months, but we got on so well and she really is the perfect tenant. Who knows what I would get if I were to terminate our agreement? And house prices have escalated so much the past ten years.'

'Does she entertain much?'

'I really could not say, but I would doubt it. Miss Mondaine leads a very active social life when she is working; I think she regards this as her – dare I say bolt hole? When she is here she lives very quietly.'

'Are you acquainted with any of her clients?'

A blank look. 'How could I be? They never come *here*.' Patiently, as if explaining to a fool: 'I have told you that her clientele is international.'

'Have you ever heard her mention a Mr Reza Dominitian?'

'No. Is he a client? She never discusses her work with me, Superintendent.'

Pause.

'But you are friends?'

'I think I may say that we are.'

Her smile was prideful. 'She trusts me with her cats, and they mean the world to her.'

Sipping her tea, she watched him giving the kitchen a comprehensive scan, noting the expensive Italian tiles, the Smallbone kitchen units and worktops, the operating theatre cleanliness of it all.

'But you are not her only friend, surely,' he commented idly, sipping his own tea.

'I am sure I am not, but I cannot name you any of her others.' For a moment an imp of mischief prodded at her to give him Philip's name, but caution kept her mouth shut. It was not that Philip had anything against the police; he had more than one 'old friend' in their ranks, from the highest to the lowest, but this was nothing to do with him and it was already becoming a dangerous mix as it was.

'All I can tell you, Superintendent,' Miss Eleanor Jordan said primly, 'is that Miss Mondaine has never, in all the years I have known her, ever given me the slightest cause for concern. She is the perfect tenant, she has a very good job, and she keeps my house in excellent condition. I cannot for a moment think that she would ever knowingly be mixed up in *anything* unlawful.'

'Our enquiries concern Miss Mondaine only insofar as people she might know are concerned,' he replied disarmingly, throwing her a smile that was his equivalent of throwing an obedient dog a bone. It made her wish it *was* a bone and she could brain him with it.

'Then I am afraid I cannot assist you.' Her eyes widened, alarm flooded her voice and she put a hand to the high neck of her dun-coloured crimplene dress. 'Unless – you are not investigating *me*!' she gasped.

'No. Nor Miss Mondaine. I merely wish to speak to her again to ask if she can assist us further with our enquiries.'

'Oh . . . .' A gusty sigh of relief. 'That's all right, then.'

'Perhaps, when Miss Mondaine returns, you would ask her to get in touch with me. She has my telephone number but in case she may have mislaid it in her very busy life – ' the irony clanged as it met Eleanor Jordan's one-way mirror but only she heard it – 'I will leave it with you so that one of you has it.' He scribbled his name and telephone extension on a piece of paper he tore from his loose-leaf notebook and pushed it across to her. 'I will put it with her post this very instant,' Eleanor said earnestly. As she had known he would, he followed her into the sitting room, where she slid the piece of paper in front of a sheaf of envelopes held by a brass spring that spelled FOR ATTENTION. 'There, she cannot fail to see it.' Two of the envelopes were ones that had come that morning and had not yet been opened. Since one was from the Inland Revenue and the other from her accountant, she had put off the evil moment till later. Fortunately, both were addressed to Miss Cleo Mondaine. It was the ones behind that had come for Miss Eleanor Jordan, but unless he took them out and leafed through them there was no way he would know this. Since he was merely 'making enquiries' he would need a search warrant to proceed further. Anyway, hadn't she already bluffed him good and proper?

He was examining the room, and though his was a good policeman's face in that it kept quiet about his feelings, her own internal radar, honed by years of experience of intimate encounters with strange men, told her that he was surprised. No, it's not your average bordello, is it? she asked him silently. You are not the only one who has come a long way, you know. And yes, I do have a lot of books, don't I! What's more, I've actually read every single one of them – at least twice. And that *is* quite a record collection, isnt it? 'You can see how neat and tidy she is,' Miss Eleanor Jordan praised.

He made no comment. There was no telling what he thought. Was it experience that gave policemen their impassivity or was it part of their training? One of the things she had remembered about the Nice Young Inspector was his smile, but since the one the Superintendent had given her at their first encounter it had been off duty. Just then he turned to look at her, caught her pensive stare and gave the smile an airing. It intensified the colour of his eyes and she noticed that either he had an expensive dentist or he was blessed with perfect teeth. What did a Superintendent earn nowadays? £30,000 – £40,000? plus overtime, of course. He obviously spent money on himself since his suit was beautifully cut and his Burberry was the real thing, as were his hand-crafted highly polished lace-ups. She had noticed that the watch on the wrist that was exposed as he held his tea-cup was wafer thin on a crocodile strap. She was willing to bet that the name written on its face was Boucheron. She had an American client who had one just like it.

'Thank you for being so helpful,' he said smoothly. 'And you will ask Miss Mondaine to get in touch with me on her return, won't you?' The velvet glove was of as good quality as the rest of him but there was no getting away from the steel it covered.

'Oh, I most certainly shall,' Miss Eleanor Jordan twittered.

'When is she expected back?' It was casual but she was ready.

'One day next week. She will ring me, as usual, once she knows which day that will be. She always takes a night flight and gets home at about nine in the morning, then I know she always goes to bed to get over her jet lag, so it will probably be the day after her return that you hear from her.'

She was leading the way to the front door as she spoke, opening it to allow him to pass through it to his car – a beautifully maintained BMW whose black paintwork gleamed wetly – parked and waiting for him.

'Goodbye, Superintendent,' she said, smiling brightly.

'Goodbye, Miss Jordan.' She shut the door on him but put her eye to the spyhole. He crossed to his car but did not get in it. He stood back and gave the house a leisurely once-over before doing a 360 degree turn to take in the other houses, the warehouse, the dead end at one end, the exit to Wigmore Street at the other.

That's right, Nell fulminated. Advertise your presence. Not that there was anything about him that said 'copper'. It was just that the only men who ever came to the house were those who read her gas and electric meters, the occasional workman and Philip Faulkner. Finally, he got into his car, did a perfectly executed three-point turn and at the Wigmore Street end turned right.

Only when he had disappeared did she let out a breath. Its gusty relief was that of coming to the end of a performance. She felt drained; at once relieved it was over but anxious as to how her performance had been received. She thought she had fooled him, but unease sent her to the mirror. No . . . there was absolutely no resemblance between the greying spinster with her unflattering hairdo and frumpish clothes, eyes owlish behind the steel-frames of her glasses, and Cleo Mondaine, the worldy hooker with her designer dresses and exquisite face. The one face was unadorned and lined at the eyes and mouth corners; the other was a work of art. No, she thought, reassurance reinflating her confidence. He has no way of knowing we are one and the same person. But she knew, as she went upstairs to shower and change, that if he really got down to it, he could peel the two apart like sticky tape from plastic. To tell the truth she had not meant to do it; had done so only because he had caught her on the hop, so to speak.

What she was really doing, she supposed, as she took off her 'ageing' make-up and brushed the grey streaks from her hair, was fighting a delaying action. Sooner or later she would have to stand her ground and fight. But maybe, by then, they will have arrested whoever murdered that poor child and won't need me any more. I hope, she thought, as she stepped under the shower. There might be a chance – albeit a slim one – that my deep cover won't be blown and the five years I need to achieve unassailable security are still possible. All I can do is wait and see.

'So you think Eleanor Jordan has no idea what her "perfect tenant" actually does for a living?' Bill Ross asked.

'If she does she's a very convincing liar. She's everything Cleo Mondaine is not. Ultra respectable, very prim and proper. Not the kind to let her house to anyone – and unfurnished. It was far too luxurious for someone as self-effacing as she is.

The decor is obviously to the tenant's not the landlady's taste,' Mark Stevens answered.

'Early whore?'

'Anything but. Late *House and Garden*.' Mark cocked an eye at his sergeant. 'Have you ever been inside a high-class call-girl's house?'

Bill Ross had to admit that he had not. Plenty of prostitute's bed-sits, but that was all.

'There is a whole world of difference between the two – like the fees they charge.'

'Is this Cleo Mondaine a specialist, do you think? I mean her having Reza Dominitian for a client? If he's the money-man behind the porn ring and also provides the studios and the equipment . . .'

'He comes up sweet as a rose. A highly successful, extremely rich entrepreneur; one of Margaret Thatcher's go-getting boys. He came to this country at the time she won the election in 1979 – from Germany, where he'd been for the previous six, and his passport says he was born in Smyrna – like Aristotle Onassis, only he's not Greek, he's Armenian. He has every single finger in a rich pie of one sort or another, and in the eleven years he's been in this country he has pulled out one plum after another. He is on first-name terms with a lot of very powerful and highly influential men – as the Dorset County Constabulary discovered when they called on him. Very politely, of course, and ostensibly to warn him that there was a gang of house-breakers operating in the vicinity, and was he happy with his security arrangements etc. He showed them round without a qualm and the place was as clean as a whistle. He even showed them the wing he'd told Cleo Mondaine was kept locked. No sign of anything. In the garages he had nothing but Rolls and Mercedes and the absolutely latest Porsche. No mini-van.'

Bill Ross's mouth turned down at the corner. 'Well, county constabulary . . .'

'I was at Bramshill with the DCI who's handling the case. He's a good copper; only left the Met to go to Dorset because his wife wanted to take care of her ageing mother. He says the place was absolutely clean. Lots of workmen, ladders, smell of paint – they went through each and every room and he told me that there was nothing; that if there had been, every trace had been most carefully removed. The one thing that was revealing was the house's electricity supply. It has its own generator, and it is powerful enough to supply power to the sort of lighting needed on a filmset. And in one large room, though a trestle had been moved in front of it and wallpaper artistically draped to hide it, the power outlet was big enough to supply a whole street of semi-detached houses equipped with every electrical appliance known to man.'

'Tyre tracks?'

'None. But Cleo Mondaine said the van was parked on the grass, and that was being cut with a power mower at the time of the "inspection". It was either brought in specially for the job or it belonged to somebody who has since got rid of it because it has not been seen since.' Mark shook his head. 'No . . . we are dealing with a well organised ring here, with money to back them up. Either they will have moved their base of operations elsewhere or they'll wait until they feel the coast is clear and start up again. What would be of great assistance would be another visit by Mr Dominitian's own personal whore. Which is why I want to keep in touch with her. As soon as she gets back from the States I intend to have another go.' Mark Stevens looked down at the sheet of information his sergeant had provided. 'I see no telephone number for Cleo Mondaine. I doubt very much if her clients call her through her landlady so check and see if she is ex-directory. Lean a little and get the number. Give them the usual story about helping with our enquiries but don't press too hard. I don't want to start people wondering. And why isn't she on the Voting Register? Only Miss Jordan is down as being eligible to vote. It may be that Cleo Mondaine doesn't really live in that house but uses it as a base of operations as far as her clientele is concerned. Yet that's the address she gives in connection with her driving licence and it is the one on her passport. I've got that itch at the back of my neck that tells me something is not quite kosher here. Keep on digging, but tactfully. Something is being hidden. I want to know what it is and why.'

'Do you think her information was suspect?'

'No. I believe she saw what she saw. She came out of deep

cover to give it to me. I thought I knew – if only by word of mouth – all the courtesans in this town, but she's been very discreet indeed. Either she peddles the sort of services that her clients can't possibly afford to have known, or she herself has something to hide.'

Bill Ross pursed his lips and whistled soundlessly. 'I wouldn't say she hid her light under a bushel the other night.'

'Then why has she gone to ground? Miss Jordan says she is in America, but she was not particularly forthcoming when I asked her for information about her tenant.'

'Well she's got no record – under either Elly Little or Cleo Mondaine.'

'Did you check the fingerprints from the glass I gave you?'

'Yes. They are not on file either.'

Their eyes met. 'Fake as a fifteen pence piece,' Mark said succinctly. 'That's another thing. What's her real name? Where is she from? I don't like mysteries, Bill. I only like solving them, and something about this one has got me bent and determined to get it sorted out.'

'Move over Inspector Morse?' grinned Bill.

A couple of days later, the Dorset police raided a video rental shop in Swanage on a tip-off that behind its façade of normal box-office hits obtainable for £2 a night there was a second, even more lucrative rental trade in pornography. Surveillance revealed that certain favoured clients were allowed through to the rear. This turned out to be an even larger shop whose shelves were lined with videos of the hardest porn. They were seized by the police as evidence, and as such had to be watched so that a report of their contents could be made for the prosecution once the case came to court. It was while one of them was being watched by a PC who felt he was overdosing on sex that a member of another relief came in to see if there was anything worth watching.

'Not after the first couple of hours,' he was told sourly. 'I never thought I'd hear myself say this but it is true; when you've seen one you've seen them all, and there's only so many things you can do with it anyway.'

'Don't be like that,' the young policeman said, eyes riveted to a pneumatic blonde of impossible proportions who was performing incredible feats with a man who was hung like a horse.

'She'll never swallow *that*!' exclaimed the young policeman, even as she did. As the camera moved in for a close-up it swung slightly – obviously it was hand-held, because for a couple of frames it lost its subjects and focused on what seemed to be a huge fireplace before sweeping down to the rug in front of the flames – which was all that had previously been seen of it – and the man and woman making an exhibition of themselves.

'Hang on a minute. Go back a bit . . .'

'What for? I've got dozens more of these sodding things to view yet – '

'Here . . . let me have it.' The young policeman picked the remote control from the arm of the chair in which his fellow officer was slumped, and ran the video back to that point where the camera swung upwards and focused on the fireplace proper rather than just the enormous grate. Then he put it on hold before going forward to crouch in front of the television screen.

'I knew it!' He exclaimed. 'I know that coat of arms. I saw it somewhere recently, a big shield and an axe and a sword and some Latin underneath. I can't read it from here but I'm sure it's the same one . . . that big house we went to . . . a reccy for the studio that makes things like this. Don't move it on. I want the guvnor to see this.'

When he had: 'You're right,' his chief inspector said. 'It's the one we saw. Huge great thing . . . took up practically all one wall. Roast a couple of oxen in that fireplace. Well done, Crawford. You've got sharp eyes.' He turned to the original viewer. 'Keep your eyes peeled, Mason. Anything else out of the ordinary apart from the sex – and you report it, along with the name of the video and the counter number.'

'Yes Sir,' said PC Mason, gloomily. He had hardly made a dent in the piles of videos stacked around the room. Thank God somebody else would be taking over soon.

'Any sign of children being sexually involved?' the CI asked.

'No, Sir. So far just – well – ordinary stuff,' the young PC answered disgustedly. He'd heard they videoed women with animals, group sex, daisy chains, homosexuality et al, yet of the dozen videos he had checked so far all he's seen was close ups of every kind of sexual intercourse between fabulously endowed men and insatiable women.

'Then keep looking,' he was ordered, before the CI took the tape away with him. A copy of the frames featuring the fireplace appeared on Mark Stevens's desk a couple of days later along with an explanation as to their origin.

'So her information was spot-on, Sir,' Bill Ross said, as they both looked at them.

'It would seem so, Bill. It would seem so. But I still can't get hold of her. She's not yet back from America.'

'Well, now that you've verified her information there's not much more she can do for us, is there?'

'It depends on the outcome of any further investigation after the discovery of this very interesting piece of film and the result of the surveillance we will keep on our friend Mr Reza Dominitian. I want the best we've got on this one. There's no doubt Dominitian is implicated; Cleo Mondaine's evidence and these two frames prove it to my satisfaction even if it is all circumstantial. I need to know much more about this man; where he goes, who he sees when he sees them. I want the numbers of the cars he drives as well as those of the people he meets and I want every single one of them checked out. He's a powerful man and he has a lot of highly-placed friends so it has to be softly, softly, right? If anybody causes him to so much as raise an eyebrow in our direction the culprit won't get any overtime for the next ten years! We've got his London address, and if he leaves for the country we tip the wink to Dorset and they can handle their own end. I want to know *everything*, Bill. This is a powerful and dangerous man and he's in a filthy business. If anything comes in from Dorset about a video using children I want to know, but I've got a feeling that they are tightly restricted to members of the paedophile ring. And I want an eye kept on Tony Panacoulis. We know him of old, but I want to establish the connection with Dominitian beyond the most reasonable of doubts. That's why I want to see Cleo Mondaine again. I want to know everything she knows about this particular client of hers. I also want pictures; lots of lovely sharp black and whites of the subject, his life, his lifestyle, his friends, his family – the lot. That had better be

Davis; he fancies himself as a Lichfield. Put Scott and King on his tail; they're the best double act we've got and he'll have to have eyes in the back of his head to spot either of them. Tino Constant will do nicely for Tony Panacoulis since it often takes a Greek to know just exactly what gifts another Greek is concealing in his pocket. I want to be able to produce an exact map of the lines on both their faces by the time I've finished and since we won't have much time in these cost conscious days and surveillance costs both arms and legs we must make the most of it. An intensive effort, Bill, for as long as we can manage it, so as to find out whatever there is to know before analysing it.'

The cobalt blue eyes met the brown ones, and Bill Ross recognised their light.

'Super's got his teeth into this one,' he reported back to the squad. 'He wants this collar so go to it lads. There's overtime a-plenty but it won't last for long and if the hours don't show results it'll be the last you'll see until they start turning up bodies buried in Buckingham Palace gardens. Do I make myself clear?'

A week later, on checking her answerphone, 'Cleo' found a message from Mark Stevens requesting a further meet, and asking her to ring him with a time and place. Her first feeling was a nervous realisation that he had obviously been busy digging deeper into her life. He'd got her ex-directory number, for a start.

Although she had diligently scanned the papers there had been nothing more about the Dorset murder, and none of the television programmes, either the detailed appeals for help or the two minute flashes between commercials had mentioned it, so why did he want to see her again? She had not heard from the client since talking to the police about him, and she had not been aware of anything untoward as far as the even tenor of her life was concerned. She simply had nothing more to tell them, and when she finally called Scotland Yard and was put through to him she told him so.

'I am not after direct information,' he cut in, using the voice that made people feel they'd been put in their place. 'I want to show you some photographs; find out if the people in them are known to you. It would be best done in private. Could I come and see you?'

'To my house!'

'I *am* a plain-clothes detective.'

'So is Lieutenant Colombo,' 'Cleo' snapped. 'Haven't I made it plain enough, Superintendent? I can't afford to get involved with the police!'

'I won't look like one. I can promise you that. And if you want to make it even more natural I could pick you up somewhere and we could arrive at your house together – as if we were good friends.'

God, but he was persistent. The original irresistible force. She had the feeling that all she would get out of coming on as an immovable object would be exhaustion.

'All right,' she conceded grudgingly. 'Come on Friday evening.'

'What time?'

'Six o'clock?'

'I'll be there.'

For some reason she could not as yet define, he got right up her nose. God, but he had changed. 'Will Success Spoil Mark Stevens?' Yes, she thought rancorously. He thinks he's God's gift: probably wants to have *his* show on television. She mourned the nice young inspector, with his kind smile and his interested concern. Well, they said police work hardened you. They had told her that when she first went on the streets.

'There's some right bastards out there,' Paula had warned. 'One wrong look and they'll have you. They hate prostitutes except the word *they* use is slags or whores. They talk to you as if you were something they'd trodden in and in their eyes you are sub-human because you fuck for money. Which is not to say that if you were to offer them a freebie they wouldn't say no, but even then you can't trust them. I had one like that when I first started. Offered to look the other way if I did the business with him. *And* he got his no-money's worth. After which what does he do but arrest me, and when I try to tell about the deal he accuses me of making unfounded allegations against a police officer! Bastard! He got caught, though, by somebody sharper and wiser than me who stitched him up a treat when he offered *her* a deal. The Vice Squad has got some real nasties so be careful. Always look at their eyes; don't go by their voice. Some of them can sound ever so reasonable and sympathetic but it's all a con. Stick with me as much as you can and follow my lead until you know your way around.'

By the time Nell did, she knew enough to spot a genuine kindness when it came her way. But all the girls had liked him; thought him dishy, sighed that *he* could arrest them any time . . . And she had to admit that even this time he had not been anything other than perfectly polite. Those very blue eyes had met hers head-on and he had not been in the least bit thrown when she'd gone across and kissed him. And what imp of hell had made her do *that* she still didn't know, except that the moment their eyes met in the mirrors behind the bar her every hackle had fixed bayonets. Which was only natural. She had always been very careful to give the police a very wide berth, ever mindful of the security and confidentiality her clients paid for and of those names she would have had to erase from her list had they for a moment thought she had anything to do with a policeman, apart from traffic offences, of course. 'Discretion is all,' Philip had quoted to her back at the beginning.

Now I've got a high-ranking policeman coming to my house – I must be mad, she despaired.

'Cleo' was at her most immaculately soignée when she let him in at six o'clock on the dot. A crisp shirt of heavy pure white silk organza with bishop sleeves and a wide, deeply collared neck worn with black crêpe narrow legged trousers, her bare feet in thonged sandals, toenails to match those of her hands, which both picked up the silky scarlet of her mouth. The black hair shone and her eyes had been made smoky with clever makeup. She smelled of *Knowing*.

He was casually dressed; beige chinos, a checked shirt and a beautiful suede jacket. He carried a large manila envelope and he looked like anything but a Superintendent of the Metropolitan Police. She did not know whether to be pleased or piqued. He kept meeting her when she rounded corners.

She offered him a choice of coffee or a drink.

'A drink, please. I see you have some Wild Turkey over there. Straight, on the rocks.'

'You know America?' she asked, as she poured it.

'I spent six months there studying their big city policing methods; three months in New York, three months in Los Angeles. How was New York this time?'

'Hectic,' 'Cleo' lied smoothly. 'I was told of your visit,' she went on as she handed him his drink. His hands were large but well-shaped; long fingers, well-kept nails. He wore no rings.

'You have a very contented landlady. She says you are the perfect tenant.'

'She is every bit as perfect as a landlady.' 'Cleo' sipped her own small gin and large tonic.

'Is all this hers or yours?' He gestured to the creamy tranquillity of the sitting room, calm and elegant with its warm ivories and yellow and black fabrics, its fresh flowers and gleaming mirrors.

'Mine. I took the place unfurnished.'

'Nice,' was all he said, but it warmed as the gin did not.

'So these are all your books?' he went on, gesturing at the shelves above the cupboards on both sides of the fireplace.

'Yes.' Her voice was honeyed when she asked: 'Haven't you ever met an educated whore, Superintendent?'

'Several times. I know one who has a Master's Degree in Economics and a PhD in Philosophy, but she earns more from her research into the perfect orgasm – and she got no grant for that.'

When she could, 'Cleo' said: 'I don't think I know her.'

'Not surprising. She doesn't operate in London any more. She did all the research she could here. Now she has done a stint in Paris, one in Rome and she is at present in Brussels. Lots of scope within the EEC.' His face was straight, his voice matter of fact but 'Cleo' did not dare look at him. She concentrated instead on looking at the big envelope which he had laid on the black lacquer coffee table.

'Are those what you want me to look at?' she asked.

'Yes.'

'Have you had any results from the information I gave you – or aren't you allowed to answer that.'

'We have had results but not enough to justify laying charges against anyone.' Laying down his glass, he sat forward, and 'Cleo' noticed that when he did so there was no bulge above the leather belt that held up his chinos. Something that could not be said of any of her clients. But he had to be a good ten years younger than the youngest of them. There was no blur to the chin, either. His jaw-line was clean and though his face showed his approaching middle age those lines he had were laughter and smile lines only. The eyes were as blue as ever. What was it she had heard one girl say about them all those years ago . . .? 'Talk about My Blue Heaven . . . I'll bet that's where he could take any girl.' And somebody else had said: 'Chance would be a fine thing. He don't do no trade-offs on account of he don't need no sexual favours. He gets it for free . . .'

He raised his head, caught her staring and for a moment their eyes held then he was opening the envelope with those long fingers and laying out, like a hand of cards, a succession of black and white photographs, six by eight. For a moment, as she stared at them, they made no sense to her; all she saw was a blur, then as her vision cleared and her mind steadied she recognised the face of Reza Dominitian.

'It is not him we want to know about, it is the people he is with,' Mark Stevens said. 'Do any of these faces strike a chord in your memory?'

She went through them slowly and carefully, aware of him watching her, which made it difficult to concentrate, but when she said: 'No. I don't recall seeing any of these people before,' she was telling the truth. She raised her head to look into the blue flames again.

'None of them are present or former clients?'

'I have no "former" clients, Superintendent, except those who are no longer alive.'

Their eyes collided. His were penetratingly intense; all she could see was blue. She had a feeling that if she were to put out a finger and touch them they would smudge.

Without removing them from her: 'Would you label this particular client as being out of the ordinary in any way?' he asked.

'No. He is a very predictable man. He laid down a set procedure from the start about which he was very particular. He gets irritable if it is not followed.'

'So you were surprised when he asked you down to Wiltshire?'

'Yes, I was. Previously we had always met in London.'

'Here?' He pushed across with one long finger a photograph of Dominitian leaving a tall narrow house in Chelsea.

'No. We always meet at a service flat in St John's Wood.'

'May I have the address?'

She gave it to him and he wrote it down in a flip-over notebook. 'Have you a key?'

Her silence made him say: 'It will be copied and returned to you, but we have to investigate all leads.'

She got up from the sofa and went out. He heard her ascending the stairs. Instantly he was up and investigating the books, reading spines and running his fingers along bindings to see if anything was concealed between them. She had catholic taste, he discovered, surprised by his own surprise. Everything from Montaigne to Mary McCarthy. In the cupboards underneath was a state of the art hi-fi system on one shelf; racks of CDs and LPs below. And again the range was wide. She had a lot of Stephen Sondheim, he saw approvingly. He never missed a Sondheim himself. Lots of Sinatra, Carmen Macrae, Edye Gorme and someone he found people had often never heard of – though again he was a fan – Blossom Dearie. She also had Stravinsky, Ravel, Debussy, Aaron Copeland as well as Beethoven, Brahms and Berlioz. He heard her coming down the stairs but only closed the doors on the records. When she came in he was leafing through a well-thumbed copy of *Vanity Fair*.

He was about to say something but he saw the look on her face so merely replaced the book and returned to his chair. She laid the key on the table with a snap.

'I need hardly remind you that I am literally putting my livelihood in your hands.'

'Where it will be taken care of,' he promised. 'I am aware of the risks you are taking, Miss Mondaine – that is not your real name, by the way, surely?'

'No. But it is the one I use for working purposes – which is the only area of my life that concerns the police right now.'

He backed off. 'Fair enough. I'll get this key back to you as soon as I can.'

'Drop it through the letter box,' she said coldly. 'Now, is there anything else?'

'Yes. Do any of the faces in these photographs strike a chord?' He put away the first batch, spread a second one in its place.

'That's Tony Panacoulis,' she said, identifying a face in the first one. Her glimpse of him in the house that night had been brief, but it had been him all right. He still dyed his hair; too densely black to be real above his doughy face. It always would remind her of an over-ripe fruit; slightly bruised looking and pulpy to the touch. And that mouth; always pouting, as though about to blow a kiss. He had given her the creeps then and he did so now.

'Do you know the man with him?'

'No.'

'Or any of these others?'

She examined them carefully. 'No . . . wait . . .' She picked up a photograph of a group of men leaving a Soho club. One of them was pulling up the collar of his overcoat and his arm partially obscured his face but there was something familiar about what she could see of it. 'I think . . . only think, mind you – that he is the man I saw carrying the roll of carpet. The way his hair falls over his forehead, and his nose – it's been broken.' She chewed her lip. 'The man I saw had his face partially obscured by the carpet but there is something familiar about what I can see of this one . . .'

'Did you notice anything about his hair – apart from the way it falls over his forehead.'

He saw her frown.

'No . . . except I think it was auburn. There's a lamp at the edge of the drive and as he passed under it I remember thinking it was the colour of marmalade.' She looked up, met his expression and asked involuntarily: 'That's good?'

'You've just identified "Ginger" Telford. A known associate of Tony Panacoulis. A fixer, a gofer and a carrier-out of dirty jobs. Like disposing of bodies.'

'So can you arrest him?'

'Not yet. We only have your word that you saw him and Panacoulis, and knowing them they will be able to furnish cast-iron alibis that they were not within a hundred miles of that house. We need something more than – '

'The word of a whore?'

He did not pretend. 'Yes.'

She sat back, picked up her glass and emptied it. 'Then I have done all I can – until you call me to give evidence at the trial, of course.' The edge of her voice would have shaved ice.

'You have been of enormous help, and I'm grateful. I know the risk you took.'

'Do you?' Her doubt was that of Saint Thomas.

'Yes. And I promise you here and now that if there is any way I can keep you out of whatever transpires in this investigation, I will do so.'

'You mean not produce me as a witness?'

'I hope to get evidence that will make such a thing unnecessary.'

'But you can't say for sure.'

'Not possible in my line of work.' He smiled and she blinked. 'But trust me.'

'That's why I called you in the first place.' It was out before she could stop it; quite involuntary and instantly regretted. He would think she was spreading the butter far too thickly. So she shrugged and added: 'You were one of two police officers who treated me other than as a body wearing a For Sale sign all those years ago.'

As she had known he would: 'Who was the other one?' he asked.

'A WPS at Kings Cross. She was known as "Ma" because she was motherly and used to scold rather than condemn.'

'Ma Parkes.'

'Yes . . . I'd forgotten her other name. Probably because I only ever thought of her as Ma, but I reckoned she was probably long retired . . .'

' – she is.'

'So I called you.' There, that should take the gilt off his gingerbread. She saw his glass was empty. 'Would you like a refill?'

'Please. It's not often I get offered a liqueur bourbon.'

'I bought it because I occasionally like a whisky sour.'

'And you use a bourbon like this! Sacrilege! It should be drunk unadulterated by anything other than ice because it is best cold. If you want a whisky sour you should use Jack Daniels or Old Grandad.'

'I do.'

Bossyboots, she thought. Six months in the States and he's an expert. But she poured him a double – let's see him drink *that* and drive, she thought, and took it back to him. His smile as he took it also took the sting from her *amour propre*. Whatever it was that had entranced the street girls, he still had it.

'You spend a lot of time in the States, don't you?' he asked.

'I go about a dozen times a year, usually brief trips; a weekend, normally, but now and then three or four days. It all depends on the client.'

There was a pause, during which he examined the beautiful Waterford crystal of his glass.

'Would it be out of order if I asked you how you made the transition from the pavement to the hotel suite?' he asked, but in such a way as to make it clear to her that his object was not prurient curiosity, nor was it professional; she sensed a real interest.

To gain time she picked up her own glass, took a mouthful, let the gin and tonic trickle down her throat before answering: 'I was lucky enought to be spotted by a remarkable lady who was coming to the end of her active life and wanted to pass on the benefit of her knowledge and experience to someone she thought worthy of it; someone to carry on where she left off. She . . . trained me, changed me, made me over, in fact. Everything I have, all I am, I owe to her.'

'She must have been remarkable.'

'She was.'

'And is she in honourable retirement?'

'No. She is dead.'

There was another silence. She was still on guard for the particularly intrusive question, the careless reference to something which could, if equally carelessly answered, lead him in directions she would rather remained unexplored.

'How did you get to be a superintendent so quickly?' she asked divertingly.

'I entered the Met as part of a special university intake and went from Cambridge to Bramshill . . .' He told her what had happened to him since Kings Cross.

'And this Squad you head – it specialises in pornography?'

'In serious crimes against children. Like the murder of Darren Henry.'

'Are you any further forward?'

'Not far enough to make an arrest. We have confirmed that there is a well organised, financially backed group making pornographic films, and that within that group there is another, smaller group of paedophiles who make other, more specialised films for their own delectation. Over the past two years the bodies of five children have been found in various Metropolitan Districts. They were all killed in the same manner as the latest one, and they had all been appallingly sexually used and abused.' He paused. 'Sexually tortured, in fact.'

She made herself get up slowly, when what she wanted to do was jump up and run, and turn her back on him to go over to the drinks trolley where this time she put more gin into her glass than tonic.

'We are dealing with sick people,' Mark Stevens said in an even, uninflected voice. 'I'm sorry if I upset you, but it is as well to know what your client is involved in.'

She gave him ten out of ten for perception, and then reminded herself that he was trained to be so.

'You are sure he has never been anything other than – '

'Normal?' The edge was back to her voice.

'He may be using you as a blind. You don't see him that often, do you?'

'Four or five times a year. I know he is no longer a young man but either his sexual appetites are diminishing with age or he satisfies them in other ways. I have never, ever, received from him so much as the slightest impression that he has deviant sexual tastes. In fact, considering that he is a man who likes order to an almost obsessional degree I would say that he would regard that kind of sex as gravely disordered.'

'Disordered enough not to be invested in?'

'No.' There was no hesitation. 'First and foremost he is a businessman.'

Now, he thought, let us see if it is true that prostitutes are experienced judges of the male. 'Why do you think so?'

'Because his approach to sex is wholly businesslike. More than once I have had to change an appointment because some business which was much more important came up. He likes value for money, but he also likes money.' She frowned slightly, as if sorting things out in her mind. He waited. 'He is the kind of man who would never put pleasure before business, and if there is a lot of money to be made in the making and renting of paedophile films then he would not hesitate to invest.'

Mark Stevens nodded. That fitted with the information they had received from Holland. Reza Dominitian had been heavily involved in the porn trade there while ostensibly living in Germany, where his business activities were entirely above board. Ergo, it was likely that he *was* the money-man behind the UK operation.

'You have no other information about him which might be useful to us?'

The extraordinarily beautiful green eyes – deep and dark as the Atlantic – looked straight into his as she said calmly and flatly: 'I know nothing about the private lives of my clients, Superintendent, except what they choose to tell me, and Reza Dominitian is the type who does not. He pays me to have sex with him every now and then. End of story.'

'Why?'

If she was thrown by the question she did not let on. 'Because he likes uncomplicated sex. He has no time for the rituals, I think was the word he used at the time, of male-female behaviour. He prefers not to clutter his mind with emotional involvements. When he wants sex he pays for it.'

'Did you know he has a wife in Smyrna?'

'No.'

'Of some thirty years or more. Tell me what you do know about him if you will.'

'He is self-made and proud of it. He seems to know Europe very well and is an expert on the EEC. I know he speaks several of its languages.' She paused. 'But the one he was speaking with Tony Panacoulis was Greek. It came to me the other night.' She thought again. 'I think his financial base is Zurich – '

'One of them. He has bank accounts in the Cayman Islands, Hong Kong and various other tax havens. His holding company is registered in Panama. In fact – as befits his nationality

– his business affairs are byzantine in their complexity. He has shareholdings in just about every large company on the Stock Exchange and thus privy to the secrets of a thousand board-rooms. We believe he supplies the financial backing for Tony Panacoulis.'

He saw her shudder.

'You said he contacts you every ten or twelve weeks as a rule?'

'Yes.'

'If and when he does – play along with him.' Over-riding her protest. 'We cannot afford to arouse the slightest suspicion on his part.'

'What about my part?' Indignation vaulted on to its high horse.

'It could be performed under surveillance.'

Horror-struck, she could only gape at him until she fumed wrathfully: 'No way!' She jumped to her feet, such was her agitation. 'That would be fatal!'

'Not the way we do it.'

'There is no way I would allow you to do it in the first place! Haven't you understood a word I've said? I cannot afford the slightest risk of my prized discretion showing so much as a hint of blight!'

'It wouldn't. I give you my personal guarantee.' He paused. 'And I don't go around handing them out like warrants.'

For a moment she was taken aback and her eyes met his, held them until she read their message, when they tore themselves away.

'He hasn't contacted me yet, so aren't you jumping the gun?' she asked, but she was referring to something else and they both knew it.

'My offer stands, nevertheless.'

So near and yet so far, he thought. She wants justice done but she doesn't want it to jeopardise her earning capacity. Which must be considerable. Probably twice – even three times – my own. She had a life-style that was expensive no matter which way you looked at it. Like her. In no way did the cheap words used to describe the women of her profession fit her. Slag was ugly and woman-hating; tart was cheap; whore was hate-filled, hooker was hard, courtesan euphemistic. The word the Americans had coined fitted the bill perfectly, as usual. Call-girl. Except this was no girl. This one was a woman in every sense of that multi-meaningful word. And incredibly unsoiled. How did she manage to be so unsoiled? There was no way he could match up what she did with how she looked. She fitted another American word perfectly. Classy. Sexually elegant. Not your average woman. But he had known that the moment he had set eyes on her; she had assaulted his senses like the 100 per cent pure, triple-distilled cocaine he'd been offered by the Hollywood sex symbol, who had been honestly astonished when he told her he should, by rights, arrest her for it. No more astonished than he was though, at allowing himself to indulge in fantasies involving a woman who made her living helping make such fantasies come true.

Who was she, anyway? Where was she from? She gave very little away and guarded her privacy with all the ferocity of the female guarding her young. For all he knew she might have some tucked away where nobody could get at them or connect them with her. He just did not know enough about her for his own satisfaction, and he wanted to know it all. He could not rid himself of the feeling that Cleo Mondaine was self-invented and self-created; that behind the exquisite façade there lurked another woman, one quite different. He'd come across it once before. A woman whose academic researches had been funded by her extra-curricular activities, about which her colleagues in the senior common room knew absolutely nothing. A professor by day and a prostitute by night. Perhaps Cleo Mondaine had another, secret life. She had no police record. Not as Elly Little. Not as Cleo Mondaine. Not so much as a parking ticket. She paid her bills and taxes and kept her head below the parapet. But she was hiding something. He knew it like he knew the sun would rise next morning. Just as he knew he would not let her go until he had found out what it was. More important, what *she* was.

15

'You are not yourself, my dear Nell. I sense a certain – *distrait* quality. If there is something worrying you, then allow me to quote the age-old cliché that a trouble shared is a trouble halved,' Philip said.

'I'm not in any kind of trouble,' Nell answered.

'Come, come. Remember to whom you are speaking. Faces are my fortune. All the truths and lies of humanity are there to be seen in the human countenance provided you know what to look for. Yours has a quality I would describe as – absent. You are with me – and I appreciate the visit since hospitals are not my idea of fun places – yet you are somewhere else. *With* someone else, dare I ask?'

'What sort of drugs are they giving you?' Nell riposted.

'Those that combat the kind of virus pneumonia which clobbered me yesterday morning. I was perfectly well when I went to bed – I had met this perfectly *delicious* young Tunisian. My dear, his body . . . I saw one just like it once, but it was a statue carved by Praxiteles.'

'They told me that you had collapsed.'

'Yours was the first name that came to mind . . .'

'Because it is one not likely to cause speculation?'

Philip met her smile with unruffled calm. 'One has to be circumspect in our position – whatever that happens to be at the time.'

'But they would have to be told that you are HIV positive.'

'It was the very first thing I did tell them once they got me here. But then, of course, once my own doctor arrived I left it all to him. He saw to it that I was moved into this private room – all those years of paying medical insurance are finally beginning to pay off – and I have to admit that after living in the vicinity of Westminster Hospital for so long it is fortunate that it is still open and able to receive patients.'

'And what is the prognosis?' Nell asked.

'I have AIDS,' Philip answered flatly. Then he shrugged, the public persona banishing the sudden anguish behind the mercury glitter of his eye. 'It is no longer a matter of being HIV positive. It is because my immune system is now under attack that I succumbed to the virus so quickly. From now on, time is also my enemy.'

Nell was silent.

'It is not as though it was not expected,' Philip said, patting the hand she had laid on top of his, but for the moment, the silence was as heavy as Nell's heart. She did not love Philip Faulkner as Liz had done. He was not her idea of a lovable person. But she had become used to having him around. In spite of her reservations he had woven himself into the fabric of her life and would leave a dreadful hole when he was no longer around to supply his own particular weft and warp. In his own way, she knew he was fond of her. She had been prepared, she had thought, ever since he had told her he had tested positive, but this had still caught her on the hop. It was a situation not unlike that of her mother's MS. She had known for four years, because her father had been careful, in his scrupulous way, to tell her exactly what the situation was; that her mother was dying, yet the shock had still been more than she could handle. Which was, no doubt, why what had happened as a consequence had been even more impossible to accept, never mind handle. The difference was that this time she was old enough to understand.

She drew a deep breath, held it a moment then released it. 'Then we must do what we can,' she said, 'with the time you have left.'

'I take the view that for once in my life, I really do have nothing to lose.'

Their eyes met and they both began to laugh.

'So you can tell me what it is that is on your mind,' Philip continued smoothly. 'It will go no further.'

Oh yes it would, Nell thought. Something as juicy as this would leak through Philip's maliciously thin promise because other people's troubles were his pleasure, and dissecting them in the course of deeply interested discussion with like-minded gossips would have it disseminated like pollen on a spring breeze. The only secrets Philip could be trusted to keep were his own.

'Nothing is on my mind,' she said, but with a sigh. 'I suppose, to tell the truth, I am bored . . .' She paid him a compliment in his own coin. 'But now I shall have something to take up my time, won't I? Now whom do you wish me to notify? Shall I go back to the flat and fetch your address book? And is there anything else you want? I am at your disposal.'

Philip scowled. Liz would have told him without having to be asked. Asked his advice in fact. Nell never willingly solicited advice from anyone, and imprisoned in this damned hospital bed there was no way he could find out. Well, he would just have to employ surrogates . . . 'Yes, I do need my address book – amongst other things. Perhaps if I give you a list . . .'

'Westminster Hospital?' Mark Stevens asked. 'What was she doing there?'

'Visiting a Mr Philip Faulkner,' his sergeant told him. 'Quite a well-known "gentleman" in certain circles, Sir. You've heard of the King of Kings? Well, Mr Philip Faulkner is known as the Queen of Queens.' A dramatic pause. 'And he has AIDS.' Bill Ross met the blue eyes. 'I have a contact at the hospital, Sir.' He consulted his notebook. 'Seems Mr Faulkner and the lady are old friends. She has a key to his flat by Westminster Cathedral; took him a bag with things she got from it. I've made some enquiries about Mr Faulkner. No record. With us, that is. But *very* well known in certain other circles. Comes from a very old family but gossip has it that though his birth certificate says he's the son of the late Mr Hugh Faulkner, his real father was even more blue blooded; purple-blooded, in fact. He certainly acts very grand. And his love life reads like *Who's Who*. This is a list of the visitors he's had over the past few days. Some very important people on it, as you'll see.'

'Also known to Miss Mondaine?'

'Couldn't say, Sir. She wasn't there when they were. She goes in the afternoon; they go in the evening.'

'And Miss Mondaine herself? What's been happening with her?'

'Well, Sir, something's been added.'

Bill Ross laid before his boss a sheaf of photographs, taken by a policeman concealed in a van parked outside the warehouse next to the little mews house. 'There's a third member of the household.'

'What!'

'This young lady, Sir.'

It was Nell; hair down, wearing Nell-type clothes from Marks and Spencer.

'Who the hell is she?'

'No idea, Sir. But I'll tell you another odd thing. None of those three women ever go anywhere together. You only ever see them one at a time. They don't seem to be around in a group. And Miss Jordan, the landlady? She's there Tuesday, Wednesday and Thursday; Miss Mondaine comes out only at night, and the other one, she's there at weekends. And she drives Miss Mondaine's car.'

'Are there any other visitors?'

'Nary a one.'

Mark Stevens studied the photographs of the new yet unknown quantity. Soap and water face, but a nice, open one. Lots of soft brown hair, sleek and shiny clean. Nice figure; the breasts beneath the plain round-necked T-shirt were full and firm, and the jeans revealed a nicely rounded rump. She was wearing dark glasses yet there was an elusive familiarity about her. Where had he seen her before . . .? And who was she? A friend? A relation, maybe? Yes, his mind seized on it. That was the connection. She reminded him of Miss Jordan; a much younger edition. A niece, probably? Someone who kept an eye on things when her aunt was otherwise occupied? Oh, Hell, he thought, this gets more complicated by the minute. Why do the other two spend so much time at the house? When Cleo Mondaine is away the cats have to be looked after. But she isn't away. So why are they still paying unnecessary visits?

An idea so ridiculous it was risible struck him. Was it possible – could it be that Miss Jordan; nicely spoken, ultra respectable, prim and proper Miss Jordan was the brains behind the call-girl? Fixed the fees, found the clients, banked the money? Perhaps this third female was also in the same business but catering to a slightly downmarket clientele, and the mews house was their base of operations? Not one but two call-girls, on different levels with differing schedules and differing fees but all adding up to a shared whole. I think, he thought, a further visit to Miss Cleo Mondaine is called for.

'I want to know when Cleo Mondaine is at home,' he said. 'The moment she is seen going into that house tell me. Pass that along.'

He fell to studying the photographs again, compared the third woman with Miss Jordan. It was the glasses, he decided. Miss Jordan's were tinted, the kind used to protect weak eyes from strong light as well as to aid vision; the unknown's were sunglasses – he took a magnifying glass from his desk drawer, examined the photographs closely – 'Raybans,' he said out loud. 'Fifty pounds the pair minimum, yet she's wearing jeans and a chain-store T-shirt.' He examined her shoes. 'Topsiders,' he said, recognising them to be just like the ones he had bought in San Diego. He'd paid sixty dollars for them then – about forty pounds. He shifted the glass to the shoulderbag hanging from one shoulder, nodded in satisfaction. It fastened with a gilt clasp in the shape of an H. For Hermès. And on the arm which held the strap close to the top of the bag was a wristwatch. The powerful glass enlarged it to the point where he recognised it as the twin to the one he'd seen Cleo Mondaine wearing. The Cartier Rivoli watch. Vermeil with a sapphire in the winder and a crocodile strap. Six hundred quid a time. He leaned back in his chair. So . . . the house was not so much a brothel as a base. Miss Jordan came to check the answering machine, kept the appointments book. The other two kept the appointments. No wonder she was so keen to play her cards so close to her chest. They must be earning a fortune, one they would be very loath to lose. A very nice little set-up, he thought admiringly. The house in a quiet mews, not much coming and going except to the warehouse. Neighbours away most of the time. No nosy parkers to wonder what the three women did for a living.

Yes, he thought. Time for another little chat. He had felt

that odd, uneasy dissonance which meant that what he was being told and what he believed would never make a match, all the time he had been speaking to Cleo Mondaine. But not with Miss Jordan. He had taken her at the value she had given him. Conned? he wondered. A very clever lady under the Womens' Institute cover? They were playing a game, he realised, feeling chagrin put a match to his anger. And playing me for the proverbial sucker. Some kind of women's co-op? Fiercely women's lib, perhaps? Or even, as he had been told but never managed to believe, man-haters, as so many prostitutes were supposed to be? Whatever, she had a few questions to answer, and by God, she had better come clean this time.

By the time he got round to the little house, his first rush of anger had abated. Only his professional pride had been hurt, because he had been fooled so easily and thoroughly. He had absolutely nothing on either Miss Jordan or the third woman. They had committed no crime. If they were operating from the little house as call-girls that was still not illegal. Just so long as they did not use the house itself. And the surveillance had revealed that they most certainly did not. Business was done elsewhere. And she – Cleo, that was – *had* come forward. Risking *her* business. Which was, strictly speaking, none of *his* business. But he hoped that this time he could catch her on the hop.

She must have been in the bath, because he had to ring twice more before the door finally opened, to reveal her in a mandarin-collared towelling robe with another towel wound turban-fashion around her head.

'Now what?' she demanded frigidly.

The flame blue eyes seemed to burn into her, but his smile was easy. 'Just a few more questions,' he said.

'God, why did I ever get mixed up in all this . . .' she turned, leaving him to find his own way in, and stalked down the hall and into the kitchen. Closing the front door behind him he followed her there to find her waiting for him, arms akimbo, in the style of the seaside postcard mother-in-law. 'You are hounding me, Superintendent,' she accused angrily. 'Why?'

Because it is the only way I can get to see you, he admitted to himself. If I asked you out you'd refuse and that would not be a sensible thing to do anyway because I'm on the up escalator and the people travelling with me will be as closely scrutinised as I am on the way to the top. 'I have some more photographs for you to look at. There might be a face from your past.'

'I doubt it. That I saw Tony Panacoulis was purely by chance, not, repeat *not*, design. I did not like him then and I do not like him now. It is highly unlikely that the people in his world have anything to do with the people in mine.'

'All the same. We are not making much progress. Any piece of information, no matter how small, would be of enormous help in completing the jigsaw.'

She was not happy, he could see that. She seemed on edge. Before, she had been calm, composed. Now, he noticed the way her long fingers – she had lovely hands, he thought, imagining what they must feel like in full caressing mode before slamming his mind up against the wall, clearing it wonderfully – fiddled with the wide folds of her towelling robe. He must have been staring because she stopped abruptly, decided instead to re-tie the belt of her buttoned-up robe and quellingly stared him down when his eyes came back to hers.

'Look, erm . . . if you want to go upstairs and finish what you were doing I'll see to some coffee,' he offered.

'No, thank you.' With the chill politeness of one who could not wait to get rid of an unwelcome visitor: 'Let's get on with whatever it is you want and be done with it.' She turned away, reached down cups and saucers, took a tray from a set of three standing against the tiled wall next to the huge American refrigerator. 'You might as well go and sit down,' she ordered.

'Can I take anything?'

'The liberties you are taking are quite enough, thank you,' she snapped.

Oh, nice one, he thought, but his grin met with no response. Definitely not very happy. She'd probably been lying back in hot bubbles up to her chin, or perhaps in the shower, water streaming down that long, slender body, black hair plastered to her head. He'd had that feeling when she'd opened the door to him; that he had disturbed her. Which makes two of us, he thought.

When she came in, carrying the tray, she sat across from

him, the big coffee table forming the great divide. He did not break the silence as she poured the coffee; strong and black and fragrant, held out a cup to him. The silence held its breath. One of the cats strolled in, leaped effortlessly on to the arm of the sofa next to her and began to wash its face.

'The photographs,' she reminded.

'Here . . .' He laid them out, another half a dozen black and whites. Tony Panacoulis, each time with different people. She examined them, slid three aside, but when she came to the fourth, of the Greek and a blonde, he saw her expression tighten. For a moment she stared at the picture and then she put it away before examining the last two. Finally, she returned to the fourth, picked it up, studied it again before laying it down to say: 'I used to know her back in 1979. She was one of the girls Mickey Shaughnessy ran when I was with him, only she was his particular girl. Her name was Cindy Lewis. I heard – later, after I'd left Mickey, that she'd done the same thing because he'd beaten her up and broken a nail or two. She had a thing about her nails; they were long, curved talons but she thought they were lovely; the mark of a woman who has other people do the jobs that would ruin such perfection. She hasn't changed, except she looks much more sophisticated and her hair wasn't worn in that Dolly Parton style when I knew her.'

Picking up the photograph, Mark examined the hand patting the spun-sugar bouffant, not because it needed tidying; more the preen of a woman who went to the hairdresser every day, as well as to show off the five-pence size diamond on the third finger and the extraordinarily long painted nails which curved over the ends of her short, stubby fingers like the talons of a bird of prey. Each of them had to be at least an inch from nail bed to tip.

'She is now known as Cindy Searle and she is Tony Panacoulis's mistress, has been for the past five years, since when she has starred in several of his pornographic epics. What can you tell me about her?'

'Venal, vain, vicious and totally self-serving. Thick as sixty planks but with the sort of shrewd cunning to know who and where and when and how will do her the most good. Friendly enough to those she regards as no threat; dangerous to those she does. She soon got rid of a girl Mickey Shaughnessy recruited and showed interest in – apart from her earning capacity. I wasn't there at the time but I was told she didn't warn the girl about a well-known punter who liked to see a girl suffer . . . Cindy was out with her showing her the ropes and also showed her this – pervert. He tied her up in such a way that when he finally raped her, her struggles strangled her. He was caught and tried for it but it was too late for the girl. Cindy denied everything, of course. Said she had warned the girl, who wouldn't be told and thought she could handle anything. But when I was part of Mickey's stable I was warned not to trust her. The last I heard of her she had gone back to Salford after shopping Mickey – all because he broke her precious nails. Since, as you told me, he is now dead, I presume she thought it safe to come back and in her eyes, go up in the world.'

'That diamond is real and so is the mink. Tony is making more than enough to keep her in the style to which she thinks she is entitled. You don't know any of the other men or women?'

'No.'

'They are all former prostitutes, now in the keeping of Tony Panacoulis's associates.' He paused to sip his coffee appreciatively.

'Were you and Cindy friends?'

'No. We knew each other, that's all.'

'You never saw or heard from her once you went your separate ways?'

'I had forgotten her until I saw that photograph.'

'Are you surprised that she is living with a man like Panacoulis?'

'No. Cindy was never particular where the money came from as long as there was plenty of it.'

The cat, who had finished its ablutions, now decided to change seats and jumped lightly onto the lap of its mistress. She rubbed it absently behind the ears and it purred like an outboard engine, rearing up on its hind legs to push its face against hers. It was a big cat and its attentions were forceful.

'Bundle, behave yourself!' But it was so lovingly said that the cat, encouraged by the tone of voice, proceeded to rub its head against her with such force that her towelling turban, its end tucked under itself next to one ear, became loose. Before she could snatch it the whole towel had slid from her head to fall about her shoulders, revealing swathes of nut brown hair. Bone dry.

The cat, alarmed by the falling towel, did a runner.

She did not move, she was so rigid she looked frozen. His gaze was pasted to her hair; not short, black and wet but long, brown and dry. His expression was a study. Hers was a study in scarlet.

'There is only one of you . . .' Mark Stevens said at last, in the voice of one who now understood. 'You are Cleo Mondaine, Miss Eleanor Jordan and the mystery woman.'

He saw her expression darken as she took in the implication of that sentence then, with a shrug that said: What the hell . . . so now you know. She undid her robe before peeling it off, revealing a yellow T-shirt and jeans rolled to the calves.

Mark Stevens's laugh was short. 'Congratulations. You had me fooled. You are a very good actress. I was wholly taken in by Miss Jordan. When would I have met the real you? I am looking at the real you, aren't I?'

'Yes. I really am Eleanor Jordan, but always known as Nell. It is the other two who are my . . . creations.'

'Self-invented? Your own, unholy trinity?' He felt as much as saw the quick flick of her glance and knew he had hit the bull. 'But – why?' he asked when he could, torn between admiration and surprise.

'I have my reasons, and they have absolutely nothing to do with the matter in hand. I would also appreciate it if you did not – reveal – my . . . secret. It does no harm and it is not illegal.'

'But – ' he said again.

'Miss Jordan is my alter ego, if you like. The absolute opposite of Cleo Mondaine – '

'Eleanor Jordan – that is you in the future? Far distant, of course.'

'Another side of me. Eleanor is my given name, but only my father ever called me by it.'

'So Elly was genuine?'

'Yes. I was always known as Nell until then, and Nell is how I think of myself – my *real* self.'

'But Miss Jordan did not have green eyes,' he said suddenly.

She bent her head, did something to her eyes and when she looked up again he saw her eyes were a clear, brilliant grey, with darker, anthracite rings around the irises.

'And the greying hair?'

'A coloured hair-spray.'

He shook his head admiringly. 'You had me fooled,' he repeated. 'It was the third one – you – that had me flummoxed. I thought you had a third person living here.'

'No, only me and the cats.'

Bundle, hearing the voices and realising they were not raised, came back, made a noise like a rusty hinge then leapt up onto Mark's lap.

'Bundle!'

'No. It's all right. I like cats.' Mark unerringly found the sensitive spot behind the ear and the cat settled itself on his lap, folding its paws like the wings of an aeroplane and purring like its engine. 'Thank you, Bundle,' Mark told it gravely. It looked up at him as he said its name and blinked its eyes in acknowledgement.

'If you had me down as a mystery woman that means you have been following me, doesn't it?'

'No. But I will admit to having your house watched.'

'Why?' Outrage quivered.

'Just to make sure that you were what you said you were. And I believed you until I saw Nell.' He shook his head. 'That threw me.' Then he asked: 'Is that why you were so keen to protect your – anonymity.'

'No. I told you why. Cleo is the one who makes the real money, Eleanor is only – her alter ego, if you like. Something to do during the day.' Defensively: 'It does no one any harm and it gives me pleasure, so what is wrong in it?'

'Had you reasons for becoming Cleo?'

'Yes. She had to have absolutely nothing to do with Elly Little. She had to have no past, no problems, only a future.'

'The friend who died – was she a part of it?'

'Yes.'

'And Philip Faulkner?'

He saw the clear light grey eyes darken to smoke. 'You *have* been following me.'

'I am conducting a murder investigation.' He was unapologetic; Superintendent Stevens rather than Mark Stevens.

She lowered her lids, leaned forward to pick up her cup and he saw her breasts move under the thin cotton of her T-shirt, realised they were unsupported.

'Philip played his part,' she admitted after a moment. She looked up suddenly. 'You must know by now, then, who he is,' she challenged.

'Yes.'

'He was a very dear friend of the woman who befriended me. He was her . . . mentor, I suppose you could call him. Since she died he has acted as my adviser. There is very little Philip does not know and even fewer people – worth knowing, that is. He is the most appalling snob.' Before he could ask she said: 'No. He knows *nothing* of this. He is not *my* father confessor.' Which made it clear the capacity in which he had acted for Cleo's own mentor.

'Good,' Mark said simply. 'Better he knows nothing since it would be a secret he could not possibly keep.'

Cleo's smile flickered again. 'I see you have had him investigated too.'

'Not in any criminal capacity. Like you, what he does is done with the utmost discretion, even in the days when it was against the law. His list of lovers reads like *Who's Who*.'

'Philip would say that it is because of him they appear there in the first place.'

They smiled at each other, which turned into a laugh, which faded as their eyes continued to hold. Then she sat back; an actual physical retreat, a warning that he was getting too close.

'So it took you so long to answer the door because you were getting into your disguise,' he surmised.

'Yes.'

'And how long would you have kept it up – your act, I mean?'

'As long as it suited me. Why, is there some new law which says I can't?'

He tried another tack. 'When you ran away from Mickey Shaughnessy – were you afraid he would try and find you?'

'Until I heard Cindy had shopped him, yes.'

'But you have had no contact with that world since?'

'None whatsoever.'

She made herself sit under his examining eyes until she realised they were entirely impersonal; that he was following some train of thought.

'You had facial surgery, didn't you?' he asked at last. 'That's why I didn't recognise you.'

'I had facial surgery, yes. Mickey broke both my nose and my jaw. I also had a star fracture to my left cheekbone. The surgeon took the opportunity to make one or two – improvements. But that is not why you didn't recognise me. You did not recognise me because you did not remember me.'

She was not in the least put out. A fact was a fact was a fact.

'So it is highly unlikely that Cindy would recognise you?'

She was there before he had stopped speaking.

'Oh, no! There is no way I am having anything to do with that lot!'

Her voice was indignant, while her grey eyes were as turbulent as storm clouds. 'I climbed my way out of that sleaze long ago. In my case it is not a case of "once a scrubber, always a scrubber". I scraped all that stands for from myself and my life a long time ago. I have done my duty as a citizen, Superintendent. I took a risk when I told you what I saw that night. I've identified the man and now I've given you Cindy Lewis. What more do you want?'

'To put an end to the child murders, and put away the men who get their sexual satisfaction from seeing children sexually abused and finally snuffed out like a candle.'

He saw the storm warning lowered, and the sudden paleness of her face was the white flag of surrender.

'Why do you think I called you in the first place?' she demanded. She subsided back on to the couch. When she looked at him the anger had been replaced by guardedness. He knew she was weighing up his power – that of the law – against her own; which was not very much – since when the chips were down her VIP clients would not want to know; would deny all knowledge, in fact. Her sole power lay in her usefulness to him and how much leverage it would take, against the pressure he could bring to bear by threatening to expose her. He hastened to disabuse her.

'I am not threatening you,' he said quietly. 'I have no

authority to do that. I cannot make you do what you don't want to do. This is not a police state. Nor can I blackmail you into doing anything. All I am doing is asking for your help. If you could somehow contrive a meeting with Cindy; talk over old times, ask her what she is doing, where she has been, and give her a carefully re-arranged version of your own life since you were both with Mickey Shaughnessy. She might even want you to meet Tony Panacoulis. We know she recruits for him. No . . .' he saw the outrage gather again, 'I would not want you to go so far as to work for him.' Pause. 'But if he was to ask you, it would be an opportunity for you to find out things we need to know.'

Sarcastically: 'And would I also be introduced to his partner, Mr Reza Dominitian?'

'He is out of the country. I told you that before. Besides which, Dominitian is the sleeping partner; I doubt if he has anything to do with the actual making of the films.'

This was said with a straight face but she had come to appreciate his sly and subtle sense of humour by now. Besides, the vividly blue eyes held an unholy light. She controlled her impulse to break into a grin. As their eyes held, all desire to laugh fled. She was conscious of a powerful impulse to follow it; forced herself to sit still.

'Would you think about it?' he asked eventually. 'You understand that I have to investigate what lies under every stone, and believe me, I've turned over a great many of those in the last two years. I'm not too proud to beg. Right now I need all the help I can get and you, Miss Jordan, are the best means I've had in a long time. Through you I can get into the life of a man who keeps it under lock and key. It is a godsend that you know Tony Panacoulis's mistress, even if it was a long time ago. I would not send you into a dangerous situation. That desperate I am not. But if you would consider what I am asking . . .'

She considered. He waited. How pretty she is, he thought. Softer than Cleo, nowhere near as striking, but she's got the kind of face that lingers in a man's memory. Extraordinary eyes. Exquisite skin. She even sounds different. Cleo's voice is much more husky, based on a bedrock of sex. Miss Jordan's was hesitant, apologetic even. Nell's is natural; her own voice.

Which was when he began to appreciate her skills as an actress. He was pretty sure, though, that she was not acting now, because Nell did not need to. This was the Nell nobody knew existed. Philip Faulkner would know her, but who else? I owe you one, Bundle, he thought. No wonder she had intrigued him from the start. Three women, one body. Three different and distinct women at that. But Nell was the base of the triangle, of that he was sure. What remained to be discovered was why she had needed to create the other two sides. And discover he would. He wanted to. Very much.

It confirmed instincts his reason had tried to pass off as purely physical. What one of his instructors at Bramshill, wise with the experience of many years in the Metropolitan Police, had warned him to beware of when dealing with attractive women in the course of duty. 'The kind that lead you into thinking with your cock. I've seen many a promising copper come to grief because he lost his ability to distinguish between thinking and feeling: between being a copper and being a man. There will be times when you have to decide which it's to be.'

Like now, Mark thought. He laid down his coffee cup. 'How much time do you want?' he asked.

'Don't call me. I'll call you,' she answered, softening the command with a mocking smile.

He did not return it. 'Not too long, I hope. All the time we are trying to get somewhere the ring is operating, children are being abused.'

He saw something flicker across her face but too quickly to be caught and examined. 'How do they get them – the children, I mean?'

'They are usually runaways, street children. Some of them quite deliberately become rent boys because it is the only way they can make money; others are – persuaded – into it.'

He saw her shudder, but she was dogged. 'Mostly boys?'

'Mostly, but we do come across girls. The ones who don't like having to obey their parents' rules and come to London to be, as they think "free". And those who have already been abused, of course.' He paused, then hit her with the rest of it. 'We know of five bodies; how they died, why they died. What we don't know is the whereabouts of another twenty-odd more; all runaways, all missing for many, many months now, some for years. There may be other reasons why they have not been found; they may not want to be; it is possible for people to evaporate like water in strong sunlight. But some parents worry and we don't forget them.' Pause. 'With the police, it is not a case of out of sight, out of mind.'

Her head came up and she shot him a glance that hit him right between the eyes. 'Nor mine!' she said, in a voice that had the cat taking flight. 'I put my job on the line to tell you what I knew. I happen to care very much about children at the mercy of sexually unscrupulous men. I happen to – ' But she must have seen something in his suddenly alert expression because she did not finish her sentence. Her professional cool took over. 'You learn some pretty unpleasant things in my profession,' she said, 'but in my opinion the sexual abuse of children is beyond the pale.'

'I've come across thirteen-year-old prostitutes,' he said, matter-of-factly.

'So have I, and it was invariably their fathers who were their first clients.'

Distaste put a shudder into her voice, but there was something else underlying her obvious disapproval; a vibration that he recognised as anger. He also saw by the way it was erased, as though a damp cloth had wiped her face and eyes clean, that she was cross with herself for allowing him to see it. There were certain places, he realised, where that inner anger had eroded the wall she had erected about her essential self. When it went on the boil the weak spots gave. Like now. She must have had a pretty lousy time on the streets. Too much, too soon. Perhaps, he thought, and even as he did so he knew that he had stumbled on the key to this woman's unholy trinity, far too soon.

He rose to his feet. He wanted to think about this, then he wanted to talk to someone who would be able to tell him if he was on the right track. Right now, it was important that she had no idea how she had exposed it.

'All right,' he said, with the air of one accepting that he would get no further this time. 'I'll let you think about it. I know what I am asking.' He looked straight at her; he wanted her to understand that.

She stared at him and then she looked away, his message

having been received and understood. 'All right,' was all she said.

'I'll call you after the weekend?'

A nod. She was impatient for him to be gone, he realised. She wanted to think too, to go over the ground they had covered and see if she had left clearly recognisable footprints.

Only to me, he thought, as he strode to his car. And only because I've talked to my fair share of sexually abused women and children. Anger becoming guilt, guilt becoming corrosive. Lives twisted and mangled beyond repair. Except he did not want this one to be beyond help. That she was an emotional mine-field was beyond dispute; that she felt a need to create two other personalities, each with a distinctly defined role (for Nell, their creator, had no other than to act as their control) showed that Nell could not cope with being what Cleo was but wanted very much to be what Eleanor was. Cleo the bad, Eleanor the good. Nell the catalyst.

This is turning out to be much more complicated than I had bargained for, he thought. He could not wait to get to grips with the truth of it all.

Nell took the cups into the kitchen, washed them up, put them away, methodically going through the motions while her mind ran in blind panic like the mice Bundle occasionally caught and brought into the house to play with; toying with it, tossing it, flinging it, the tiny creature already half-dead with fear, until Nell was able to throw a towel over it, gingerly pick it up and then put it out of the door. Only there was nobody to rescue her. She had made her own blunders, allowed herself to be caught – and by Bundle!

She paused, her hands deep in soapy suds, as she admitted to herself something she had not been willing to accept for some time now. *He* disturbed her. She did not feel comfortable around him; she was far too *aware* of him even as she knew he was equally as aware of her. Whenever they talked there was a tension that was palpable. She said the wrong things – oh, boy, she thought with a wince at her own blunders this evening – did the wrong things. He made her feel clumsy, gauche, defensive. She could not remember when any man had made her feel so filled with a queer sort of excited dread. She never felt like this with clients. Which was when she understood why. With a client, *she* was in control. Not so with Mark Stevens. He went his own way and in so doing came perilously close to areas that were strictly off limits; forbidden, in fact to anyone other than herself. Not even Liz had been allowed to set foot in that zone. She knew, like she knew she had made what could be a disastrous blunder, that with this superior height, he had seen over the walls she had erected; not everything, not all the horrors, but enough to arouse his curiosity, to make him want to see more.

Which means I have to cut him off here and now, she thought. Seeing Cindy Lewis would be bad enough, with its own dangers. Seeing him again would be disastrous. I can't afford him. Time to pull in the drawbridge and lower the portcullis. From now on, Nell my girl, you are in a state of siege . . .

16

Mark Stevens strode rapidly into the pub and over to a table by the window at which a man was reading the *Daily Telegraph*. 'Sorry I'm late . . . I had a call just as I was leaving my office. Another body has come to light; this time in Hereford. A fourteen-year-old. Been there for some time but identifiable because of the soil conditions.'

'Same kind of death?'

'Yes, sexual asphyxiation, just like the others, and sodomised beyond belief. There are also signs of torture.' Mark's face was taut. 'What kind of men get pleasure from such sickness? I need a drink. You?'

'Got one, thanks, and since I've got an appointment this afternoon with a multiple murderer whom the defence claim is schizophrenic, I need my wits about me. He's a clever bastard and faking like hell. Trouble is, he's done his reading and is as knowledgeable as I am about what he is *supposed* to be suffering from. What he is *really* suffering from, of course, is amorality. He is also totally conscienceless, and arrogant with it.'

'It's your professional knowledge I want to tap into,' Mark said, after ordering his drink. 'In the course of my investigations on this child porno case I've come across a woman who has volunteered valuable information.' He paused. 'What I have discovered for myself, however, puts me at a disadvantage because I don't have enough information about her psychology to help me lead her where I want her to go. You are the best behavioural psychologist in the business so I thought if I told you what I think is her trouble, you could either confirm or correct my theory.'

'You were always probing my theories at Bramshill, as I remember,' the psychologist, whose name was Jerry Pierce, said. He had first met Mark Stevens when he was lecturing at the police college. Mark had been one of his brightest students on a course intended to help a policeman read body language, voice patterns, behavioural signals. He himself had interviewed and written reports on many murderers, usually of the more twisted, psychopathic kind; those who killed serially, through extended torture, or those who killed children. He had discussed cases many times with Mark, usually those in which he was the investigating officer, but this was the first time he had been asked about a possible witness.

'Is she an oddity?' he asked curiously.

'She plays roles as three different people, for a start.'

Mark saw Jerry's pale blue eyes warm with interest.

Over lunch, Mark gave Jerry the story on Nell Jordan and her two alter egos.

'She has full knowledge of these women and whilst playing them is aware at all times that she is playing a role?' Jerry asked.

'Yes. It is not a case of the Three Faces of Eve. Cleo Mondaine was created quite deliberately as a high–class courtesan by Nell and the woman who groomed and changed her to take over as successor. Eleanor Jordan is Nell's own creation. Nell is the *deus ex machina*, if you like.' Mark leaned forward. 'What I want to know is why a woman would want to create two other separate personalities to fulfil different functions? She was on the streets as Nell/Elly, after all.'

'Cleo is a whole flight of steps up from the gutter, so it is not at all unusual that she should have evolved as someone utterly different from the streetwalker. It is Eleanor who poses the question. Cleo's opposite. Ultra respectable, no longer young, unattractive to men; content to live a life of safe, quiet obscurity. And Nell . . . their creator. Doing what? It is the other two who have the jobs. What does she do? The planning, the creating? Is that where she finds *her* fulfilment? Sitting back and pulling the strings? In other words – in control. Indeed, all three women are in control. Cleo decides who will be a client;

Eleanor runs the office of the plastic surgeon – your information is pukka?'

'From the doctor himself, ostensibly as a character reference for a bank loan. He could not stop himself from singing her praises. Awesomely efficient, yet anything but awesome. Quiet, discreet, self-effacing unto oblivion. The kind of woman you don't really notice except insofar as the wheels never need oiling. The kind of woman you take for granted – until she is not there. Except that Miss Jordan is *always* there, Tuesdays, Wednesdays and Thursdays, without fail. She runs him like clockwork and he doesn't even feel her wind him up.'

Jerry nodded. 'In control, as I said. And the courtesan – what is she like?'

'Stunning. Everything Eleanor is not. Sexy, exquisitely dressed, very . . . fragrant, wholly feminine. But again, in charge. She decides who she will take on, and when and where. Very discreet. No hard information as to her clients but I'm working on it. A lot of them are international.'

'She must be good? A specialist?'

'Undoubtedly, but not in the usual S&M sense. I was able to get a whiff of information that her speciality is fantasy.'

'There's a need for that in today's world.' Jerry leaned back, sipped his drink. 'Where does she come in to your present case?'

Mark gave him an edited version.

'And you think she is motivated by her strong feelings about abused children?'

'Yes. I think she was an abused child herself. She does not want what happened to her happening to others.'

'You did listen to my lectures,' Jerry observed, pleased. 'Because I think you are right. That is why Cleo is separate from Nell. Cleo is the whore her father made her – Elly Little when she was on the streets and again removed from Eleanor Jordan. Miss Jordan is yet another role; the safe, eminently respectable woman Nell would like to be, but Nell can only ever be a shadow-woman. That is her punishment.'

'Punishment?'

'Self hatred,' Jerry explained succinctly. 'Guilt – a feeling that it is all her fault, since most fathers tell their daughters that "you made me do it. I could not help myself," etc. etc. Shifting the responsibility. Nell was the one her father abused, not Cleo, not Eleanor. Nell hates Nell for allowing it, so the less time spent as Nell the better. Only one third instead of three.' Jerry nodded in the face of Mark's dawning comprehension. 'Nell feels guilty because her father made her feel so; he probably told her that if she said anything he would be sent away and it would be all her fault. As a child you see no way to stop what is being done to you. As an adult you hate yourself for not having striven to stop it. Whichever way you look at it you just can't win. It is emotional blackmail, impure and anything but simple and it twists and corrupts, distorts and destroys. I've seen women whose only desire is to kill themselves – as painfully as possible, in order to obtain some sort of peace. I've known them mutilate themselves, become promiscuous, because they come to associate sex with affection since they have had so little in their lives; others cannot bear to be touched by any man. Some drink, others take drugs.'

Mark shook his head positively. 'She doesn't do drugs and her drinking is the social kind.'

'So she became what her father made her into; a whore, but as Cleo, thus allowing Nell some measure of relief. And to make up for that she created Eleanor. 'Look, daddy, what a good girl I am . . .'

'Christ!' It was violent.

'You have got yourself one very mixed-up witness, Mark. One who needs sorting out.'

'I know,' Mark said.

'Is she vital to your case?'

'She could – if I can persuade her to – get me closer to the centre of this very nasty little web.'

'At some danger to herself?'

'Not if I can help it. I don't want her hurt.'

'She is already an emotional paraplegic, Mark. But she will help you. Her guilt won't let her do anything else. Also, it will assuage her need to be punished. There is a danger involved which she will find very satisfying to her need to suffer. She will struggle – all part of the complex role playing, but in the end she will do what you ask.' He surveyed his friend. 'This is not just a friendly witness enquiry, is it? There is something more – on your part, anyway.'

'Yes,' admitted Mark, able to since it was Jerry.

Jerry scratched his nose absently, a piece of body language Mark recognised as showing concern. 'That could be dangerous.'

'I know.'

'Is there any interest in you on her part?'

'There could be if she allowed it.'

Jerry nodded. 'That fits. Only Cleo is sexually active and then only in the role her father cast her for. Eleanor is neuter and Nell is . . . Nell is not allowed the luxury of emotions. All part of her self-punishment. I have no doubt that she is possessed of very wide sexual experience but has absolutely none when it comes down to what we are pleased to call normal human relationships, especially those between men and women, probably because she considers herself barred. Then again she would have great difficulty in handling an emotional approach since it is not something she has ever known. Women with that background tend to regard themselves as unfit to be any man's partner. Clients are punters, not men. No more than erect penises.'

Jerry observed Mark closely before advising: 'Go careful with this one. Normally, it is extremely difficult for a child whose relationship with her father was incestuous to form any other relationships with men, but if they do, you cop the lot. I can't say for sure that Nell Jordan is such a child since I have not talked to her; I am going by what you have told me and what she has both told you and done for you. In that sense the evidence points to her being just such a damaged human being. Handled badly she will, like her carefully constructed tri-partite existence – I will not dignify what she has as a life – likewise break up.' He smiled. 'No doubt you have heard that women tend to fall in love with their psychiatrists. What happens when a whore falls in love – for the very first time in her life – with a copper?' Pause. 'Or he with her?'

Mark held his eyes, nodded. 'I am well aware of possible consequences.'

But won't let them deter you, Jerry thought, reading the signs, which impelled him to take it further. 'If you do get her through this, then I'll be glad to do whatever I can in my professional capacity.'

Mark's flame blue eyes burned brightly. 'Thanks, Jerry. I appreciate that.'

'What are friends for?'

Since she had none, for Philip was out of the question, Nell had no choice but to go through her travail alone. She had always been able to sleep; deeply and tranquilly. Now she lay awake, listening to the clock and the little noises the cats made as they dreamed. She read until her eyelids were heavy, usually until about 2 a.m., but as soon as her lamp was out, the engine of her mind started up.

It was not that she was afraid of meeting Cindy Lewis again. She could handle Cindy, who had been doing her nails when the queue for brains was told to line up and so had to be content with an empty head. It was the further risk she was taking in exposing herself to the world that existed outside the Life. What exposure? Cleo asked her derisively. You know better than to contact Cindy as *Cleo*, for God's sake. This would be Elly, remember? The little scrubber from those far-off days with Mickey Shaughnessy, except she would, like Cindy, have 'bettered' herself; made some money, found herself a protector who was not a pimp . . . an American, say. Yes, that would put her out of sight and mind for a few years; render her natural unfamiliarity with the current scene perfectly believable. The United States was so totally insular that you could be there for a couple of weeks, as she herself had, and hear nothing, see nothing, read nothing that had to do with England in any shape or form.

A serviceman, Nell thought – an airman from Mildenhall met while on leave in London whom Nell married in all good faith, not knowing that when he took her back to California he had a wife in Chicago who finally caught up with him demanding years of non-maintenance for her and the kids . . . which meant Nell had to go back on the streets again, and in LA the sidewalks were *very* mean. Nell had 'Elly' perfectly fleshed out in her mind's eye. Still the old mass of hair but a definite California gloss and just the hint of an American accent. There'd be no difficulty with the clothes. 'Cleo' had a wardrobe full of American clothes, from designer labels to mall chainstores. I could do it, Nell thought, feeling the old adrenalin powering her internal combustion engine. I could convince Cindy with my hands tied behind my back. All I have to do is be word perfect, know the new character inside out, *become* her . . .

She bounced upright in bed, making the cats leap up in alarm, fur bristling. 'See . . .?' she accused herself out loud, voice despairing: 'Already you are into rehearsal!'

That weekend, Mark went up to Cambridge to see his mother, who still lived in the big house left her by her father, a Circuit Judge who had doted on his only child as she herself was to dote on her only son. Joan, Mark's sister, five years older, had got out as soon as she could and gone as far as she could, currently to Hong Kong where her husband managed a British bank.

Mrs Stevens's ambitions for her husband had come to naught because the raw material which when she first saw it had seemed pure gold had turned out, twenty-five years later when he died, still a barrister though a QC, to be fool's gold. She never forgave her husband for not making her Lady Stevens, wife of the Lord Chancellor of England, and when her son, instead of following his father into the law and doing what he had failed to do, became instead a policeman, of all things, her displeasure had known no bounds. But whereas her monumental sulks and frigid silences had abraded her husband's non-combatant spirit they struck no sparks from her son, who merely removed himself from her house and her life and made it clear that what he was living was *his* life and not something she owned merely because she had had a hand in creating it. It both infuriated and alarmed her, but it was not until he made Chief Inspector that she relented. If her son could not be Lord Chancellor then Commissioner of the Metropolitan Police would have to do. Accordingly she staged a reconciliation, predicated on the sudden collapse of her health – she was a diabetic – by judicious manipulation of her insulin dosage.

She had not turned up at her son's passing out parade at the Police College, nor offered congratulations on his promotions until he reached a rank she considered high enough to be worth talking about. When she heard, via other sources of information, that he was in line for Superintendent and was regarded as material for an Assistant Chief Constable in another few years, she assured him of her wholly-committed support. Which was why she flatly refused to sell the big house off the Trumpington Road and move into a flat which could be more easily managed.

'I was born in this house, I lived my married life in this house, my children were born here and I shall die here – when I am ready.' That was her unshakeable conviction. She said she would only move on one condition. 'The day my son brings his bride to this house.'

In spite of the eligible girls she diligently sought out and kept presenting to him as eminently suitable to be the wife of the Chief Constable, Mark showed no signs of wishing to settle down. This particular weekend, while she had her son under her roof in order to celebrate her sixty-eighth birthday, she was determined to find out why. He would be forty far too soon. He ought to have married at least five years ago. Like all people who, though quick to point out other people's mistakes never admit to making any of their own, she had no hesitation in making it her business to select a wife for her son.

When Mark arrived, he found his mother in the drawing room, her face delicately made-up, her grey hair neat as ever, her lips the same overly-vivid pink of his childhood. She was wearing her best navy silk dress, she had pearls in her ears and the small circle of diamonds that meant 'Company coming' pinned to one shoulder.

'Who is expected?' Mark asked, after he had bent to kiss the cheek she proffered, giving him a whiff of Floris Lily of the Valley.

'Nobody in particular; Lucy Golding and Mary Warton said they would come for a cup of tea. As you are taking me out for my birthday dinner tomorrow I asked them to come today instead. Oh – and a friend of Mary's, someone she and George knew when they were in Bahrain.'

With a daughter of marriageable age, Mark thought wearily. Here we go again. The tea-tray was already laid, and as he threw himself into the chair on the other side of the fireplace, Doris, who had worked for his mother for years and known Mark all his life, brought in the freshly-made tea.

As Doris handed him his cup, Mark noticed that it was the

Rockingham china. Definitely a fishing expedition, Mark thought. As he did so, he caught Doris's eye. It winked. She knew only too well what his mother was up to. 'Can't help arranging things,' Doris had said to him a long time ago. 'Has this mania for wanting things *her* way. Always knows best, your mother, and don't want to know what's worse.'

Everyone was expected to defer to Marianne Stevens's judgement. She never said 'maybe' or 'perhaps'. She instructed precisely and firmly. If that did not work she turned to manipulation. This Friday afternoon was one of her little exercises in 'the hand is quicker than the eye' magic.

When Doris went out: 'So who is the sacrificial lamb this time?' Mark asked.

His mother's lips thinned and her blue eyes, every bit as vivid as his, surveyed him reprovingly. 'I instructed Doris to make one of her superlative Victoria sponges,' she said calmly. 'Not sacrifice anything.'

'Come off it, mother. You are pandering again.'

'Do not use that sort of language in this house, if you please.' Then she sighed. 'Is it so unreasonable of me to want to see you settled with the right woman? I am sixty-eight tomorrow, Mark. I do not have many years left in which to see you – '

'Arranged to your satisfaction?'

Her eyes and face composed themselves into an arrangement of mother-love.

'Happy,' she said, allowing a wistful little smile.

'I *am* happy. With things as they are.'

'But you are no longer – involved – with that actress, are you?'

His mother had a web of contacts, kept up from her husband's day, and from them she obtained all the gossip.

'No. That was over some time ago.'

'Then what is wrong with me trying to find you the right wife?'

'Right for whom? You or me?'

'Why, for you, of course,' she told him imperturbably. She leaned forward, took a cigarette from the silver box by the tea tray, lit it with a matching lighter. She had been told to stop smoking but maintained that the ten a day she got through was her only luxury.

326

'I am old enough to know what I want, mother. And we both know by now that it is not what you want.'

'A man in your position – now and in the future – needs the *right* wife. How many times have I told you that the right wife can make or break a man on his way up. She must be able to hold her own – '

'Not to mention his,' Mark said helpfully, with a straight face.

'Don't be vulgar,' his mother said coldly, and then her face moved without a break into a welcoming smile as the drawing room door opened and Doris ushered in the first of the afternoon's visitors.

Never had a weekend seemed so long, to Mark. As he had known, the sacrificial lamb was of the meek and mild variety; what his mother termed a 'biddable girl'. Well brought up, right schools, given a season (even now the 'right' girls were given a season) during which she did not 'take' and thus had to get a job instead of walking down the aisle: with the 'right' estate agent or the 'right' art gallery, or perhaps take a Cordon Bleu course. This particular candidate was, he was assured 'an absolutely splendid cook'. She was also painfully aware of what their respective mothers were up to, and when at their urging Mark 'showed her the garden' she said as much. 'I don't know who is the more overpowering; your mother or mine. They simply refuse to take account of the fact that times have changed; life has moved on, and one does not arrange a suitable match as if one was royalty. *They* may have to do it out of duty but I'll be damned if I will.'

Mark liked her honesty. And she was not wholly unattractive. Just – ordinary. She had a good body though. Athletic. Firm. No excess flesh.

'I jog,' she explained.

'So do I – well, run.'

They arranged to meet next morning for a six-miler, and Mark was pleased to see that she ran well, was not gulping for air when they had done their circuit. In very brief shorts and a singlet her figure was well worth a second look. She was obviously intelligent, easy to talk to, had a nice sense of humour. Why then, was she being touted around by her mother?

'Because I had the bad judgement to get myself involved with a man who was as unsuitable as it was possible to be; because I fell for him so hard it warped my judgement and emptied my bank account, and when I told him I was pregnant he cut my strings. So ten months and a discreet abortion later here I am, constantly being reminded of "what we have done for you" and that "it is my duty to make up for all the trouble I've caused". Oh, and not to breathe a word about being damaged goods.'

As a policeman, faced with liars who would not have known the truth if it walked up and spat in their face, Mark was impressed. Honesty was a trait he prized. This was the direction in which he ought to be looking. By the time he had dropped her off in front of her own large house, he had her phone number. She lived and worked in London during the week. 'I do directors' lunches in the City' – but came dutifully home most week-ends. 'A sort of trade-off. That way I don't have her breathing down my neck *all* the time.'

She was twenty-eight and her name was Alison Moody. His mother oozed satisfaction at her birthday dinner that night and they parted, after lunch on the Sunday, more amicably than they had done for years.

But it was of Nell Jordan that he was thinking as he drove down the M11 towards London.

17

Coming out of yet another nightmare, soaking sheets wrapped about her, hair and body drenched in sweat, Nell knew she had to make up her mind. But before she did, she made a phone call. That afternoon, she drove North.

Margaret was no longer in the original home; that had been pulled down some years before. She was now in the specially adapted wing of a large area hospital, a special unit which looked after the severely mentally disturbed. Margaret was one of them. Over the years, her autism had become progressively worse. She now never spoke; she sucked her thumb obsessively, and she rocked; she rocked for hours. But there were times when she came out of her silent rocking to exhibit a high degree of violence. After her last visit, Nell had been advised to leave well alone. Margaret no longer knew her sister; she no longer seemed to know anyone except for one nurse who somehow managed to get through to her, and was, when she went into one of her rages, the only person whose voice Margaret would heed. Just now, though, she was quiet. When Nell was taken in to see her, she was in her favourite chair, a bentwood rocker placed by the window which overlooked the beginnings of the Northumbrian moors. Her hair, which had been long and curly, had been cut very short, but it still curled, and she wore a sack-like green check dress with a square neck and no buttons or belt, short white socks and shoes without laces or buckles. Her left thumb was in her mouth and her right hand held a grubby white terry-towelling napkin under her nose. Nell's heart contracted. Margaret had always loved

329

what she termed 'Clutchy'; her clutcher, without which she would never, ever go to bed.

'She gets very upset if it is taken away,' the attendant with Nell said. 'Now, then, Margaret, look who has come to see you.' Margaret did not. She went on rocking and sucking.

'I brought her these . . .' Nell brought out a box of liquorice allsorts from her shoulder bag. 'She always used to love these. Is she allowed them?'

'Not the whole bag, but try her with one. Her favourite, perhaps . . .'

Nell brought out the small round of liquorice covered in nonpareils, bent over her sister and said: 'Do you remember how you loved these sweeties, Margaret?'

No answer. Margaret seemed not to hear or even be aware of her sister. Nell looked at the attendant who advised: 'Don't be upset. This is the norm for Margaret.'

'Does she *ever* talk?'

'I've never heard her and I've been here five years.'

'But what does she *do* all the time?'

'Rocks, sucks her thumb.'

'Does she eat?'

'If someone will feed her. She has not used a knife and fork for some years now. But she does eat. As you can see, she is not thin.'

The attendant, who had things to do said: 'Here, draw up a chair, sit with her for a while, see if she realises you are there. She is totally unpredictable sometimes, other times you can set your watch by her.'

Nell sat for half an hour, during which time Margaret never looked at her, never ceased her rocking, her sucking, or ceased to stare out at the moors. Finally, she gave up, but on the way out, she asked if she could speak to someone about her sister. After a wait she was conducted to an office where a middle-aged man with a harassed look and a smoker's cough sat behind a desk. He had a file in front of him.

'You are Margaret's sister?'

'Yes.'

'I don't think we've met.'

'I have not been here for some years. I was told it was a

waste of time. Now I ring every few weeks.' Nell's tone was bleak when she said: 'She did not know me then and she did not even acknowledge me now. I see why they told me not to bother to come as it was a long journey for nothing.'

'Where do you come from?'

'London.'

'I see . . .' He looked down at the file then said bluntly: 'I can offer no hope concerning your sister. She will never progress beyond what she is now. Her autism is such that she has gone beyond reach. She will never be able to go back into the community, unlike some.'

'I was told she never speaks.'

'Never.'

'What hope has she, then?'

'She knows nothing of hope, or anything that we can understand. She will have to be cared for for the rest of her life.'

Nell was silent a moment then asked: 'You know she was sexually abused by our father?'

'Yes.'

'Could that have aggravated her autistic tendencies?'

'Possibly. Autism is still something about which we know very little as yet. What causes it, what aggravates it. Your sister has a violent aversion to men so it is possible that she has memories of what was done to her. Her retreat into silence may have been her only means of protecting herself. Where autism is concerned it is difficult to make firm diagnoses or give hard opinions. Sufficient to say that she has violent episodes, becomes very destructive, very hate-filled at these times. Once she has expelled her rage she is quiet again. Until the next episode.'

'Is there any point in my coming to see her, then?'

'To satisfy yourself as to her physical condition, yes. Other-wise, no.' He closed his file.

That's it, then, Nell thought, numb with despair as she walked back down the long corridors. I hope you are in hell and *burning*, father. For what you did in your rightness, using the authority you insisted we accepted unquestioningly. I hope you suffer eternally for what you did to us in the name of that authority.

331

She was so angry she could not trust herself to drive until she calmed down. She sat in the car until she no longer felt murderous before starting it up to go and do something which would finally shut the door on her early life.

The suburb of the City of Newcastle where she had been born and lived for the first seventeen years of her life had changed. A big new by-pass led to it, there were new shops in the formerly old-fashioned High Street, big new blocks of flats, a brand new Metro Station. But as she climbed the hill familiar landmarks appeared. The church, the police station – except the handsome old Victorian original was now a red-brick monstrosity – and finally, her old school. There was a supermarket where the George Hotel had stood but Warwick Avenue had not changed at all. Still the same Edwardian-solid big, detached houses with their immaculate gardens, though some of them had been divided into flats, since there were many door bells instead of just the one, and several cars parked in the driveways. But Number 17 was still in single occupancy, and the beautifully maintained car in the drive was a Volvo Estate. The house had been painted; the wood trim was now a bright, spanking white instead of the black Nell remembered, and the brickwork had been cleaned and repointed, while the old conservatory, built along with the house at the end of the 19th century, had been replaced by a new one in the Victorian style, as gleaming white as the house-trim. The garden had been redesigned. The rockery had gone; so had the rose-beds and the high hedge of privet behind which the house had hidden. A beautifully manicured lawn ran down to the pave-ment, while the gravel drive was now flagstones.

Somewhere behind the house a dog barked and Nell heard the high shrill voice of a child. She had parked by the pillarbox, which stood opposite the house, and now she heard the irritable beep of a horn. Looking in her mirror she saw that a post office van wanted to get in to empty the box so she drove off, but slowly, right up to the top of the hill where she turned and drove back down again. The white paint made the house look lighter, younger, and the curtains at the windows were bright, without the concealing nets that had shrouded them when she lived there. She could see flowers in bowls – her father had never allowed flowers to be picked from his garden – and the walls were white and hung with paintings. All gone, Nell thought, as she picked up speed and left the house behind for the very last time. Nothing there now of me or Margaret or my father or the horrors. The cellar is probably filled with wine racks and new, bright fluorescent lighting, the surgery has become a summer sitting room. And no brass plate on the gate so no doctor lives there now. No whitened sepulchre. No – Stop it! she ordered herself. There is nothing you can do for Margaret now. It is too late. It was always too late for Margaret, if I had been able to do something . . . stop him . . . I should have told the truth long before I did. If I had spoken out sooner then I could perhaps have saved my poor demented sister. She looked to me all her life, and at the one point where I could have – *should* have – realised what would happen, I should have spoken *then*.

Well, she resolved, hands tightening on the steering wheel, I have got the chance to do something now; something to atone for my cowardice. I was too late for Margaret but if I play my part and manage to insert myself where I can do some good, then maybe I can save some other children. It is, she thought self-laceratingly, the very least I can do.

When Mark Stevens rang the bell of the little mews house a couple of nights later his eyes widened at the familiar stranger who confronted him.

'Elly?' he hazarded at last. Once again she confounded him.

'Yes. What do you think?'

He followed her in to the sitting room where she twisted and turned like a model. Her hair was the fashionable bird's-nest and a mass of curls; her face was made up in the current style – emphasised eyes and deeply glossy mouth, and her nails were long and scarlet. She wore the ubiquitous clinging black dress – an Azzedine Alaïa copy which ended some eight inches above the knees, and her ear-rings almost touched her shoulder blades. Her black tights – stockings were not possible because of the shortness of her dress – were sheer and her heels high. Picking up the silver-fox jacket on the nearby chair she draped it over her shoulders. 'Silver fox made a comeback last year in New York – they don't have to contend with our Animal Liberation Front – and though it went just as quickly I think

Elly would still have hers since she can't afford to dump it. Everything I am wearing has an American label and if you look closely is not new. Cindy will look closely, it's her way. She did not like anyone to have better things than she did then and I doubt if she has changed her point of view. She did use to ask me for pointers as to what was good taste; she had no idea. So she will expect me to be fashionable but it will not do to look more expensive than her. I noticed in the photograph you showed me that she was wearing a diamond watch. Elly, on the other hand, would wear this.' She held out her wrist to show the Cartier Rivoli watch he had seen before. 'Again, not new. The impression I am trying to give is someone who has had it good but is now having a struggle trying to hang on to it. Also, the meeting *has* to be accidental. If Cindy thinks I have made a point of looking her up she'll think I'm after her man – she's that jealous. She has to recognise me, if possible by name. So how do we go about it?'

She was all level-headed business, brisk and matter-of-fact, but 'What changed your mind?' he asked.

'I thought about it.'

And what else? he wondered. He knew she had been away for the weekend; he had rung several times, got the answer-phone but left no message. Perhaps she had gone away to think things through. Whatever, he was grateful, even if she was proving Jerry's theory.

'We know her movements – Cindy's, I mean,' he said. 'She goes to the hairdresser every other day – ' He named a fashionable West End Crimper. Nell frowned. 'Not good?' Mark asked.

'Not in my book. You pay the earth and come out looking as if you had slept under a hedge.'

'We all have to make sacrifices,' Mark said, straight-faced.

'When does she go next?'

'Day after tomorrow. Always the same time – eleven-thirty. She lunches under the drier.'

'Then I'll have to be there while she is; just as she is, in fact. I know that hairdresser's; once she is collected by her shampoo-ist she's out of sight of the reception area. I have to get there just after eleven thirty – or even at the same time, and make a fuss about an appointment . . . normally they make you get

334

down on your knees and beg; they think it gives them some sort of social cachet. One look at their clients tells you different. But it is the sort of place Elly would go to because it is *the* place right now, among a certain set. The ones who dress like this. Help yourself to a drink while I go and change.'

'No – don't do that,' Mark said quickly. 'Let me get used to Elly . . . that way I'll know how she would act, what she would say, do.'

'I've thought of that,' Nell said. 'God, these heels kill me.' She kicked them off, padded in her stockinged feet towards the drinks trolley. 'It will be how are you, where've you been, what have you been doing, have you heard; a general question and answer session before she gets down to satisfying her real curiosity, and – if you are right in your assumptions, she decides to recruit me.' She came back with the Wild Turkey and he thanked her appreciatively. 'You said that the girls in these films are not street tarts?' she reminded.

'By no means. They are – considering what they are and what they do – quite surprisingly classy.'

'What about their bodies? Big, small, tall, short . . .'

'No particular type, but all good looking and all with spectacular assets.' He saw a slight frown knit Nell's well-shaped brows.

'The best I can do is a 36B . . .' He saw her chew her lower lip. 'Hang on a minute . . .'

He heard her running up the stairs, but not before he had watched her enticing rump, enhanced by the clinging black crêpe dress, do a Marilyn Monroe wiggle out of the room. He took a hefty swig of his bourbon.

When she came down again she was wearing a bikini; two small triangles of black silk, the bottom half no more than a *cache-sexe* with a thong between the buttocks. Mark was instantly aroused. Her body was slender, yet lush, the curve between waist and hip the sweetest he had ever seen, breasts firm and high and her bottom the kind that made a man's hands cup themselves instinctively.

'Will I pass muster?' she asked, 'because if I don't then the whole thing is off. I have to be what they are looking for physically as well as experience-wise.'

335

She sounded anxious; he felt reverential. He had to clear his throat before he could speak.

'I don't think you'll have any trouble,' he said, making the understatement of this or any year. Her smile drenched him, then she took that lithe and lovely body upstairs again, leaving him able to compose himself, mentally and physically. This, he warned, will do you no good at all. She is a high priced whore. You are a career policeman. Alison is what you need. Yes, and Nell is what I want. So want he told himself coldly. Put things in perspective, for God's sake. If and when this thing is over and done with then take her for what she is – and pay for it. But even as he thought it he knew he would not – could not. The very thought was loathsome. He did not want *that* with her. Not just sex. He wanted more, the more he knew she was capable of. Only not as she was right now. All that had to be shed, like a dead skin. All the hurt and pain and guilt and self-hatred. Parts of her were deadened; he wanted to be the one to bring them back to life. He did not want Cleo, or Elly or Eleanor. He wanted Nell; the real Nell locked away deep inside where her father could not hurt her.

She came back downstairs again, changed once more into jeans and a baggy shirt. She looked about seventeen, for she had cleaned her face. She is a chameleon, he thought. Able to change at will. How many women has she shown me? She creates them out of thin air. And enjoys doing it. Like Jerry said, a different woman to cope with every different situation. But it is the one at the heart of her I want to come out and face things, the world – me.

He became conscious that she was looking at him quizzically. 'Have I developed horns?' she asked lightly.

'Oh, no, sorry . . . I was planning the campaign,' he lied.

'Wouldn't it be better to play this first meeting by ear? See what she says and from that what transpires? She may not recognise me. I might have to make the first move. In fact, I rather incline to that view. Cindy's mind – what there is of it – rarely leaves her own area of concern. The thing that might run in my favour is her curiosity. It's like that of a cat. And she *loves* gossip. If I can salt our conversation with some juicy tidbits and drop names she has probably only read about it might make her want to see more, know more. But everything

336

will depend on her. She has to make the running, don't you agree?'

'It would be best. I'll leave the staging of this act to you. You are the expert.'

His dry tone had her saying delightedly. 'I fooled you, didn't I? And you a long-serving police officer.'

'Not *that* long,' he protested.

'How long?'

'Eighteen years. I joined the Met when I came down from Cambridge in 1972.'

'I'd have liked to go to university.' There was both wistfulness and envy in her voice.

'What prevented you?'

'My father wanted me at home. My mother was dead and I had a younger sister who needed me.' Pause. 'She was – is – autistic. She is in a special home.'

He nodded by way of acknowledgement, filing away the information she had let slip. Her father had 'wanted' while her sister had 'needed'.

'So,' she said, her tone indicating that she was not going down the cul-de-sac of her past any further. 'I get to the hairdresser at about 11.30 on Thursday and once I see Cindy I play it by ear. Are there any specific questions you wish me to slide in?'

'No. Renewing your acquaintance is the object of Thursday's exercise. What I am hoping is that she suggests meeting you again.'

'What if she wants to see where I live?'

'You don't have a permanent address yet. Right now you are staying with a friend – one who could get you fixed up with her pimp right away, but which offer you have flatly refused because you gave that up a long time ago. Even in the States you didn't solicit; you worked for a call-girl agency. If she should want to verify – Tony Panacoulis is a very cautious man – I have a contact on the New York Vice Squad who likewise has one in Los Angeles who can provide the necessary back-up. Be as cautious as you like first time round; give the impression that there was some trouble back in California. Hint at deportation but don't actually admit to it. You are not on the run, far from it, but you do need to work. Ask her what things are like in the Life nowadays over here, what the prospects are, what pays best. Be most interested in that last answer. You are broke. You need to earn the maximum and now, not next month.'

'She nodded; she was looking at him but not seeing him. He could almost see her writing the script she would use, plotting her moves, visualising her direction.

He found himself asking: 'You are quite sure you want to do this?' because suddenly he found he didn't want her to. It was dangerous. Panacoulis was dangerous. He probably made a very great deal of money from his various activities, and he would stop at nothing to protect them. The thought of Nell walking, of her own free will, into a den of such iniquity terrified him as a man, even though as a Detective Superintendent he had coolly assessed the risks and found them well worth taking. She was capable, she was intelligent, she was quick thinking and she had a healthy respect for the man she would be dealing with, even if it was based on fear and loathing. Which is why she will be the last person to do something foolish, he decided. And if she does it right she is the one person who can get you into places you've been trying to enter for a very long time. Through her you have a chance to get to grips with something that has kept slipping from your grasp because somebody, somewhere, is oiling his wheels and keeping his engine tuned.

Nell must have seen something in his intent face because she said crisply: 'It is a bit late to be asking me that now, isn't it? Have you had second thoughts as to my capabilities?' She was so frosty as to be iced.

'I don't doubt your acting abilities for a moment. It is what you will be getting into I don't like. The kind of people they are, what they do. If they should somehow find out who and what you really are . . .'

'But Reza Dominitian is abroad still, you said.'

'True, and under surveillance, but Panacoulis will have you thoroughly checked.'

'Then it is up to you to see that my cover stands up to his scrutiny, isn't it?' She softened. 'Look, in my job you get a nose for danger. To spot the punter that is a wrong-un. I've had my share of run-ins. I've had knives pulled on me, one who tried to choke me, another who attempted to suffocate me . . .' Her laugh had him asking instantly:

'What did you do?'

'Bit him. Almost severed his prize possession. While he was writhing I ran. If I get that itch between my shoulder blades I'll know something is wrong and act accordingly.'

'I get an itchy neck,' he contributed.

'I *always* trust my instincts.'

'So do I.'

They smiled at each other.

'Well, then,' she said.

On the Thursday morning, Nell loitered until she saw Cindy Lewis alighting grandly from a milky-coffee coloured Rolls-Royce and ascending the steps to the hairdresser, before crossing the road and following her in, crowding her ever so slightly but apologising nicely before crossing to the reception desk to ask about an appointment. Cindy was met with the smiles given only to regular customers who tipped well. Her mink coat was taken, but she held on to her black crocodile handbag – fake, Nell sniffed to herself: too glossy and far too big – when she sat down in a comfortable armchair to await her own, personal stylist who would be with her 'directly'. Until then – perhaps a cup of coffee?

'Nothing at all for six weeks!' Nell said in disbelieving tones. 'But I was told that this was the one hairdresser where you didn't have to put your name down at birth! Even with Kenneth I never had to wait *that* long!' She was aware that Cindy was looking at her, taking in the clothes, the hair, the *real* crocodile handbag. She turned, as if in haughty exasperation, letting Cindy get an uninterrupted look at her face as she checked the Cartier watch. 'Oh, well, I suppose it will have to be Michaeljohn again, then . . .'

Out of the corner of her eye she saw Cindy rise, but did not stop as she made for the door until she heard: 'Excuse me . . . but – aren't you Elly Little?' Nell turned, absolutely no recognition in her face as there was on Cindy's Barbie-doll vacuity.

'I *was* Elly Little.' Allowing a touch of hauteur, not to say *froideur* to chill her voice, Nell asked, 'Have we met?'

Cindy had always been more than a little in awe of Elly's education, background and accent though she had been at pains to deride even while she emulated. Now, the old superiority had her saying humbly: 'You don't remember me? Cindy Lewis as was?' Sidling closer to hiss: 'We was with Mickey Shaughnessy, remember?'

Nell made her hang in suspense for a moment while she appeared to search her memory. Then: 'Good Heavens!' she exclaimed blankly. 'Cindy Lewis. It must be all of ten years . . .'

'Eleven,' Cindy offered helpfully. 'Comin' up to twelve.'

'Well of all people!' Nell held out a hand. 'How are you, Cindy?'

'Very well, thank you.' It was repeated as it had been learned, by rote.

'Was you wantin' to have your 'air done, then?'

'Well, I was told in New York that this was as good a place as any – and good hairdressers are as scarce as hen's teeth . . . but they can't take me because I should have booked ages ago.'

'Leave it to me,' Cindy said confidently. 'I'll get you in. I come 'ere three times a week regular. Just you wait there.'

Cindy turned to head importantly for the reception area, only to turn on her heel after a few steps and head back again.

'What's yer name nowadays, then?' she hissed.

'Lytel – Elaine Lytel.' Nell pronounced it the American way – Lie-tel.

Cindy raised the pencil line of her eyebrows, which made Nell remember the fact that she had shaved them off years before and had had to create false ones ever since, before commenting snidely: 'Very posh, I'm sure, but you'll always be Elly to me.'

Having established the status quo she went off to demonstrate the power of her own, changed circumstances.

Nell moved discreetly away to where the waiting chairs were arranged.

In a moment Cindy came back. 'They'll fit you in,' she said, smug with triumph. 'Elly' looked suitably impressed.

'Heavens, you do have clout! But then, you said Cindy Lewis that was . . . who are you now?'

'My married name is Panacoulis.' Lie number one. She was not married.

Elly frowned. 'That strikes a chord . . .'

'Tony Panacoulis, remember? Used to do business with Mickey.'

Elly's face cleared. 'Of course . . . didn't he make – '

'Not 'ere,' Cindy hissed. 'Tell you what,' she said loudly, 'why don't we 'ave lunch. I've got a table booked at my regular place. They keep it for me most days . . . we can have a lovely long chinwag. What do you say?'

'That would be lovely,' Elly said.

As she had known, her hair was indifferently done after being washed with the wrong shampoo in water that was far too hot. She would have to rewash it herself when she got home that night. But it had got her the necessary 'in' with Cindy.

The restaurant was Greek, in Soho, and Cindy was greeted with obsequious smiles.

'Tony owns it,' she confided. 'He owns 'alf the 'airdresser's too. Put up 'alf the capital seein' as 'ow Kenny – that's the owner isself – is the brother of one of Tony's oldest friends.'

'No wonder you had clout,' Elly observed with a smile.

'What about you, then? Been in the States, have you?'

Elly told her story, leaving Cindy wide-eyed with a mixture of envy and superiority. 'I been with Tony five years, now.'

'You don't turn tricks any more, then?'

'Tony don't like it. He still runs a stable, of course, but I'm not one of them any more.'

'I seem to remember that he was in the film business . . .'

Cindy's day-glo face blanked out. 'He dabbles in a lot of things,' she said evasively. 'But tell about you, what was it like in America? I've always wanted to go but Tony don't like it over there. I think 'e ran into a bit of bother, like, when he went. So I've never got to see it. What was New York like – and California? Is it like what you see on the telly?'

She listened raptly as Elly described her life in the United States, and what it was like to be a call girl, how they had undercover plainclothes policemen whom the law permitted to use entrapment, but how the earnings, for a skilled hooker, could be very high.

'You look like you been earning' 'igh,' Cindy commented, taking in the dress, the fur, the handbag.

'I was, then I got landed with a bad john and lost the lot.' She spun the story of how she had met this man in a singles bar – 'not on a working night, you understand. This was pleasure, not business. He turned out to be kinky, beat me up and cleaned me out. I had eight thousand dollars tucked in the toe of my winter boots – he must have known where to look because he took it, every last cent, and on top of that he called the Super of the apartment house and told them I was a hooker. That got me evicted, and the fact that I was what they termed an illegal alien without my green card, plus the fact that my marriage to an American had been bigamous were of no help. I was deported. Given a plane ticket – Economy, when for years I'd never travelled anything but First – and told to go back where I came from. So here I am. Almost on my beam ends – fortunately I wasn't wearing my diamond ear-rings, which was a godsend because right now I'm living on what I got for those when I sold them – and in need of somewhere to live so that I can set myself up in business. I've been away so long I've lost contact with everybody. I don't know what is going on or who is running things or even how to get into somebody's good books.'

'What was you doin' then, when you was 'ooking?' Cindy asked, Salford coming on strong via a tongue loosened by several glasses of retsina which Elly had only sipped at, since she loathed it.

'You name it, I've done it,' she shrugged. 'I've been in a couple of movies – the price was right – but what I'm trying to do is set myself up the way it was in the States. A nice little flat and an even nicer list of regular customers, but rents are so high!'

'Where you stayin' now, then?'

'With an old friend who used to be in the Life but is now retired. It's only temporary, but beggars can't be choosers.'

Cindy nodded, but it was obvious she was doing what inside her head passed for thinking.

'Tony owns a lot of property,' she said finally, 'but he don't rent to just anybody. Seein' as you was one of Mickey's girls 'e might look on you as bein' what 'e calls "the right kind" but I'd 'ave to ask him first.'

'Well, it would depend where the property is . . .' Elly made it clear she had come a long way since Islington. 'If I want to earn big money I have to have the right place – '

'Tony 'as property all over the West End, and 'ad it a long time.' Pride burned brightly. 'My Tony's a Mr Big, these days.'

'Really,' Elly said. Then a shrug that accepted just how much things have changed. 'I'm glad somebody has turned up trumps.'

Cindy picked up her cue. 'I can 'andle 'im,' she said confidently, a creamy smile on her lips and a wholly knowing look in her eyes. 'Just you leave it to me. What's your number?'

Elly gave her Eleanor's number.

'I'll give you a ring in a day or two,' Cindy promised, printing it with a gold pen in a small notebook and underlining the name Elly.

'You are a godsend,' Elly told her gratefully. 'And now I simply must dash. I've got to go and visit an old friend who is in hospital.' Something told her not to mention why. Cindy was the kind to believe every wrong rumour there was about AIDS.

'Anybody I know?' Cindy asked.

'I doubt it. He has no connection to the old life, the way you and I do. He came after that.'

'Old boyfriend?'

'No. Just old friend – and I mean old. Pushing seventy.'

'Oh . . .' Cindy's interest expired.

'Can I give you a lift?' she asked, as they left the restaurant and the Rolls, which had obviously been called, glided to a stop in front of them.

'No, thanks. I've got some errands to do on the way to the hospital. It's been lovely seeing you again, Cindy, and I'm glad you are doing so well.' She added an extra dollop of cream. 'Better than any of us, in fact.' Cindy preened, gathered her mink about her, the knuckle-duster on her left hand glittering ferociously. 'I always used to say I'd make my mark, didn't I?'

'Yes,' Elly agreed, remembering how often that had been

and how wrong she had been to think that it would never be more than a cross.

'Never mind. I'll give you a tip or two,' Cindy said confidently. 'Put you in the picture as to what's what and what's not, OK?'

'Any advice gratefully appreciated,' Elly answered earnestly.

As the liveried chauffeur opened the door of the Rolls Cindy could not resist one, last, triumphant dig: 'Brains *ain't* everythin', you know.' The door shut on her and she smiled graciously, before bestowing a Queen Mother wave as the car slid silently away.

Nell let out a breath as if to blow away the heavy smog of the 'Poison' with which Cindy had been drenched, totally obliterating her own 'Y'. Then she set off towards Piccadilly Circus where she would pick up a bus for Westminster.

Philip stared. 'And what part are you auditioning for today, might one ask?'

'A call girl down on her luck.'

'Of course; one could *never* say that about Cleo. Am I allowed to ask why?'

'No,' Nell said. She withstood the full blast of Philip's chill-factor-one-thousand stare.

'If and when it comes off then you shall know all,' she promised.

'Ah . . . so there is something to know?'

'Just think of the fun you will have imagining what it might be.'

'Considering there is nothing else to do in this enclosed convent I must be grateful, I suppose.'

'No sign of being discharged, then?'

'Every time they *appear* to be satisfied something else insists on upsetting the applecart. Now they do not like the look of my lungs, or some such thing.' Casually, as if it was a bore: 'Just because they had to put me on oxygen the other night.'

Nell examined him. His high-bred, well-boned face was paler than usual and he had lost weight he could not afford since by nature he was, like Cassius, lean and hungry looking, but his eyes were as alert as ever and his voice as purringly powerful. When it commanded her to tell him what gossip she had for him, it sharpened to Sweeney Todd proportions when she confessed that she had none.

'Why, then, do you waste my time in coming to sit by my bed when you have no reason for doing so?'

'To see how you are, of course.'

'You know perfectly well how I am. Dying. The least you could do was your very best to see that my declining months were spent amidst the *on dits* I love. Since you have nothing to say that could be of any interest then you may take yourself off. Kindly do not return until you have a valid reason to do so – no, you may leave the books, since they are the ones I asked you for. And you have brought me green grapes when you know perfectly well I only eat black. I am *not* a herbivore. You may take them away with you.'

'What about the Turkish delight?'

'That stays – so long as it is of the plain chocolate variety?'

'It is.'

'One red mark, then – but no star. Now be gone about whatever your nefarious purposes are and I hold you to your promise. The *full* story as and when.'

'Promise. Cross my heart and hope to die.'

'*That*, is *my* line.'

The pub was behind Scotland Yard; one Nell had never been to before. It was quiet, there was no music, and the tables were well spaced. She got there first, ordered herself a drink and opened her *Evening Standard*. Nobody took any notice of her, though she was the only woman in the place. Her black crêpe suit was unremarkable – not the drop-dead chic that would have caused stares, she wore no jewellery but small pearl studs in her ears, her skirt was of a discreet length and her shoes were plain black pumps with two inch heels. Her hair was neatly upswept in a French pleat and on the leather-covered seat beside her reposed a black leather briefcase. Some high-powered executive having a restorative drink after a hard day, was the image she sought to establish. When he pushed through the swing doors Mark's glance at first swept over her then returned as recognition dawned. *Another one!* was his instant reaction.

'Are they for real?' he asked, indicating the horn-rims perched on her nose.

'Real. I need glasses for reading.'

'So the contact lenses are not just for disguise?'

'No.'

'Ready for another?' He indicated her almost empty glass.

'Please.'

He brought her a fresh gin and tonic, a beer for himself.

'So . . . how did it go?' he asked.

'Like a dream. She knew me at once, but I'd taken pains to re-create the Elly she knew, if somewhat up-market. She commented on the fact that there was something different about me and I told her I'd had plastic surgery – which I have.'

'And she accepted your story?'

'It is not Cindy I have to fool. It's Tony Panacoulis.'

'But you think you'll get the chance?'

'Oh, yes. She can't wait to show off her power, the position she now holds, her clothes, her jewels. She seems to think she has Tony right where he wants to be.'

'And you? How do you feel about it?'

'Confident,' she answered unhesitatingly. 'There was no strain, no suspicion – no "why is she here all of a sudden after all this time". She was only too pleased to have someone to brag to. Cindy was never one to keep her good fortune to herself even if all you ever got of it were detailed descriptions.'

But he did not smile. 'You are sure there was no suspicion?'

'Absolutely none. Why should there be?'

'Because Panacoulis is paranoid about secrecy. He and Dominitian meet regularly but they always arrive and leave separately and they never meet in the same place twice. Panacoulis is a Greek Cypriot, but he is Sicilian in his distrust of anyone who is not what he regards as Family. If Cindy sits as high on the hog as you say then by all means cultivate her because it means her power and influence are considerable.'

'I'll wait and see the proof of it first. Exaggeration is part and parcel of Cindy, and for all I know she has told me her highly-coloured version of the truth. Mind you, if memory serves, Tony Panacoulis always had a thing about blondes, probably because he is so dark. Cindy is not naturally blonde, and she wasn't platinum when I knew her; more golden.'

346

'Will he recognise you so easily?'

'I hope not. I never knew him as well as I did Cindy.' And did not want to, she thought. She stole a glance at her watch.

'Am I keeping you?' It came out more tart than he had intended because he had hoped to entice her to have dinner with him.

Cool as an iced lager: 'I can't stay long. I'm working tonight.'

For her it was a statement of fact, but it utterly changed his mood for the worse. Her words blew his hopes away leaving a gaping hole in their place.

'Oh,' was all he said but she was on to it like a flash. He saw the way her eyes cooled, while her face shifted imperceptibly, like a slow dissolve. Her gaze moved over him, unsmilingly green and stand-offish, as if he were no more to her than a nuisance. Full Cleo mode.

'When I agreed to help you, Superintendent,' she said levelly, 'nothing was said about my ceasing to help myself. I am what I am. I would advise you to accept that fact.' Gathering bag and gloves she rose. So did he. 'If and when I have anything further to report on the matter in hand you will hear from me.'

She nodded, as if to a very new acquaintance, one who had no importance in the scheme of things. Then she was gone, leaving nothing behind but the evocative headiness of her perfume.

He could have killed her. Since that was not feasible he decided to drown his sorrows. Bitch! Tart! Whore! He shot off the epithets like bullets, firing them straight at her image, which fragmented, fell apart and instantly reformed itself.

Well, now you know, he told himself. And not before time, either. You and your own little fantasies. Because that's all it is; all *she* is. Realise it once and for all and act on it!

Just as well, he told himself, emptying his glass and going to the bar for another – a whisky this time, and a double at that. His car was back at the Yard – he had walked the short distance to the pub. You were becoming far too immersed in that little fantasy. Because that *is* all it is, you know. All it ever can be. Just because you want a thing to be true doesn't make it so. You should know that by now. All right, acknowledge your want and then know once and for all that as your mother takes such delight in saying: 'What you want and what you get are two very different things.' Which train of thought stopped next at Alison's station. Yes, he thought, feeling the whisky hit the spot. Alison is everything that the other one is not. Made to measure for an up and coming copper like you. Use your common, Mark, and check your mirror. There is always someone on your tail waiting to cut you up. Nell Jordan is the kind of knife certain people would dearly love to wield to cut the rope you are climbing. Use her as she should be used; as an informant. Solve this case and your next Board will be the kind you skate on – right up to the door marked Det. *Chief* Superintendent Stevens. Do it *right*. Alison is *right*. Feeling in his pocket for loose change he went to call her.

'I'm sorry,' he said, later, knowing he had compounded his felony, but too miserable to feel anything, so heavy-hearted his gravity field must have altered.

'No need. These things happen.'

'Not with me, they don't.'

'Not even when you drink too much?'

He was silent then on a sigh admitted it.

'I knew something was wrong the moment I saw you. You were as uptight as it is possible to be without being strangled.'

He felt guilty, and resentful of her making him feel that way.

'Is it work?'

'Yes.' He seized on the half-truth. 'The case I'm working on. It's a headache.' And a heartache, he thought.

She was silent and then she said: 'I know you are ambitious, Mark, but you have come a long way in a short time. I have no doubt that you will get what you want and where you want to be. Just – be a little more patient, that's all.'

'Not one of my strong points, I'm afraid.'

'Nobody's perfect.'

'You are very understanding,' he said truthfully.

Her smile was wry. 'Oh, yes. And kind, and compassionate and – ' A shrug. 'All the "good pal" virtues. I'd rather be told I was desirable and sensuous and unforgettable; the kind of woman who would make the Member for Mark Stevens vote yes no matter how halfcut he was.'

She flung the covers back, reached for her Japanese kimono and he appreciated once more the firm athleticism of her figure: the flat stomach, the almost flat bottom, the small but firm breasts. But even as he admired it he saw superimposed the slender yet lush curves of Nell Jordan's body and felt hollow with wanting. He was also hard. What he could not achieve with Alison, knowing it was Alison, was effortless when he thought of Nell. He reached out a hand. She turned queryingly and then, when she saw how fine and upstanding he was, raised her eyebrows and asked: 'Was it something I said?'

'And something I saw . . .' Another half-truth but it had worked, hadn't it? The thing to do was put it to the test.

He passed with flying colours. 'A gold, I think,' Alison sighed, replete unto boneless satisfaction. 'Yes, definitely a gold. Plus an E for effortless.' There was a fine sheen of sweat on her body and a little pulse throbbed rapidly in the hollow of her throat. 'Sex is the best workout there is, don't you agree?'

'Certainly the most pleasurable.'

She went pink. 'Do I really – give you pleasure, I mean?'

'Yes.' It wasn't really a lie, he thought uncomfortably. It had been Alison's body, Alison's response – but Nell he had held, Nell he had pleasured, Nell whose sighs and catches of breath and body-arching gasps he had heard. I'm not the first and I won't be the last, he thought. That thing we carry between our legs has no conscience, and who was it said that at night, all cats are grey? But looking at Alison's delighted face he felt guilty, and soiled by it. He got out of bed quickly. 'I must shower and go,' he said. 'I've got a long, hard day tomorrow . . .'

But before he left he put his hands on her shoulders. 'Thank you,' he said.

'For what?'

'Being there.'

She made a mock salute. 'Any time, Superintendent.'

As she locked the door behind him she wondered, with the bitter dispassion of one who had played second fiddle in the orchestra of life ever since she learned how to play a scale, who Nell was. Mark had uttered the name with a shout that was a cross between exaltation and despair, as he climaxed, so deep

349

in his imaginings – as he was deep in her – that he was no longer in control of his responses and no longer in control of himself. That had never happened before. She had had a sense tonight, powerful and all pervasive, of a nakedness about him that had nothing to do with his being without clothes. He was a good lover; strongly passionate, skilled yet sensitive and he knew how to give pleasure before taking his own, but always, before, she – who had developed a seventh sense because of her sixth sense of always being second best – had been aware of a gulf; a deliberate detachment of mind from body, so that while he was doing one thing he was thinking another; that while he was ostensibly heart and soul into his endeavour, she had known very well that his heart had nothing to do with it. Hers was the one which had been done harm to; GBH in his parlance. All he'd done was smile, shake her hand, and it was done. She was done. Done for.

It was nothing like the despairing, hopeless hunger of her infatuation for a man who had no interest in her beyond the money she'd inherited. This was a recognition of someone whom she could trust, who would mean what he said, live up to his obligations and be friend as well as lover. This was the kind of man she had hoped but never expected to meet, and she had wanted to die of embarrassment when, on making contact with his eyes, she had read there that he knew exactly what their respective mothers were up to. But it was not them that had made him ask her out; not their plots which had led to them ending up in her bed on only the second time of asking. She had known that she did not have his full attention, not in the way she wanted, but she knew what she was and what she could expect and was grateful. She had been picked up and dropped so many times there was nothing left to break, which was why she was surprised that it should hurt so much. Cole Porter said it all, she thought, as she stripped her bed and remade it with fresh linen. 'I've got you under my skin,' except it is not me who is in his blood. He had made love to her tonight with a passion and tenderness which proved how true the old saw was: third time was indeed lucky. There had been no detachment tonight. He had given all of himself in such a way as to make her painfully aware of just how much he had shortchanged her the first two times. Except it had not been her. It had been a woman named Nell.

Cindy got back to Nell the very next day. 'I spoke to Tony and if you want to have a chat with 'im, tell 'im what you been doin' since Mickey and 'ow you come back to this country, 'e's willin' to listen.'

Nell was cool. 'Who is doing the favour here, Cindy?' she asked. 'I'm not the two-bit scrubber he remembers. I hope you told him that.'

'Oh, I did, I did. But – well, you remember Tony? 'ow particular 'e is? This ain't 'ollywood we're talkin' about you know. Tony 'as to be careful, very careful, and since 'e's a cautious man by nature it stands to reason 'e's even more cautious than normal. 'E don't trust nobody and it's only 'cos I spoke for you that he said 'e'd see you in the first place. I told him you was a bit o' class and it just so 'appens that's what 'e needs for a new movie waitin' for the right girl to start shootin'. If your face fits you're in.'

Nell sensed that Cindy had painted a picture so rosy as to be in a permanent state of blush. But she'd never been able to leave well enough alone. Who else but a female Baron Munchausen would wear such unbelievably long nails? God knows what he expects, Nell thought, but it will be as well if I live up to it.

'Where and when?' she asked crisply.

'Tony's club in Soho – the Orchid House. Tomorrow mornin', eleven a.m.'

'I'll be there.'

As she hung up she wondered whether or not to tell Mark Stevens. Decided not to. The outcome of the proposed meeting was what mattered. She went upstairs to prepare for her role.

The Orchid House was a strip club, sleazy and unappetising in the harsh light of day; dark, stuffy and smelling of cigars and cheap scent. A cleaner was desultorily moving a vacuum over puce-coloured wall-to-wall carpet. Silk curtains several shades paler hung across the entry to the club proper. The foyer was hung with life-size photographs of nudes; all blonde, all young, all Marilyn Monroe clones. A man behind a counter, stacking cigarettes and cigars looked across to ask: "Elp yer, love?'

'I have an eleven o'clock appointment with Mr Panacoulis. My name is Elly Little.'

''Ang on a minute.'

He came round the counter, went through the curtains. The cleaner, who had a permanent squint caused by the smoke which drifted past her eyes from the cigarette which drooped at one corner of her mouth, glanced over at Nell, sniffed in a way which spoke volumes before aiming the vacuum at the ash which had fallen when she did so.

'This way, love.' The man stood in the curtains, jerking his head. Nell followed him. The club was small, crowded with tables, banquettes along two walls, a small stage at the back. More puce carpet, plastic crystal chandeliers, lamps made out of Chianti bottles with candles stuck in them. Nell followed her guide through the tables and to a door at the rear of the stage, which he opened, announcing: 'Miss Little.'

Nell went past him and he shut the door behind her.

Tony Panacoulis sat behind a desk in a windowless room lit by one green shaded lamp. He lounged in a swivel armchair, tilted so that his feet rested on the edge of his desk, and he was paring his nails. To Nell, it was an instant replay of their scene all those years ago. The curly hair was still very black, but now the dead black of dye (no wonder he owns a hairdresser's, Nell thought), and his eyes were still small pieces of obsidian which regarded you steadily, unblinkingly, from a face that still reminded her of an over-ripe fruit. It was the mouth, she decided: too wide, too full, too soft; that and the unnatural pallor of his skin, which obviously rarely saw sunlight. He wore a pale grey silk suit, a heliotrope silk shirt and a parma violet tie. His hands were small, pudgy, like his face. He wore a heavy gold ring with a diamond in it on one little finger, a heavy 22-carat Rolex Oyster with full complement of diamonds on one wrist, chain-link gold identity bracelet on the other.

Nell sniffed without moving her nose and realised he still wore the same aftershave; more important, it was the one also worn by his good friend Reza Dominitian. No wonder she had taken a dislike to it.

'Sit down, Miss — Little,' he said. He still had his Greek Cypriot accent, though there was no hesitation in his English. He indicated the wooden chair in front of his desk.

'Thank you.' Nell seated herself, crossed her legs, the pure silk of her taupe shirt-waister slipping back from her knee to her thigh. She had heavy gold twists in her ears to match the brooch pinned to her left lapel, and her shoes and handbag were of rich brown silky calf, the clasp of the latter bearing the entwined C's of the Chanel logo.

'Well,' Tony Panacoulis said at last, after a contemplative, unhurried examination, 'you have come a long way.'

'Snap,' Nell returned coolly.

'Tell me how you did it.'

Nell gave him the story she had given Cindy, but unlike her, he asked questions. He was especially interested in her experiences as a high-class call girl, and the only sign of life to him was when she told him how much she had earned per trick.

'So there's a lot of money in it for the right girl,' he said at last, thoughtful with interest.

'Yes; more if you work on your own and not from an agency.' She let a few seconds go by then hit him with it. 'On that level there are no pimps. The kind of girl who can earn that kind of money knows it and has no intention of not keeping it.'

'You like money?'

'I like my own money.'

'How come you're sitting in front of me, then, asking for a job?'

'Because I was robbed of eight thousand dollars. Because Cindy suggested I might fit in with your . . . set-up. I've not done much skin-trade stuff; in the States it's a big-time operation with a high turnover of girls, added to which a lot of it is controlled by men I have never cared to work for. The kind of men who tend to get shot in barbers' chairs or the backs of cars.' She levelled her gaze at the dead black eyes. 'If it wasn't that I need the money I wouldn't be here, and if it is not what I consider worth my while I won't do it. I still have a few contacts here and I can still turn a good trick with men prepared to pay for something . . . out of the ordinary.'

'Like what?'

'That is my business.'

'Not if you work for me; then everything you do is my business.' It was calmly said and absolutely decisive, but Nell was picking up vibes which contradicted his words. Something at the back of those dead eyes . . . a little flame she recognised. She decided to call his bluff.

'In that case, there is no more to be said. I bid you good-day, Mr Panacoulis.'

Her hand was on the door knob before he said: 'Don't be so hasty. Let's discuss this a little more.' The movement of his mouth was obviously meant to be a conciliatory smile. 'I'm not used to dealing with such a high-class hooker.' Sarcasm dripped.

'Be advised, Mr Panacoulis,' Nell told him quellingly, 'that is exactly what I am. Disabuse yourself of the idea that I am what Mickey Shaughnessy made me. I left him and his sort behind me a long time ago.'

'I can see that.' He swung his feet to the floor, pocketed his nail-parer. 'But I think you should see the quality of the home movies I make. They aren't your average street-crap either.' When he walked over to her he was quite short, a good head below her in her heels. 'I'll give you a private screening,' he said. 'I think it will surprise you.'

It did. The sets were lavish, the colour good, the camera-work expert, even though some of the acts were perversions of the baser kind. And there was an actual story, even though, once the clothes came off and the heat was on, nobody cared about it by then. The images were extraordinarily artistic in places, and one scene in particular had Nell utterly intent on the screen, though she was careful to give no indication of why. Tony Panacoulis sat next to her and his arm, sharing the arm-rest between them, touched hers so that he would have felt the slightest tension in her as she recognised just where it was that the act was taking place: the colonnaded marble folly that stood in a circle of trees some half a mile from the house in which she had spent the weekend with Reza Dominitian.

'Well?' Tony Panacoulis asked as the lights came up.

'I have to admit that I am impressed.' It was the truth. This was obviously no penny-ante operation. Money had been spent, care had been taken.

Tony had come a long way since the Islington days. He was quite obviously what he would call Big Time, now, and she was confirmed in her beliefs that he was running a vastly profitable hard-core pornography business, backed by Reza Dominitian certainly, and perhaps by other, equally wealthy men who were not too particular as to the means they used to increase that wealth.

He was still a man she found utterly repellent, personally and professionally, but she was confident that knowing him as she did she could use that knowledge to help Mark put him away for a long time. Had there not been an ulterior motive of such vital importance she would not have come near him again for anybody's sake, but sexually abused children were an issue about which she held almost violent opinions; a matter her conscience would never have allowed her to ignore. Added to which, she was no longer a nobody. She now had the confidence of years of experience as a high earning, highly-skilled courtesan. And she was not a mistress of fantasy for nothing!

No. She could play her part. This little interview had made that clear. In order to put this horrible little creep in the dock looking at a long sentence she would give him a performance that would knock his socks off.

She felt Tony Panacoulis's arm ooze around her shoulders, forced herself to remain apparently unmoved while he put his face close to hers, leered lasciviously and said confidently: 'You are the perfect fit for my next leading lady – and I do mean lady. Lady Chatterley, in fact. I'm going to make the only really honest and true version of that little masterpiece. How'd you like to play Lady Constance?'

18

'We start shooting next Monday,' Nell told Mark Stevens.

'You had no trouble, then?' There was nothing to be deduced from his voice. She could not see his face as they were speaking on the telephone. Ever since she had sensed what he felt that night in the pub she had resolved not to exacerbate what her intuition told her could turn out to be a very tricky situation. Remote control was called for.

'None. In fact, since you mention it, I did make a sale. Tony Panacoulis now wears a red sticker. He made it quite plain that he fancies me.'

No answer to that.

'Where will you be working?' he asked instead.

'Don't know. I'm to report to his club at ten o'clock. Then I'll be taken to wherever they propose to shoot. There will be some location work – he says he intends to follow the book closely – '

'What is he, the producer or the director?'

'Somebody called Bill Myers will direct but my impression is that Tony has the final say.'

'No hint of anything else?'

'Absolutely none. I can only surmise that the straight porno stuff is handled by one set of people; the specialised, paedophile material by another and never the twain do meet except through Tony Panacoulis. I made enquiries about Bill Myers through certain contacts I have. Considering the business he's in his reputation is a good one. He was once headed for Hollywood but went via heroin. He's an eight-year addict but provided he has taken his shots he is a fast worker. They reckon a week is his usual schedule.'

Another silence. 'And will there be a follow-up?'

'It depends on how well I do as Constance Chatterley.'

'Which will depend, surely on who plays Mellors.'

She disposed of his savagery by taking him seriously.

'A man named Harry Hall. The lead in all Panacoulis productions. Looks like Mr Universe. I saw him in action and have no doubt he is why so many women hire his videos. He even gets fan mail.'

Don't take me on, Superintendent, she warned him. I am in no mood to argue. Not after encountering Tony Panacoulis. So when she heard Mark ask: 'You are sure you want to do this?' she knew that he didn't.

'You were the one who pointed out that I could be of inestimable value to your investigation. You were the one who suggested I make contact with Cindy Lewis again, you – '

'All right!'

At the tone of his voice she backed away. 'I am doing this for one reason only,' she told him, 'to give back a little for all the good luck I've had. I'm not superstitious but my benefactress was. It was her firm belief that if you don't give back a little of your good fortune there won't be any more coming your way. This is my way of giving back. I have a thing about child-pornography, about children and sex – ' now she said what she knew would push him right back over to his side of the line. 'And it is not as though the job is something I have never done before. All right, it is downmarket and it will be filmed, but I can handle that.' When he heard her laugh he winced. 'Besides, according to Mr Panacoulis I am about to participate in the making of a work of art.'

'You seem to have had quite a discussion.'

'I was trying to pump him.'

No. That's *his* intention, Mark thought savagely.

'It is the perfect opportunity for me to look, listen and learn. I was told that the search for the perfect Constance has been going on for some considerable time. One look at me and Tony knew he had found her. I shall wear a blonde wig, of course – '

'Because his thing is blondes?'

'No . . .' Nell sounded surprised. 'Constance Chatterley is blonde.'

'Yes, yes. Of course.' He forced his mind back into official channels. 'So apart from being hired you have nothing else to report.'

'It's a beginning, isn't it?'

'Just be careful. This is not – '

'I know exactly what this is, Superintendent, and I will get as much information for you as I can without compromising my position although . . .' the sly amusement he had come to appreciate lightened her dead-even inflexion, 'it has to be said that it is pretty compromising to begin with. I'll be in touch.'

It took five days. She called him on the Friday evening, and he did not like the sound of her voice. 'It's all in the can. We "wrapped" as they say at five o'clock this afternoon.'

'How did it go?'

Her voice was so expressive he could see her shrug. 'It went.'

She sounded down, he thought. Very dispirited. Whatever had gone had not gone well.

'Where are you?' he asked.

'At home.'

'I'll be there in twenty minutes.'

'Suit yourself.'

She looked like she sounded. There was a droop to the wide mouth, she looked pale – but that could be because her face wore no make-up. Intuition, allied to his training and experience, diagnosed a dangerously low flashpoint.

'Want some coffee or would you rather have a drink?'

'Coffee, please.'

He took off his Burberry, flung it over the back of the couch, sat down on it. She came back with two mugs, handed him one and then went to sit, yoga-style, on the sofa opposite. She had on jeans and a T-shirt, her usual in-house style, and her feet were bare. Her hair was skewered carelessly atop her head.

'So . . .' she said, after dipping deep into her coffee, 'you'll be wanting my *report*.' Sarcasm dripped. 'The "studio" is an abandoned warehouse due for demolition on the south side of the river opposite Greenwich. It was due for development but the money ran out and demolition stopped. The upper floors are a ruin but we worked on the ground floor.

The board outside said Athena Investments. I think it belongs to another Greek Cypriot. It is obviously in regular use because they have a power supply for light and heat – and it was damned cold, believe me; it is right on the water's edge. They had one corner of the ground floor set up as a set, supposedly Mellor's cottage. We worked there Monday to Thursday – very fast, very time-is-money but everything had been worked out in advance and Bill Myers knew exactly what he wanted. Sex. And more sex. With giant close-ups. So much for Tony and his "art". It was all very brisk, very businesslike. The crew were all right, all part of a group Bill has worked with for years. All close-mouthed. Whether that was because for the first two and a half days Tony haunted the set I don't know, but small talk was not their forte. However, on the Friday we "went on location" and guess where?'

His experienced ears read her tone. 'Wiltshire? Reza Dominitian's house?'

For a moment her mouth hung open then she asked in disappointed tones: 'How did you know?'

'Bits of the house's interior have been recognised in more than one video from a haul of pornographic material. And it makes sense that they would use somewhere entirely safe for outdoor work of their particular kind.'

Her eyes raked his face suspiciously but when she sensed no ridicule she relaxed and said: 'That's exactly what we did. Outdoor scenes. We shot a couple in and around a little marble temple I spotted when I was shown round that weekend. Me pushing Sir Clifford – it was a long-shot so one of the electricians played him all wrapped up in a rug – in his wheelchair, and one inside the temple: the famous flower decorating scene. I was on tenterhooks all the way down because although nobody told me where we were going I recognised the route once we got into Wiltshire. But you had told me Reza Dominitian was still out of the country so I just sat tight.'

'He's in Brussels.'

'Well, it was obvious Tony had the run of the place, and that it was known he was there because he had a phone call. It must have been top secret because although he carries a phone in his pocket the servant came from the house to tell him, so it must have been of the kind that needs a secure land-line. When he came back he said he'd been called away and left Bill in charge.' There was a pause. 'Along with Cindy.' She nodded to the query in his eyes. 'Yes . . . she was a part of the set-up all week. Anyway, that was the last we saw of Tony until this afternoon when we got back to London and he paid up. In cash. A thousand pounds. He seemed to think it was a fortune.' The imp of mischief escaped from its cage and hovered around her mouth. 'He wasn't impressed when I failed to be, but he told me to stand by for more action so I think I gave a good performance. Bill was more than happy, anyway.' Dry as dust: 'He said I was a born actress.' Some secret knowledge glimmered. 'But I don't think there is any point because I learned absolutely nothing. Either they don't know or they won't – or daren't say – and I incline to the latter, because they are a decent lot; all quite straight. They know what they do is illegal but it is very well paid because of that and there is a huge market – they can't turn them out fast enough, evidently. To them it is a job, no more. They showed a bit of interest in me, because I was new and I suppose they wanted to check me out, but for the most part they showed more interest in the result of the snooker championship. I chatted, I told them about the States but there was absolutely nothing to be got from them. They told me stories – a hoot some of them – about certain now frightfully snooty ladies who began their careers in the skin trade – but there was no sign of any warning glances, any signal head-shakes or conferring in undertones.' She sighed. It came from the lower depths. 'It was a total waste of time.'

She sounded so disappointed, so defeated, he was impelled to set down his mug, get up and go and sit down next to her. 'No you didn't,' he disagreed. 'You confirmed the link between Dominitian and Panacoulis; we now know that they are still using the house as a base of operations.'

'But I got no – what is it you call it – hard evidence about when they make the other movies, who makes them and where. I spent a whole week fishing and caught absolutely nothing!'

'I've spent months – this case has been going on for two

years – and been just as frustrated. Cases are solved in an hour and a half only in the movies.'

'I suppose so.' But she didn't sound like a believer.

'Have I complained?'

'No, but you have every right . . .'

'No, I haven't. Police work is for the most part a slow, hard slog through question and answer, digging holes that nine times out of ten contain no body, sifting evidence until you find something, often previously thought insignificant, that looked at in a different light, opens a door you've been battering at for God knows how long. Over the past two years six bodies have come to light but there are still many missing children unaccounted for. This is a very well organised and protected ring. We know that only those people participating have knowledge of when and where and how, but we have no idea who they are, where they come from. The bodies have been found as far apart as two hundred miles; it may be that the members of the ring come from all parts of the country as and when circumstances are right and they have a suitable victim. That may be at frequent intervals but it is much more likely to be infrequent. Once a body comes to light there is a general damp–down because the boys they are after take fright and become very reluctant to be enticed. The phone call you mentioned might possibly have concerned the ring or it might not. Panacoulis is still being watched and he has done nothing untoward or been anywhere suspicious; we have the pictures to prove it. Later on you can take a look at them. There may be another familiar face.'

'I doubt it.' She would not be cheered up.

'Why was it so important that you come away with incon-trovertible proof?'

'That was the whole point of the matter, wasn't it? And as you very well know, I don't like the thought of children being sexually abused.' She rose to her feet. 'More coffee?'

He knew he had touched a nerve so said: 'I've got a better idea. You need cheering up. Why don't I take you out to dinner?'

'No, thank you.' It was as incontrovertible as the evidence she had hoped to find.

'Don't take this set-back as a hopeless failure. Mark it as unsuccessful and go on to the next thing.'

'But I was so sure I could come up with something.' She sounded so forlorn he wanted to take her in his arms, offer her comfort; knew that was not possible yet.

'You have got yourself into the slough of despond for no good reason. You need warmth, good food and company, not to mention a few glasses of wine.'

'I said no!' Thank you was tagged on as a sop.

Her curt refusal put a match to his own smouldering fire. 'God, but you are a hard nut to crack. What do I have to do? Become a customer? Don't you ever *give* anything of your self?'

Lightning flashed behind the storm clouds of her eyes; her mouth tightened and her hand came up instinctively, heading for his cheek, but his was there to grasp and stop it, gripping it so forcefully she winced, though it did not stop her trying it on with her other hand, which received the same treatment. They stood facing each other, feelings clashing, temperatures raised. He had her helpless, literally in his grip, unmoved by the Medusa-like glare she was giving him.

'You are determined to sulk, aren't you? Don't tell me you can't take failure? I had thought you made of stronger mettle. I've told you; this is not some hot-shot girl detective movie, it is real life, and that being so it cannot be controlled. And you have to control everything, don't you? That's the only way you feel safe, and not being safe means being sorry!'

She struggled to free herself, white-faced with temper, teeth bared. It was useless. His hands were commensurate with his size and he had locked them around her wrists like handcuffs.

'You are not a robot; you wouldn't be feeling such a failure if you were, so why won't you allow yourself some relaxation?'

From between her teeth: 'I volunteered to do a job for you, and that is all you'll get from me. What I was feeling was sorry that I was not able to do a better one.'

'Have I complained? You expected far too much far too soon.'

Again she tried to wrench her arms free; again she failed. He could see the beginnings of panic in her eyes as she realised she was not in control. He was.

'Use that intelligence of yours,' he commanded, 'and your much-vaunted common sense. Would *you* tell a total stranger things that could get you banged up for years for even being implicated in one of the filthiest trades there is? These are sick people we are dealing with here; twisted and perverted and sadistic, who get their kicks from inflicting unthinkable indignities on children! You waltz on to the set and think that a nice little heart-to-heart will have them confiding in you! What makes you think you are so special?'

She exerted all her strength and pulled one wrist free, face contorted, voice wild: 'Because I know all about child abuse, that's why. I know what is done because it was done to me – and by my own father! *That's* why!' As soon as it was said it was regretted. Mortification flooded. There was a long, crackling silence, then at the look which came into his face she bit her lip hard and he saw the bright glitter of tears before her overwrought, self-lacerated nerves gave way and she put her face in her hands and burst into noisy, angry tears. He went over to her, and as if he were handling something infinitely and fragilely precious, enfolded her in his arms.

'My poor dear love,' he whispered. 'Why in God's name didn't you tell me.' He'd intended to open her up gently, not goad her to self-humiliation.

'I've never told anyone,' she said through her sobs. 'It's not something you talk about.'

He drew her down on to the sofa again, but this time on his knee. He took out his handkerchief, put it into her hands and then let her cry it out. The past week must have been sheer hell; trying to find out about something connected to events she had spent her life trying to forget; thinking of it constantly, trying to find the right way to frame her questions, wanting desperately to help by finding out and failing. No wonder she could not handle her failure. All she had gained was another load of self-hatred.

But she had made the step, a giant one. Now it was up to him to help her the rest of the way. Crying her heart out helplessly was not her style; the one she had created for herself, that is. But it had always been the soft, vulnerable Nell at the heart of Cleo's shellacked sophistication that had called to him. The woman at the heart of this deeply-felt, yet wholly shared emotion was the one he wanted, and he had not dared hope that the crack in her façade would be so deep or spread so quickly. Back at the beginning, when he had realised that what he felt for a high-class call-girl was more than he had ever felt for any woman, he had asked himself bluntly: 'Have you any idea what you are getting into here? This is no *happy-ever-after* fairy tale. There is no possibility of that kind of ending in this particular case. You don't even live in the same universe never mind world! And there is no separating this sheep from the rest of goats, either.' He had told himself, on meeting Alison, that this was more like it. Except that what was right and proper and what he wanted had nothing to do with each other. Hitherto his career had suborned all else; it had been 'When I get to Chief Inspector' then 'When I get to Superintendent' and lately 'When I make Chief Superintendent'. Now, as he held her, warm and yielding and still crying her heart out, he knew that if they were to offer him Commissioner on condition that . . . etc. he would say thank you, but no thank you. If this is as far as I go so be it, as long as I can have Nell too.

She wept until all she had left were dry heaves, and when she began to speak it was without prompting, and in a voice drained of everything but exhaustion.

'It started when I was eleven. After my mother died my father informed me that I was to take my mother's place. In everything. I didn't understand wholly, but I knew enough to know that it was not right. When I pointed this out – timidly, because you questioned my father at your peril – he said that what other people said was right was not necessarily *his* right, and as my father he had absolutely every right. I was the elder daughter; he had no wife. Ergo, I must perforce take her place. In the household. In the house. In his bed.' The flat, uninflected emptiness of her voice told of years of solitary anguish, not knowing where to turn, who to tell, how to deal with the horror of a life twisted when it was far too young to offer resistance.

'He did not come every night, but I soon learned that if I showed anything but absolute obedience punishment would follow. He used to take me down to the cellar, tie my wrists to metal rings fixed to one of the big beams, leave me hanging there in darkness, feet just skimming the floor. At first I used to scream, but he never came, so I learned to wait it out in silence. He never hit me, never used any kind of force on me. He had no use for physical violence. His violence was emotional. It was only when I was fully grown that I realised my mother had died of emotional starvation as well as multiple sclerosis. When I was little she used to sing about the house and play the piano, but my father liked a quiet house so there came a time when she did not play or sing any more. She faded, like a picture left in strong light, under my father's dominance. Everything had to be according to his instructions. When I had my periods and he could not have use of my body – he was a very fastidious man – he taught me how to fellate him. And while I was on the pill he was meticulous in his checking of my blood pressure, his examinations as to my physical well-being. When I became pregnant and I still don't know how because he gave me my pill every morning and stood over me until I had swallowed it – he aborted me. It was during that period, when in his perverted, scrupulous way he left me alone to recover from the D&C, that he started on my sister. She woke me one night, screaming and crying for me. When I went to her room she was not there. She was with my father, in the big double bed, and as always, his door was locked. I hammered on it, shouted, screamed, and he came out and told me to stop making a spectacle of myself before taking me down to the cellar. That's when I made up my mind to tell on him. I was seventeen and it had been going on for six years. I could not let him ruin her too. So one morning, after he had been with me, I went straight down to the Social Services, told them what he'd done; that I had not bathed; that the proof of what I was saying was still inside me. I told them everything once they had done the swabs and had their proof, and when my father had gone out on his rounds they came to the house and I showed them the cellar and tried to get Margaret to tell them what he had done to her – she used to talk, then – but all she would say was "daddy hurt, daddy hurt". So they swabbed her too and then they waited for him.' Her empty voice trailed off. Mark said nothing, only held her close, keeping the lid on an anger which was by then at a rolling boil. Finally: 'He didn't deny any of it. He told them what he had told me, that it was his right. He was my father, I was his daughter. Nobody – *nobody* – had the right to tell him what he could or could not do with his own daughter in his own house. And all he said to me as they took him away was: 'I am disappointed in you, Eleanor. I thought I had taught you better than this.'

She closed her eyes. She looked and sounded deathly tired. But she struggled to finish. 'They put me in care, but once I knew Margaret was safe and my father could never get to her again I ran away. Just – packed a bag and took what money I could find and left. The house, my so-called life – everything. I went to London and there I became what my father had made me. I had been his unpaid whore; now I did it for money. I knew nothing else except how to clean, cook, wash, sew. And it was all I was fit for. I was on the streets for more than two years and then I met Elizabeth. The rest you know.' Her lids fluttered closed again.

A sense of the utter hopelessness and helplessness of the seventeen-year-old girl impermeably stained, she believed, by her father's incestuous behaviour, swamped him so totally that he felt his throat thicken and his own eyes prick. Jesus Christ, he thought, and I thought I had seen everything.

'It's all right,' he murmured, holding her close, rocking her slightly. 'You are safe now. You will always be safe with me. That's a promise.'

It was as though her outpouring of pain, stifled through all the emotionally starved years of her childhood had formed a link between them, invisible but strong. 'Thank you for telling *me*', he said softly. 'Thank you for needing *me*.'

But she did not hear for she was already deep in exhausted sleep.

She slept for three hours. After covering her with a quilt he found in a bedroom cupboard he had sat and read, helping himself – he was sure she would not mind – to her Wild Turkey. She had a good selection of books but he finally settled for a thriller: an American police procedural. Nothing like his own daily grind. The cats came in from wherever they had been and made it clear, by means of rusty-hinged miaows, that they were hungry. He found a tin of cat food and shared it between them, re-filled their milk bowl. Licking their lips, they returned to the sitting room where they proceeded to wash and groom, after which they investigated the sleeping figure of their mistress, who did not stir. So they climbed up on to his chair, and while Blossom made herself comfortable on his lap, Bundle stretched out on the top of the deep cushion at his back. Mark could feel the throb of his purr.

She had created a haven for herself and no mistake. Warm colours, comfortable furniture, soft lighting, books, music, television. Probably everything her childhood home had been not. Except she had never really been a child; her mother wheelchair-bound from the time she was seven; her father ruthlessly destroying any chance of becoming a normal teen-ager. His own mother was very ambitious for him but he had never doubted her love, or the pride she took in him. Likewise his father. They had doted on their children, and whilst his mother had preferred him, so his father had turned to his daughter, so that each had one parent whose devotion was unquestionably to be relied on; two parents united in wanting the best for their children. From what she had told him earlier he doubted if Dr Jordan had been capable of love. Duty and filial obedience had taken its place. Only what *he* wanted had mattered. Mark doubted if what Nell had *needed* had ever come into it. She's screwed up all right, he thought, still feeling the anger that had seared him as he listened to her story. It will take time and patience and a lot of tender loving care to unscrew and straighten out what her father crumpled in his ruthless palm, but I'm willing to have a damned good try.

When Nell opened her eyes, sat up, yawning and stretching, he watched her unguarded expression congeal as she saw him in the chair. A squirming look that was half confusion, half embarrassment, with a dash of consternation crossed her face in marching order then she said stiffly: 'I'm sorry. I didn't mean to go to sleep on you.'

Her voice held all the careful control of one who is holding in a state of screaming panic. She was remembering what she had told him and bitterly regretting it.

'You obviously needed it. Do you feel better for it?'

A nod. Not looking at him.

'Good. I fed the cats, by the way, and helped myself to a drink.'

'Thank you . . .' She stood up, raked her hair back. 'I feel like a nice hot cup of tea . . '

'That's a good idea. I'll do it. Don't worry. I know my way around a kitchen.'

Blossom protested as he lifted her up so he handed her to Nell. 'Here, try another lap for a change.'

'She was on your lap!'

'And him behind me.' He jerked his head to where Bundle was regarding them somnolently.

'Good heavens, you are favoured! They don't normally go to anyone – not even Philip!'

As Mark went into the kitchen: 'Traitor!' Nell whispered fiercely against the smoky blue-grey fur. But she also felt unaccountably pleased. While it was never a case of 'Love me, love my cat' she had found that the people they did not care for were not likely to appeal to her either.

'Hungry?' Mark called from the kitchen.

Another surprise. She was ravenous. Putting Blossom in a chair she went into the kitchen.

'Do you know what I would like?' she asked. 'A plate of fluffy scrambled egg and a couple of slices of hot, buttered toast.'

'Got any bacon to go with that?'

'And mushrooms . . .'

They ate at the kitchen table; she with her scrambled egg – 'You can cook!' she exclaimed – he with his fry-up. 'To hell with cholesterol for once.'

They did not talk much; both hungry, they concentrated on their food. Not until they took their cups into the sitting room, where the cats had settled down in front of the fireplace, did Mark ask: 'Do you feel up to telling me what upset you about your week – apart from what you consider your failure to come up with any information?'

For a moment she regarded him over her cup. 'How did you know?'

'I'm a detective, remember?'

A dour smile. 'Which I am obviously not.' The smile faded. Finally: 'I made a disconcerting discovery,' she said. 'I didn't like what I was doing because it was in front of an audience. It made me feel – for the first time since I left the streets – like the whore I am. Grubby, degraded, second-hand. It was all so – cold and clinical. And it was also ridiculous. Time after time I had to force myself not to laugh. They took it all so seriously. Between the distaste and the hilarity I had to keep reminding myself why I was there, what I was supposed to find out. I kept thinking of things I had not – would not allow myself to think about – for years, with the result I got uptight. I suppose that's what made me blow a fuse tonight. It has been rumbling away beneath the surface and all it took was one well-placed remark and – up she went.'

'It was only a matter of time. And I am partly to blame for allowing you to put yourself in such danger. It won't happen again.'

The expression on her face had him asking: 'Now what?'

'Tony wants me back. Fanny Hill, remember?'

'To hell with Fanny Hill. No more pornography. We'll find some other way.'

For a moment Nell became Chloe as her gaze went up and down him, ice-cool and drop-deadish. 'Are you giving me orders, Superintendent?' Her voice was silky.

'If you want my protection and that of the force I work for, yes.' That turned the silk into sackcloth and ashes. And then she totally disconcerted him by saying meditatively: 'I think I might just have found one – another way, I mean.'

'Tell me.'

'I told you Cindy was part of the set-up all week? Well, we became *very* friendly – or at least, I let her think we did. You know, all girls together and talk about the old days and "do you remembers," as though we had been the best of friends instead of the worst of enemies. Cindy is always prepared to make a friend of a former enemy if that enemy happens to have done very well for herself. It is what you are now – and what you have, of course, which matters to Cindy. She is a worthy mate for that horrid little man. Both of them are their own prime interests. But I thought if I cultivated her and played along with her delusions of grandeur I might manage to glean some odds and ends of information about Tony, so I polished away at her ego assiduously – talk about self-obsessed! – but she is very close-mouthed where he is concerned. Though I continually managed to turn the conversation in his direction she always ended up steering it in her own, so I'm afraid I didn't get much information about him, but Cindy's very appearance on the set was cause for gossip, to which I bent my shell-like whenever I got the opportunity.'

Mark's nod was approving, so Nell continued her story.

'Evidently, it is not usual for Cindy to be on the set unless she is actually appearing, which is not very often nowadays – too grand, so I was told, along with the murmur that she was here now only to protect her investment.' Nell paused for effect. 'Not against me. Oh, no. Tony was not her concern, in spite of the fact that he made it plain from the start that he fancies me something rotten.' Here Nell shuddered convulsively. 'I wouldn't let him touch me with a ten-foot barge pole.' She paused to sip coffee. 'No, Cindy's interest was not in him two-timing her, but in her own bit of cheating. Cindy is absolutely besotted with Harry Hall, our own Mr Universe, though being as crafty as a whole container full of monkeys, she was very careful to give the impression that she was playing up to me in order to make sure that I didn't move in on her property. She had the set fooled but I know Cindy of old. She was always one for smoke-screens, so I watched her. I remembered how she used to be with Mickey Shaughnessy; the way she is *not* with Tony Panacoulis, but the way she *is* with Harry Hall. She is two-timing Tony. I proved it by following her and Mr Universe to a secluded part of the gardens while everyone else was packing up . . .' They were making arrangements to meet and she was all over him, like a leech. She fastened herself to him as if she wished she could drain him dry, and she teased him with some very poisonous barbs about not having anything left for her after giving it all to me.' Nell's smile curled at the edges. 'And I must say that he really does thoroughly immerse himself in his part.'

Mark's face betrayed nothing of the bolt of jealousy which, for a moment, misted his vision. 'So what are you leading up to?' he asked, in a get-to-the-point voice. Two can play at your game, he thought.

He saw her eyes darken, before she snapped: 'Blackmail,'

with the air of one laying down a Full House. 'I confront her with my knowledge of her little *affaire* and tell her that if she doesn't provide me with the necessary information regarding the where, when and who of the next meeting of the paedophile ring to film their activities, I will shop her to Tony.' Now her smile was baleful. 'Cindy may like her Mr Muscle – and believe me he has them in his head instead of brains – but she likes her mink and diamonds better.'

'And her life? What importance do you think she attaches to that?'

A tiny frown hooked her eyebrows together at his tone of voice.

'What you propose is not only highly dangerous it is also highly unlikely. You told me earlier of the way your father punished you for disobedience. How do you think they would punish Cindy, these men who murder children on film for their own sexual gratification, if she revealed who they are, where they meet and when? She would lose far more than her mink and diamonds. So would you. The very first thing Cindy would do if you tried to blackmail her would be to go to Tony; not to protect him but to protect herself. You told me she was venal and self-serving, remember? Don't you realise that if Tony was caught he would see no reason to protect his mistress? She would go down too, since she is involved by reason of prior knowledge. She may not know as much, but I agree with you that she does know. She is the kind who would not rest until she did. And at the first sign of trouble she would run to her protector, who would be that much more likely to forgive her little peccadillo in the light of her having saved both his life and his livelihood.'

During this little speech her frown had slipped its hook, and her expression had blanked out.

'So what *do* we do?' she asked stiffly.

He ignored the tiny echo of resentment. 'We go on watching and waiting and hoping.

'For how long?'

'As long as it takes.'

'But you said it is already two years!'

'So . . . you'll just have to put up with me for another two.'

Her glance flicked at him and then away. He decided to bring a little pressure to bear.

'The idea doesn't appeal?' he asked.

'You know I can't afford to be connected with the police in my job.'

'I am not the police. Only one policeman.' He underlined the man. Let a beat go by. 'And hardly a heavy-handed one. I've gone along with you as much as I can. Besides, I think we've gone beyond the formal stage, don't you?'

Again her glance bounced off him, but she did not answer. He sensed the by now familiar withdrawal. This, he thought, is where all that training comes in handy. How to look, how to listen, how to observe, how to threaten, how to coerce, how to charm. How to comfort. But he'd already done that. Studying her, he detected a familiar stance; that of shutting off. Something she had learned to do when her father began her sexual initiation. To abstract her *self*, leaving behind only her shell. It was that shell she had filled with first Cleo, then Eleanor. That shell she retreated to when she felt threatened. Which was usually when faced with something she could not control. Like me, he thought.

'Don't go away from me,' he said. 'I don't like it when you do that, and there is no need.'

Still not looking at him: 'I know what you want,' she said flatly, 'and it is not possible.'

'Why not?'

'You know very well why not.'

'Humour me. Explain.'

Once again her glance flicked him, like a feather duster, before she got to her feet as if her feelings would not let her be still.

'Because of what I am.'

'What difference does that make?'

She stared, then: 'Oh, come on, Superintendent.'

'My name is Mark. Why won't you use it?'

When she did not answer: 'Because you are afraid I'll use it as a jemmy to open you up?'

'I am a whore, you are a policeman destined for higher things. We are connected professionally, that's all, and not for long. Don't expect anything from me except professional help insofar as I can give it.'

'Because you can't or because you won't?'

As if he had her up against the wall at the end of a blind alley she turned on him. 'Both!'

He studied her. 'I know why you feel you can't,' he said, 'but I'd like to know why you won't.'

'I don't get involved. Ever.' It was finality's self.

'That is no answer. I asked *why*.'

She closed her eyes for a moment as if praying for patience. 'Look, I'm not – this is not something I want to get into right now. I've had a bad week and I've got my most demanding client tomorrow night. Just go away and do whatever you have to do and leave me to get on with my life.' It was a plea, but he knew she had introduced the client quite deliberately, like throwing a banana skin under his feet. Which means, he thought, that she is down to last resorts.

'Would it be so bad if our lives became involved? You said you knew Tony Panacoulis fancied you. Why then, won't you admit that I do? Is it because that with Panacoulis it didn't matter so he posed no threat?'

She tried to stare him down and failed.

'You seem to find it necessary to keep me at several arms' lengths, why? I am a man as any other.'

'Who just happens to be a policeman!'

'That's not a reason, that's an excuse.'

'It's a damned good reason and you know it! You are destined for higher things in the Metropolitan Police, I am a whore! Now tell me about excuses! You can't afford me because I'd cost you a hell of a sight more than a thousand pounds!'

'I'll be the judge of that since it is my career.'

'But the jury will hand down the verdict and I can tell you now it will be a unanimous Guilty!' When he did not reply his silence encouraged her to say scathingly: 'You tell me to use my common when you can't even find your own!' Confident she had won, she softened her tone to one of kindly understanding. 'It won't do, you and I. It just won't do.'

'What? Work? I disagree. There is no earthly reason why it should not work except one – your fear to come out of hiding and try to make it work.' He shook his head. 'You may be a great success as a thousand a trick call girl but you know damn-all about being a woman.'

'Spare me the bit about meaningful relationships *if* you please.'

'What would you know about them? You've never had one. Have you?'

When she did not reply: '*Have you*!' He did not raise his voice but it had her bridling instantly.

'None of your damned business!'

'I, on the other hand, have had several, lasting from ten months to five years; I've had my fair share of one night stands but they are now proscribed since AIDS made them suicide missions; I've been seduced – by a woman whose house had been burgled – and done the seducing; I've been dumped and done my own dumping – in short, I have had experience of what we are pleased to call relationships and the concomitant aches and pains the flesh and the human heart is heir to. What have you had except heartless, emotionless, commercial transactions? That's your trouble, don't you see? You know absolutely nothing about emotion; not surprising considering the lengths you go to avoid it. Like now, for instance. Come out of hiding, Nell. Take a chance; on me, on what we can give each other. The last person to love you was your mother and that was twenty long years ago; far too long to be without the warmth and comfort of another human being.'

Her jaw was clenched tight as if to prevent unbidden words issuing from her mouth. '*Will you be told*!' she hissed from behind her teeth. 'I never get involved. I made that vow when I left my father's house. I swore that no man would ever again control me or my life; that *I* would run it all by myself, as I wanted, how I wanted, when and where *I* wanted. I have kept that vow. My independence is very precious to me and I see no reason to sacrifice it now.' Then she went and ruined it all by bursting out: 'I can't . . . don't you see? I can't . . .'

'You mean you daren't. And I have no wish to control you. I don't feel threatened by the independence of women. That's what intrigued me about you from the start: that you *were* independent, so obviously "in charge". I happen to like strong women; doormats bore me and clinging vines strangle. I have no wish to put you back in your cage. There are liberated men too, you know.' He shook his head. 'It won't go away just because you chose not to acknowledge it. Why won't you permit yourself the luxury of emotion? Allow a powerful attraction on both our parts to proceed to its logical conclusion? Use your feelings. I know you have them – I've seen you with your cats.' He paused. 'But there is no risk with them, is there? Whereas with me . . . that's probably why the very idea scares you so much. You like to be safe, and considering your childhood and adolescence I understand why.' He frowned, thinking. 'Why did you send the others away – for there have been others, haven't there?'

'No. Never.'

'Never!'

His astonishment brought to mind New York and the brash young actor who had given her such a fright. 'Well . . . one. He was a nuisance; far too full of himself.'

'If that is how you see me then say so. I don't pursue where I'm not wanted. All you have to do is tell me – no, don't look away. Just look into my eyes and tell me that you don't want me.'

She was a consummate actress but you had to be inhumanly good to be able to lie with your eyes. That was one of the things he'd learned on Jerry Pierce's course. And sure enough, though her eyes had darkened, the anthracite of her irises devouring her pupils, he saw the lightning flicker of panic illuminate their depths. When she spoke her voice was all over the place; a sure sign he was getting to her.

'I only know it won't do.'

'That is not what I asked.'

His remorseless pressure broke her fragile hold on her feelings like a thumb on an eggshell. 'I can't give you what you want!' she shouted at him. 'I don't know how! All I know is sex; uninvolved, unattached, unemotional sex!'

Her words ricocheted in the following silence like echoes rebounding from rock. She put up her hand to her face as if to hide, whether from him or from herself.

'An emotional virgin . . .' Mark said into the ringing silence. 'Of all the men who have paid for the use of that delectable body not one of them has ever really had *you*, have they? Because the essential you is not, never has been for sale.'

Wide-eyed she stared through her spread fingers, as if mesmerised, into the vivid blue eyes. She looked as astounded as he felt, for suddenly, with an almost audible click it had all fallen into place.

Mark sighed. 'Oh, Nell, Nell . . .' he said plangently. She dropped her hands from her face, he picked them up, held them a moment than slid his hands up her arms to her shoulders. When he pulled her gently but surely against him she offered no resistance. They stood in silence, and after a moment, her own arms came up and around his big shoulders. Now that he had done it, Mark felt no triumph; he was conscious only of a deep, melancholy tenderness for her, yet his mind was busy making connections, fitting pieces into place, finally standing back, looking at the picture and at last, understanding what it meant.

He put her away from him slightly, looked down at the face she raised to him; pale, eyes dark with her own comprehension yet still heart-catchingly lovely, and calling up every protective instinct in him. He bent his head and kissed her.

19

Nell sat cross-legged on a big brocaded Indian silk cushion, a souvenir brought back from a client-sponsored, all-expenses paid trip to Kashmir Liz had taken years ago, and kept by Nell as a remembrance of things past. On the coffee table in front of her stood two tall scented candles, providing the only illumination, and the remains of a bottle of Corton-Charle-magne, bought at auction on Philip's urging and meant for special occasions. Since she regarded what had recently hap-pened as a very special occasion she had decided to celebrate it. On the CD player a husky voice was singing and at a distance the cats sat together like a pair of ornaments, their molten gaze fixed on her face as she drunkenly (for the bottle now contained no more than a mere top-up) and dreamily swayed to the music, mouthing the words along with the singer:

Is this
what they mean
when they talk about love
Is this really what it seems to be?
Have I, at long last
met up with the man
who is meant to be
my destiny?

He touches my heart
as no one before
He invades my dreams at night

Where once I knew nothing
and felt even less
can it be – is this
love at first sight?

'You can't tell me, can you?' she asked the cats drunkenly.
Bundle uttered a sympathetic chirrup of understanding but
Blossom only yawned hugely. 'I mean – why now? All these
years love never bothered me and I never bothered it. We
respected each other's territory. So why does *he* have to come
along and put the boot in? It's not as though I was looking for
it or expecting it. It's not something I've ever had much to do
with – love. Not since my mother died. I thought my father
had dug it up by the roots, like he did any and every weed in
his precious garden. So how come I can't sleep, can't concentrate, can't think of anything but him, keep remembering those
chills up my spine . . .' Her stomach dropped like a stone yet
again at the very thought. She had felt dizzy, disoriented, had
to hang on to him for a minute when he lifted his mouth from
hers, unable to look at him, to let him see what she knew she
could not possibly hide. The knowledge that they had crossed
a frontier; that there was no going back now.

She was acutely aware that he had read her response with his
instinctive sensitivity to her moods. It was as if she were a
book he knew so well he could quote from it.

'*Why*?' she asked the cats. 'Why me? Why now? I never
expected this. I don't know how to handle it. It scares me. I
don't like not being in control. What am I going to do?'

She emptied the bottle into her glass, which she then
proceeded to drain.

'I had it all worked out,' she said, blinking blurredly at what
now appeared to be four pairs of yellow eyes. 'I knew where I
was going and I had a rough idea of how long it would take
me. Now, here I am going around in circles and it's not
because I'm drunk – well, not on this, anyway. On him.' Tears
welled, spilled, dribbled down her cheeks, dripped from her
chin, yet she was laughing rather than crying. 'For God's sake,
all he did was kiss me . . .' She caught her lower lip with her
upper teeth. 'More men than I can shake a stick at and every
one of them no more than a necessary evil, raising nothing

more than the occasional yawn. This man does nothing more then kiss me and every nerve ending is screaming its throat hoarse – why?' Eyes as round as the cats, she said in an awed voice that verged on panic: 'Can you imagine what it will be like when – ' Her voice dried and she felt her heart race, her skin prickle. 'I've had sex,' she said finally, 'and then some, but I've never made – *love* – before . . . and that's . . . what this . . . would be.'

She fell silent, staring into the candle flames, feeling strange, sweet, thick stirrings deep inside her. Her mouth opened and her tongue rimmed her lips. She drew in a deep breath, released it on a small shuddery sigh.

Then somebody leaned on the doorbell. Starting like a guilty thing she knocked her empty glass over and it fell off the table and on to the carpet. The cats did a runner as Nell lurched to her feet, attempting to blow the candles out at the same time. The doorbell went on pealing. 'I'm coming, I'm coming . . .' Oh, God, it's him, she thought, a-quiver with desirous dread. A flick of her eyes at the clock revealed the time to be 10.40 p.m. If he was late turn he came off duty at ten o'clock – but then strictly speaking he did not work shifts; just very long hours. The bell was insistent. She slammed the candlesticks back onto the mantlepiece before running for the door, switching on the lamps as she went with one hand, smearing her wet eyes with the other.

'All right, all right, I know you are impatient but – ' her voice dried as she flung open the front door.

'Thank God!' cried Cindy, rushing past a suddenly shockingly disappointed Nell. 'I don't know where I would've gone if you 'adn't been in.' Her voice was high, her face a mask of rage. 'Honest, Elly, I dunno when I been so mad! Look what 'e's done, the bastard!' She held out shaking hands. Every single nail had been crudely hacked off, leaving only ugly misshapen remnants, some of them painfully close to the quick. ''E 'ad one of 'is goons 'old me down while 'e 'acked away with the kitchen scissors! I'll pay 'im back though, you see if I don't! Nobody does this to me . . . nobody! Not even God-Almighty Tony Panacoulis!'

She paced back and forth wildly, so deep in her anger that she failed to notice Nell's tear-stained face or the way she hastily drew her tailored silk dressing gown about her and re-tied the belt. Cindy was wearing her treasured leopard skin coat – 'Somali' she had told Nell proudly, 'cost several small fortunes, it did'; over a tight, white, much sequinned and bugle-beaded dress; her bouffant newly sculpted, which meant that she had been ready to spend the evening at Tony's Soho Club when events had overtaken her.

'Calm down,' Nell told her soothingly. 'I'll go and put the coffee on; I was just going to make myself a cup.'

'Not for me, thanks. I'd rather 'ave a drink. Scotch – straight, no ice, no water.'

When Nell handed it over she swallowed it in one gulp. 'That 'it the spot. Got another?'

With it in her hand she followed Nell into the kitchen. 'One thing's for sure,' she said in a voice that threatened dire retribution, ''e won't do it again. Once is too many. Mickey rued the day 'e spoiled my nails and so will that bastard Tony Panacoulis, you mark my words! I know things as would put him away for so long 'e'd forget there was a world outside.'

Nell felt those words like a douche of cold water which shocked her from her semi-inebriated state into coldly aware sobriety. 'I'd be careful what I said', she cautioned, speaking her first line in the role of The Understanding Friend. 'He's not a man to cross, is our Tony. And you must have given him cause. *Everybody* knows how much you pride yourself on your nails.'

She saw Cindy turn away slightly, shrug, as though her mistake had been nothing more, really, than a mild misde-meanour. 'That jealous sod Spider Costas told him I was 'aving it off with Harry on the side. 'E's always 'ated me, that Spider. Dead jealous. Can't stand Tony to be fond of anybody but him. Oh, it ain't that 'e's queer, none of that . . . just – well, 'im and Tony go back a long way, since they was at infants school together back in Cyprus. Childhood friend 'n all that.'

'You were doing the business with Harry behind Tony's back?' Nell let her amazement show plainly.

'Only when Tony was away!' Cindy sounded holier-than-thou. Then, furious again. 'Which ain't been often enough, lately. Tony's a good provider, I'll grant you that, and 'e don't stint, but he's no bloody good in bed. No sooner gets in than 'e's gone, leavin' me at the startin' gate! I tell you, Nell, I got so frustrated I was becomin' ratty. And 'arry's a different kettle of fish.' A sly look. 'As you should know. I never seen him so 'appy in 'is work as on that film set when you was goin' at it.'

Nell shrugged. 'I'm a good actress,' she said. 'But I take your point.'

'And you 'ave to admit 'e's very well endowed. Tony's cock is about the size of my little finger even when its standin' to attention! I ask you, what use is that to a girl who 'as to 'ave her oats regular or she starts gettin' edgy.' She flounced off the stool on which she had been sitting in order to pace again, voice rising, face white with rage. 'So when that little toad Spider tells Tony I've been doin' the business with 'arry he gets 'is dander up and does this!' Cindy looked at her ruined nails and burst into tears. 'Years it took me to get them to this length. I looked after them as if they was my very own babies . . . now look at them! I'll kill 'im for this, I will! Either that or I'll shop 'im. Nobody does this to Cindy Lewis and gets away with it. Nobody!'

Nell was expressing shocked sympathy even as her mind was working overtime.

If she could somehow encourage Cindy to shop Tony in the right direction – that of the paedophile ring, she would have something to bring to whatever relationship evolved from her involvement with Mark Stevens, for like it or not, she *was* involved, and in a way she had been careful all her adult life to avoid. Emotionally.

The information about the next meeting of the paedophile chapter would be a gift she could give Mark, proof of her worth to him, her love for him. She would have to act her pants off, of course, but even the thought of the performance necessary had her adrenalin doing a four-minute mile. Challenge had always been her spur. The thought of the award that would be hers for this one was already drawing blood.

'I doubt if Tony would go down for making pornographic films,' she demurred practically. 'He's probably got himself well covered and arrangements made for somebody else to carry the can. I don't particularly care for him, Cindy – I'm being honest here; I never did back in the old days with Mickey, but I respect him as a very shrewd operator. And I would not care to be the one who shopped him. Greeks have a long tradition of revenge.'

Cindy's face took on the craftiness of a fox. 'I'm not talkin' porn! That's a sideline. 'E's involved in somethin' that could see him put away for a very long time. It's 'igh risk and 'e gets very well paid for the facilities 'e provides, which include security. The right judge and Tony wouldn't see daylight for twelve years minimum!' Cindy smiled. It made Nell shiver. 'By that time I'd be long gone. Mickey never found me, remember? I know 'ow to disappear. And the thought of seein' that bastard suffer for what 'e did to me is one I could sit and dream about on long winter nights.'

'If it is something so secret then how come you know about it?' Nell led Cindy where she was meant to follow.

Cindy's smile was hooded, making Nell, who recognised its message, exclaim: 'You've been listening at doors again!' She had been warned of Cindy's eavesdropping tendencies when she had first joined Mickey's stable. 'She's a sneak,' Paula had warned her. 'Drop anybody in it if there's anything in it for her.'

'A girl 'as to 'ave some kind of insurance, don't she? 'Course I found out what I could; I wasn't born yesterday, you know. If you don't look out for yourself nobody else will, that's for sure, 'specially where punters is concerned, and I 'ad me first one o' them when I was fifteen! So I put my ear to certain keyholes – and I took good care not to be caught, neither – and what I know Tony don't know I know, see?' A derisive sniff. ''Im and 'is tight security!'

Nell re-filled Cindy's glass. Alcohol was the only way she knew to loosen Cindy's tongue. She would probably do for the entire bottle, and it was twelve-year-old Johnny Walker Black Label, but it was a small sacrifice to pay for priceless information. First, though, she had to play devil's advocate.

'I'd think twice before crossing Tony,' she cautioned. 'Unless you have proof it is a waste of time anyway.'

'Of course I've got proof! What do you take me for? I 'appen to know where and when – and there's people oo'd give a hell of a lot to know what I know. I could sell this information for immunity, I could. Plus a sworn promise that Tony wouldn't see daylight for a long, long time.' Cindy examined her ruined nails again, after which she swallowed her double Scotch. Nell poured her a refill – a triple. ''E 'ad no call to go and do this. 'E knows I set great store by my lovely nails . . . mark of a lady, they are. If 'e'd belted me I wouldn't have minded. 'E's entitled after all . . . but to 'ave me 'eld down while he gets to work with a pair of kitchen scissors . . . That's goin' too far, much too far. I won't stand for that. No way I'll stand for that . . .' The triple followed the double. Next time Nell poured a good two inches of Scotch into the empty glass.

'I've a good mind not to go back 'im,' Cindy said, once it was empty again. She was becoming maudlin, a sure sign that she was well on the way to loosening up. 'Five years I've stuck with 'im . . . five long years. Never stayed with nobody that long before.'

'Changed your mind about shopping him, then?'

Cindy blinked owlishly. 'Why shouldn't I?' she asked bellig- erently. 'After what 'e done to me? If 'e wants me to go back then 'e'll 'ave to apologise. Go down on 'is bended knees . . . if 'e won't . . . Well, then that's a different matter, innit?'

'Why should Tony apologise? You were the one having a bit on the side. Greeks are very touchy about that sort of thing. You will have to make the apology.'

'Me!' Cindy reared like a stung horse, and Nell took the opportunity to pour her another hefty slug of Scotch before refilling her own cup for the third time.

'Then the only other alternative is to shop him. If you have this top-secret information you say you have.'

'I do, I do 'ave it!'

But it took the rest of the Scotch and Cindy weeping into her empty glass before Nell, plying calculated sympathy along with carefully planted prods, arousing Cindy's dying ire to sullen threats of revenge, managed to inveigle the information out of her. And then it had to be done by feigning flagrant disbelief, inciting Cindy to lose her temper with Nell, accusing her of being a snob and always holding her, Cindy, in contempt.

'Think yourself so bloody superior . . . and I know Tony 'appens to fancy you, not that it'll do 'im any good. You always was a snob. Looked down on me didn't yer – but oo's the one with diamonds and the mink and the Somali leopard coat, and oo's the one as 'as the goods on a kiddie-porn ring the coppers would give their next ten years overtime to nab – me, . . . Cindy Lewis.'

'If you are so hell bent and determined to shop Tony then there is the telephone. Pick it up and call Scotland Yard. Don't keep going on and on about information you don't have.'

Nell made her voice short, contempt-filled and worst of all – bored. 'Either put up or shut up, Cindy. I'm tired and it's late and I want to go to bed.'

Cindy attempted to get to her feet and failed; they would not support her. Her eyes were blurred and her tongue thick, but she managed to utter: 'Don't you talk to me like that, you ungrateful cow! After all I done for you!'

'And haven't I sat here for hours listening to you going on and on about how you are going to get back at Tony because he massacred your beautiful nails? But you've done nothing!'

Cindy raised her hands, reminded of her tragedy, and her wails broke out afresh. 'I will,' she screamed. 'I *will* tell the police there's a meet next week at ware'ouse down by the river next Tuesday night . . . where's that bloody telephone . . .' She heaved herself to her feet, took a step forward then fell flat on her face on the carpet. Out cold.

Nell sprang forward, turned her over. Cindy was a lump of inert flesh. Nell slapped her face, hard. Cindy made a whimpering noise, managed to get a hand up off the floor before it fell back. When Nell picked it up, let it drop, it was useless.

Leaving Cindy where she was she ran upstairs to her bedroom, opened the sliding drawer where she kept her client answerphone and dialled Scotland Yard, giving Mark's extension to the operator. There was no answer for some time then a strange voice answered: 'Superintendent Stevens's office.'

'Is he there? I need to speak to him urgently.'

'I'm sorry. Superintendent Stevens left some time ago.'

'Do you know where he is? A number where he can be contacted?'

'One moment, please . . .' More silence, then: 'If you would care to leave your name and telephone number I will see that Superintendent Stevens calls you at the first opportunity.'

'But this is a matter of great urgency!'

'If you will leave your name and telephone number – '

Nell crashed down the receiver. Sodding bureaucracy! Where are you Mark? she fretted. Why aren't you there? Then her eye fell on her bedside clock. It was 12.08 a.m. No wonder he wasn't there! He was no doubt at home, getting some much needed sleep. She just had not been thinking straight . . . But there was no answer there, either, only his own machine. Now what do I do? she thought. In the meantime she went downstairs, managed to get Cindy, a deadweight, up off the floor and on to the sofa, where she took off her stilettos and covered her with a quilt. She would have a head and a half tomorrow morning but, unless her metabolism had changed, she would not remember a thing. Cindy was the kind of drunk whose reaction to an excess of alcohol was total amnesia. When she surfaced in the morning Nell would tell her as much of the truth as was practicable; that she had come looking for sympathy after Tony's barbaric act and the two of them had killed a bottle of Scotch before passing out. Before then, Mark would be in possession of the information Nell had obtained for him. Please God, she prayed, as she washed up. At one o'clock she called Mark's private number again and got the answering machine. She went to bed but lay awake until two when another try got the same result. This time she left a message. 'It's me. When you get home, call me. It's vital.'

It never entered her head that he was not working, but he wasn't. He was with Alison Moody.

Nell did not sleep much; her thoughts did not allow it. By eight next morning she was downstairs. Cindy was still fathoms deep and the cats were waiting expectantly for breakfast. Once the coffee was made Nell tried Mark's number again. Only the answering machine responded. So. He had not been home all night. Her first thought was that something had broken in regard to the case, but there was nothing in the paper, not even in the stop press. All right, so he had been working on something else. Except her understanding was that he spent most of his time heading the Serious Crime Squad that had been set up to solve the child murders and break up the paedophile ring. So why aren't you there to take the information I've got for you and act on it? she asked the silent telephone. Where were you last night? What were you doing – and who with? And why haven't you called me . . .

Cindy began to make groaning noises around nine, but she did not wake, and when Nell bent over her she muttered something and huddled into the quilt. Nell recalled that Cindy had ever been a late riser. After last night's intake she was good for at least another three hours. Oh, Mark, where *are* you? She called his office at the Yard. He had not arrived yet but he was on his way; he had called to say he would be in about ten. He had a call to make first. Oh, yes? On whom? Nell thought miserably. She felt grievously wounded. Had he not said he would always be there for her? That she could call him at any time, day or night? So why had he not been there when she had?

She felt betrayed, lied to, *used*. She had spent time and a good bottle of Scotch in order to obtain information which, as Cindy said, was worth its weight in gold; doing it as proof of her wish to help him, of her feelings for him. Which you did not put into words, she reminded herself. No need, that self retorted knowingly. He knew. It was in his eyes, his voice . . . He *knew*. So where the hell *is* he? And where was he last night? Cultivating some other important informant? Getting her in the same state you are, all your circuits shorted? Oh, Mark . . . she thought in anguish. Where *are* you? Don't leave me like this, hanging in mid-air. She put her head in her hands, sat at the breakfast counter slumped in misery. The cats, attuned to her mental state, leapt up to head-butt her, purring loudly as if to say: 'It's all right. *We* still love you.'

When the bell rang she ran for the door. It was the postman. He had a large packet that would not go through the letter-box. It was an unwanted catalogue. She dumped it in the bin and was on her way upstairs to shower and dress when it rang again.

'Now what.' She scowled her way back down to the door, flung it open. 'I don't want any more – Mark!' Her relief was such that euphoria reinforced with confidence turned to anger. 'Where the hell have you been? I've called your flat umpteen times – the last at 2 a.m. this morning – I've called your office – where were you all night?'

'That's what I've come to tell you. I –'

She seized his arm, dragged him inside, shut the door, put a finger to her lips. 'Cindy's here.'

She saw the twin blue flames deepen as he read her face and voice and the importance of her urgency sank in. Nell nodded. 'The kitchen,' she mouthed. But first he had to inspect Cindy, invisible under the quilt but snoring lightly. Mark winced at the sight of the wreckage, looked queryingly at Nell, who lifted a shoulder: 'Almost a whole bottle of Black Label.'

He winced again, but as always his agile mind went unerringly to the whys and wherefores. 'Worth it?'

Nell's smile had him reaching for her. 'You'll never believe . . .' She closed but did not shut the kitchen door, dropped her voice low.

'Just in case. I don't expect her to surface for another couple of hours at least, but I never did trust her. Coffee?'

'Please. About last night – '

Nell, secure in the knowledge that she was the call he'd had to make, was able to brush his explanation aside and give him the story of her coup. Mark listened, amused at first then, as he heard her out, his face tautening with excitement and something else which, as Nell felt it down to her bone-marrow, had her voice faltering as she asked: 'It is enough, isn't it? I know the time is vague but I told you exactly where the warehouse is and you can put men around the place to see who arrives and . . . why are you looking at me like that?'

'Because you are, as they say, a fucking marvel! Two long years I worked on this, sifting information through sieves, following God knows how many dead-ends and red-herrings, coming up against stonewall after stonewall. Patient, hard slog – which is what police work is all about no matter what the TV or books say. And then, out of the blue – and my past – you appear, and straightaway things start to happen; one piece of information leads to another, all falling like ninepins culminating in, of all things, a mundane domestic quarrel.' He laughed exultantly, gathered her to him and kissed her soundly.

When she could, her voice wobbling all over place: 'So it is enough, then? For you to act, I mean? I didn't dare press for more in case she twigged.'

'Enough? she asks me. More than enough, you clever girl. You parlayed a never-real friendship into the one place a woman's vanity, damaged by a man's pride, could turn to. You were the right person in the right place at the right time. I had my doubts about that porn movie but you were right: it worked beautifully. Almost as beautiful as you are . . .'

Later on: 'I never thought of myself as a fatalist,' Mark mused, Nell perched on his knee as he sat on one of the high kitchen stools, 'but I think I have to admit that you turning up in my life again is a very definite stroke of fate. We were marked, you and I, from the very first time I cautioned you. Fate spins very complex webs, and for a long time you and I were at opposite ends of ours, yet all the time we were moving along predestined strands until they met at a particular junction. From then on we travelled the same strand. I always thought life was what *you* made it, but I've come to realise that some things are inescapable.' He tipped her chin. 'Like you.' He paused. 'That's what I was doing last night. Telling a woman who, in other circumstances, I might have married and settled down with, that fate had other plans for me, and that they were plans I accepted with all my heart. That *you* are my fate, and that what had happened since we met up again had confirmed that fact beyond any kind of doubt. We'd had the date for some weeks – the theatre and then a late supper, after which I took her back home and we talked. Or rather I talked, because I told her all about you. Nothing about what brought you into my life, just – you as a person and why I knew that while I could have achieved a pleasant, undemanding, secure kind of life with her, I wouldn't have any kind of a life at all unless it included you. That I loved you, and it wasn't pleasant, or undemanding or secure; that you are independent to a degree, sharp-tongued and quick-witted, fast on the draw and accurate in your fire, yet vulnerable in a way that makes me want to protect you to the death; that you turn me on as no other woman ever has; that you have a skin like satin and a mouth like wine . . .'

'Oh, you didn't . . .' Nell was appalled. 'I'd have hit you with the poker!'

Mark threw back his head and laughed joyously. 'There, you see! That's why I love you. Alison would never – could never – do that because she accepts too easily. You are a fighter. If you weren't you would never have come so far so fast. You have all the spirit that she lacks, and that I need. She asked me to be honest with her so I was.'

'All night?' Jealousy's smoke was a signal plainly written on Nell's voice.

'Until almost 1 a.m. when my sergeant rang me – I'd left her number with him – to say that a child's body had been found in suspicious circumstances.

'Was it – another – ?'

'No. It was a sudden death but it was natural. A four-year-old who had been missing for the past week. He'd wandered off from his parents while they were on a picnic in Epping Forest, fallen into a ditch and drowned. But we had to make sure there was no connection. That's why I was out all night.'

But Nell's mind was several steps back. 'Was she hurt – Alison?'

'More resigned. I think. There was nothing between us. She was someone my mother produced for me. She keeps trying to marry me off to women of her choosing when she knows perfectly well that I will make my own choice. I liked Alison and we went out a few times, and had I not already met you things might have been different. But I had met you. And it was different. *That* is what I told her.'

'Had you slept with her?'

'Yes.'

Nell was quiet, then she smiled. Mark's stomach jolted. 'Nobody has *ever* relegated me . . .'

She slid off his knees. 'How much time have you got?'

'How much do you want?'

Upstairs, in her bedroom, he said: 'No tricks. You are not turning one with me. I don't want Cleo or one of her performances. I want Nell, the essential you I spoke of the other night . . . I told you, remember, that sex with love and sex without are two very different things? Let me show you what I meant.'

Deprived of her alter ego. Nell felt naked, though she was pleased to lie under his eyes and let him look, touch and taste. She felt unaccountably nervous, shy, even, did not know what to do with her hands because each time she went to touch him he put her away. 'Just lie back and enjoy it,' he told her. Since this was something she had never done she wondered at his confidence, only to jump as he drew his nails lightly over the skin of her lower belly, his palms brushing the thicket of curls at the juncture of her thighs. And when he swept his hands from her ankles to her breasts he left behind a definite after-burn. She wanted to stretch and purr. But suddenly he was cupping her buttocks and lifting her against him, pressing her against his hard, hot arousal. She heard him laugh softly as he felt her belly flutter, and when he put his mouth and tongue to nipples that had hardened into tiny thimbles she bucked like a spooked horse and clutched hard at his shoulders.

For a moment she had the sensation of falling from a great height; regarded her skin with amazement for it was covered in a light dew of moisture yet she had not done a thing! Which was when she realised that it was not the perspiration of concentrated effort but the sheen of physical excitement! Something else that had never happened before. Like the violent inrushes of sensation which robbed her of breath, or swamped her in great tidal waves of feeling which zig-zagged like a bolt of lightning from the breast he was suckling to the pit of her belly.

As he proceeded with his leisurely exploration, her eager impatience to show him, give him, take him to the heights, fell by the wayside because he already had her at thirty thousand feet. She would have died if he had stopped what he was doing. No man had ever sucked her toes before, sending spears of feeling zinging to her very core, or kissed his way up her spine while his hands cupped the globes of her breasts, his long thumbs teasing her aching nipples, or lasciviously licked away the fine sheen bedewing her flesh. She had never been the object of such concentrated sensuality, and it had the effect of sending her programming wildly haywire. She thrashed around the bed, making noises the like of which had never issued from her throat before, arching her pelvis and pushing it against the moist heat of a mouth and tongue which produced sensations not unlike a series of electric shocks. Again and again he took her to a peak before pushing her off it, making her scream with pleasure as she did. By now her mind was clouded, her body bathed in moisture, but never had her senses been so acute: she was aware of the sleekness of Mark's own skin, of the roughness of his legs entwined with hers, of the faint flavour of toothpaste and aftershave, of the rapid thump of his heart as his hands became more demanding and his mouth more urgent. They were breathing as though from a shortage of air, their mouths juicy with moisture, and as Mark's found hers once more she could taste herself in him. If somebody had fired a double barrelled revolver above their heads they would not have heard it. They were deaf, dumb and blind to all but the touch, taste and scent of the other. When, finally, Mark moved over her she instinctively looped her legs over the big shoulders to felicitate the long, slow, delicious slide of his entry, and as he completed it, Nell perceived, as if through a blinding light, something she had never been able to understand before. What was meant by the phrase 'one flesh'. She had fused with many men but always remained apart; with them but not of them. She had rejected it as a part of the gigantic con perpetrated by organised religion to persuade poor fools of people that sex was much, much more than a bodily urge or purely and only biological. Her reaction had been: 'Oh yes? Pull the other one, it's got Big Ben on it!'

Shocked to her core she now opened her eyes only to find his already fixed on her. Without ceasing their perfectly synchronised movements they gazed long and deeply into each other then she saw Mark smile; it was one of satisfaction that he had proved his point. As if to confirm it, once more he palmed her buttocks, lifting her towards him so as to penetrate her even more fully.

Time had ceased to exist; their only reality was each other. So attuned were they that they were able to read each other's slightest movement; the writhings and circling of her lips, the ripples that were the convulsive movements of her vaginal muscles clasping and massaging his almost agonisingly sensitised penis, his gasps and harsh, indrawn breaths of a seemingly unendurable pleasure. The tide of their blood surged in a single heartbeat and his thrusts, at first deep and measured, picked up speed until, as Nell felt her ultimate climax gathering itself, her muscles clamped themselves tightly on him, letting him know she was ready. Only then did he let his own climax carry him over the edge and she felt him flood her with a final, triumphant roar of total fulfilment. Her internal muscles milked him as he subsided, his breath harsh in his chest, his rigid muscles softening, but he did not shift in order to slide out of her. They lay still fused, his face in the hollow of her shoulder, breathing deeply and coming back to themselves. Finally: 'Oh, my God . . .' Nell said in a totally stunned voice, 'How long has *this* been going on?' And she burst into shattering sobs.

Mark gathered her to him, held her close, abstracting a handful of tissues from the box on the bedside table.

'I'm sorry,' she wept, 'it's just that – I had no idea . . . it was never like this before . . . not ever . . . there was never anything in it for me, because I was never there. It never touched me. I learned how to go somewhere else.'

'That's because you have never known one moment of freely offered, absolutely normal, unmanipulating love since you were eleven years old and the only human being who gave it was lost to you. So you carried an intolerable burden alone, believing there was no atonement, no forgiveness, no absolution. Go ahead and cry; God knows you have reason to.'

Nell was deeply moved, by a feeling so sweet, so intense, that she felt her throat thicken and her eyes well again as it dawned on her what it was. *She was feeling like a woman*; soft, vulnerable and wholly feminine.

For so long – always, it seemed – she had been forced to replace feelings by rationality, emotions by cold logic, since feelings were dangerous. Had they not caused her such monstrous hurt that she dared not trust them ever again?

Mark had released her from the prison of her own making; liberated feelings and emotions from long years of solitary confinement, made love, not just had sex. She had not dreamed there was such a difference; that a man *loving* a woman was utterly different from a man using her to relieve a sexual itch.

She felt soft and supple again, after years of arid dryness. I was withered, she thought; like a grape placed in a hot sun to dry and shrivel into a piece of dried fruit. I had distanced myself from life, from love, because I thought myself unworthy of both. But I was not wholly dead; Mark saw it and gave me what I needed; gave me back to myself. I had gone as far as I could from what I really was. He has brought me back again.

She looked at him, eyes brimming, found him watching her.

He smiled. Wordlessly, she laid her head on his chest, felt him gather her close.

When, much later, he stirred, sighed, said: 'I have to go . . . I've got a very full day ahead of me,' Nell murmured, 'Your days are your own to do with as you wish, but your nights – your nights are mine.'

'I was hoping you would say that . . .'

While he showered, Nell tiptoed downstairs to check on Cindy who was still stertorously sleeping and obviously would do so for some time yet.

'What do you wish me to do with the body in the living room?' she asked Mark.

'Nothing. Just follow her lead but be careful. Don't let her know what she let slip last night.'

'And if she wants to stay here?'

'Let her – if you can put up with her. I'd be happier if I knew where she was and what she was doing. And if she should want to contact her erstwhile lover, listen to what she says if you can without being too obvious.' He paused in the act of shrugging into his jacket. 'If she asks any questions – ' he broke off. 'Why am I telling you?' he asked wryly. 'When it comes to dissembling I bow to your undoubted mastery.'

'I wasn't dissembling with you,' Nell protested, in hurt tones, watching him from beneath her lashes. Suddenly it was vitally important that she be reassured that all this was real and true; that it had indeed all happened and – best of all – would happen again . . . and again . . . and again.

'Nor I with you.'

Their eyes met and Nell tore hers away hurriedly, feeling breathless but guilty. He had work to do!

'Will you ring me?' she asked, trying not to sound as if she was begging.

'Yes, but it will have to be when I can. I've got – '

'A very full day . . .'

Mark picked up his Burberry. As they walked to the front door – after a making-sure look at Cindy: 'Once this is over and done with we can devote some time to ourselves,' he said. 'But right now, I have to put this first. What you have discovered is the kind of information you get only when the Gods have got out of the right side of the bed that particular morning, and when we have world enough and time I will show you my appreciation.'

'I'll hold you to that.'

'Don't tempt me.' He kissed her once, hard, then he was gone.

Nell went slowly and dreamily back upstairs. Stripping the bed, she buried her face in the sheet, inhaling the scent of him, of her, and the glorious, revelatory sex he had introduced her to. Liz was right, as usual, she thought, remembering something she had said about knowing when it was love: 'Casablanca had it all wrong: a kiss is not just a kiss when it is from the right man.'

'And just how do you know he is "right"?'

'Because it will blow your socks off but leave your shoes still on.'

Nell smiled to herself. 'Which it did', she said, hugging the knowledge to her. And not just my socks. Wait until I tell Philip – Damn! It was Monday, her afternoon to visit him. The thought of taking Cindy along was one she dumped along with the dirty laundry. She was dressed and putting it into the washing machine when she heard moans and groans and imprecations from the sitting room. When she went in Cindy was rising to a sitting position, doing it very slowly as if being lifted by an invisible hoist. Her eyes were closed, an expression of intolerable pain on her face, which was streaked with mascara and smeared lipstick. One set of false-eyelashes hung drunkenly from the corner of one eye. She was keeping her head very still, as though if she moved it – even ever so slightly – it would fall off her neck.

'Oh, my Gawd . . .' she moaned, 'I got an 'ead like a steam 'ammer.' She blinked as she saw Nell, stared in surprise before her features sharpened. 'Wot you doin' 'ere?'

'I'm staying here . . . my friend's house. You came here last night, remember?'

Cindy frowned uneasily, indicating that she didn't before she lied: 'Oh, yeah . . . that's right.'

'You were upset about your nails,' Nell reminded sympathetically.

'Me nails?' Cindy raised her hands. 'Oh, my Gawd . . .' she wailed again but this time it was more of a howl. 'Me nails

394

'. . . me lovely nails . . .' Her voice disappeared in a squeak and tears welled. 'That bastard Tony. I remember now. 'E 'acked them off with the kitchen scissors.'

'So you came to me for some tea and sympathy, only you preferred Scotch. Almost a full bottle. I had wine. We both ended up under the weather.'

Cindy's face cleared. 'That's right. I remember now.' Casually: 'I didn't get out of order or nothin', did I?'

'No. Just cried into your whisky, as you – as *we* mourned your nails. Then you passed out, so I covered you with a rug and left you to it. I've not long been up myself. How about some black coffee?'

'I'd rather 'ave tea. 'Ot and strong and plenty of sugar.'

'Want a shower?'

'Tea first. I ain't fit or nuthin' till I've 'ad me tea . . . and a couple of Alka Seltzer.'

At the breakfast bar she sat with her head in her hands. 'Christ, I dunno when I got so pissed!'

'You were very upset,' Nell soothed tactfully.

'So would you be n'all if somebody 'acked your nails to bits.'

The bitterness was back, but a brooding quality had been added. One which boded ill. Probably for Tony Panacoulis.

Nell said little, left her to drink the tea she made; dark as treacle and equally sweet.

Finally: 'I don't suppose Tony rang?' Cindy's enquiry was casual in the extreme.

Nell showed surprise. 'You told me you stormed out in tears without telling him where you were going, so how could he?'

'I didn't ask you to tell 'im I was 'ere?'

'No. I told you, you were very upset.'

'But not – out of order?' Cindy was fishing, Nell realised. She wanted to know if she had made threats.

'No. You said he'd soon find out he couldn't do without you but that you'd let him do it the hard way; pay him back for his spite,' Nell fibbed.

Cindy's face cleared like a heavy sky before a strong wind. ''An I will, n'all. 'E 'ad no right to do what 'e done, no right at all!'

'Well, you were having it off with Harry. What else did you expect?'

Cindy threw Nell a look. 'In my book what's sauce for the gander is sauce for the goose. I know what Tony gets up to with those girls 'e "auditions" for the club.' If 'arry had between 'is ears wot 'e's got between 'is legs it might be a different story, but as it is Tony knows 'e can count on me on account of 'e 'as other – redeemin' qualities.'

Yes, thought Nell. Like money.

Cindy said: 'I think what I said last night was right on the button. Do 'im good to sweat for a day or two. Show 'im 'e can't treat me like a slave – and I'll 'ave myself a set of brand new nails that will cost a fortune, you see if I don't.' Cindy brightened; had she not been so hung over she would have sparkled. 'So can you put me up for a couple of nights? I mean – you got the room?'

Nell saw Cindy's eyes do a speculative cost-accounting scan of the kitchen. 'I told you before, this is not my place', she lied. 'It belongs to a friend of mine who happens to be in hospital right now. As a matter of fact, I'm due to go and see him this afternoon – '

''*Im!*'

'Yes. He's a very old friend, helped me a lot when I moved upmarket.'

'On the game 'isself, is he?'

'Not any more.' Nell paused then let her have it. 'He's got AIDS.'

Cindy's recoil was that from a double-barrelled shotgun. 'AIDS! I ain't goin' near nobody with AIDS, an' you shouldn't, neither!'

'He's in hospital, Cindy, and cleared for visitors.'

'All the same . . . if you're goin' to see somebody with AIDS I don't think I'll bother, thanks. I'll go and 'ave me new nails fitted – it's a long job so I'll be gone all afternoon. If you've got a spare key I can come back . . .'

'I have no spare key,' Nell lied. 'Only the one. I should be back here at about half past four.' She wasn't having Cindy prowling around.

'All right, then.' Cindy shoved her cup across. 'Pour us another cup.'

*

They left the house together, and as they walked up the mews: 'Nice little 'idey-'ole this, innit? Nobody'd know as you was 'ere. What's your "friend" do, then?'

'He was in the Life, like us, but on a very much grander scale. You would not believe the famous names he lived with at one time or another.'

"'E's gotta be rich, then?"

'He does not have to count his pennies.'

Which brought Cindy to a full stop. "Ere . . . I ain't got no money! I'm used to goin' everywhere by Roller. Bung us a few quid, Elly. I'll pay you back, honest. I got money back 'ome – it's just I dunno when I'll be able to lay me 'ands on it.'

Nell handed over two twenties and a tenner. 'It's for the cabs, see. I can 'ave me nails put on me account, but I gotta 'ave a tip,' Cindy explained. As a cab answered her hail: "Ere, where you goin'? I mean which 'ospital? Maybe I can give yer a lift.'

'It's the Westminster Hospital, that's Millbank. If it's in your direction that would be fine.'

'Well, then . . . I'm goin' to Battersea – ' As if to correct the impression that she was going downmarket: 'They tripled Patsy's rent so she 'ad to move, but she's got a thrivin' business. 'Op in. I'll drop yer on me way.'

As Nell got out of the cab Cindy said: 'See you about half past four, then.'

Nell was back home much sooner that that. When Cindy did return it was gone six, and she had obviously had her hair done too. She found Nell sitting on the sofa, an empty glass clasped in her hands, staring blankly into space.

'Now that's more like it,' Cindy preened smugly, flourishing her hands in front of Nell's unseeing face to display her newly-manufactured talons. 'Ain't they lovely? Cost a hundred quid they did, and serve that toad Tony bloody-well-right . . . Elly?' It finally penetrated Cindy's self-absorption that something was not right. 'Elly! You all right?' She peered uneasily into Nell's colourless face.

'Philip's dead,' Nell said disbelievingly. 'He had a heart attack . . . they were working on him when I got there. I waited, but not very long, then they came to tell me it was no use.'

Cindy straightened. Shit! she thought. She studiously avoided anything which she deemed 'nasty' and death was top of her list. Death meant long faces and whispers and black and funerals. And besides, this was an AIDS death. She made up her mind. 'Oh, I am sorry,' she said sounding more put out than sad. 'Still, if 'e 'ad AIDS it was only a matter of time, wasn't it?' Her mind leapt unerringly to what was important. 'Which is what you've not got much of now, 'ave yer – I mean, living' ere.'

Nell did not answer.

'And you'll 'ave lots to do. Unless 'e 'as relatives, o'course.'

'I don't know,' Nell said. 'I don't think so. I've got the telephone number of his solicitor. I suppose I had better ring him . . . there isn't anybody else that matters . . . except all Philip's friends, of course.' She looked distracted, lifted her glass, found it empty, put it down again. 'I have to go back to the hospital tonight to collect his things.'

'Well, then, under the circumstances I think I shouldn't add to your burdens,' Cindy said virtuously, her intention being not to add to her own.

Nell roused herself from her stunned shock. 'You can stay if you like,' she said. 'Philip wouldn't mind . . .' Her smile was half-hearted. 'He's beyond minding anything.'

'I wouldn't dream of it,' Cindy denied. 'I'll go to me sister in Paddington. Let Tony stew a day or two more. And I ain't seen Trace in a month o'Sundays anyway.' She patted Nell's shoulder consolingly, admiring her new nails as she did so. Nobody'd ever know they weren't real, she thought happily.

'Well, if you are sure . . . but what about Tony?'

'You ain't seen me, you ain't 'eard me, right? I want him to suffer the way 'e made me suffer. When I'm good and ready then I'll go back . . .'

'All right.' Mark had said not to push.

No mention was made of the fifty pounds, but it was the last thing on Nell's mind, which Cindy shrewdly counted on. Call it 'for services rendered', she thought. She'd also borrowed another hundred from Kevin, at the hairdresser's, but that, she reckoned practically, was part Tony's money anyway. She'd drop Trace a couple of tenners – a fortune to her with three kids, all from different fathers, and only the Social to live on. But then, Trace'd always been useless with men.

'Would you like me to make you a nice cup of o'tea?' Cindy offered generously.

'No, thank you.'

'I'll leave you to your grief then.' She'd read that once, in a story, and thought it sounded ever so nice. 'I'll give you a ring in a couple of days, let you know how things 'as been sorted out, all right?'

'Yes.'

This Philip must 'ave been a very good friend, Cindy thought, as she closed the front door behind her. Elly was really shook up. Still, worth a bob or two, and no family. Cindy surveyed the mews house. Who knows, Nell might 'ave done 'erself a bit of good. Which would change things with Tony, of course, on account of she wouldn't be so strapped for cash. That would put another spoke in 'is wheel . . . Cindy was well aware that Tony's plans for Nell went beyond starring her in another porn 'classic'. An' I'll bugger them, an' all, she thought vindictively.

20

When Mark rang, at exactly nine thirty, Nell was sitting with Philip's personal effects on the table in front of her. His beautiful thirties' Cartier watch, his wafer-thin and well-worn Louis Vuitton wallet with its matching note-book, his treasured address book, thick as a telephone directory, his keys on a holder that looked like a pebble picked up on a stretch of shingle somewhere but was, in reality, a diamond in its original state; his heavy plain gold cuff-links and the ring he had always worn on the little finger of his left hand. Nell had not known there was an inscription on its inside. 'Philippe le Beau – Paris 1938. Je t'adore.' In a carrier bag, as they had given it to her, was his suit, his silk underwear, his Lobb's shoes, his Charvet tie. He had given up cigarettes but still carried his gold Dunhill, also pre-war. There had been a case to match, she remembered, with his initials in sapphires. Probably back in the flat in Ashley Gardens. Or sold.

Mark asked at once, at the sound of her voice: 'Is everything all right? No trouble?'

'Not with Cindy. She's gone to her sister's in Paddington.'

'For how long?' Mark's voice was sharp.

'She said a day or two. I'm sorry. I should have found out where . . .'

'No matter,' Mark said. 'I can do that. So what's up, then?'

'Philip died this afternoon. I went to the hospital but he was already in intensive care. I've just been to collect his things.'

'I'm sorry,' Mark said, meaning it. 'He was an old friend, wasn't he?'

'That's the odd thing. We were never close. He was Liz's confidant, never mine, but – I feel like somebody has just taken a knife to my life. He had a hand in remaking it, you see. He taught me so much.'

'I'll come as soon as I can.'

'No, really . . . you have more important things to do – '

'I thought I had made it clear that nothing is as important as you.'

Nell closed her eyes, released a silent breath. 'I'll wait,' she said humbly. 'No matter how late it is.'

When he arrived she went straight into his arms, seeking a comfort she had not expected to need.

'Love me, Mark . . . right now I very much need to be loved.'

He provided it, and more.

Afterwards, drowsing in his arms: 'Philip was loved many times in his life – and he was very proud of that fact, but he told me he only ever loved once. And couldn't have the man. Sometimes I wonder if that is what made him so cynical about everything. Philip is the kind of man who could never get used to wanting and not having.'

'You will miss him, won't you?'

'Yes. That is what I find so strange.' She frowned slightly. 'I could never – how shall I put it – commit myself to Philip as a friend as Liz did. There was always a – a gulf I could never manage to cross. Liz trusted him implicitly – and I have to say that I never knew him to let her down – but I never could. And I know he was a very long way from one hundred per cent for me, either. But we got along. We – used each other, I suppose, but not unkindly. I needed his expertise and connections, he needed the fees I paid him – plus the kudos I let him take unto himself of being Cleo Mondaine's mentor.'

'Wasn't he rather like a godfather to you?'

'Only in the style of Vito Corleone!'

Mark laughed, but his own feeling at the death of Philip Faulkner was one of relief. One more strand attaching Nell to the Life cut away. And who else knows, now? Only Cleo's clients. And when the time is right she can walk away from them too.

His arms tightened around her. I'm as selfish as the next

man, he thought. I want it all. Nell *and* the next rung up the ladder. It will be risky, but worth it. Oh, yes, very much worth it. All I have to do is get that paedophile ring broken up and put Tony Panacoulis away. He thought about the preparations he had made for the next night's raid; the surveillance teams ready to be set up around the warehouse in buildings at the back, on either side and in front, which was the river, on a boat. He would have men stationed at the approaches to the road where the warehouse lay, dogs and their handlers ready in case any of the paedophiles tried to do a runner, plus a member of the welfare services to take care of the child or children who would be the centre of the evening's orgy. Each and every one of them would be connected by tested radio links. He also had a photographic team ready to capture the faces of the men arriving, using night-cameras, plus an additional two men on the floor above where the meeting would take place. He had inspected everything himself, entering the warehouse from the back, unseen just in case the ring – made up of extremely cautious men – were mounting their own surveillance prior to the meet. He had found the big empty cavern at the front, overlooking the river, where Nell said they had shot *Lady Chatterley*; found stuff from the sets that had been used, noted the powerful electricity supply. This would be no scratchy, dark, badly lit video: this would be sharp, crystal clear and on good-quality film to enable all the prints required to be run off. These men got off not only by participating but by watching the copies Tony Panacoulis would provide, over and over again. Only one thing disturbed him. Something Nell had told him Cindy had said in her drunken ramblings. About the members of the ring.

'Names 'as would make you blink, I can tell yer, and the faces to go with them.' At Nell's deliberately expressed disbelief: 'No names, no packdrill, but there's two of 'em from the 'ouse of Lords, for a start, and more than one MP – one is *very* well known . . . but the real laugh is the judges. Oh, yes, the very men as is supposed to be sendin' down these evil perverts is perverts theirselves. 'Ow about that for a lark? That's why Tony's laughin! *Nobody*, especially the bleedin' God Almighty Establishment, is goin' to allow that piece of news to get out. If somethin' *was* to go wrong the lid would be on and the pot buried before you could say Not Guilty! There'd be a cover-up the like of which 'as never been seen before in this country and as Tony says, God knows there's been enough of *them*! Nobody does a cover-up like the British 'cos nobody 'as 'ad as much practice at protectin' their own, especially them as run things.'

'Then what is the point of shopping him?' Nell had asked.

''Cos they'll make 'im the scapegoat same as they did that bloke in the Christine Keeler scandal . . . that was sex and the bleedin' Establishment, wannit? They'll get away with it, like always, but *'e* won't. They'll drop 'im in it quicker than they'd drop their pants for a juicy twelve-year-old!'

Given Cindy's tendency to boastfulness, Mark still felt uneasy. He knew the Establishment protected their own; he had experience of it. As a young Sergeant he had been a member of a team investigating a sex and bribes scandal which had suddenly turned nasty in that they began coming up with names which, as the investigation proceeded, began to ascend the social and power scale until, as it was about to penetrate the very top, was ordered to stop. Without explanation the order came down: This investigation is now closed. All files had been handed in and speculation was that they had been destroyed; that the order to halt had come from the Home Office itself.

Well, nobody has told *me* not to go any further, he thought. But then, nobody has any idea of the identity of the members of the ring. And we are talking multiple murders here. This is not sex only; it is perversion and unlawful killing of children. Let them try to put the lid on *that*! *If* Cindy is right, of course. And we shan't know that until we've got them in custody. But a sense of unease remained.

'You are worried about tomorrow, aren't you?' Nell, who had acquired her own special sensitivity towards *him*, asked.

'No. It's all set up as well as anything can be. I was thinking about what you told me Cindy said concerning the men who make up the paedophile ring.'

'Don't believe everything she says. She'll say anything to appear more important than she really is,' warned Nell, 'and if they were really *that* important would she have been allowed to set eyes on them? I doubt it. I doubt if anybody has – perhaps not even Tony Panacoulis. Anyway, tomorrow night will tell us if she was lying or not. Let's concentrate on tonight instead. Can you stay?'

'I was hoping you'd ask.'

And he'd made his arrangements to allow for it, such as being away before the two–man surveillance he'd set up on Nell arrived to take up their position in the fake British Telecom van. It would not do for the Superintendent in charge of this particular investigation to be seen leaving the house of a female informant very early in the morning. On the other hand, there were hours to go before then. He set himself to making them as pleasurable as possible.

She got up with him, cooked him breakfast. 'You'll let me know the outcome as soon as you can?' she requested, trying not to seem anxious.

'I will,' promised Mark. 'Try not to worry about it meanwhile.'

'I won't have time, thank God. I've got a very busy day ahead of me because Philip had me down as next of kin. That means places to go, people to see.' Thank God, she thought, as she prepared to go and get on with it.

Between visiting the various authorities which had to be notified of anyone's death Nell went to see Philip's solicitor, to find that he had made her his Executor.

The solicitor, a very old friend, explained: 'Philip sought to avoid sulks and a general falling out among his – circle. He felt he could not be seen to favour one over the other, all being childishly jealous. So he chose you. Outside the inner circle, yet very much a close friend, with no axe to grind. He has left you several small mementoes. He also left you this note. It concerns the clearing out of his flat.'

'What will happen to it? He lived there so long.'

'There are still some years remaining on his lease. I shall be dealing with that. You have his keys?'

'Yes.'

'Then once you have sorted everything out you will let me know, won't you?'

'Of course. What about his funeral?'

'Oh, that was all arranged years ago. He was very precise in his instructions. No religious service, no mourners, nobody in attendance but the undertakers and myself, to see his wishes carried out. Once they have been, then his friends are at liberty to remember him as and how they like.'

'I know he always said he wished to be cremated.'

'That is so.'

'What about his ashes?'

'To be thrown to the four winds.'

They shared a smile. 'How very Philip,' Nell said.

It was late afternoon when she got back, and she paid no attention to the British Telecom van parked opposite. As her front door closed behind her: 'This is a waste of time,' one bored policeman said to the other. 'Not so much as a squeak all day. What are we supposed to be watching for, anyway?'

'Any callers.'

'But she hasn't had any.'

'She's still the Super's snout and I heard that she passed on some very tasty information about that toe-rag Tony Panacoulis.'

'Never! What would a woman like her have to do with a bubble porn merchant?'

'Because I also heard that she's on the game herself.'

'Get away! Somebody's having you on! That's no tom!'

'Will you listen? I said on the game but I mean a different one from the kind that's played on the streets. I mean a high-class, high-charging call girl; the kind that costs an arm and a leg.'

'Says who?'

'I'm only telling you what I heard.'

'If she can afford to live in a house like that you'd probably have to remortgage your own to be able to afford her!' Then, tone sharpening. 'Hang about . . . who's that . . .'

A taxi was drawing up and a blonde got out. 'Stone me! that's Tony Panacoulis's bit of stuff! What's she doing here . . .?'

'Never mind that; get her in the frame so we can prove she was . . .'

Nell was surprised, Cindy unapologetic. 'You said as 'ow I was welcome to stay and it's no go at me sister's on account of she's got a new boyfriend and don't want no distractions. So I come back.' She barged past Nell, sure of her welcome. 'I don't suppose you've 'eard from Tony?' she asked.

'No. Why should I?'

'Well, 'e rang me sister but I got her to say she 'adn't seen me, so I thought maybe 'e'd rung you 'n'all.'

'I've been out all day,' Nell said. 'I've only just got back.'

'Oh, that's right . . . your friend, the one that died. You doin' the funeral, then?'

'He had me down as next of kin,' Nell answered obliquely.

Cindy nodded, none the wiser. 'I could murder a cuppa.'

Nell's heart sank. Cindy was not the company she wanted right now.

By eight o'clock everything and everyone was in place, cameras at the ready, radios tested, but it was nine before the first arrival was spotted, parking five streets away. His collar was up and his hat-brim was down, but he was photographed anyway. As were the rest of them when they arrived, one by one, all of them approaching the building carefully and cautiously, disappearing into the blackness once they entered through the gap in the chain-link fence, which appeared to have been made by vandals. A dozen were counted in by the time the object of the evening's entertainment arrived, accompanied by two men. He looked to be about fourteen; well made for his age and showing no signs of drugs or fear. A rent boy, Mark surmised, examining the peach-bloom face through his night glasses; there was a cocky wisdom about it that belied its youth.

His radio murmured. The men positioned above the ceiling had something to report.

'What is it?' Mark asked.

'You'll never believe this, guv, but they're all wearing masks.'

'What kind of masks?'

'The kind kids wear at parties, except they are rubber; cartoon characters. There's a Porky Pig, Mickey Mouse, Goofy – I've just spotted a Superman – blimey, at least he's got a sense of humour . . . this has to be seen, guv; every one stark-bollock naked and wearing a mask.'

'By their pricks shall ye know them,' murmured Mark.

'Say again, guv?'

'Get it all down on film.'

They waited until things were moving; it was reported that the boy was being had by his first customer – 'being run in' was the even-voiced comment, watched by an interested group fondling their own or someone else's erection, some indulging in oral sex, others going at it doggy-fashion. As the boy's first customer withdrew he was replaced by another without a break, while a third positioned himself so that the boy could fellate him. The orgy picked up tempo.

After a little while: 'Jesus!' Mark heard over his radio. 'Things are getting out of hand, guv, there's two of them at the boy and he's in trouble . . .'

'Keep your cameras turning,' Mark insisted. He wanted as much evidence as possible on film. There had to be no possibility of these men escaping arrest, but at the same time he could not allow the boy to be harmed, so he ordered in a decisive voice: 'Stevens to all units – go!'

There was a concerted cry of 'Police!' as doors burst open and uniformed officers rushed in. Naked men scattered, panic-stricken; some struggled with the officers who captured them, others, paralysed with fear and shock, offered no resistance. Within minutes it was all over; the expensive state of the art video camera and the film it contained were taken into custody along with the men who had hoped to view it at leisure. In a cupboard a stack of videos was also found and impounded. White-faced and crying, the boy was taken away to be examined forensically; while the men, masks removed and avoiding each other's gaze, were handed their clothes and told to dress, after which they too were taken away. By ten-thirty the empty and derelict warehouse was silent and deserted once more, the surrounding streets gleaming wetly under the streetlamps in the gently falling rain.

Mark was at his desk, chin propped on both fists as he studied the names on the list in front of him; those of the men who had been apprehended, when his sergeant came in, obviously cock-a-hoop.

'One of them is singing like a bird, Sir. The accountant –

Eardley. Terrified out of his life – he's married, three kids, ultra respectable. Says he's ruined; swears he knows nothing about the other videos – the ones that show the killing of Billy Knowles and Kevin Peel; says he has never been part of any orgy where a boy was killed; that they always used a rent-boy, like tonight. And Billy and Keviv *were* abducted. He admits to being a paedophile but that's all. Others are singing the same tune, one or two are refusing to say anything until their lawyers arrive, but I think congratulations are in order. It took two long hard years but you did it.'

Mark looked up and smiled his thanks, but his sergeant thought it lacked both pleasure and satisfaction. Well, he's tired, he thought. Probably a sense of anti-climax.

'It's been a long day, why don't you go home?' he suggested. 'Leave the rest to us.'

'I might just do that,' Mark agreed.

When his sergeant had gone he drew his telephone towards him.

'You are up late,' he said, when Nell answered on the first ring.

'I was waiting for your call. Is it over?'

'For tonight.'

'Was it successful – the raid?'

'Oh, yes.'

'You don't sound very happy.'

'I'm not. I need to talk to somebody and I can't think of anybody I'd rather talk to than you.'

'Cindy's here,' Nell said morosely.

'What!'

'Her sister has a new boyfriend who – reading between the lines – didn't want Cindy there so back she came to me.'

'Where is she?'

'Watching the late-night movie. I'm in the kitchen . . . hang on a minute.'

Nell tip-toed out of the kitchen, pushed open the sitting room door. Cindy was on the sofa, a bag of crisps on her lap, munching her way through them as she watched yet another re-run of *The Godfather*.

'She's deep in Al Pacino,' Nell reported back.

'I'd rather she was deep in the Atlantic,' Mark said savagely.

His sigh was dredged up. 'Oh, well, it was a nice thought.'

'I'm sorry . . .' Nell sounded so desolate he forced himself to say: 'It's not the end of the world. What about tomorrow?'

'I'm going across to Philip's flat to do some clearing up.'

'That's Ashley Place, isn't it?' Mark asked, perking up. 'Just across Victoria Street.'

'Yes.'

'I'll be there as soon as I can. Don't start the party without me.' Nell was laughing as they hung up.

Next morning, when he called into his office to check the latest state-of-play there was a message his secretary, a comfortably plump fifty-year-old, handed to him with the sort of reverence rendered only to those that came from on high. Mark was summoned to the Home Office.

'Damned fine job, Superintendent,' the Permanent Under-Secretary told him in his polished-to-a-shine Old Etonian accent. 'It was a long, hard slog but worth it, what? Put these beggars away for a long time, eh?' When Mark said nothing he went on: 'I understand they found certain highly unpleasant but undoubtedly incriminating videos at the scene.'

'Yes, Sir. But since the participants are masked it is some-what difficult to identify particular individuals. However, there are other ways.'

The pale blue eyes, hard as paving stones, offered a fish-like stare.

'Quite . . .' It was short and it said plainly: we will not discuss *that*.

Stony eyes, stony heart, Mark thought, and the hide of an armadillo. Governments may come and governments may go, but Permanent Under-Secretaries go on for ever. And I would not trust this one as far as I could throw Big Ben.

'So how did you do it, Hmm? Seemed to be getting nowhere then suddenly the off is given and you are thundering home by several lengths.'

'Patience and persistence, Sir.'

'And putting the boot in a little, eh?'

'Now and again, Sir. In the hopes that somebody, some-where might begin to realise that we would never give up; that it was only a matter of time.'

'And did you hear from someone?'

'A person did come forward, Sir.'

'And the information was spot-on?'

'It proved to be very – enlightening, Sir.'

'But you are not allowed to say who?'

'Like journalists, we protect our sources, Sir. We have to.'

'Of course, of course.' The urbane voice – he must shave it every morning, Mark thought, was thoughtful. 'Where would the Metropolitan Police be without their – snouts, I believe you call them?'

'Among other things, Sir.'

'What? Ah, ha-ha, yes, quite.' The fingers in the waistcoat pockets felt the gold half-hunter; the sort of gesture that made it unnecessary to check its time. 'So now you have every member of this pernicious ring?'

'No, Sir. Its protector is missing.'

'Protector?' Mark withstood the onslaught of voice and eyes.

'The man who arranges the venues, provided the victims then disposed of the bodies. A Greek Cypriot named Tony Panacoulis. He has vanished.'

'But you will find him, won't you?' It was an order not a question.

'He is being looked for, Sir.'

'Good, good. Mustn't let him get away. Sounds a nasty piece of work.'

'No worse than the men who employed him, Sir.'

Armadillo reinforced with rhinocerous, Mark thought, as the cold, pale eyes interrogated him.

'Well, it is still a very nice piece of work, Superintendent, which will not be forgotten by those who have it within their power to show you their appreciation. I am sure you will go on to even better things.' A perfunctory smile and a handshake which steered him in the direction of the door. 'Good luck.'

And that was that.

Nell was at Philip's by half-past ten, just as Mark was walking up towards the Home Office. She had left Cindy still asleep, but had taken the precaution of locking away everything that might prejudice her cover story, taking with her, in her big shoulder bag, such choice items as Cleo's client book, since Reza Dominitian's name was in there. It was in code, and nobody but Nell knew that code, but better safe than sorry, since she was already regretting the necessity of having to give Cindy a spare key when she had asked for it. 'I won't lose it, honest, but we're both comin' and goin', right? And if I can't get in the 'ouse it means I've got to 'ang about waiting for you to come back and Gawd knows 'ow long that'll be. It's only for a couple of days 'till I know for sure 'ow the land lies where Tony's concerned. Once I've got me arrangements made I'll be off.'

Nell had been tempted to lie and say she was carrying the only spare key, but knew Cindy would only offer to have a copy cut. So she contented herself with a dire, if mendacious, warning.

'Do be careful with it, Cindy. This is not my house, as I told you before. I'm a guest just as much as you are and responsible for it. By rights, I should not really have you here in the first place, but since you helped me in my hour of need, the least I can do is return the favour. Just keep it safe. If this place was to get burgled I'd be in deep trouble.' Which *was* no more than the truth.

Cindy had sworn that she would more or less guard it with her life, with which Nell had to be satisfied. She did not like the thought of the key to her private life – for her house was very private to her – being held by an acquaintance (there was no way she would have described Cindy as a friend) whom she had never really trusted, but Mark had been very emphatic in his insistence that everything appear to be normal in every casual sense of the word. And giving your front door key to someone who was staying with you for a few days was normal behaviour. For other people, Nell thought, as she double-locked the heavy mortice behind her. Not for me. But then, she thought wryly, most people would probably consider my whole lifestyle abnormal!

She ignored the fake British Telecom van as though its presence outside her house was also entirely normal, reflecting that it was very satisfying to know that Mark was so concerned for her safety, but since Tony Panacoulis had no idea where Cindy was, the possibility of him coming to look for her here was really a very remote one. Still, Mark was the policeman so he should know.

She was already looking forward with tingling anticipation to seeing him, loving him – for by now they could not keep their hands off each other – again. Philip would approve, she thought mischievously. The first thing she did on entering his enormous flat – far too big for one person, really – was to use his keys to open up the myriad of locked drawers, cupboards and chests, only to find that apart from everything else he was, Philip had been a magpie. He had kept every single gift bestowed on him by his lovers. He had cupboards crammed with crystal and silver, drawerfuls of trinkets: cigarette boxes, lighters, photograph frames, all made out of precious metal and in many cases encrusted with precious stones. There were dozens of fine leather wallets, umpteen fitted dressing cases in crocodile or coach hide, made for the days when travel was by train or boat and weight unimportant. He had parted with nothing that had any value, but Nell would not have been able to say for what reason: sentimental or pecuniary. When she opened a locked drawer and found it crammed with studs, cuff-links and watches, all of gold or silver or precious stones, she was amazed, for she had never seen him wear any of them. 'God knows what a treasure-trove you built up over the years,' she said aloud, as she sorted through heavy silver photograph frames – all empty; likewise engraved cigarette boxes – all of them given 'With Love'. 'I know you had been disposing of what you called your "trifles" but why were you always pleading poverty? There is enough here to have seen you through the next twenty years without lowering your lofty standards. So why did you accept fees from me?'

In the wardrobes were suits and shoes, shirts and silk underwear; so many and so much they would have stocked a shop, all of the very best quality. 'These are the wages of sin?' Nell asked herself, which was when she began to perceive the solution to the enigma that had been Philip Faulkner. 'You always used to say: "Put not your trust in princes", didn't you? So you put yours in perquisites. Oh, Philip . . .' A deep sadness filled her. 'You were never a happy man, were you? So very many acquaintances, so few friends. Liz was the truest, wasn't she?'

It was to Nell that Philip had passed on what Liz had left to him, plus one other thing. The clock which stood in the hall; an eighteenth-century longcase of walnut and marquetry.

She took out the letter the solicitor had given her, slitting open the heavy, parchment-type envelope with a curved dagger, its hilt inlaid with rubies set in silver. Philp had always used it as a letter opener. The letter was brief.

This clock tells much more than the time. It also tells my life. If you apply pressure to the marquetry vase in the centre of the base, a concealed door will spring open. Inside is a second door. This opens by means of the filigree key hanging on the back of the outer door.

Inside the hidden compartment you will find my journals.

Yes; I know I always *said* one should *never* keep a written record of *anything*, but if I had not said so – many times – who would have confided in me?

I had intended to write my *Memoirs*. The journals were to be my *aide memoire*. Life has decreed otherwise. Punishment for leaving it too late, I suppose.

I leave the journals to you. Read them and enjoy. Marvel at the life I led. Publish, if you will. And overcome the libel suits. You will understand what I mean when you read the names of the august personages I encountered in my travels. And as you know, I have been simply everywhere. Except for the unknown country which will always remain unknown until such time as someone is able to return from it and describe what it is like. Just the sort of challenge to appeal to me, don't you think?

Expect me when you see me.

À bientôt

Philip

There were ten of them; thick, leather-bound, nothing but the years stamped in gold on their spines. Philip had obviously had them specially made for each had a bookplate inside with the Faulkner coat of arms and the words EX LIBRIS PHILIP HUGH DELACY FAULKNER.

Nell abstracted the one that covered 1979, the year she had first encountered a man she had never quite managed to trust, but was only now that he was dead, finally beginning to understand.

It was all there. She flinched, flushed, bit her lip at his comments on the nineteen-year-old scrubber. 'A piece of cheap bijouterie'. But she applied his later, more approving comments as a mollifier. It was when she came to his musings as to her motivation that she became totally immersed. His inability to open her up rankled, so he had to make assumptions rather than piece together facts. And what he had written, in his thesis on the whys and wherefores of Cleo/Eleanor/Nell was pure fiction.

For one so steeped in the history of vice and all its myriad ramifications, Philip had never seen the truth staring him in the face, as Mark had. But that, Nell understood now, was because Philip's self-absorption – as thick as rubber – acted as insulation for a sensitivity that was focused inaccurately on supposed flaws and/or weak spots. Though he had her father dead to rights – 'cold, unloving, ungiving, emotionally sterile; a despot' he had not divined that Nell had been her mother's surrogate in her father's bed, for to Philip, sex meant passion, and Nell's father was incapable of it.

True, thought Nell, but he was passionate as to his *rights*. And where I was concerned he used them. Philip believed she had run away because she wanted to be an actress, and when she failed she became the next best thing: a prostitute who specialised in fantasy. Thus she gained the best of two worlds. Her father's, in that she was revenged on him by showing the world what he had made her; and her own, inner one, by acting her pretty little head off, even if all her roles were sexual. How strange, Nell thought, that one man could know me all those years and never divine what made me tick, while another man takes only days. Probably because, to Philip, I was never flesh and blood; only a specimen. He never did see people as human, only as the sum of their faults.

Philip always spent so much time picking over faults that he never saw the virtues shining away at the bottom of the pile. This was confirmed when she read – bits here and there for she had little time and the journals were thick – his comments on the people he had known; the men who had wanted him, paid his way, fallen in love with him. Her jaw dropped and her breath hissed as she read the names. My God! Not him! And a little later on: Never! It's not possible! But it was. With the deadly pen of the emotionally uninvolved Philip detailed commercial and physical transactions, as well as sexual abilities, physical dimensions, particular sexual preferences. It was numbingly heartless. Except for once. The one time in his life Philip had loved rather than been loved. He wrote then with feeling; pain-filled longings and despairing dreams, for the man he loved was heterosexual; knew Philip, even liked him, but would have been appalled to know how much Philip loved and wanted him.

Oh, Philip . . . Nell thought, emotion sweeping away distaste. You did know what it was like but it was unrequited. Is that what soured you? Made you so cynical? Then she realised that Philip had been forty-four years old when he had met the only love of his life.

The doorbell rang. It was Mark. Her heart gave a little hop, skip and a jump at the sight of him and her kiss was such as to make him ask 'What was that in aid of?'

'Love. I've come to the conclusion that I'd rather have it than not.'

Then she saw he wore a bitter, brooding look. Something had obviously gone wrong.

'I could use a drink,' he said. 'A stiff one.'

'Of course. Come on in and I'll get you one.'

She did so, and he swallowed it at a gulp. Then he stood, sunk in thought staring at nothing until, as though making a conscious effort, he roused himself to say: 'Sorry . . . bad mood. Not your fault. Come here.'

She sat on his knee and he kissed her thoroughly and at some length. Then he leaned his forehead against hers, eyes closed and said: 'I've just had a patronising few minutes with a very superior person at the Home Office who kindly threw me a bone after giving me a pat and telling me I'd been a good dog.'

'You sound as if there was no meat on it?'

'I have no taste for human sacrifice.'

'Tell me,' she soothed, 'but first let me get you another drink.'

He sipped it as he told her his suspicions that his 'successful' raid had been a set-up. 'What we netted were small-fry. Pathetic little men who scuttle around corners or blustering braggarts who keep telling you who they are and what a mistake you have made. There was not a single specimen of the names Cindy hinted at. Last night's gathering was of the second eleven. Moreover, the boy was rented, already known to us. He keeps running away from the children's homes he gets sent to every time he is picked up. The murdered children were abducted, and except for Darren Henry, much younger. Oh, they are paedophiles all right, but they are not the men who murdered those children. I'd stake my life and almost twenty years in the job on that. Why would Cindy say that there were extremely important persons involved if there were not? Names she obviously recognised, if not faces; they always wear masks in case a video should ever fall into the wrong hands.'

Nell was silent, listening intently as Mark thought aloud.

'No, I think that in this instance she was telling the truth. Why else was Tony Panacoulis nowhere to be found when we went to arrest him? Who told him to do a runner? And why a rent-boy? The real ring doesn't rent its boys, and this one told us he was hired in plain view. It doesn't add up, Nell, but my instincts keep telling me I've been fitted up! There has been a great deal of interest in this case from certain elevated quarters right from the beginning; resources were made available at a time when every department in the Met was screaming for its share of a cake that gets smaller and smaller. "Public confidence must be restored," they said. "Can't have these tabloids braying on about 'mothers' fears' and saying our children aren't safe. These people are obviously perverts and queers and they must be stopped. Set up your squad, Superintendent. We are told you are a comer and a very good detective. Prove it, with our blessing. Oh, and er – keep us fully informed." '

Nell said nothing. She was too taken aback.

'I'd heard a whisper that there were people at the top involved in paedophile activities but I tended to dismiss it as the usual spite and animosity people always show to those who become successful and/or powerful. We know how our lords and masters protect their own, from Kim Philby to Anthony

Blunt. If they will protect people who betray their country and its people, why should they not go to equal lengths to protect those who happen to be sexual deviates? Why not have someone keeping an eye out for the *real* members of the ring, who are so very important that the slightest whiff of the truth could precipitate a scandal that could shake the establishment so badly it would collapse. When there is that much at stake, nothing must be left to chance. Last night was too pat. For two years they have always been one – even two – steps ahead of me. Suddenly there is a cupboard of incriminating videos – this in a derelict riverside warehouse that is a vandal's paradise!' Mark's voice would have ground glass. 'Somebody, somewhere is playing games and I'm damned if I'll allow myself to be used as a football! That warehouse meet was a set-up, staged by but not for the ring I'm after. Last night was *not* kosher, Nell, I know it! My copper's instinct is yelling it in my ear all the time. The men we captured last night are not the ones involved in the serial murders I've been investigating. Oh, they'll be touted as such, I have no doubt, but one of them has a very expensive lawyer; too expensive even for a successful TV producer such as he is. A lawyer with a title who is known as Counsel for the Establishment. Before we can come to court with his client or any of the others there is still a lot more to do, a lot of questions to be answered. And how he comes to have such a lawyer is one of them.'

Mark's voice vibrated with angry frustration. 'Do you know what one little shit said to me last night? "Since when have you begun to arrest men for buying sex, officer? That boy had been bought and paid for. He is the prostitute. I suppose it is his age . . . but he was not coerced. I assure you. He has committed the crime, not us." ' Bitterly: 'I now understand how one-sided the law is concerning prostitution. There is a seller and a buyer; both take part in the act. Why, then, is only the seller punished?'

'Because she is usually a woman,' Nell pointed out, 'and men make the laws.'

'On behalf of my sex I apologise,' Mark said sombrely. 'We have no right to punish you for *our* sexuality; *our* desires.'

'No, you haven't,' Nell said without rancour, 'but you'll go on doing it just the same.' Her smile had a sting to it. 'Say what you like about prostitution, it gives you enormous insight into the male psyche. And speaking of that, let me give you an insight into that of one particular man.' She brought him Philip's journals.

Mark's first reaction was incredulity. 'Not *him*!'

'Yes. Him.'

A little further on. 'Jesus! It's like defaming God! Do you know what these men are – what they do – the power they wield?' He read on, avidly. 'They don't come any higher than this! If I had not seen it I would never have believed it!' His depression had melted in the heat of his excitement. 'I can't make any arrests on this sort of hearsay, but by God I can keep an eye – both eyes – on what this lot get up to.' His laugh was gleeful. 'They thought by elevating me to Chief Superintendent they'd bury me at my desk under an avalanche of paper, safely where I could not stick my nose into where they did not want it. But there is nothing to stop me forming a special squad and keeping that fact to myself.' Nell's eyes and mouth had formed circles. 'Yes, that was my bone . . . the news that my next Board would be a formality. They are shoving me upstairs and off the streets – they hope. These . . .' he brandished one of the journals, 'make it possible for me to look as if I'm deskbound while my squad watches and waits and collects evidence. Thank God for Philip Faulkner!' Mark's elated face sobered. 'And most of all thank God for you. I owe you so very, very much, Nell. For being in the right place at the right time; for telling me about it; for so much invaluable information gained at considerable risk. And now for being a friend of The Man who Knew Everybody!' He followed up his verbal eulogy by a wholly satisfying physical demonstration of his gratitude.

Curled up against him: 'How Philip would have relished all this,' Nell said.

'Did you ever tell him what you had got yourself mixed up with?'

'No! You have just been reading his journals. Would you have told him anything?'

'God forbid.'

'Exactly. And you have to bear in mind that a lot of what he says is what people said to him; there is a great deal of hearsay. I'd go carefully if I were you. His spite was legendary.'

'Oh, I'll go carefully all right. I'll be the very model of a Chief Superintendent shuffling my in and out trays and all those administrative pieces of paper. Then, when I'm good and ready and absolutely certain of my case, I'll bring it.'

Nell shook her head. 'Another case that will never come to court?'

'Of course it won't – but it will stop a few in their tracks and show them that *nobody* is – or should be – above the law. That they should have thought they were, protected by their power and their privilege, sickens me!'

'It might also ruin your career.'

Mark's grin was pure wickedness. 'By that time I'll be a Commander . . .'

Nell gazed at him admiringly. 'You've got it all planned, haven't you?'

'When I was a tree-climbing twelve-year-old the apples I wanted were *always* the ones at the top of the tree. Now let's put these journals back in their hiding place and I'll remove the clock to your house myself. It is far too valuable to leave to any removal men.'

21

When Nell got back home there was no sign of Cindy but a note was pinned to the bulletin board in the kitchen. 'Gone to get some things while the coast is clear. Back later. Cindy.' Nell sighed with pleasure. A little time on her own to sit and think, ponder on what had happened. Then she noticed that the cats had not come to greet her.

'Bundle . . . Blossom . . .' she called. 'Come on, my loves, I'm home . . .' Silence. No sound of them jumping off her bed and on to the floor, no sound of bells jingling as they raced lightly down the stairs, no rumble of deep purring as they wound themselves around her legs.

She went to the glass door leading into her tiny garden, flapped their cat door. They did not come. It was the very first time they had failed either to be there, waiting, or to come at the sound of her voice.

'They can't have wandered off,' she told herself, feeling panic set in.

The thought of losing her two closest companions was not to be borne. 'They can't be far,' she said out loud. 'I've never known them to go beyond the sound of my voice.' Then she thought of the garage. It had an interior and an outer door; a couple of times she had inadvertently shut them in because they had slipped past her like drifts of smoke, unseen and unheard. Only their insistent miaows had alerted her to the fact that she had closed the door on them. Now she went to the door, opened it and put on the light. 'Come on then, if you are in there,' she said. But they weren't.

She was sure she had not shut them in a room upstairs; she never shut any door for they had the run of the house. But she'd had so much on her mind of late it was quite conceivable that she had absent-mindedly done just that.

But all the doors were open, as usual. It was not until something made her look under her bed, lifting the frilled valance to do so, that she saw them, huddled together at the far end by the wall. 'Darlings . . . what is it? Come along . . . it's all right.' At the sound of her voice they untwined themselves and crawled towards her. She picked them up, felt the intensity of their purring. 'What frightened you, then . . . Was it that awful Cindy? Did she shout at you? I know she has no time for animals. Stupid idiot! Well, I've no time for people like her. I don't give a damn what Tony Panacoulis does to her, she is not staying here!' She got to her feet, crooning to them.

'That's all right then,' said a voice, 'because she won't be back.'

Nell whirled, clutching the cats in her arms. Tony Panacoulis lounged in her bathroom doorway, smiling at her. He was immaculately dressed in a pale grey raw silk suit with a royal purple tie, and Nell could smell his cologne. His dead-black curly hair gleamed and in his right hand he held a gun, small, not much more than palm-sized, but aimed directly at her.

Nell gawked at him stupidly, too shocked by his sudden appearance to do anything else for a moment or two. Her voice sounded rusty when she managed to ask shakily: 'How did you get in here?'

'Cindy let me in.'

'But – she's not here. The note downstairs . . .'

'We – er – met up at the 'ouse when she came to collect her things, and when I asked her nicely to 'and over your key she let me 'ave it – ' Tony's pulpy melon-face split in a grin that reached across and squeezed Nell's heart so that she gasped for air. 'After which I let her have it . . .'

The shiny black eyes flared momentarily and Nell knew instantly that Cindy – foolish, venal Cindy who thought she was always one step ahead of the game – was dead. She also knew that unless she could think of a way to circumvent it, her own death was imminent. I shouldn't have given her the key.

Oh, God! *Why* did I give her that key? Because the raid was over and done with and I thought – we both thought – that Tony was on the run. Mark was right. Mark! His men were outside! She had forgotten his copper's instincts.

Her relief was such she almost laughed until she also realised that had they spotted Tony he would not be here now.

'She shouldn't've grassed,' Tony said sorrowfully. 'She knew full well what happens to people who grass . . .' The melon split again. 'Even if she was set up for it . . .'

Nell stared numbly, holding tightly to her cats as though they were now all she had left to hold on to. Sensing her fear, Bundle, bigger but without his sister's belligerence, pressed closer to her, while Blossom growled softly.

'Set up?' Nell repeated. If she could keep him talking, she thought, perhaps she might think of a way out of this. But her mind was so possessed by her terror it seemed to have seized up.

Tony's smile was gleeful. 'Thought yourself so clever, didn't you, coming on as a down-on-her-luck call girl? That was a nice touch and I'd have fallen for it if Reza hadn't thought there was something not quite kosher. You looked familiar but you wasn't the Cleo he laid and paid for – oh, and he says you were worth every penny, by the way. In the end it was your voice. That's a very distinctive voice you've got there, did you know that? Anyway, he wasn't absolutely sure so he said to take you on but keep an eye on you. He's the money man, see? He likes to vet all my girls, so he was on the other side of the one way mirror behind my desk the day you come to be interviewed.'

'But – he was abroad . . .'

'Only his passport, carried by his very own look-alike, whose been doin' it for as long as I've known Reza, and that's about eight years now. 'Course . . . once the cops paid him a visit down in Wiltshire he soon put two and two together. Very sharp, is our Reza. Mind like an old-fashioned strop razor. He worked it out that you'd seen something that weekend he had you down – and that was a slight miscalculation on his part which won't happen again – so we strung you along from then on; had an eye kept on you at all times, you and that flash copper from the Yard. And when you turned up at Cindy's 'airdresser . . . well, you was signalling your moves, love. Still, it 'elped us keep one step ahead of you all the way. And we knew Cindy'd been listenin' at doors and spyin' through keyholes so we give her something to use. Then I did for 'er precious nails and just as we expected, she come straight to you. Talk about mad! She was spittin' tacks, but that was what we wanted, see? Cindy'd made threats once too often to be anything but a nuisance so we thought it would be just as well to dispose of you both.'

'You won't get away with it,' Nell repeated the cliché with as much confidence as she could muster. Keep him talking, keep him talking, she told herself feverishly, even as she was thinking 'we'? Who was 'we'?

'But we have.' Tony tut-tutted. 'Whatever you know, we know. But what we know you don't know, see?'

'You're bluffing,' Nell managed to sound amazingly derisive, though she was having difficulty controlling her voice.

'Don't need to, do I? Not now. Your copper 'ad 'is little raid and collared a dozen or so of those nasty little men who like sex with children, and we saw to it that there was a fair selection of the videos he's been after for so long. The ring is finished, as far as he is concerned, while you are finished as far as we are concerned.'

Nell was trying to think through what she had just heard, especially the fact that Mark had been spot on; last night *had* been a set up and the real ring left untouched.

'You've got a mole, haven't you?' she asked, sounding as if it was something she had not realised until now.

'You could call 'im that, I suppose, but 'e don't live in no underground tunnel.' Tony's laugh was a guffaw. 'Not 'im. Six bedroom town house, a country house and twenty thousand acres is more 'is style.'

Oh, Mark, you were so right Nell thought. I *can't* let him kill me now; I have to tell you what I've learned . . . oh, God, please, help me . . . I can't think of anything.' Her eyes roved the room and stopped as they met the telephone; if there was only some way she could manage to reach that . . . dial 999 . . .

'No go, love,' Tony said, following the direction of her stare. 'I pulled the jacks, every man jack of them.' He giggled at his own feeble joke. 'And your minders won't be kickin' no doors down seein' as 'ow they was sort of kicked theirselves, if you take my meanin'?'

'I'm expecting Superintendent Stevens any minute – '

'No you 'ain't. He's gone back to the Yard. I told you, we got our own eyes and ears.'

Nell bit hard on her lower lip. Oh, God, you can't mean it to end like this . . . is all I get just a glimpse of Paradise? That's every bit as mean and spiteful as this murdering bastard! Underneath her fear she could feel her rage building. 'Why is it necessary to kill me anyway?' She wanted to know.

'Because you grassed to the cops once Cindy had grassed to you.'

'But they will know at once who has done it! Superintendent Stevens is already looking for you.'

'Not very 'ard seein' as most of 'is time is spent with you . . . on the job in more ways than one, is 'e?'

The insulting leer on his pulpy, over-ripe face only served to turn up the heat under Nell's already simmering fury.

'Besides, I shall be takin' a nice long 'oliday. See the world, soak up some sunshine. It's all arranged. As for you,' – the leer became a very cold, very deadly smile – 'well, you'll just be the victim of another nutter passin' 'isself off as a punter but who gets off on other people's pain . . . you've met more'n one of them, I'm sure. There'll be nothing to prove I was within miles of this place. And they won't find Cindy neither; word will be that we've both gone on 'oliday. No, you'll be just another up-market tart got 'ad once too often, that's all.'

'Why the gun, then?'

'All the better to frighten you with.' His giggle was high-pitched but it served to inflame Nell's already smouldering sense of injustice. Unconsciously her anger made her clutch her cats tighter, making Bundle struggle to free himself, alarmed by the fear he could sense and the taut quivering of his mistress's body. He dug his back legs into Nell's arms, seeking purchase in order to leap for freedom, and as his claws sank into her flesh she yelped, flinched and released her hold. In an instant he had sprung from her arms, intent on leaving by the door but making Tony Panacoulis recoil as the cat leapt towards him.

'Keep that thing away from me!'

His fear and revulsion were such that Nell at once knew her attacker was phobic about cats. Some people were so terrified of them that they could not remain in a room with them. Tony Panacoulis, Nell perceived now, was one of them, and it gave her an idea.

Seeing Bundle flee to safety Blossom struggled to follow, protesting loudly as only she could.

'I said keep it away!' The fear had banished the shrillness; his voice was now hoarse with panic. The gun was still aimed roughly in her direction but his attention was wholly on the cat in case it too should make a move in his direction.

'All right . . . all right!' Nell had no difficulty in sounding the note of her own panic. She shifted the cat in her arms, appearing to hold her more tightly while at the same time shuffling, inch by inch, over the floor until she was facing Tony Panacoulis – by now inside the bathroom – four square. Blossom was making threatening noises but Nell held her so that her lethal claws could find no purchase.

'I'm putting her down . . . see . . .' she said loudly, bending forward from the waist as if to set the cat down on the ground.

As Blossom saw the ground coming up she struggled to reach it, in such a way as to make Tony Panacoulis retreat further into the bathroom, his eyes riveted to the object of his fear and loathing. Just as Blossom seemed about to set her paws on the carpet Nell straightened suddenly, in the same movement throwing the cat directly at the cowering man. Blossom shrieked in fury at this *lèse-majesté*, which made Tony lose his bottle completely. He fired in panic-stricken terror. The bullet struck Blossom in mid-flight, producing a howl that made him fire again, but miss, the bullet burying itself in the wall above Nell's bed. Nell did not notice. All she saw was the body of her beloved cat fall to the floor like a dead thing.

That did it. 'You murdering bastard!' She launched herself at him, fingers curved to rend and tear. He fired again but his aim was by now wild and missed Nell by yards as her hand reached instinctively for the bronze statue that stood on the chest of drawers next to the bathroom door. Before he could fire again she had hit him with it – hard. He was knocked off balance, staggering backwards, already unconscious, to strike the edge of the bath with the back of his knees which had the effect of making him fall backwards into the bath, hitting his head a second time on the tiled wall, after which he slid downwards, the gun falling from his useless hand. Out cold.

Nell dived for the gun, dropping the bronze as she did so, and once she had it in a somewhat palsied grip managed to stand up on legs that threatened to dissolve, holding the gun in the two-handed grip she had seen used in so many thrillers and pointing it straight at the unconscious man. But he had his eyes closed, and the left-hand side of his face was covered in blood which was dripping on to his lilac raw-silk suit. Cautiously Nell edged forward, laid her fingers on the side of his neck as she had been taught by Liz long ago ('I once had a client succumb to a heart attack just as he was coming so I learned what to do in case it ever happened again'). There was a pulse. She had not killed him. Feeling her legs going she staggered to the door, closed it behind her, locked it and then, leaning against it, slid slowly down it to collapse in a heap on the carpet, shaking violently. Even her teeth were chattering.

Then she saw her wounded cat valiantly trying to lick her shattered hind leg. 'Bloss . . . Oh, Bloss . . .' Nell crawled towards her, moaned when she saw the state of the mangled leg. 'Oh, God, I'll get help . . .'

Terror galvanised her, firmed her legs and fingers as she found the phone jack, plugged it into the wall, jabbed out a number.

'Mr McGregor, please . . . this is an emergency. Yes, I'm a patient – or rather my cat is . . . Blossom. British Blue. Yes, yes . . . she's been shot . . . what? Oh . . . left back leg . . . she's bleeding badly, please send someone right away . . . otherwise she is going to bleed to death . . . please, please . . . what? Oh, Jordan . . . Nell Jordan . . . yes . . . Wigmore Mews, that's right . . . hurry, please, for God's sake *hurry* . . .'

She hung up, sniffed, wiped away tears with the heels of her hands, then with fingers that were once more shaky, punched out 999.

When Mark entered the house at the run it seemed to be full of people. Nell was not among them. 'Upstairs, Sir, in the bedroom,' a policeman told him.

Nell was crouched on the floor by an elderly man who was

busy with a limp bundle of grey fur. She was weeping soundlessly, her huge eyes drowning in tears.

'I've managed to stop the bleeding,' the man was saying in a soft Highland burr, 'but she'll need surgery. The leg was pretty badly smashed when the bullet exited.'

'What happened?' Mark asked.

Nell looked up. 'That bastard Tony Panacoulis shot her!' her voice was acrid with hatred.

'She'll be a pretty sick cat for a wee while and I doubt she'll have a limp but she'll live,' the vet said.

'You're sure?' Nell begged for reassurance.

'Aye, she's in prime condition and very well looked after. A wee bit overweight but I've told you about that before. Now, then, if you'll lift the door of that cage there, I'll get her into it and back to my surgery. I'll have to operate right away.'

'I'll come with you.' Nell got to her feet eagerly.

'No,' said Mark.

She whirled on him. 'No! this is my cat and I'm not leaving her. Didn't you hear what I said? Tony Panacoulis shot her!'

'Which is why I want you to stay and tell me why and how.'

'I've already told the other policemen. Ask them.'

'I prefer to hear it first hand from you.'

Sensing a collision course the vet said: 'There's nothing you can do now, Miss Jordan. I'll get her on the table as soon as I get back and as soon as I know the full extent of the damage to tissues and such I'll put her together again as best I can.'

'You are sure . . .'

'You may as well wait here as sit in a hard chair at the surgery. I'll let you know how she does just as soon as I know.'

'Promise?'

'Cross my heart. I know how attached you are to this little Madam, here, and her brother . . .'

'Oh, my God, Bundle!' exclaimed Nell in consternation. 'I've been so worried about Bloss I forget my poor Bundle . . . He managed to get down and did a runner. He's probably cowering in terror somewhere. I must find him.'

Blossom safely in her special cage, they all went downstairs where Mark raised his voice to say: 'Everybody, please . . . a grey cat with yellow eyes, the brother to this one. He's somewhere in the house or garden, hiding. When you find him, bring him to Miss Jordan.'

'He won't come,' Nell said practically. 'Just tell me, I'll come and get him.'

He was found cowering deep in an azalea bush by the wall. Nell had to flatten herself and crawl in after him, coax him out with soft words and a piece of chicken liver, his favourite.

'Blimey! All this fuss over a couple of cats,' Mark heard one policeman say to another. 'And she doesn't look the type, either . . .' Mark was about to issue a blistering reprimand when he thought better of it. His knowledge of Nell was not supposed to be any better than theirs.

'I suppose you think I'm ridiculous, making all this fuss,' Nell said some time later, Bundle on her lap, purringly secure once more, 'but you have to remember that for a long time Bloss and Bundle were all I had.' Penitently: 'I'm sorry I bit your head off. I was upset.'

'Really,' Mark said drily. 'Most women would have been having hysterics. Tell me again just how you did it.'

Nell did so.

'And you lifted this statue?' Mark reached across to heft it, now shrouded in protective plastic, 'and hit Panacoulis with it?'

'Yes.'

'In God's name how? It weighs a ton.'

'I don't know. I just did. I was so *angry*. I thought he had killed her so I wanted to kill him.'

Mark replaced the bronze; of a young girl in a flimsy, clinging dress with a wild mane of hair and an expression of wide-eyed innocence.

'Liz gave it to me years ago,' Nell said, eyeing it. 'She said it reminded her of me but I've never been able to see it.' Her expression darkened. 'All I could think of was clouting him for shooting Bloss.'

'Oh, you clouted him all right. Severe concussion and a fractured skull, but it's just as well you didn't kill him otherwise I would have had to arrest you for murder.'

'W-H-A-T!'

'That's the law, when you kill someone other than by

accident. Then, the charge is manslaughter. You hit Panacoulis deliberately – '

'You bet I did!'

There was a cough and Mark looked up to see his two-man surveillance team, looking very hung over, standing in the doorway.

'How are you feeling?' he asked.

'Like we had at least two over the eight,' one of them said miserably.

'The effects of the gas he used. Quick acting but slow to dissipate. Best thing is to go home and sleep it off. You won't be fit for anything else.'

'If you're sure, Guv . . .'

'I'm sure. See you in the morning.'

'What did Tony Panacoulis use on them?' Nell asked curiously, when they had gone.

'Some kind of aerosol anaesthetic. Reza Dominitian owns a company which manufactures such things.'

Nell shuddered. 'Do you think his is the hand behind this?'

'I doubt it. He is a behind-the-scenes operator and a very cautious one. The fact that he uses a *doppelgänger* indicated how deeply he is involved in things he wants left unknown.'

'Like the mole – whoever he is?'

'Yes. I'll have a better idea of where he might be hidden when there is some action on what has happened here, depending on who and where it comes from.'

'Do you think it will be from on high?'

'I'm sure of it. He is somebody who remains in place no matter which government is in power. He might be a fixer, or a sweeper-up-of-messes to the Establishment, but he's pretty powerful. He's had the drop on me from the start, but I want him to think I've been dealt with; that I believe the set-up he obligingly created for me and am quite prepared to go happily one more rung up the ladder from where I will mind my own business.'

'But you won't'

Mark's vivid eyes looked at her and she felt them slide into her.

'I've spent two long years on this case and I hate waste.'

'So do I.'

His grin was followed by: 'Something else we agree on.'

That evening they went to see Nell's beloved Blossom. 'She saved my life,' Nell said to Mark seriously. 'The least I could do was do my best to save hers.' She was still under the anaesthetic but had withstood the operation very well.

'She's got a heart like a steam engine,' the vet told Nell.

'When can I have her home?'

'Och, it'll be a wee while. I have to make sure there's no infection. I'm afraid the leg won't be the same shape as the other one, I had to pin it, but she'll be able to use it just fine.' He said Nell could return next morning. On the way home she was a different person, but once there she dropped into a chair, leaned her head against the wall, closed her eyes. The tension releasing its hold was all but visible.

'You need a drink,' Mark said.

'I need something restorative, that's for sure.'

He gave her a strong gin and tonic – 'That's better . . .' she sighed. They sat in silence until Nell asked: 'What happened to Cindy? You never said.'

'She was found at the bottom of the stairs in the house in Islington where she lived with Panacoulis. Her neck was broken and one of her shoes was minus a stiletto heel. That was found half-way up the stairs caught in a tear in the carpet.'

Nell opened her eyes and sat bolt upright. 'But – he told me he had let her have it! I thought that meant – '

'Oh, I have no doubt he broke her neck. But I also have no doubt we'll never prove it. There was not a mark on her and the pathologist says her broken neck is consistant with the way she fell.' Now Mark sighed. 'All we've got him for is threatening behaviour – and shooting a cat.'

Nell stared at nothing. 'It's all my fault Cindy is dead . . . me and my big ideas. It is all because I stuck my nose into her business, looked her up, got her drunk, made her tell me things.' Her look was filled with self-hatred. 'My father was right, I am neither use nor ornament. I spoil everything I touch. I will go my own way because I won't listen to advice.'

'Balls!' Mark said robustly, in such a voice she shut her mouth and looked chastened. 'Cindy had information that made her a party to as nasty a business as I've ever dealt with in twenty years. She was the mistress of a man who made his living from running girls and selling porn; she had been arrested times out of number for soliciting – '

'There, but for the Grace of God . . .'

'But you did have the Grace of God. In no way are you to be compared to Cindy Lewis!'

'Oh, yes I am. We were both whores. That's how Tony was going to make it look . . . like I'd been murdered by a trick that had gone wrong.'

'Except you never, ever brought a punter into your house. He didn't know that, and it would have gone against him. But *I* would have known and come hell and high water I'd have made sure he went down for it.'

There was such savage conviction, even passion, in Mark's voice that Nell bit her lip, but she said firmly: 'It won't do, Mark. I've been thinking about this – about us. You are going to be a Chief Superintendent and I could harm your future career. My past has the power to do for your future and I should never be able to forgive myself if it did. I love you too much – no . . .' She placed a hand over his mouth so that she could go on: 'Think of the publicity, my darling. Fatal to you . . .'

'There won't be any. I know a clamp-down when I see one even if they have not gone so far as to issue a D-Notice – that means you are prohibited by law from so much as discussing the case,' he explained to Nell's querying look.

'All right, no publicity, but it will still have to come to court which means I shall have to give evidence. You can imagine what Tony Panacoulis's lawyer will do then! "Look at her, members of the jury, this woman whose profession is selling her body. Do not be fooled by her looks. This woman is nothing more than a common whore!"' Nell shook her head, sighed deeply. 'It won't do my love, it just won't do . . .'

Mark leaned forward, took her hands in his. 'Let me correct a few misapprehensions on your part. First off, I very much doubt if this case will ever get to court. We have no proof that Panacoulis murdered Cindy.'

'But he told me – he said – '

'That he had, and I quote – "given it to her". A good lawyer could make that into anything, but most of all misunderstanding on your part. Not surprising considering the situation you were in. I *know* he killed Cindy, but here . . .' Mark tapped his forehead, 'and warrants are not issued on a policeman's gut feelings. There is not a shred of proof. All we can get Panacoulis for is threatening behaviour and illegal possession and discharge of a firearm. It will be your word against his, but it will never come to that. Take my word for it.'

'It's not fair,' Nell said, aflame once more at the injustice of it all.

'No, but it is eminently practical. Don't you see, *they* – whoever they are – won't want a word of this to come to court. It could mean a hairline crack becoming a fissure. I think that Panacoulis did all this off his own bat. He got angry and decided to wreak a little revenge. But he told you things he should never have told anybody because he was going to kill you – he thought. He had not taken into account either your cats, your love for them or your own, inimitable resourcefulness. No . . . the clamp-down is already in operation. The press has been muzzled, the word has gone forth. Too much at stake. The bogeyman they always flourish when they want to hide something has been brought out yet again: security.' Mark said a rude word. 'Tony Panacoulis is no supergrass with information too sensitive to be discussed in public. He's a professional villain, but he is *the* villain. They *own* him. And they will deal with him. Just so long as the way they do it does not involve you. The whole thing will be allowed to die in indecent obscurity, you'll see.'

Nell nodded. 'Like Cleo.'

Mark felt his heart leap but he said only: 'Yes. You can dispense with her now, can't you? You don't need her any more.'

'Or Eleanor. She is about to tender her resignation – she's been on leave of absence. Now she just won't ever return to work.'

'Which leaves only Nell . . . I'm glad,' Mark said simply.

Nell pressed his hands, held tightly in his. 'I could not have done it without you. You changed my life.'

'What do you think you've done to mine?'

'I did!' Nell pretended innocence. 'How? Could you perhaps show me . . .?'

Well, Mark thought later, Nell asleep in his arms, all I need now is for everything I told her to come to pass. He felt reasonably confident. There had not been so much as the smell of ink from the press; the officers who answered the 999 call had been told that anything concerning Tony Panacoulis was *sub judice*; there had been no nosy neighbours to gossip; the hospital had been given nothing but barest details, and the officer left outside his private room had reported that on regaining consciousness, the first thing Tony Panacoulis had asked for was a telephone. Within thirty minutes a minion from the high-priced lawyers whose senior partner was Counsel to the Establishment had turned up. Already the wheels were turning, the deals being done, the hole repaired. Not so much *sub judice* as *sub silentio*. It suited Mark because it kept Nell out of things.

If, for form's sake, they decided to allow Tony Panacoulis to appear on a charge of threatening behaviour and illegal possession of a firearm Mark was willing to bet that the end result would be a fine and bound over or some such thing. For while everybody knew Tony Panacoulis was a villain he had never ever been prosecuted for any crime, thanks to his friends in high places, which meant his counsel could proclaim him blameless. No . . . chances are the CPS won't even open a file, or if they do they'll lose it. What are the odds that Nell will be advised not to make charges? They'll trot out the story old Jubb gave to me: that Tony Panacoulis is a valuable source of information on matters much too sensitive to be made public. Pardon me while I laugh up both sleeves.

Nell stirred in his arms and he soothed her disjointed mutterings. Her face was flushed and her lids were fluttering. Reaction, of course. Brushes with death always turned people on to life. And wasn't she now prepared to face hers head on? Renouncing both her alter egos had taken courage, for now she would have to face the world as her real, her only self. What was it she had said to him when he had asked her why she felt the need to become other people: 'When I become someone else I can do things I could never do as myself. I become a separate person who is not me at all, who has access

433

to and the means to express feelings that in me – in Nell – are blocked. I'm not me so it doesn't matter what I do which gives me enormous confidence because not being me I have no responsibility.'

Well, she was now accepting responsibility for what she was, all that had been done to her, what she had become and what she thought she had become. No more Cleo or Eleanor to hide behind. Only Nell. Who was the woman he wanted anyway.

He only hoped he was right in his reading of the situation; that *they* would erect the usual 'Security' screen behind which they would do the usual cover-up. That Nell would be left alone because that was the lesser of any two evils, and as long as their mole was safe they had no interest in her. As for Tony Panacoulis. Well, if there is any justice – and sometimes, even now, I still wonder if there is – he will no doubt be dealt with.

He smiled to himself, shook his head. What a fluke! Maybe somebody up there really does take an interest in things down here. What was it he suffers from again? Ailurophobia. Morbid fear of cats. So what does he do? He comes to a house where there are two of them! Nell had not only managed to use his fear, she'd clunked him with that damned great piece of bronze! What a woman! he thought to himself, proud and admiring, and now that the real Nell is out from under who knows what more there is to be revealed? He counted himself lucky to have been there at the unveiling!

Who would have thought it, he mused to himself. Who in God's name would have thought it. My mother will have a fit!

He shook with laughter, so much so that Nell muttered crossly and Bundle, curled up in the curve of Mark's legs, raised a head to chirrup protestingly.

The copper and the call-girl, that's what we are. The Chief-Superintendent – well, almost – and the Courtesan. I don't care if it is Laurel and Hardy, he thought, just so long as it is me and Nell. They can paint Tony Panacoulis as an icon of the Greek Orthodox Church for all I care. Just so long as it leaves Nell free and clear for me.

My God, he thought. How many times have I been in love – or thought I was, anyway. Just shows how little I knew. And when it comes down to hard evidence I know even less about Nell yet I know her like I know the back of my own hand. A phrase he had heard somewhere dropped into his mind: she filled a long-felt want.

Yes, he thought. That is it exactly. Not one of those other women ever filled the vacuum. They only rattled around in it and then left when they heard how hollow it was.

Nell fills it completely.

He was not surprised that Tony Panacoulis had wanted her. What man would not want Nell Jordan?

He yawned, wondered fuzzily if Panacoulis really was some kind of supergrass then answered his own surmise without a second thought. No way, he thought. Never in a million years . . . Then he wondered no more because he fell asleep.

Nell had not intended to go to Philip's cremation. She remembered him saying to her once, with the inimitable curl of the lip: 'La Rochefoucauld had it right, as always, when he said: "The pomp of funerals has more regard to the vanity of the living than to the honour of the dead."' Which was why, no doubt, he had arranged his own in so spartan a fashion. No pomp, no circumstance, no people, and, especially for a man who had been so vain in life, no vanity. Which was what determined Nell to attend. That and her own near-miss with death.

It had set her to thinking who would attend her own funeral, had Tony Panacoulis been successful.

Mark, certainly. But who else? She had made no friends, since that would have entailed explanations she was unable to give, and they had not been missed, since what you have never had you can never miss.

Now, she thought of Philip's inhuman disposal and it gave her the shudders. There ought to be *somebody* there who had been a friend. She resolved to go to the cremation and advised his solicitor once she had ascertained the date, the time and the place. He gave her no argument. Rather the reverse. He seemed pleased.

Mark went with her. She was, she said, absolutely all right and he had so much to do. He heard her out and still came with her. He knew from experience the delayed effects of shock, and he wanted to be there in case the sight of Philip

Faulkner's coffin brought on any unpleasant reminders. She was strong, but not *that* strong.

So he was there with her when they saw the coffin, lying on a trolley being pushed by a crematorium attendant, Philip's solicitor and the undertaker following behind. There was not a flower, nothing but the coffin, and on Philip's instructions that too was nothing more than a wooden box.

As the trolley continued on its lone way, for only crematorium staff were allowed beyond the swing doors, Mark, who was holding Nell's arm, felt her shudder convulsively, then even as the doors swung to she had turned and begun to walk rapidly away.

'Horrible!' was all she said violently, as they left the building. 'But so very Philip. A thundering anti-climax. Wherever he is I'll bet he is laughing himself silly.'

'But you will miss him.' It was a statement, not a question.

Nell took a deep breath, released it. 'Yes – and no. I shall miss his wit, his elegance, his trenchant common sense. I shan't miss his jaundiced view of life.' She turned to smile at the man she loved. 'From now on, all that looks yellow will not be to the jaundiced eye but because the sun is shining!' In mocking, dulcet tones she shook her head at him reprovingly. 'See what you've done to me? Now you see why I wouldn't tell him about us. He would have spoiled it somehow . . .'

In accordance with Philip's wishes they repaired to his flat for the last toast he had suggested. Nell had put the undrunk bottle of Krug back in the chill cabinet and got out a couple of his Baccarat glasses.

'Works of art,' Mark commented appreciatively. He tasted the Krug. 'And so is this!'

'Philip led a champagne lifestyle – paid for by other people, of course. No wonder he always said it was the cheapest in the long run!'

Mark twirled his glass. 'Will you be sorry to leave your own champagne lifestyle? I don't do badly and I'll do better as a Chief Superintendent, but policeman aren't in the top ten earning bracket, I'm afraid.'

'I only drank champagne when it was bought for me,' Nell told him candidly. 'I was brought up by a father who never spent a pound where a penny would do. I've lived on next to nothing and even now I don't spend a quarter of what I earn. Most of it is in a numbered account in a Swiss bank – one of my clients – ex-clients – is a gnome in Zurich. I'm a prudent housekeeper and I like value for money. We won't lack for cash.' She paused. 'Or don't you like the idea of not being the sole provider?'

'I don't give a damn! I told you, I like strong women.' He grinned. 'Even better when they've a strong bank account.'

Struck by something suddenly: 'Do you know, I don't even know where you live?' Nell exclaimed.

'In one of the Inns of Court, as it happens. My father's old stamping ground and his father's before him. It's old and only big enough for one but it's convenient and it suits me. Unfortunately . . .'

'What?'

'No females are allowed. Something to do with the old eighteenth century by-laws.'

'Then you'll just have to come and live with me,' Nell offered hopefully. 'Or would that be flying in the face of Providence?'

'I'm not flying in the face of anything until I know how things turn out concerning Tony Panacoulis.' He held out his glass for more champagne. 'I think,' he said, 'that we leave the status very much quo for now, wait until the dust has settled, my new job is confirmed and Blossom is her old cantankerous self again. In the meantime, of course, there is absolutely no reason why we should not see as much of each other as the traffic will bear. It's not as though we know each other very well is it?'

His face was dead serious but his eyes were dancing. She, however, took him seriously.

'I think that would be a very good idea,' she agreed. 'I have been thinking about – well, us. Being confronted by your own mortality concentrates the mind wonderfully. Thanks to you a lot of rage and darkness have fallen away from me and I've begun to unfasten the shackles of a past I've been carrying around like the chains of Marley's Ghost. I think,' she went on carefully, 'that what you say is eminently sensible. We don't know each other very well, do we? I've been on my own such a long time and unlike you I've never lived with anybody – a man, I mean. All I've ever had are my cats, and you know I love them dearly – '

'I'd noticed.'

' – but I'm set in my ways and I've probably got habits that might very well prove highly irritating, while I don't even know what yours are. I'm never going back to the Life; that's over and done with; something I don't need any more. She paused to swig champagne as if to imbibe courage. 'What I am trying to say is that – once we do really know each other, if – if it doesn't all come together and we decide it won't work then I'll understand, and it will still have been worth it because I'll have learned so much and changed even more . . .' She looked at him anxiously. 'Am I making sense?'

'Yes.'

One word but it said it all.

He had paid her the compliment of listening to her rather than just hearing. She wondered if she would ever stop wanting or loving him; if her heart would ever cease to give a little hop, skip and jump of pleasure every time she saw him.

'And there's something else,' she went on. 'If I'm giving up Eleanor as well as Cleo that means I've got time on my hands. I've decided that I'm going to take some kind of a course that will train me to work with women – and children – who were sexually abused by their fathers. I think somebody who has been there and knows what it is like is the kind that could do most to help.'

'I quite agree.'

'If it needs a degree then I'll take that first . . . I always wanted to go to University.

'Why not?'

'I don't need a grant or anything because I've got more than enough to pay whatever it costs.'

'I'm with you,' Mark repeated, as if to soothe away her obvious anxiety that he would not be.

'You wouldn't mind? I mean – you wouldn't rather I put the whole thing behind me; buried it along with Philip and the Life and a past I am no longer chained to?'

'No. Whatever you want, I am happy to go along with it. Just so long as we are together while you do it.'

'But . . . if things don't go as you hope . . .'

'What are you? Devil's Advocate?' But his smile took any sting from his words. 'If things don't go as we hope then we deal with them as and when they arise, to the best of our ability.'

The plural wreathed itself around Nell like a ribbon of roses. One thing Mark had in abundance was confidence; that of a man who knew his own capabilities. How lucky I am to have found him, she thought. Maybe there is something to fate after all, like he said. It never so much as entered my mind all those years ago, yet his was the name and the face I remembered when I needed them. Something Liz had once said to her surfaced from the depths of memory, prodded by her thoughts. They had been discussing love and sex, or rather Liz had been trying to explain to Nell the difference between the two. Exasperated by Nell's genuine lack of understanding, Liz had been reduced to say: 'You'll know when you find the perfect equation.'

'Which is?'

'One plus one equals one.'

Nell had smiled tolerantly. 'That is a mathematical impossibility.'

'Who is talking mathematics?'

Mark, who had been watching her expressive face now asked: 'What is so funny?'

She smiled dazzlingly in the face of his puzzlement. 'I was thinking about a certain mathematical equation.'

At his obvious mystification her smile became a laugh. She stood up, held out a hand. 'Let's go and see Bloss,' she said, 'then we'll go back home where I will show you exactly what I mean . . .'

SANDRA BROWN

Mirror Image

She was living another woman's life . . . and loving another woman's husband

AVERY – A talented TV reporter, she was suddenly and tragically in possession of another woman's identity and deadly secrets – and suddenly in love.

TATE – A handsome, charismatic senatorial candidate, he was targeted for death by an unfaithful wife he had come to despise – who was now a charming woman he couldn't resist.

EDDY – He was Tate's best friend and campaign manager, and he'd play any dirty trick or bed any pretty woman who would help him get what he wanted.

FANCY – Tate's restless niece, she told too many family secrets and slept with too many men – until one lover taught her games of pain and power.

They were all entangled in lies of power, loyalty and love.

'Sandra Brown sizzles! A heart-stopping mixture of sex and murder, passion and politics.'

Susan Elizabeth Phillips,
Bestselling Author of FANCY PANTS

SUSAN LEWIS

Stolen Beginnings

Madeleine and Marian dream of success and escaping from their dreary lives. But they are very different. Madeleine, a stunning beauty, seeks fame and fortune as an internationally famous sex symbol; Marian, older, kinder and more serious, lives in her dazzling cousin's shadow.

These are the happy beginnings that are stolen by the arrival of the devastating Paul O'Connell. The cousins' lives are changed forever as they take separate paths to very different kinds of success . . .

'A force for Judith Krantz and Jilly Cooper to reckon with'

Options

A Selected List of Fiction Available from Mandarin

While every effort is made to keep prices low, it is sometimes necessary to increase prices at short notice. Mandarin Paperbacks reserves the right to show new retail prices on covers which may differ from those previously advertised in the text or elsewhere.

The prices shown below were correct at the time of going to press.

☐	7493 0576 2	**Tandia**	Bryce Courtenay	£4.99
☐	7493 0122 8	**Power of One**	Bryce Courtenay	£4.99
☐	7493 0581 9	**Daddy's Girls**	Zoe Fairbairns	£4.99
☐	7493 0942 3	**Silence of the Lambs**	Thomas Harris	£4.99
☐	7493 0530 4	**Armalite Maiden**	Jonathan Kebbe	£4.99
☐	7493 0134 1	**To Kill a Mockingbird**	Harper Lee	£3.99
☐	7493 1017 0	**War in 2020**	Ralph Peters	£4.99
☐	7493 0946 6	**Godfather**	Mario Puzo	£4.99
☐	7493 0381 6	**Loves & Journeys of Revolving Jones**	Leslie Thomas	£4.99
☐	7493 0381 6	**Rush**	Kim Wozencraft	£4.99

All these books are available at your bookshop or newsagent, or can be ordered direct from the publisher. Just tick the titles you want and fill in the form below.

Mandarin Paperbacks, Cash Sales Department, PO Box 11, Falmouth, Cornwall TR10 9EN.

Please send cheque or postal order, no currency, for purchase price quoted and allow the following for postage and packing:

UK including
BFPO

£1.00 for the first book, 50p for the second and 30p for each additional book ordered to a maximum charge of £3.00.

Overseas
including Eire

£2 for the first book, £1.00 for the second and 50p for each additional book thereafter.

NAME (Block letters) ....

ADDRESS..

....

☐ I enclose my remittance for ....

☐ I wish to pay by Access/Visa Card Number

Expiry Date